W9-AZF-040

FALL ON YOUR KNEES

A Novel

ANN-MARIE MACDONALD

SIMON & SCHUSTER

SIMON & SCHUSTER
Rockefeller Center
1230 Avenue of the Americas
New York, NY 10020

This book is a work of fiction. Names, characters,
places, and incidents either are products of the
author's imagination or are used fictitiously. Any
resemblance to actual events or locales or persons,
living or dead, is entirely coincidental.

Copyright © 1996 by Ann-Marie MacDonald
First published in Canada by Alfred A. Knopf Canada
All rights reserved,
including the right of reproduction
in whole or in part in any form.

SIMON & SCHUSTER and colophon are registered trademarks
of Simon & Schuster Inc.

Illustrations by Gina Wilkinson

Designed by Irving Perkins Associates
Manufactured in the United States of America

1 3 5 7 9 10 8 6 4 2

Library of Congress Cataloging-in-Publication Data

MacDonald, Ann-Marie, date.
    Fall on your knees : a novel / Ann-Marie MacDonald.
        p.   cm.
    I. Title.
PR9199.3.M2985F35   1997
813'.54—DC20   96-34186
                                                      CIP

ISBN 0-7432-3719-6

(continued on page 510)

Dedicated with love and gratitude to
Cheryl Daniels and Maureen White

Thanks and Acknowledgments

The author wishes to thank the following individuals and organizations, as well as to acknowledge certain books that were particularly helpful in the course of her research. David Abbass, Sister Simone Abbass CND, The Canada Council, *Cape Breton's Magazine,* Cheryl Daniels, Diane Flacks, Lily Flacks, Rita Fridella, Nic Gotham, Malcolm Johannesen, Honora MacDonald Johannesen, James Weldon Johnson's *Black Manhattan,* Paul Fussell's *The Great War and Modern Memory,* Daphne Duval Harrison's *Black Pearls: Blues Queens of the 1920's,* Arsinée Khanjian, Suzanne Khuri, Margaret MacClintock, Cuddles MacDonald, Dude MacDonald, John Hugh MacDonald, Katie MacDonald, Laurel MacDonald, Sister Margaret A. MacDonald CND, Mary Teresa Abbass MacDonald, Harold MacPhee and The Black Cultural Centre of Nova Scotia, John Mellor's *The Company Store,* Bill Metcalfe and the Cape Breton Highlanders Association, *New Waterford Three Score & Ten,* ed. Ted Boutilier, Beverly Murray, Michael Ondaatje, The Ontario Arts Council, Bridglal Pachai's *Beneath the Clouds of the Promised Land,* Pearl, John Pennino and The Metropolitan Opera of New York Archives, Archival Staff of The Metropolitan Toronto Reference Library, Father Principe of Saint Michael's College U of T, Shari Saunders, Wayne Strongman, Lillian MacDonald Szpak, Kate Terry and The Beaton Institute of The College of Cape Breton, Mrs. Helen Vingoe, Maureen White, Gina Wilkinson.

"Why canst thou not always be a good lass, Cathy?"
"Why cannot you always be a good man, father?"

WUTHERING HEIGHTS

Silent Pictures

THEY'RE ALL DEAD NOW.

Here's a picture of the town where they lived. New Waterford. It's a night bright with the moon. Imagine you are looking down from the height of a church steeple, onto the vivid gradations of light and shadow that make the picture. A small mining town near cutaway cliffs that curve over narrow rock beaches below, where the silver sea rolls and rolls, flattering the moon. Not many trees, thin grass. The silhouette of a colliery, iron tower against a slim pewter sky with cables and supports sloping at forty-five-degree angles to the ground. Railway tracks that stretch only a short distance from the base of a gorgeous high slant of glinting coal, toward an archway in the earth where the tracks slope in and down and disappear. And spreading away from the collieries and coal heaps are the peaked roofs of the miners' houses built row on row by the coal company. Company houses. Company town.

Look down over the street where they lived. Water Street. An avenue of packed dust and scattered stones that leads out past the edge of town to where the wide, keeling graveyard overlooks the ocean. That sighing sound is just the sea.

Here's a picture of their house as it was then. White, wood frame with the covered veranda. It's big compared to the miners' houses. There's a piano in the front room. In the back is the kitchen where Mumma died.

Here's a picture of her the day she died. She had a stroke while cleaning the oven. Which is how the doctor put it. Of course you can't see her face for the oven, but you can see where she had her stockings rolled down for housework and, although this is a black and white picture, her housedress actually is black since she was in mourning for Kathleen at the time, as well as Ambrose. You can't tell from this picture, but Mumma couldn't speak English very well. Mercedes found her like that, half in half out of the oven like the witch in Hansel and Gretel. What did she plan to cook that day? When Mumma died, all the eggs in the pantry went bad— they must have because you could smell that sulphur smell all the way down Water Street.

So that's the house at 191 Water Street, New Waterford, Cape Breton Island, in the far eastern province of Nova Scotia, Canada. And that's Ma on the day she died, June 23, 1919.

Here's a picture of Daddy. He's not dead, he's asleep. You see that armchair he's in? That's the pale green wingback. His hair is braided. That's not an ethnic custom. They were only ethnic on Mumma's side. Those are braids that Lily put in his hair while he was asleep.

There are no pictures of Ambrose, there wasn't time for that. Here's a picture of his crib still warm.

Other Lily is in limbo. She lived a day, then died before she could be baptized, and went straight to limbo along with all the other unbaptized babies and the good heathens. They don't suffer, they just sort of hang there effortlessly and unaware. Jesus is known to have gone into limbo occasionally and taken a particularly good heathen out of it and up to heaven. So it is possible. Otherwise. . . . That's why this picture of Other Lily is a white blank.

Don't worry. Ambrose was baptized.

Here's one of Mercedes. That opal rosary of hers was basically priceless. An opal rosary, can you imagine? She kept it pinned to the inside of her brassiere, over her heart, at all times when she wasn't using it. Partly for divine protection, partly out of the convenience of never being without the means to say a quick decade of the beads when the spirit moved her, which was often. Although, as Mercedes liked to point out, you can say the rosary with any objects at hand if you find yourself in need of a prayer but without your beads. For example, you can say it with pebbles or breadcrumbs. Frances wanted to know, could you say the rosary with cigarette butts? The answer was yes, if you're pure at heart. With mouse turds? With someone's freckles? The dots in a newspaper photograph of Harry Houdini? That's enough, Frances. In any case, this is a picture of Mercedes, holding her opal rosary, with one finger raised and pressed against her lips. She's saying, "Shshsh."

And this is Frances. But wait, she's not in it yet. This one is a moving picture. It was taken at night, behind the house. There's the creek, flowing black and shiny between its narrow banks. And there's the garden on the other side. Imagine you can hear the creek trickling. Like a girl telling a secret in a language so much like our own. A still night, a midnight clear. It's only fair to tell you that a neighbor once saw the dismembered image of his son in this creek, only to learn upon his arrival home for supper that his son had been crushed to death by a fall of stone in Number 12 Mine.

But tonight the surface of the creek is merely as Nature made it. And certainly it's odd but not at all supernatural to see the surface break, and a real live soaked and shivering girl rise up from the water and stare straight at us. Or at someone just behind us. Frances. What's she doing in the middle of the creek, in the middle of the night? And what's she hugging to her chest with her chicken-skinny arms? A dark wet bundle. Did it stir just now? What are you doing, Frances?

But even if she were to answer, we wouldn't know what she was saying, because, although this is a moving picture, it is also a silent one.

All the pictures of Kathleen were destroyed. All except one. And it's been put away.

Kathleen sang so beautifully that God wanted her to sing for Him in heaven with His choir of angels. So He took her.

Book 1

THE GARDEN

To Seek His Fortune

A LONG TIME AGO, BEFORE you were born, there lived a family called Piper on Cape Breton Island. The daddy, James Piper, managed to stay out of the coal mines most of his life, for it had been his mother's great fear that he would grow up and enter the pit. She had taught him to read the classics, to play piano and to expect something finer in spite of everything. And that was what James wanted for his own children.

James's mother came from Wreck Cove, the daughter of a prosperous boat builder. James's father was a penniless shoemaker from Port Hood. James's father fell in love with James's mother while measuring her feet. He promised her father he wouldn't take her far from home. He married her and took her to Egypt and that's where James was born. Egypt was a lonely place way on the other side of the island, in Inverness County, and James never even had a brother or sister to play with. James's father traded his iron last for a tin pan, but no one then or since ever heard of a Cape Breton gold rush.

It used to make his father angry when James and his mother spoke Gaelic together, for his father spoke only English. Gaelic was James's mother tongue. English always felt flat and harsh, like daylight after night-fishing, but his mother made sure he was proficient as a little prince, for they were part of the British Empire and he had his way to make.

One morning, the day before his fifteenth birthday, James awoke with the realization that he could hit his father back. But when he came downstairs that day, his father was gone and his mother's piano had been quietly dismantled in the night. James spent six months putting it back together again. That was how he became a piano tuner.

All James wanted at fifteen was to belt his father once. All he wanted at fifteen and a half was to hear his mother play the piano once more, but she was dead of a dead baby before he finished the job. James took a tartan blanket she'd woven, and the good books she had taught him to read, and tucked them into the saddlebag of the old pit pony. He came back in, sat down at the piano and plunged into "Moonlight Sonata." Stopped after four bars, got up, adjusted C sharp, sat down and swayed to the opening of "The Venetian Boat Song." Satisfied, he stopped after five bars, took the bottle of spirits from his mother's sewing basket, doused the piano and set it alight.

He got on the blind pony and rode out of Egypt.

The Wreck Cove relatives offered him a job sanding dories. James was meant for better things. He would ride to Sydney, where he knew there'd be more pianos.

Sydney was the only city on Cape Breton Island and it was many miles south, by a road that often disappeared, along an Atlantic coast that made the most of itself with inlets and bays that added days to his journey. There were few people, but those he met were ready with a meal for a clean clear boy who sat so straight and asked for nothing. "Where you from, dear, who's your father?" Mostly Gaelic speakers like his own mother, yet always he declined a bed or even a place in the straw, intending that the next roof to cover his slumber be his own. Moss is the consolation of rocks, and fir trees don't begrudge a shallow soil but return a tenfold embrace of boughs to shelter the skinny earth that bore them. So he slept outside and was not lonely, having so much to think about.

Following the ocean a good part of the way, James discovered that there is nothing so congenial to lucid thought as a clear view of the sea. It aired his mind, tuned his nerves and scoured his soul. He determined always to live in sight of it.

He'd never been to a city before. The cold rock smell of the sea gave way to bitter cooked coal, and the gray mist became streaked with orange around him. He looked way up and saw fire-bright clouds billowing out the stacks of the Dominion Iron and Steel Company. They cast an amber spice upon the sky that hung, then silted down in saffron arcs to swell, distend and disappear in a falling raiment of finest ash onto the side of town called Whitney Pier.

Here homes of many-colored clapboard bloomed between the

blacksmiths' shops and the boiler house of the great mill, and here James got a fright, never having seen an African except in books. Fresh sheets fluttered from a line, James guided the pony onto asphalt, across a bridge where he looked back at the burnt-brick palace a mile long on the waterfront, and contemplated the cleanliness of steel born of soot.

Plaits of tracks, a whiff of tar, to his right a dreadful pond, then onto Pleasant Street where barefoot kids kicked a rusty can. He followed the screech of gulls to the Esplanade where the wharfs of Sydney Harbour fanned out with towering ships from everywhere, iron hulls bearded with seaweed, scorched by salt, some with unknowable names painted in a dancing heathen script. A man offered him a job loading and unloading—"No thank you, sir." New rails in a paved street mirrored cables that swung along overhead and led him to the center of town, an electrical train carriage sparked and clanged right behind him, the sun came out. Charlotte Street. Fancy wood façades rose three stories either side, ornate lettering proclaimed cures for everything, glass panes gloated there was nothing you could not buy ready-made, McVey, McCurdy, Ross, Rhodes and Curry; Moore, McKenzie, MacLeod, Mahmoud; MacEchan, Vitelli, Boutillier, O'Leary, MacGilvary, Ferguson, Jacobson, Smith; MacDonald, Mcdonald, Macdonell. More people than he'd ever seen, dressed better than Sunday, all going somewhere, he saw ice cream. And at last, up the hill where the posh people lived.

The pony sagged beneath him and cropped the edge of someone's fine lawn as James came to the conclusion of his traveling thoughts. He would have enough money to buy a great house; for ready-made things, and a wife with soft hands; for a family that would fill his house with beautiful music and the silence of good books.

James was right. There were a lot of pianos in Sydney.

His Left Eye

THE FIRST TIME JAMES saw Materia was New Year's Eve 1898, at her father's house on the hill. James was eighteen.

He'd been summoned to tune the Mahmouds' grand piano for the evening's celebration. It was not his first time in the Mahmoud house. He'd been tending their Steinway for the past year, but had no idea who played it so often and so energetically that it needed frequent attention.

The piano was the centerpiece in a big front room full of plump sofas, gold-embroidered chairs, florid carpets and dainty-legged end tables with marble tops. A perpetually festive chamber—even slightly heathen, to James's eyes—with its gilt mirrors, tasseled drapes and voluptuous ottomans. Dishes of candy and nuts, and china figurines of English aristocracy, covered every surface, and on the walls were real oil paintings—one, in pride of place over the mantelpiece, of a single cedar tree on a mountain.

James would be let in the kitchen door by a dark round little woman who he initially assumed was the maid, but who was in fact Mrs. Mahmoud. She always fed him before he left. She spoke little English but smiled a lot and said, "Eat." At first he was afraid she'd feed him something exotic and horrible—raw sheep, an eyeball perhaps, but no—savory roast meat folded in flat bread, a salad of soft grain, parsley and tomatoes with something else he'd never before tasted: lemon. Strange and delicious pastes, pickled things, things wrapped in things, cinnamon. . . .

One day he arrived to find Mrs. Mahmoud chatting in Gaelic with a door-to-door tradesman. James was amazed but glad to find someone with whom to speak his first language, since he knew few people in Sydney and, in any case, Gaelic speakers were mostly out the country. They sat at the kitchen table and Mrs. Mahmoud told him of her early days in this land, when she and her husband had walked the island selling dry goods from a donkey and two suitcases. This was how she had learned Gaelic and not English. Mr. and Mrs. Mahmoud had made many friends, for most country people love a visit, the mercantile side really being an excuse to put on the kettle. Often the Mahmouds carried messages across counties from one family to another, but good news only, Mrs. Mahmoud insisted. Just as she did when she read a person's cup—"I see only good." So when she peered into the tea leaves at the bottom of James's cup he was neither frightened nor skeptical, but felt himself drawn in with an involuntary faith—which is what faith is—when she said, "I see a big house. A family. There is a lot of love here. I hear music. . . . A beautiful girl. I hear laughter. . . . Water."

When the Mahmouds had saved enough, they had opened their Sydney shop, which thrived. Mr. Mahmoud had bought his wife this splendid house and told her to stop working and enjoy her family. And yet James never saw a sign of the family. Her children were all at school, and the big boys were at the shop with her husband. Mrs. Mahmoud missed her Gaelic friends in the country and looked forward to grandchildren. She never spoke of her homeland.

On this New Year's Eve day, Mrs. Mahmoud greeted James with *Bliadhna Mhath Ūr* but didn't show him into the front room, remaining in the kitchen to work alongside the hired Irish girl, who had a lot to learn. He proceeded there by himself, quite comfortable now in this house, took off his jacket and got to work.

He had already removed a few ivory keys and was bent under the lid behind the piano's gap-toothed smile, so he didn't see Materia when she stepped into the archway.

But she had seen him. She had spied him from her upstairs bedroom window when he came knocking at the kitchen door below, toting his earnest bag of tools—a blond boy so carefully combed. She had peeked at him through the mahogany railings carved with grapes as he entered the front hall and hung his coat in the closet beneath the stairs—his eyes so blue, his skin so fair. Taut and trim, collar, tie and cufflinks. Like a china figurine. Imagine touching his hair. Imagine if he blushed. She watched him cross the hall and disappear through the high arch of the big front room. She followed him.

She paused in the archway, her weight on one foot, and considered him a moment. Thought of plucking his suspenders. Grinned to herself, crept over to the piano and hit C sharp. He sprang back with a cry—immediately Materia feared she'd gone too far, he must be really hurt, he's going to be really mad, she bit her lip—he clapped a hand over one eye, and beheld the culprit with the other.

The darkest eyes he'd ever seen, wet with light. Coal-black curls escaping from two long braids. Summer skin the color of sand stroked by the tide. Slim in her green and navy Holy Angels pinafore. His right eye wept while his left eye rejoiced. His lips parted silently. He wanted to say, "I know you," but none of the facts of his life backed this up so he merely stared, smitten and unsurprised.

She smiled and said, "I'm going to marry a dentist."

She had an accent that she never did outgrow. A softening of consonants, a slightly liquid "r," a tendency to clip not with the lips but with the throat itself. What she did for the English language was pure music.

"I'm not a dentist," he said, then rushed pink to his ears.

She smiled. And looked at the loose piano teeth scattered at his feet.

She was twelve going on thirteen.

Had she hit E flat things might never have progressed so far, but she hit C sharp and neither of them had any reason to suspect misfortune. They arranged to meet. He wanted to ask permission of her mother but she said, "Don't worry." So he waited for her, shivering on the steps of the Lyceum until he saw her come out the big front doors of Holy Angels Convent School across the street. The other girls spilled down the steps in giggling groups or private pairs, but she was alone. When she caught sight of him she started running. She ran right into his arms and he swung her around like a little kid, laughing, and then they hugged. He thought his heart would kill him, he'd had no clue what it was capable of. His lips brushed her cheek, her hair smelled sweet and strange, an evil enchantment slid from him. The salt mist coming off Sydney Harbour crystallized in the fuzz above his lip and alighted on his lashes; he was Aladdin in an orchard dripping diamonds.

She said, "I got five cents, how 'bout you, mister?"

"I have seventy-eight dollars and four cents in the bank, and a dollar in my pocket, but I'm going to be rich someday."

"Then give me the dollar, Rockefeller."

He did and she led him to Wheeler's Photographic on Charlotte Street, where they had their picture taken in front of a painted Roman arch with potted wax ferns. He felt, before he learned anything about where she came from, that the photograph had made them one.

They continued on to Crown Bakery, where they shared a dish of Neapolitan ice cream and melted their initials onto the window. He said, "I love you, Materia."

She laughed and said, "Say it again."

"I love you."

"No, my name."

"Materia."

She laughed again and he said, "Am I saying it right?"

She said, "Yes, but it's cute, it's nice how you say it."

"Materia."

And she laughed and said, "James."

"Say it again."

"James."

It was when she said his name in her soft buzzy way that his desire first became positively carnal—he blushed, convinced everyone could tell. She touched his hair, and he said, "Do you want to go home now?"

"No. I want to go with you."

They walked to the end of the Old Pier off the Esplanade, and looked at the ships from all over. He pointed. "There's the Red Cross Line. Someday I'm going to get on her, b'y, and go."

"Where?"

"New York City."

"Can I come with you?"

"Sure."

She really was betrothed to a dentist, promised when she was four. The dentist was still in the Old Country but was coming to marry her when she turned sixteen.

"That's barbaric," said James.

"It's old-fashioned, eh?"

"Do you like him?"

"I never met him."

"That's so . . . backward, that's savage."

"It's the custom."

"What does he look like?"

"He's old."

"For God's sake!"

They walked back up the Old Pier hand in hand. To the right of them sank the tepid sun, while to their left the blast furnaces of Dominion Iron and Steel erupted into a new day's work. A light orange snow began to fall.

Sydney is only small. By then several people had seen them together and word reached Mrs. Mahmoud, who kept it from Mr. Mahmoud. Materia was forbidden to have anything to do with the piano tuner. She was cross-examined. "Did he touch you? Are you sure?" And the nuns were alerted. She was never alone, and at night her mother locked Materia's bedroom door.

Materia had been just six when they docked in Sydney Harbour and her father said, "Look. This is the New World. Anything is possible here." She'd been too young to realize that he was talking to her brothers. On the night of her thirteenth birthday, Materia climbed out her window and left the Old Country forever.

Come with me from Lebanon, O my sister. February 17 1899, a moonless night, *I am the rose of Sharon, and the lily of the valleys.* They set out before dawn on a hired horse and got married that day at Irish Cove, in a Protestant ceremony performed by an ex-navy chaplain who asked no questions in exchange for a quart of rum. *Thy lips, O my bride, drop as the honeycomb, honey and milk are under thy tongue.* They snowshoed in to a hunting cabin on Great Bras d'Or Lake that was used by rich Americans in the fall, *thou hast ravished my heart, my sister, my bride.* It was all boarded up but he set to work—*thou hast ravished my heart with one of thine eyes*—prying planks off windows, healing the blind. Inside, he wouldn't let her open her eyes till he'd swept, lit a fire and laid the table. He'd thought of everything; there was rose-hip wine, new linen sheets, and the mothbally tartan from his late mother's hope chest, *and the smell of thy garments is like the smell of Lebanon.* He sang her a Gaelic lullaby which made him cry because, if such a thing was possible, he loved her more in his mother tongue, *a garden inclosed is my sister, a spring shut up, a fountain sealed.* He kissed her so gently, didn't want to frighten her, he'd mail-ordered *What Every Husband Should Know* but decided never to touch her in that way if necessary, he'd rather die than frighten or hurt—she reached up and stroked the back of his head,

"Habibi," she whispered, *"BeHebak."* With my own hands I opened to my love.

On the second day she said, "Let's live here forever, let's never go anywhere except New York City."

And he said, "Don't you want a lovely big house and fine handsome children and to have your parents say, 'Well, you were right all along, Mrs. Piper'?"

"No," rolling over to lie on him, her elbows on either side of his face, "I want to stay right here for a long long time," curving her belly against him, "forever and ever. . . ." *kiss me with the kisses of your mouth.* "And ever and ever . . ." he sighed.

When he came out of the woods for provisions on the third day, James was seized by two large men and taken by cart to Sydney and the back room of Mr. Mahmoud's Dry Goods Emporium on Pitt Street. Mr. Mahmoud sat on a pressed-back wooden chair, a long narrow man with leathery cheeks and black wavy hair.

"Sir—" said James.

Mr. Mahmoud had splintering brown eyes. James looked for Materia in them. "Sir—" said James.

Mr. Mahmoud raised his forefinger slightly and the two younger men removed James's boots and socks—James noted with some distaste that they both of them could use a shave.

"—where's my wife?"

Mr. Mahmoud took a leather thong and whipped the soles of James's feet so that for days they swelled and peeled and leaked like drenched onion paper.

They put him in the YMCA and brought him meals. When he could walk again with the aid of a cane, the two men escorted him to Sacred Heart Roman Catholic Church. "Take your hands off me," James said, but he hadn't heard either man speak a word of English. "Oily bastards," he added.

Materia was waiting for him alone at the altar, veiled in black. She wouldn't look at him. Her hair had been cut off. They exchanged vows once again, this time before a priest of Rome. It was James's first time in a Catholic church. Smells like a whorehouse, he thought, although he'd never been in one of those either.

At the back of the church Mrs. Mahmoud's heart broke, because how could that pale boy with no family and no real religion possibly know how to treat a wife? It's a terrible thing for a mother to know that her daughter will not have the happiness she herself has had. But more than that—more than sorrow—was a chill. For she had seen something in his cup.

Mahmoud didn't beat his daughter, and he counted it a weakness that he'd never been able to bring himself to raise a hand to any of his girls for there was the root of the problem. The day after the horrible wedding, he instructed his wife to purge the house of Materia. He went to his shop and sealed himself in his back room while Mrs. Mahmoud burned, snipped and bundled off his daughter's memory.

Materia's favorite little sister, pretty Camille, cried for days. She and Materia had dreamed of marrying two handsome brothers: they would live side by side in big white houses and their children would grow up together; Materia would brush Camille's beautiful straight black hair every night and they'd share a room just like always. Camille wrote a letter to Materia in large neat printing with x's and o's at the bottom, but Pa found it and burned it. He called Camille to him in the cellar and beat her.

It wasn't so much that the piano tuner was *"enklese,"* or even that he was not a Catholic or a man of means. It was that he had come like a thief in the night and stolen another man's property. "And my daughter yielded." There was a word for all this in the Old Country: *'ayb*. There was no translation, people in this country couldn't know the depth of shame, of this Mahmoud was certain. There was no taking her back, she was ruined.

But God is merciful and so was Mr. Mahmoud. He allowed James to convert to Catholicism in exchange for his life. And Mr. Mahmoud arranged for a good-sized house to be built for the newlyweds nine miles up the coast near Low Point. This was so he wouldn't have to toss them from his doorstep a year from now when they turned up destitute. Such a thing would kill his poor wife.

As for the yellow-haired dog who stole my daughter, may he rot. May he awaken to the contents of his mouth strewn across his pillow and may God devastate his dwelling . . . well, perhaps not the dwelling.

As for my daughter. May God curse her womb.

★   ★   ★

The night after Materia's horrible wedding, Mrs. Mahmoud opened her rosewood jewelry box. Immediately the little ballerina popped up and began to revolve to the strains of "The Anniversary Waltz." Mrs. Mahmoud peeled back the red velvet lining from the bottom and placed there her daughter's long black braid, coiling it flat. She covered it with the velvet and replaced the beautiful things her husband had given her over the years—rubies, diamonds, moonstones and pearls. . . . Then she went into the big oak wardrobe where he would not hear her, and mourned.

Materia never saw her family again. Her father forbade it. Her younger sisters were taken out of school and kept home till they were married. Materia's older brothers were forbidden to kill the English bastard but, all the same, he had better keep out of their way. She was dead to them all from that day forth.

James and Materia moved into their big two-story white frame house, with attic, a month later. But just because it was new, doesn't mean it wasn't haunted.

Low Point

WHAT JAMES RESENTED MOST was that *enklese* nonsense. He wasn't English, not a drop of English blood in him, he was Scottish and Irish, like ninety percent of this godforsaken island, not to mention Canadian. Filthy black Syrians.

"Lebanese," said Materia.

"What's the difference, you're better off without them."

There was no town or village at Low Point. There'd been small mines around here, some dating back to the first days of the French, but they were all closed up now. Though scratch anywhere and you'd find coal. The closest neighbor was a Jew who raised kosher meat, and James kept his distance. God knows what rituals involving chickens and sheep . . .

In back of the house there ran a creek that emptied into the ocean half a mile away. The Atlantic was always in sight and this was something James and Materia both came to depend on.

If you followed this creek, you'd walk through long pale grasses keeled over in the damp, careful not to stumble on the rocks that sleep and peep out here and there. Past a stocky evergreen or two, their spiky scent, beaded sap stuck with rain. Startled by the scarlet mushroom, you might stop and stare. Or bend to feel the purity of the stream, refresh your eyes upon the pebbles stained with iron gleaming on the bottom there. Then you'd come, with your wet shoes and droplets in your hair, to a dirt road that stretches nine miles to Sydney on the left and all the way to Glace Bay on the right. Some called this Old Lingan Road, and others called it Victoria or Old Low Point Road, but in time it came to be simply the Shore Road.

You might cross this road and walk a few steps to the edge of the cliff. Down below is the jagged water. All day it chatters back and forth across the gravel beach, unless the weather's rough. Farther out it's mauve like a pair of cold lips; closer in it's copper green, gun gray, seducing seaweed to dance the seven veils despite the chill, chained to their rocks by the hair. And there on the cliff you might sit with your legs dangling even on a flinty winter day, and feel soothed by the salt wind. And if you were like Materia, you might look out, and out, and out, until what there was of sun had subsided. And you would sing. Though you might not sing in Arabic.

In time, Materia wore a path from the two-story white house, along the creek, across the Shore Road, to the cliff.

They didn't have much furniture at first. James bought an old upright piano at auction. In these early days Materia would play and they'd sing their way through the latest *Let Us Have Music for Piano*. Sometimes she'd slide down the bench and insist he play and he would, with gusto, the first few bars of some romantic piece, and then stop short, just as he did when he tuned pianos. Materia would laugh and beg him to play something right through and he would reply, "I'm no musician, dear, I'd rather listen to you."

He built her a hope chest out of cedar. He waited for her to start sewing and knitting things—his mother had milled her own wool, spun, woven and sewn, a different song for every task, till wee James had come to see the tweeds and tartans as musical notation. But the hope chest remained empty. Rather than make Materia feel badly about it, James put it in the otherwise empty attic.

He wasn't much of a cook but he could boil porridge and burn meat. She was young, she'd learn in time. On weekends he tuned pianos as far away as Mainadieu. Weekdays he cycled in to Sydney, where he swept floors at the offices of *The Sydney Post Newspaper* in the morning and worked as a salesclerk at McCurdy's Department Store in the afternoon. Then he'd buy groceries, cycle home, make supper and tidy the house. Then prepare his collar and cuffs for the following day. Then climb the stairs and fold his dear one in his arms.

One day in spring he asked her, "What do you do all day, my darling?"

"I go for walks."

"What else?"

"I play the piano."

"Why don't you plant a little garden, would you like me to get you some hens?"

"Let's go to New York."

"We can't just yet."

"Why not?"

"We have a home, I don't want to just run away."

"I do."

He didn't want to elope for a second time. He wanted to stay put and prove something to his father-in-law. He intended to pay for this house. He started going to school every night by correspondence with Saint Francis Xavier University—liberal arts. He knew that could lead to law and then he could go anywhere. He had his mother's best-loved books, her Bible and her Shakespeare, *Pilgrim's Progress* and Sir Walter Scott, all well worn, but he knew there were gaps to be filled if he was to become a cultivated man. A gentleman. Books were not an expense; they were an investment. He spotted an ad in the *Halifax Chronicle* and sent to England for a crate of classics.

He worked at the *Sydney Post* but he read the *Halifax Chronicle* to get a perspective on the world outside this island—the real world. The hacks at the *Post* thought he was just a broom boy, and those unctuous philistines at the store thought he was lucky to have a collar-and-tie job what with no family and no one to recommend him. He'd show them too, not that they were worth showing.

One evening that spring, he pried the lid off a packing crate and removed untold treasure: book after beautiful book, Dickens, Plato, *The Oxford Book of English Verse*—he paused over the latter, weighing it in his hands; just read that cover to cover, thought James, you could go anywhere, converse with the Queen. *Treasure Island, The World's Best Essays, The Origin of Species*. He counted them; there were twelve in the crate, that meant he now possessed sixteen books. Just imagine, thought James, all that knowledge, and it's here in my house on the floor of my front room. He sat cross-legged and surveyed the riches. Which to open first? Their gilded leaves and their crimson covers engraved with gold invited him.

He went and rummaged in the kitchen, returning with a pair of scissors. He selected a volume and lifted its front cover; the spine crackled, sending a shower of red flakes into his lap—no matter, it's the words inside that count. He took the thin blade of the scissors and carefully cut the first pages. He called to Materia—she was about the house somewhere but he hadn't seen her for an hour or two. "Materia," he called out again as he cut the last page. When she appeared he said, "Where've you been, my darling?"

"The attic."

"Oh. What were you doing up there?"

"Nothing."

He didn't pursue it, maybe she was up there secretly sewing something for the hope chest, planning to surprise him. He smiled fondly at the thought and said, "You look right pretty."

"Thank you, James."

Her hair was freshly braided and wound about her head, and she wore a rosebud print with puffed sleeves, matching ribbons and a hooped skirt.

"Look, my dear," he said, "here's a book you might enjoy."

"Let's go out."

"Out where?"

"To town. To a dance."

"But sweetheart, we can entertain ourselves for free right here, and you'll see, it'll be more fun."

He gave her a warm smile and drew her down next to him on the horsehair sofa. He put an arm around her and turned to page one of the beautiful volume. He read aloud, " 'Book One. Of shapes transformed to bodies strange, I purpose for to treat. . . .' " savoring the words and the warm weight of his wife cuddled close, " 'Then sprang up first the Golden Age. . . .' "

He read and evening closed in. " 'Men knew no other countries yet than where themselves did keep. There was no town enclosèd yet with walls and ditches deep. . . .' " He read and the coals cooled to gray in the hearth. Reaching over to the lamp and raising the wick, he remarked to his wife, "Now isn't this better than going out among strangers?" And turning to her for confirmation, he saw she was fast asleep. He kissed her head and returned to the book, " 'Of Iron is the last, in no part good or tractable. . . .' "

He continued aloud because that was how he and his mother had read together and the thought made James's happiness complete far into the night, " '. . . Not only corn and other fruits, for sustenance and for store, were now exacted of the earth, but eft they 'gan to dig. And in the bowels of the earth insatiably to rig for riches couched and hidden deep in places near to hell . . .' "

By midsummer she was three months pregnant and crying all the time. James couldn't figure it out—weren't women supposed to be happy about something like that? He tried to be extra nice. He brought her sweets from town. He tried to get her to read so they'd have something to talk about.

He was at first amazed and then dismayed by her indifference to books. He assigned her a chapter a day of *Great Expectations* in order to cultivate a love of reading and at suppertime he quizzed her, but she was a sorry student and he abandoned the effort. He racked his brains to devise some sort of seemly diversion for her, having given up hope that she'd take to housewifery. But it was no use, and he tried not to judge her too harshly; she was young, that was all.

And yet it tried his patience.

"Materia, you can't spend all your time wandering the shore and fooling around on the piano," for lately she'd begun playing whatever came into her head whether it made sense or not—mixing up fragments of different pieces in bizarre ways, playing a hymn at top speed, making a B-minor dirge out of "Pop Goes the Weasel," and all with the heavy hand of a barrelhouse hack. James found it disturbing, unhealthy even. Besides, he couldn't study with that racket.

"I'm sorry, James."

"Why don't you play something nice?"

At which she struck up "The Maple Leaf Rag" and he yelled at her for the first time. She laughed, pleased to have gotten a rise. He decided to ignore her after that. Which made her cry—again—but, frankly, he'd figured out her tricks by now, she was just looking for attention.

On Labor Day he turned down an invitation to bring the wife and come to a McCurdy employee boat ride and picnic. He told himself he had no desire to socialize with ready-made gentlemen, it was enough that he worked beside them; if he once gave himself the spurious comfort of a social life he might get sidetracked. But deep down he winced at the thought of showing Materia to anyone. He was grateful they lived in the middle of nowhere. It wasn't that he didn't love her anymore, he did. It was just that, recently, it had struck him that other people might think there was something strange. They might think he'd married a child.

★ ★ ★

By September she had puffed up and turned sallow. He began sleeping on a cot by the kitchen stove. "It's for your own good, my dear, I don't want to roll over and gouge the baby with an elbow."

Pound, pound, pound on the piano keys in the middle of the night. No wit anymore, however juvenile, no naughty ditties, just discords. Tantrums. Fine, let her exhaust herself. *Plank, splank, splunk* into the wee hours. In the mornings he would rise from his kitchen cot as though he'd slept perfectly well, pack his own lunch, pat her on the head and cycle off to work on iron tires.

By Halloween she was big as a house. One evening he came home to find her sitting at the kitchen table with a bowl of molasses-cookie dough, for that was what the ingredients lined up on the table indicated. He was delighted. Her first attempt at cooking. He even gave her a kiss to show just how pleased he was, but when he went to dip a finger in the dough the bowl had been licked clean.

"What in God's name are you doing?"

She just looked queasily straight ahead.

"Answer me."

She just sat there, bloated.

"What's wrong with you? Don't you think? Haven't you got anything to say for yourself?"

The blank stare, the flaccid face. He grabbed the bowl.

"Or are you just a lump of dough?"

No answer.

"Answer me!"

He hurled the bowl at her feet and it broke. She ran outside and threw up. He watched her hunched and huge over the back steps. You'd think by now she'd know enough not to bring it on, a dumb animal knows not to make itself upthrow. Well she can stay out there till I've cleaned up this mess.

He swept the floor and scrubbed it too. He got a lot of work done that evening, not to mention some clear thinking. He locked the piano and pocketed the key. Then he said, "I'm not cooking anymore and I'm not cleaning. You do your job, missus, 'cause Lord knows I'm doing mine."

She looked so sad and dumpy. He had a pang of pity. Did all women get this ugly?

"I'm sorry, James," she said and started crying. At least it was better than that weird staring she'd been at lately. He let her hug him, knowing it would calm her. He didn't want to be cruel. He hoped the child would be fair.

Materia went upstairs to the attic. She knelt down, opened the hope chest and inhaled deeply. James thought Materia hadn't filled the hope chest because she had nothing to put in it. But she kept it empty on purpose, so that nothing could come between her and the magical smell that beckoned her into memory. Cedar. She hung her head into the empty chest and allowed its gentle breath to lift and bear her away . . . baked earth and irrigated olive groves; the rippling veil of the Mediterranean, her grandfather's silk farm; the dark elixir of her language, her mother's hands stuck with parsley and cinnamon, her mother's hands stroking her forehead, braiding her hair . . . her mother's hands. The smell of the hope chest. The Cedars of Lebanon. She stopped crying, and fell asleep.

The Jewish Lady

MRS. LUVOVITZ HAD SEEN the pregnant woman sitting on the cliff's edge. Like a fixture warning ships, or luring them. People around here believed in kelpies. Mrs. Luvovitz's imagination had been infected. What could you expect with so many Catholics? They saw omens in everything. Where Mrs. Luvovitz came from they called them golems.

Maybe there's something wrong with the woman, thought Mrs. Luvovitz, maybe she's simple. Because when Mrs. Luvovitz had passed by on the Shore Road to Sydney with her cartload of eggs the other day, she had heard the woman singing what sounded like nonsense words. A poor simpleminded woman from down north in the hills perhaps. They marry their cousins once too often. But as yet Mrs. Luvovitz had never seen the woman's face, for she always wore a plaid kerchief that had the effect of blinkers.

Mrs. Luvovitz had asked her husband, Benny, if he'd seen the pregnant woman, but he never had.

"Mr. Luvovitz, you must have."

"I haven't, Mrs. Luvovitz."

"She's there every day."

"Maybe she's a ghost."

"Get out, Ben."

Benny laughed. He knew her weakness.

Mrs. Luvovitz had resolved to speak to the woman next time, because by now she was beginning to suspect she'd been all too Celtified. She needed to satisfy herself that the woman was human and not an omen. If an omen, it was important to determine certain things: "When do I usually see her? In the morning? Or evening?" A forerunner seen in the morning meant death was still a ways off. Seen in the evening, it meant get ready. A child meant the death of an innocent.

On this day, Mrs. Luvovitz was driving the Shore Road from Sydney as usual, having sold all her eggs.—"A dozen Jewish eggs, please."—She could hardly keep up. Likewise Benny, who delivered meat in his icebox wagon.

"Hello," said Mrs. Luvovitz, pulling up her horse.

The bright kerchief fluttered in the sea breeze; it was a nice day but that could mean anything.

"Hello there," Mrs. Luvovitz repeated.

"Hello, hello!" cried little Abe beside her.

The plaid kerchief turned and Mrs. Luvovitz said to herself, *"Gott in Himmel!"* A pregnant child. A dark little thing, too, she must be from away. Or from Indian Brook maybe. Mrs. Luvovitz forgot all about ghosts and *golems*. "Where are you from, dear, who's your mother?"—falling into the local formula.

"I haven't got a mother."

"Get in the cart, girl."

It was surprising to find out that the child belonged to that big new white house across the way. Mrs. Luvovitz had never seen her come or go, just appear, as it were, on the cliff.

"How old are you?"

"Thirteen and three-quarters."

Ay-yay-yay, and married to that young fella. It was illegal, of course. Where did he get her?—a child bride. From overseas somewhere, was she Eyetalian? A Gypsy? What was the accent? Mrs. Luvovitz made tea and entertained these and other questions. All would be revealed, she'd see to that, but first, tea. Where she came from and where she lived now, tea meant a spread. She placed a plate of cookies before Materia, who said, "What's that?"

"What do you mean, 'what's that,' that's *ruggalech.*"

Materia took a bite of the folded-over cookie. It tasted strange and familiar all at once, cinnamon and raisins.

"It's good," said Materia.

"Of course it's good."

Materia turned her attention to little Abe, playing peekaboo.

"Where's your family, Mrs. Piper?"

"I haven't got one—you can call me Materia."

"What's your maiden name?"

"Mahmoud."

For God's sake, everyone knows the Mahmouds.

"Ibrahim?"

"That was my father."

"And Giselle."

Materia nodded.

Mrs. Luvovitz remembered when the Mahmouds used to sell from a donkey, hampers swaying on each side. Hardworking people, they did what we all hope to do. Now there's the big dry-goods store in Sydney.

"So what are you saying, 'You haven't got a family'? You've got a family, they're your family."

Materia shook her head. "I don't belong to them anymore."

"Why not?"

"I'm dead."

"You're dead? You're not dead, what kind of crazy nonsense is that, 'I'm dead'?"

"It's a custom—"

"I know from the custom."

Sitting *shiva* for your own flesh and blood while they're alive and well, such a custom is better left in the Old Country. "Drink your tea, Mrs. Piper."

"You can call me—"

"And eat. You're eating for two, eat."

Mrs. Luvovitz taught Mrs. Piper to cook.

"What's this?" asked James.

"Chicken soup with matzo balls."

He looked at the bland sponge floating in broth. Broke off a fragment with his spoon, ate it. After all, not so different from a tea biscuit dunked in soup. "This some kind of Ayrab delicacy?"

"Jewish."

They weren't the first people he would have picked as friends for his wife but, after all, it wasn't as though they were sacrificing babies over there. And she had finally started acting like a wife, even if the results were on the heathen side. James figured it was just as well the neighbors were foreign; it wouldn't occur to them that there was anything strange about his being married to such a young girl. And what did he care what a Hebrew farmer thought of him?—although Mr. Luvovitz seemed like an all-right type. James had gone over there to make sure.

"Call me Benny."

"Benny."

"Taste this."

"What is it?" Looked like a plug of MacDonald's Twist.

"Taste it."

". . . hm."

"You like that?"

"Not bad. It's good."

"I smoked that myself—you want, I'll sell you a whole cow for the winter, fresh off the hoof, pick one, they're all good."

Nothing really strange about the Jew except the accent, his black beard and curly sideburns and his little cap. James bought half a cow.

"I don't want it kosher," said James.

"What do you mean, it's kosher, I butcher it, it's kosher."

"I don't want you to do anything funny to it."

"Don't worry, you see that cow?"

"Yuh."

"That's the one I'm saving for you. That's a Presbyterian cow."

"I'm Catholic."

Benny laughed. James smiled. Compared to Materia's family, the Luvovitzes seemed downright white.

1900

AT THE ELEVENTH HOUR, in her ninth month, Materia began looking forward to her baby. That's because she'd grown to love Abe Luvovitz, who was two, and Rudy, who was six months. She wanted a son of course. Her father would be hard pressed to disown a first grandson even if it came to him through a daughter. That was what she told herself. And then she could see her mother again, and her sisters—she'd be a good woman after all. She began to pray to Our Lady, please, Dear Mary, let it be a boy.

James named the baby Kathleen, after his late mother. Kathleen wasn't the first baby of the new century, but she was near enough so that James had to pelt all the way to Sydney on the old nag and drag the doctor from the dregs of a New Year's party. They arrived back at Low Point in time for the doctor to tell Mrs. Luvovitz she'd done a pretty good job. Mrs. Luvovitz thought, "You should only pass a turnip through the end of that which you have between the pants over there, then we'll see who's done a pretty good job." But she took care to think it in Yiddish.

Mrs. Luvovitz told Materia how blessed she was. "I love my boys, Mrs. Piper, but a woman wants a daughter."

Materia didn't say anything.

James said, "I love you, Materia."

She said, *"Baddi moot."*

He patted her head and gazed at the baby. "Kathleen," he said. Then, "Look, she knows her name!"

He had her baptized by a Presbyterian minister.

"We gotta get a priest," said Materia.

"It's the same God," said James. It was bad enough he'd had to go through the motions of conversion, he needn't subject his daughter to any Roman hocus-pocus.

Mrs. Luvovitz looked after Materia and the new baby for the first two weeks. Benny said, "You're interfering."

"I'm not interfering, she has no mother."

"You're not her mother."

"She needs a mother."

"She needs time with her baby, how's she going to learn?"

James felt invincible. He charted the highest sales for two weeks running. He walked into the boss's office uninvited and demanded a raise.

"I'm afraid I can't do that just yet, Piper."

"I have a child now, sir."

"So have the other men."

"I'm worth three of those other fellas."

"You've had a good couple weeks—keep it up, you'll be employee of the month."

James turned on his heel and it felt that good to walk out on the old man—let him try to replace me, he can't do it, it can't be done.

James rode home high on his rickety horse, he was going to give that girl everything. She was going to grow up a lady. She'd have accomplishments. Everyone would see. He felt like a king. A sudden drop and he was standing on the Shore Road, the horse dead between his feet. No matter. As good as a sack of money lying there in the slush, worth its weight in glue.

He walked the rest of the way and formulated a plan. Pianos only need tuning once in a while, but they need playing much more often. And who plays piano? Country folk who learn by ear, thumping to fiddles and spoons for simple enjoyment. And the children of townspeople who want their kids to have accomplishments. The likes of those uppity losers he'd worked with at McCurdy's, not to mention the really well-to-do: MR. JAMES H. PIPER ESQUIRE *offers tuition in the home to young ladies and gentlemen, in the theory and practice of the Piano Forte.*

He wouldn't bother quitting the job at the *Sydney Post.* He just wouldn't show.

James arrived home in the middle of that day to find Mrs. Luvovitz in the kitchen feeding his baby with a dropper.

"Where's my wife?"

"She's sleeping."

He took the stairs two at a time and dragged her up by an arm. Herded her down to the kitchen, whinging and whining every step of the way.

"Thank you, missus, my wife'll take over now."

Mrs. Luvovitz got up, thinking thoughts not in English, and left the house.

James plunked his wife onto the chair and put the screeching baby into her arms. "Now feed her."

But the mother just blubbered and babbled.

"Speak English, for Christ's sake."

"Ma bi'der. Biwajeaal."

He slapped her. "If she doesn't eat, you don't eat. Understood?"

Materia nodded. He unbuttoned her blouse.

James allowed Mrs. Luvovitz over that evening when Materia hadn't produced a drop and the baby was fit to be tied. The women went upstairs. The howling the mother put up, as Mrs. Luvovitz did the necessary. Downstairs in the front room, James unlocked the piano and played the opening bars of various pieces from memory in an effort to drown the sound. He'd have to invest in some sheet music and exercise books. His daughter would play.

In a few days the pump was primed and the baby was sucking. But the mother cried through every feeding. One evening in the fourth week of Kathleen's life, James snatched his child from the breast in horror.

"You've hurt her, Jesus Christ, you've cut her lip!"—for the baby's smile was bright with blood.

Materia just sat there, mute as usual, her dress open, her nipples cracked and bleeding, oozing milk.

James took one look and realized that the child would have to be weaned before it was poisoned.

James might be a Catholic convert, but he'd never forgotten his Scots Confession. Feckless Catholics believe in salvation through faith—good enough, sit on your arse and believe all you like, but some of us know that work is the only sure bet, for the night will come, etc., etc. . . . get on with it, nothing will come of nothing.

Within a month, James had enough students from Sydney to Glace

Bay to start making ends meet. All day into the evening, every good boy deserves fudge and all cows eat grass. And at night, the staring zombie he'd married. Why had he married her? It was when he sat next to twelve- and thirteen-year-olds on the piano bench and watched their eyes glaze over at the mention of middle C that it hit him in the stomach that his wife had been no older than they.

How had he been ensnared by a child? There was something not right about Materia. Normal children didn't run away with men. He knew from his reading that clinical simpletons necessarily had an overdeveloped animal nature. She had seduced him. That was why he hadn't noticed she was a child. Because she wasn't one. Not a real one. It was queer. Sick, even. Perhaps it was a racial flaw. He would read up on it.

All Materia wanted to do was get pregnant again so God could send her a son. But there wasn't much chance of that because her husband wouldn't come near her. Got angry if she touched him. Materia realized that God would not give her another baby if He saw she was ungrateful for the one she had. So she prayed to the Blessed Virgin. She prayed in the attic because there was no church for miles and miles, and James didn't like her wandering anymore. On her knees, elbows resting on the hope chest, "Please, dear Mary Mother of God, make me love my baby."

Kathleen thrived. Silky red–gold hair, green eyes and white white skin. Materia wondered where she'd come from. Surely she had been changed in the night. Mrs. Luvovitz didn't care to speculate.

James watched Kathleen grow more beautiful and hardy every day. And what a set of pipes—he'd carry her out to the stony fields for yelling contests. They'd holler till they were hoarse and hilarious. He loved to hear her laugh. She could do no wrong.

Feeding the child some lovely mush at the kitchen table, Materia leaned forward and cooed, *"Ya Helwi. Ya albi, ya Amar. Te'berini."*

The child smiled and Materia said a silent prayer of thanks, because at that moment she'd felt a faint breath of something not far from love.

"Don't do that, Materia."

"What?"

"I don't want her growing up confused. Speak English."

"Okay."

A Miner 'Forty-Niner

KATHLEEN SANG BEFORE SHE talked. Perfect pitch. James was a piano tuner—he knew: his eighteen-month-old daughter could carry "Believe Me, If All Those Endearing Young Charms" flawlessly, if wordlessly, after hearing him play it once. . . . He sat perfectly still on the piano bench and regarded her. She looked straight back at him with adult gravity.

It was a moment of equal parts anxiety and awe, like the striking of a wide seam of gold. The prospector sinks to his knees—he's only been looking for coal. At a gush of oil he'd hoot, baptize himself and buy the drinks. But the sight of gold is different. He observes a moment's silence. Then he rises, eyes watering. How to get it properly out of the earth? How not to be robbed in the meantime?

Eventually it would require real money. For now, he set aside his own studies and started teaching her himself. He read up on it. He bought a metronome, a gramophone, and began a collection of records. He ordered whole scores and song sheets from New York, Milan and Salzburg. He decided it wasn't too soon to start in on the *Vaccai Practical Method of Italian Singing*. Mozart composed at three. At three, Kathleen sang, *"Manca sollecita Più dell'usato, Ancor che s'agiti Con lieve fiato, Face che palpita Presso al morir."*

Materia was permitted to play piano again, this time exactly what was put in front of her:

scales, intervals, *i semitoni*

"this lesson must be sung *adagio* at first, and the time accelerated to *allegro,* according to the ability of the Pupil" syncopation, ornamentation, literal translation, "The flame fails rapidly/more than usual/even if it flickers/with a light breath"

appoggiatura, introduzione al mordente

"the *acciaccatura* differs from the *appoggiatura* in as much as it does not interfere with the value or the accent of the note to which it is pre-fixed," intervals of thirds, intervals of fourths, *salti di quinta, salti di sesta*

"the little bird in a narrow cage/why does one never hear it sing?"

Lesson XI, The Shake, "I would explain my anguish"

Lesson XII, On Roulades, "I cannot believe my thoughts"

Lesson XIII, Per Portare la Voce, "I cannot keep silent about everything."

Materia played. Kathleen turned seven.

Materia watched it all from a great distance, and as the years flew by she missed her father more and more, forgetting everything but that he had once cared enough for her to find her a husband. All memories soften with age, and the good ones are also the most perishable—her mother and sisters had long ago been caressed to disappearing soapstone, conjured up till they faded to nothing. Like cave paintings by candlelight, she could only glimpse them now in the dark from the corner of her eye. But her father's memory was durable. Obelisk eroded to a dome of rock, the touchstone of her loss.

"You're too fat."

Materia looked at James from afar and said, "Okay."

He shook his head. Other men went strolling with their wives of a Saturday evening. Took them to church on Sunday, sat at opposite ends of a row of children. But not James. He didn't want people thinking he'd married a woman old enough to be his mother, for one thing. But mainly, what with Materia gone slack in mind and body, he didn't want his child stigmatized. For on top of everything else, Materia was dark. He tried not to see it, but it was one of those things that was always before his eyes, now that the scales had fallen from them.

He took Kathleen everywhere. They went on long walks—Kathleen in the beautiful English pram at first, and then hand in hand. Their walking language was Gaelic. With her fairy hair and fine deportment, people stared because she looked like a princess. Her clothes came from England. Nothing showy, all quality, like a real-life princess. And James trusted his immaculate shirts to no one but himself, shaved his face clean every morning. Together they turned heads.

It was 1907 and there was a town now. It had sprung up overnight starting with Number 12 Colliery. Numbers 14, 15 and 16 followed in short order. The railroad came in and so did the miners. At first they came from all over the Maritimes, England, Ireland, Scotland and Wales. In time they came from everywhere. The Dominion Coal Company bought up land and built a sea of company houses—serviceable clapboard dwellings attached in pairs. There was a school, a Catholic church, Luvovitz's Kosher Canadian Butcher Shop and Delicatessen, MacIsaac's Drugs and Confectionery and the Company Store with enough merchandise to mephistophelize a miner's wife.

Every Friday night the miners would hand over their sealed pay packets to their wives, who'd open them and fork over the price of a drink. Problem was, come Saturday shopping the pay packet—with or without Friday's tipple—would barely feed even a small family of six. But the coal company had a solution to this: "company scrip." This was a form of credit. The missus could spend cash at those shops in town that stocked the odd item unavailable at the Company Store. And she could spend company scrip at the Company Store on food, shoes, cloth and kerosene. Her man's sealed pay packet grew thinner and thinner, until quite soon it contained only an itemized account of how much rent he owed on his company house, how much interest he owed on his debt to the Company Store and how much was still available to him in scrip to spend there. The Company Store came to be better known as "The Pluck-Me Store."

Still people poured in, filling up the streets that ran north-south, and the avenues that ran east-west, every second one named for a Catholic saint or a coal company magnate. Boom Town. It didn't exist officially and it had no name yet, but the Piper house was suddenly on a street and the street had a name: Water Street.

Materia hadn't been in a church since she'd got married. Now that there was a Catholic church right handy there was no reason she couldn't just walk over. But she felt unworthy. Our Lady had not answered her prayer. Materia still did not love her child, and she knew the fault lay within herself,

"Kathleen, *taa'i la hown.*"

Materia sat the child on her lap and wrapped her arms around it. She sang, unrepeatable and undulating:

> *"Kahn aa'ndi aa'sfoor*
> *zarif u ghandoor*
> *rasu aHmar, shaa'ru asfar*
> *bas aa'yunu sood*
> *sood metlel leyl. . . ."*

Materia rocked the child and felt sad—was that closer to love? She hoped. The child felt cool in her arms. "I'll warm you," she thought. And kept singing. Kathleen stayed perfectly still, pressed close up against the rolling mass. Materia stroked the fire-gold hair and passed a warm brown hand across the staring green eyes. Kathleen tried not to breathe. Tried not to understand the song. She tried to think of Daddy and light things—fresh air, and green grass—she worried that Daddy would know. And be hurt. There was a smell.

Materia released the child. It was no good. God could see past Materia's actions, into her heart. And her heart was empty.

Materia no longer went up to the hope chest to cry—she cried wherever she happened to be at the time—nor did it any longer interrupt her work or wrench a single muscle in her face.

"Give us a jawbreaker and a couple of honeymoons," said James.

MacIsaac's Drugs and Confectionery smelt of new pine, bitter herbs and saltwater taffy. Mr. MacIsaac reached into a tilted jar brimming with the edible rainbow. Behind him stretched shelf upon shelf of bottles and packets containing powders, essences, oils and unguents. Whatever ails you.

Mr. MacIsaac handed Kathleen a sarsaparilla candy cane as an extra little treat, but she hesitated and looked at James, who said, "It's all right, my darling, Mr. MacIsaac's not a stranger."

Mr. MacIsaac looked at Kathleen gravely, lowered his head and said, "Go on, touch it."

She touched his billiard-bald head and grinned. Mr. MacIsaac said, "I hear you got a set o' lungs on you, lass."

She nodded wisely, sucking on the candy cane. MacIsaac laughed and

James beamed. He and Kathleen left the shop together. Mrs. MacIsaac said from her perch on the sliding ladder, "She's beautiful."

"Yuh, she's a pretty little thing."

"Too pretty. They'll never raise her."

Mrs. MacIsaac watched the shop while Mr. MacIsaac limped back to his greenhouse for a drop of "the good spirit." He'd been in the Boer War.

At home, Materia stood at the counter rolling out dough for a pie—steak and kidney like James's mother used to make—and finally twigged to a thing that had been nagging her all along. It was this: Kathleen's baptism hadn't taken. It had been done by a Protestant minister. The child needed to be properly baptized, in Latin, by a Catholic priest. And then everything would be all right. She told James when he arrived home with the girl but he said, "Kathleen has been baptized. It was done by a man of the cloth, a Christian man, and that's all there is to it."

Kathleen's cheeks bulged with hard candy, her green gaze directed up at her mother. She didn't look all that baptized to Materia.

James had taught his daughter to read words soon after she learned to read music. At three and a half she'd shared his lap with a terrifyingly illustrated book more than half her size and sounded out, " 'In the midway of this our mortal life, I found me in a gloomy wood, astray. . . .' " He'd started her on Latin when she was five, teaching himself at the same time—it would help with her Italian singing. He ordered another box of books. Children's classics this time, and they read them aloud, taking turns.

He hadn't much time for his own reading, though his books now numbered twenty-three not counting the *Encyclopaedia Britannica*— "Read that end to end," thought James, as he gazed at his glass cabinet, "and you'd know just about everything. Go anywhere at all."

At the local schoolhouse Kathleen learned to sit in rows and not to gawk at those less fortunate, but little else. The lady teacher got the creeps from the porcelain girl with the mermaid eyes. The child seemed to be in disguise. Staring up at a corner of the ceiling or out the window, waiting for something, a sign—what?—yet always ready with the answer: "Wolfe died on the Plains of Abraham, miss." Hands folded on the desk, spine straight. "The square of the hypotenuse is equal to the sum of the squares of the other two sides, miss." Every feature formed to preternatural perfection. "It's i before e except after c, miss." It wasn't right in a child. Perhaps she wasn't a child at all.

In the schoolyard Kathleen came alive but in the oddest way, showing an alarming tendency to play with boys. Hurling sootballs, schoolbag raised as a shield, shrieking with joy in her linen sailor dress, ringlets flying, forever banishing herself from the society of girls.

Blackened knees and torn silk were the stuff of high spirits, and James never scolded her for ruining her clothes, but when Kathleen came home and said, "Pius MacGillicuddy gots a finger in a jar what his da found in the mine, that he b'ought up from a wee tiny sprout," it was time to send her to Holy Angels in Sydney.

The Sisters of the Congregation of Notre Dame were in the business of educating the whole girl: from grammar to botany, physics to French. But above all, Holy Angels offered an excellent music program. James had been going to wait a few years, till Kathleen turned twelve and he'd saved enough for tuition, but there was no help for it, she'd be tarnished by then. He'd find the money.

He started a garden in the backyard on the far side of the creek. He bought a new old horse and cart. He traveled across the island to the Margaree and collected topsoil with no trace of coal dust. The missus would have to learn to make soap, butter and her own clothes. From now on they'd have to pay only for meat, and Benny always gave them a special price. Benny gave James a special price on manure too.

"For you, free. That's kosher cow shit, mind you, you're going to have kosher carrots and potatoes, you'll be a Jew in no time—you want, I'll throw in a circumcision, no charge."

James went out to the woods and cut down a young apple tree. Stripped it of branches, sharpened it at both ends and drove it into the center of the garden. Nailed a plank of driftwood across it, and dressed it in one of Materia's old frocks that she'd grown out of and a fedora he found blowing over a field. It wasn't effective till he fashioned a head and torso from two flour sacks stuffed with straw to fill out the clothes, and impaled them on the stake. Every so often he changed its attire, now a dress, now a pair of trousers, but always the hat, keeping the birds on edge.

"Kathleen, come."

Materia no longer spoke Arabic to the girl. What for? Kathleen followed her mother into the kitchen. The big tin tub was full and steaming. Tomorrow was Kathleen's first day at Holy Angels and James wanted her spick-and-span. That meant hair. Materia used to dread washing the child's hair because of all the fuss. James would holler from outside the kitchen door, "Are you trying to kill the poor child?" But Materia was used to the girl's hysterics, and performed the task briskly, scouring the scalp, dunking the head, wringing the tresses, getting the comb through, keeping her still. James could holler, but he would never intrude on his daughter's ablutions.

This evening there were the customary protests—"Don't pull!—my eyes are stinging! O-o-ow, stop i-i-it!"—but when Materia took Kathleen by the hair as usual and plunged her head backward for the first rinsing, she kept it under long enough to say into the submerged green eyes, "Do you renounce Satan? Yes. And all his works? Yes. I baptize you *in nomine Patris, et Filii et Spiritus Sancti, amen."* There. In an emergency, any Catholic can baptize a child. And after nine years, Materia considered it an emergency. Now the child would be safe. Now God could love her, even if Materia couldn't, and the nuns wouldn't think ill of her. Materia let go and Kathleen's face broke the surface, gasping.

Kathleen didn't cry or complain. She stood unwontedly docile as her mother toweled her dry, careful to attend roughly to the bad parts of the body.

In the wee hours of that night, Kathleen woke up screaming. She was still screaming when her daddy picked her up, and she clung to him as he walked her up and down the hallway, struggling to make out what she was saying.

"Who's coming to get you?" he asked.

And when he had deciphered some more, "Who's 'Pete'?"

And she told him through her sobs.

He carried her downstairs, out the kitchen door, across the coal clinks in the backyard, over the little footbridge to the garden and right up to the scarecrow.

"Now beat the can off him," James ordered.

Kathleen was shaking uncontrollably, almost gagging with fear. The scarecrow's hat cast a shadow over its featureless face. She couldn't see if it was smiling or frowning.

"Make a fist, go on," said James.

She did, still crying.

"Now whack the bejeesus out of him!"

She struck out and knocked the scarecrow's head to the ground, hat and all.

"That's the stuff!" said James, and he tossed her into the air and caught her with a war whoop.

Kathleen laughed as wildly as she'd been crying a moment before. It wound up in one of their yelling contests, only there were neighbors now and before long the lights came on in a nearby row of company houses and cries of protest, obscene and otherwise, were raised. James replied at the top of his lungs, "Shut up the lot of you and listen to this!"

And he had Kathleen sing:

> *"Quanto affetto! Quali cure!*
> *che temete, padre mio?*
> *Lassù in cielo presso Dio,*
> *veglia un angiol protettor.*
> *Da noi toglie le sventure*
> *di mia madre il priego santo;*
> *non fia mai divelto o franto*
> *questo a voi diletto fior."*

That's how James got a reputation as a drinker, although at that point he was a teetotaler.

The next day he stuck the straw head back onto the stake and jammed the hat on the head. There were no more nightmares.

> What great love! What care!
> What do you fear, my father?
> In heaven above, with God,
> I have a guardian angel.
> We are protected from all misfortune
> by the holy prayers of my mother.
> This flower that you love so much
> will never be uprooted or destroyed.

The Pit

EVEN THOUGH IT WAS just an old cart, he painted it red with gold trim so she'd have something handsome to ride back and forth to school in. He did her initials in fancy gilt on the side and their joke was "Your carriage awaits without, ma'am." It meant giving up some piano pupils, but he drove her the nine miles to Holy Angels every morning and he was there every afternoon when the big double doors opened and she came running down the steps to meet him. On Friday afternoons they'd linger in Sydney, wandering down to the yacht club wharf to look at the ships in the harbor.

"One day you'll get on one of those liners, my darling, and go."

She wanted him to come with her, of course, but he didn't patronize her. "You're going to sing for people all over the world. I won't always be there, but I'll always be your daddy."

At which she would cry and he would take them for ice cream at Crown Bakery, her eyelashes still wet but her eyes smiling once more. She never stayed sad for long. People stared wherever they went because she was beautiful, and the two of them were so obviously the best of friends.

James knew that someday he'd have to hand her over to professionals, send her far away, but for now . . . There was a God. James consecrated his life to being a worthy caretaker of God's gift. It was how he could endure teaching the offspring of the petty bourgeoisie to mangle "Für Elise." I'll do anything, he told God and himself. I'll cut off my arm, I'll sell the teeth in my head, I'll enter the pit. I'll allow my wife to get a job.

"Okay," said Materia.

He prepared himself for the fact that she'd likely get work cleaning and cooking in someone else's house, or at a hotel. He told her to use her maiden name. "If people think you're married, they'll pay you less," he explained. It mustn't be known that Kathleen Piper's mother was a maid.

Imagine his surprise when Materia left the house a few evenings later wearing her good dress, her hair combed and done up under her hat.

"Where're you going, missus?"

"Work."

On Plummer Avenue, the main drag of the boom town, inside the Empire Theatre, the silver screen flickered, and down in the orchestra pit so did the piano. Trills and triplets seemed a natural counterpart to the frenetic dance of light and shadow above.

The audience leans slowly back as the locomotive appears on the horizon, tinkling toward them at first, birds singing—just another day in the country—then the first hint of doom as the train looms larger; a switch from major to minor, chugga chugga, here it comes rattling and rolling, whistle screeching, punctuated by the warning *woo-woo,* escalating through the landscape in a melody of mad elation, hurtling over the keys till all erupts in chaos, notes and birds fly asunder and the speeding iron horse thunders right over our heads and past us.

The audience is breathless, eager for the next terror, all you can take for a nickel. Materia can't believe she's getting paid for this.

The next scene is more terrifying. A man in evening clothes has cornered a young woman in a slinky nightgown halfway up a clock tower. No narrative preamble required, *all ist klar,* the shadows lurk, the tower lists, the music creeps the winding stair, the villain spies a grace note of silken hem and he's on the chase in six-eight time up to where our heroine clings to a snatch of girlish melody, teetering on the precipice of high E, overlooking the street eight octaves below. Villain struggles with virgin in a macabre waltz, Strauss turned Faust, until, just when it seems she'll plummet, dash her brains on the bass clef and die entangled in the web of the lower stave, a vision in tenor crescendos on to save the day in resolving chords.

Before long, Materia was playing for local *ceilidhs* and traveling vaudeville troupes.

In December 1909, James boarded Kathleen at Holy Angels because children were dying in the boom town. Scarlet fever, diphtheria, cholera, typhoid, smallpox, tuberculosis. Leaving a wake of little white coffins. Outbreaks of disease were far from uncommon but this was something else, this was an epidemic brought on by the miners' strike. Rows of company houses sat empty, their striking tenants evicted, yanked naked some of them, pulled off the crapper and out of the cradle, credit cut off at the Company Store. Pinkerton guards and special company constables went door to door till there was more furniture on the streets than in the houses. Even miners who had bought their own homes were evicted, the coal company having put the fear of God into the mortgage company. Families hunkered down in ragged tent cities out in the fields, no running water, less food, scant shelter from the Atlantic winter winds. Scarlet blotches bloomed on the thin cheeks of children, they suffocated on pus or died worn out from coughing.

But nothing could convince the miners back to work. Not even a Royal Canadian machine gun mounted on the steps of the Immaculate Conception Church over at Cadegan Brook—and though Father Charlie MacDonald claimed he was away at the time, the Catholic church did its bit all the same to end the needless suffering of the strike: the bishop sent a special envoy to the boom town to empty the convent, the school, the rectory and the church of the miners' families that the parish priest, Father Jim Frazer, was sheltering there. Then the bishop transferred Father Frazer right off the island.

James acted fast. There was no money to board Kathleen at Holy Angels but money would be found. She'd not be kept here in the boom town to catch her death from the miners' brats. Or wind up crippled, or scarred in the face, please God no. They've brought it on themselves, stubborn bastards, and that's why I have to board my daughter at the school I already can't afford to send her to, and who's to help me do that? The piano teachers' union? The Piano-Tuners-of-the-World-Unite Party? Jesus Christ on the cross, no. I'm on my own.

"Sweetheart, you're going to live in at school for just a little while."

She didn't want to.

"No, I won't be there, and it'll be a while before I can visit." He would observe strict quarantine. "It'll be fun, you'll see, you'll make some buddies."

She cried. He said, suddenly severe, "Giuditta Pasta was lame, and when she was asked how she was able to sing so beautifully and act so brilliantly night after night, yet give no sign of her affliction, she said what?"

" 'It hurts.' "

He patted her on the head, "That's the stuff."

It would be months before he saw her again. He thought to himself, it's good training for the both of us.

He took the ill luck the strike had dealt him and turned it to his own purposes. Before dawn one winter morning he shouldered three sparkling new picks, an undented shovel and a length of rope. He filled a teapot-style lamp with whale oil, clipped it to his peaked cap, hooked a lunch can to his belt and walked with three Pinkerton guards to the Number 12 gate, where khaki-clad Tommies guarded the coal with fixed bayonets.

The soldiers who let him in were no friendlier than the gauntlet of striking miners he'd left outside, though the soldiers didn't spit or rave and call him "scab," and accuse him of murdering their children. Nor did they promise to throw his balls to the pigs.

He entered the mouth of the pit, following the trembling light of the open flame at his forehead and the shadows of the men ahead, down the sloping shaft of the main deep along the rail tracks, reaching out to touch the steel rope now and then. The airless smell of ponies, damp wood and earth, through trap doors that swung open magically, it seemed, until a child's voice said, "Hey buddy, what's the time?" Left turn, right turn, right, then left again, down, down, through the maze of hollow branches that blossomed into dark chambers. He heard a bird chirping.

Number 12 Mine was terribly wet and gassy but James had nothing to compare it to. He shoveled coal onto a cart in a dripping room he didn't know was under the ocean. He worked alongside one other man who happened to be experienced. It was this man's job to undercut the wall, then to bore and lay and light the charges without blowing up the mine. James couldn't place the man's accent and never realized he was black, from Barbados, just knew he was Albert who never got them killed. Barbados, Italy, Belgium, Eastern Europe, Quebec . . . The Dominion Coal Company had reached far and wide to break the strike. Very few English voices in the darkness and those that there were were heavily accented. James drank cold tea and chewed tobacco to keep down the dust, and at first concealed, then shared, his meat sandwiches. The cart held just over a ton, and when it was full he and Albert pushed it from the coal face to the headway and hitched it onto a trip. At the end of ten hours they surfaced into more darkness.

The foreign men were escorted to their stockaded work camp

nearby, called Fourteen Yard, to sing, sleep or gamble while the Royal Canadian Regiment stood guard. James walked home with the Pinkerton sons of bitches, passing between lines of mangy men who would have torn him limb from limb given half a chance—for as they saw it James had no excuse, he wasn't starving and he wasn't a foreigner—past women who stood on front stoops and gave him the evil eye, muttering, "May God forgive you." One said a prayer for him, then hurled an iron doorstopper, missing him by a hair.

James was making many times what he'd made teaching piano. For the first few weeks he wept silently at the beginning of every shift, until his body got rebroken to the work. Every night at home, after he'd turned white again, he'd get on his knees, fold his hands and beg his mother's forgiveness for going underground.

The Price of a Song

"YOU'VE GOT A BIT thinner. That's good," James said to Materia over supper.

She shrugged.

"What are you daydreaming about?" James used the term loosely, she was always gawping at everything and nothing.

"Houdini," she said.

"Who?"

"Houdini."

He didn't bother to pursue it. Ask a silly question. He'd long ago given up on conversation and now merely thanked God that the idiocy and swarthiness had bypassed his daughter. And that his wife had learned to cook.

"What's this?"

"Kibbeh nayeh."

"This a Hebrew delicacy?"

"Lebanese."

Benny had smuggled her the recipe.

Anyone can make *kibbeh nayeh,* anyone can make anything by following directions, but to make it right . . . that takes a blessed finger. Some say it's in the length of the cook's fingers, others claim it's in the scent, as unique as a fingerprint, that every person carries. It is definitely a gift.

Kibbeh was the national dish of Syria and Lebanon, it had to be made from the most trustworthy meat, therefore the Mahmouds bought only from Luvovitz's Kosher Canadian Butcher Shop. While Mrs. Luvovitz and the boys minded the shop, Benny made his deliveries in Sydney, always going last to the Mahmoud house on the hill. There, a dark little round woman with a graying bun of black hair would open the kitchen door to him. Benny didn't speak Gaelic and Mrs. Mahmoud's English was still halting, but they managed to chat. Benny would go along with the pretense that Mrs. Mahmoud's interest in the Piper family was purely casual.

"Oh sure I know the Pipers, she's a nice lady Mrs. Piper, Lebanese too, I guess you must know her—no?—ah well, yes they've got a lovely daughter, Kathleen, goes to Holy Angels, sings like a bird."

And this morning, when Benny asked Mrs. Mahmoud for the *kibbeh* recipe "for my wife," she didn't raise an eyebrow but went immediately to her cupboards and pointed out ingredients. Benny noted it all on brown butcher paper as Mrs. Mahmoud mimed the whole process, including the imprinting of a cross on the prepared meat. Benny laughed and shook his head and drew a Star of David for her instead.

Mrs. Mahmoud shrugged and said, "What you like," and gave him the ritual first taste of the imaginary *kibbeh*.

"Delicious," he said.

That evening, Mrs. Mahmoud watched her husband eat and thought of her lost daughter, perhaps even now serving the same dish to her own husband. Would he appreciate it? Did he love her still?

Nine miles away, James took a forkful of *kibbeh* and ate.

"It's delicious."

"Eat with bread."

He followed Materia's example, drizzling oil over the spiced meat and soft cracked wheat, tearing off bits of flat bread, folding the meat into mouthfuls.

"Where'd you learn to cook this?"

"Is raw, no cook."

He paused.

"Kosher?"

She nodded. He resumed eating. Materia got a pang; she thought, "We're happy without the girl."

She touched the back of his neck lightly.

"What are you doing?" he said.

"Nothing," and she returned to the sink.

Up till now the vaudevillians had been white, doing their minstrel shows and piccaninny turns in blackface, but now that there was a colored migration to the Sydney coalfield, genuine colored artists started coming up from the States. Materia couldn't figure out why they too performed under cork with giant painted-on mouths, but she did know she preferred them. She acquired a big collection of ragtime, two-step, cakewalk, processionals, sorrow songs, plantation lullabies and gospel.

She got to play for the Blackville Society Tap Twizzlers when their own accompanist was arrested in Glace Bay. They were a trio of brothers managed by their mother. The eldest had named his feet. He called the left one Alpha and the right one Omega.

Percussive shoes, flashing feet that chatted, clattered, took flight and girdled the globe without ever leaving center stage at the Empire Theatre. Materia just watched their feet and let her hands go, chunks of *Rigoletto* colliding with "Coal Black Rose," "Una Voce Poco Fa" on a seesaw with "Jimmy Crack Corn," all slapped up against her own spontaneous compositions—just as for the moving pictures, only with the dancers there was a two-way feed. They hounded, flattered, talked back and twisted— ebony, ivory, and nickel clickers grappling till there wasn't even any melody, just rhythm and attitude.

Materia became a bit of a celebrity, especially among the young folk.

"Hey there, Materia, how's she going, girl?"

"That's Mrs. Piper to you, buddy," James shot back.

It was a Sunday in March, they were out whitewashing the house. He turned to Materia when the feller had slunk by. "How do you know him?"

"The show."

The Blackville Society Tap Twizzlers invited her to tour with them as their permanent accompanist. They were going to Europe. Materia said no. She cried on the way home at the thought of how happy she and James could be, seeing the world together with a traveling show. But she knew better than to ask him.

The colored artists stopped coming soon after, because word had gone down the line that the new arrivals in the Sydney coalfield were up from the West Indies and weren't too interested in American colored entertainment. But Materia still had the vaudeville and the picture shows and she was happy as long as she could play. Down in the orchestra pit she consoled herself with the occasional embellishment. Now and then a locomotive sped toward the audience through "I Love You Truly," and ran over them to "Moonlight Sonata." Villains struggled with virgins to

"The Wedding March" and tenors saved the day to "Turkey in the Straw." Performers complained, but the audience ate it up when rabbits emerged from top hats to discordant splats and women were sawn in half to "Nearer My God to Thee." Materia had always smiled as she played but now she started chuckling, though she wasn't aware of it. This further endeared her to the audience, who liked her all the better for being a bit loony.

These days, James went all the way to Sydney for provisions. With the exception of Benny and Mr. MacIsaac, he didn't darken the door of any boom town establishment. Why go in to be insulted when he was paying good money? The whole town was suffering as a result of the strike, not just the miners, so everyone loved to hate a scab. He never walked, he drove his cart so as not to give people the satisfaction of crossing the street when they saw him coming. "And all because I have the gumption to support my family." It was galling, therefore, on the rare occasion when Materia accompanied him, to hear time and again, "Hello there, Materia, how's the show business, dear?" The same people who wouldn't give him the time of day would stop to chat with his illiterate wife about her career as a player-piano. Naturally these people would appreciate a low type of music. And why were they out spending money they supposedly didn't have on the price of admission at the Empire Theatre? There were too many Irish in this town by now for James's liking. Every second house a shebeen, drunken Catholics the lot. If they worked more and fiddled less they wouldn't be in such a mess. James thought of Aesop's grasshopper and ant and made a mental note to enclose the fable in his next letter to Kathleen.

Picking up a packet of starch at MacIsaac's, James had to endure "You've got a very talented wife, Mr. Piper."

James paid. MacIsaac continued, "And how's the wee lass?"

"She's all right."

"She's got a gift, that one."

James nodded. MacIsaac smiled and added, "Gets it from her mother, no doubt."

James turned and left the store. He wouldn't be taking Kathleen in there again. He decided he didn't trust the bald man. He didn't like the way he looked at children with his watery blue eyes and his big red face. If MacIsaac liked children so much why didn't he have any of his own?

When James left, Mrs. MacIsaac said to her man, "We shouldn't let Piper set foot in here."

MacIsaac smiled softly at his wife, then retired to his greenhouse. "Sufficient unto the day is the evil thereof."

Everyone liked MacIsaac, though not everyone understood how he could tolerate a man like Piper. But MacIsaac didn't see the point in penalizing a man's family for a man's mistakes and that was what you did when you cut a feller off. People shrugged and figured maybe MacIsaac was just religious. And he was, in a way; he spent a lot of time finding medicine out in the fields where other people saw only stones and scrub. He cultivated the plants in his greenhouse. Never called in a debt. Pity about the drink.

At the end of that week, James sat down to his latkes and molasses and said, "I want you to quit your job now, missus, I'm earning enough at the pit."

No answer. He looked up. Hard to know sometimes if she even registered a word he said.

"Did you hear me?"

". . . Okay."

"And don't be traipsing around town on your own."

How unhappy are they who have a gift that's left to germinate in darkness. The pale plant will sink invisible roots and live whitely off their blood.

The first week away from the Empire was hardest. The empty house, and at night James, who required feeding and nothing else. She searched for the key to the piano, and finally pried the instrument open with a knife. But after a few numbers she fell silent. She needed a stage, not a garret. No audience, no show. Materia took her sheaf of music and put it in the hope chest.

She cleaned the house and cooked a lot. Ate. She didn't have the heart to spend much time with Mrs. Luvovitz because the boys, Abe and Rudy, were a reproach to her soul. How could it be that she loved another woman's children and not her own? The interlude at the Empire receded and became unreal. Now that Materia was on her own again, with plenty of time to think, all her badness rolled back in and enveloped her: to have left her father's house, to have disobeyed and dishonored her parents— that was against the Commandments.

I have to go to confession, she thought, but then . . . in order to be forgiven I must be heartily sorry, but to be sorry for eloping means to be sorry for everything that came from it. And she couldn't be. She still wanted her husband and that too was a sin: to want the man, and not the child that comes from the marital act. And so she would keep coming back to her original sin.

She resumed her prayers to the Blessed Virgin. It pierced her heart, and it seemed a dreadful vapor rose from the wound, when she realized she hadn't given a thought to her daughter all this time. Not a note had she sent, no package of goodies from home, she hadn't even asked James, "How's the girl?" Materia saw herself in a clear glass at last, and it was monstrous.

Whom could she tell? No one. Yet she must tell or die.

In the second week, Materia left the house and walked to the cliff but didn't linger there as she used to. She scrambled down to the rocky shore and walked. She didn't sing, she talked and talked in her mother tongue to the stones, till she grew dizzy and the day grew gray and she lost track of where she was. Finally, as sometimes happens in this part of the world, the clouds lifted. A burning sky lit the sea in rippling tongues of red and gold. Materia fell silent. She faced the horizon and listened until she heard what the sea was saying to her: "Give it to me, my daughter. And I will take it and wash it and carry it to a far country until it is no longer your sin; but just a curiosity adrift, beached and made innocent."

And so, day after day, Materia slowly let her mind ebb away. Until she was ready to part with it once and for all.

Quanto Dolor

*"I'm very fond of dividing and classifying
and examining, you see I'm so much alone,
I've so much time for reflection, and Papa
is training me to think."*

CLAUDIA, BY A.L.O.E.

THE STRIKE ENDED IN April 1910, and James got a job on the surface as a check-weighman in reward for his loyalty. He had expected to see his pit buddy Albert up there too, had hoped to get a look at him in the light of day, but Albert had been let go. He had moved on to Sydney with many others from Fourteen Yard, and settled in Whitney Pier in the neighborhood known as The Coke Ovens. There were lots of people there up from the West Indies; the Dominion Iron and Steel Company knew the value of a strong man who could stand heat. The Coke Ovens was a cozy community, its houses painted everything but white, snuggled right up against the steel mill. The mill put bread on the table and a fine orange dust on the bread.

In the boom town the company houses were tenanted once more, the Company Store took miners' scrip again, the last children were buried and Kathleen came home. James had a surprise waiting: electric lights, and a modern water closet complete with indoor toilet, enamel tub and nickel-plated taps, hot and cold.

What with his hours at the pithead, James could no longer drive Kathleen to and from Holy Angels. He hired a fellow from The Coke

Ovens who drove his own horse and buggy. James was taken aback by his youth—Leo Taylor was barely sixteen—but he was steady, James made sure.

"No detours, straight there and straight home."

"Yes sir."

"I don't want you talking to her."

"No sir."

"Don't touch her."

"I wouldn't."

"I'll kill you."

"Don't worry, sir."

James reflected that he'd rather have a timid youth drive his daughter than a leering man. The fact that Taylor was colored made James feel all the more confident of the necessary distance between driver and passenger.

Although she no longer had any buddies in the boom town, Kathleen was relieved to be living at home again. Boarding at Holy Angels had been lonely. At first she'd cried herself to sleep, comforted only by the notes and treats that her daddy sent. But she knew that sacrifices were being made, knew what was expected of her, didn't flinch. She studied hard, obeyed the nuns and never complained, though she did pray for a fairy godmother to send her a friend, for there was no one to play with at Holy Angels. No boys. No cinders embedded in her knees. Other little girls weren't interested in swordfights and adventure or in who could enact the most spectacular death scene. Other girls were preoccupied with meticulous feminine arcana of which Kathleen knew nothing; what was more, none of them had careers. Initially, her schoolmates had vied for Kathleen's friendship—she was so pretty, so smart. But she failed to decode pecking orders, declined gracious invitations to braid other girls' hair and made a lasso of the skipping rope. They put her down as odd until, finally, they shunned her altogether.

Kathleen threw herself into her work and cultivated an insouciant nonconformity—her sash low slung and tied in front, hat pushed back, hands jammed into the pockets that she ordered her mother to sew into her uniforms, her long hair waving loose. The nuns made allowances. She had a gift.

In the fall of 1911 they sailed to the mainland—James, Kathleen and her singing teacher, Sister Saint Cecilia—to a recital at the Royal Conservatory of Music in Halifax. An invited audience of professionals.

"Look me in the eyes."

She did. He invoked the spirits,

"What did Stendhal say of Elisabetta Gafforini?"

" 'Whether you see, or only hear her, your peril is the same.' "

"That's the stuff." His usual affectionate bonk on the head. "Now go out there and show 'em who's boss."

Kathleen sang Cherubino's love poem to Susanna from *Le Nozze di Figaro*. Teachers from New York City gave James their cards, they were looking for the next Emma Albani. Told him what he already knew.

Henriette Sontag debuted at six, Maria Malibran at five; Adelina Patti was younger every year, her legend already way ahead of her mortality; but James was so serious about Kathleen's career that he could wait for it to begin. Patience is the mark of the true player. Her voice would last, not burn out in a blaze of adolescent glory. He would send her to Halifax for a year to get her sea legs. Then on to Milano at eighteen.

Kathleen turned twelve.

"When Malibran's father told her she must go on for Giuditta Pasta, as Desdemona to his Otello, he looked her in the eye and swore that if she did not sing perfectly, when it came to the scene where Otello murders Desdemona, he really would kill her."

Kathleen laughed and said, "You're a melodramatic old feller, aren't you."

Materia marveled. The girl was saucy, she deserved a good slap talking to her father like that, but never got one, got a chuckle and a wink instead.

Kathleen had a way of swaggering a little even standing still, and especially when leaning against a piano. She didn't yet know how beautiful she was, but she'd begun to suspect. She'd begun to care about how she walked, to gauge her effect on others. She practiced world-weary expressions in front of the mirror. She looked up the word "languid." She adopted a tone of amused scorn and loved to kid her father about his romantic obsession with *la Voce,* ordering him to fetch her grapes and peel them too. "If I'm going to be a diva, you'd better start treating me like one."

He loved her way: acting casual, working like a Trojan, singing like an angel. Not "angelically." The voice of an angel. Winged, lethal, close to the sun.

When Malibran died too young too fast—

"Sure, sure, her voice went into her husband's violin. And pigs fly."

She had the world by the tail. A modern girl. James had read about the "New Woman." That's what my daughter's going to be.

One Friday afternoon in March 1912, while Materia is in the kitchen cooking a magnificent silent supper and James is half-entombed in the old piano, Kathleen appears in the archway of the front room.

She's wearing her Holy Angels uniform. She's grown tall. Leaning in the doorway, her weight on one hip, feeling her teens though they're a year off. A smile plays about her mouth at the sight of her old dad toiling over the strings of that decrepit war horse. She glances down, bites her lip, then steals over to the piano and strikes a chord.

James springs up and around, though the hammers barely winged him, belts her with an open hand then a closed fist before he realizes who it is and what he's done, and how he'd never, not even Materia, though God knows—

His daughter is crying. She's shocked. He's hurt her, how? With my own hands. Dear God.

He reaches out, grazes a shoulder, an elbow, finds the small of her back, crushes her to him, he has never, would never do anything to hurt you, rather die, cut off my arms. He feels so acutely what she feels, clasping her, "Don't cry," a perishing empathy, "Hush now," his throat scorched and taut, "Shshshsh," he must protect her from—he must shield her from—what? . . . From all of it. From it all.

A life and a warmth enter his body that he hasn't felt since—that he has rarely felt. She will be safe with him, I'll keep you safe, my darling, oh how he loves this girl. He holds her close, no harm, never any harm. Her hair smells like the raw edge of spring, her skin is the silk of a thousand spinning wheels, her breath so soft and fragrant, *milk and honey are beneath your tongue.* . . . Then he shocks himself. He lets her go and draws back abruptly so she will not notice what has happened to him. Sick. I must be sick. He leaves the room and bolts through the back door, across the yard, over the creek to the garden, where he calms down enough to vomit.

Materia gets her balance in the archway where she stumbled just now, when James knocked her aside on his retreat. She came when she heard the commotion, and stopped in the doorway and watched. She's still watching. She goes to her daughter.

One of Kathleen's teeth is loose. She's young, it'll mend. There's a silly amount of blood on the carpet. Looks worse than it is. Materia takes Kathleen by the hand to the kitchen, where she washes her at the pump. She puts her to bed and brings her soft food. Sings until the green eyes close. Takes a pillow and places it gently over the sleeping face.

But removes it the next instant. If Materia's heart were full, she'd know what to do. Who to save, how. Loving the girl now seems like an easy task compared with protecting her. It's because I failed the first test that I am confronted with the second.

Materia tries to think what to do. But thinking never helped in such a situation. She gets a whiff of salt air, a chill laps her cheek, she feels movement beneath her feet, the bed pitches and she is on a liner bound for New York City, the girl with the heart-of-flame hair at her side clinging to the rail. But the moment flees before Materia can get hold of it, a message telegraphed weakly over a sagging distance of time and space, every second word missing.

Materia knows now who sent Kathleen, and why. It's her own fault God is forced to work in this way. Through my fault, through my fault, through my most grievous fault.

Kathleen knew that her father had hit her by mistake, that he was terribly sorry. She knew he'd been working too hard and all for her sake. No harm done, the tooth settled back into the gum. She made him a card to tell him she loved him. She wrote a funny poem about "the lost chord." They put it behind them.

The First Solution

THE NEXT NIGHT, MATERIA conceived Mercedes.

To her own surprise, Materia began to look forward to this child, not even caring if it was a boy. She was *Hebleh* again and she liked it this time. It made her feel close to her own mother, expanding body, avalanche breasts, slow thighs. Her troubles went into remission.

James still didn't take her places, but he came alive again at night—she's my wife, after all. Her dark body and soft mind allowed him to enjoy her in an uncomplicated way. Why did he ever look to her for conversation or mental stimulation? It was unfair of him. A man looks elsewhere for those things. James finally felt normal.

He put on a little weight; she fed him, ran his nightly bath, washed his back, licked his ear and reached into the water. He let her. He was soothed. He had outrun the demon that had leaped up in him the day he hurt Kathleen.

Materia tried to conceive in sorrow, telling herself that it was only to prevent a greater sin on her husband's part that she acted the harlot with him, enticing him even when she was already pregnant. Lust in marriage is the same as adultery. Adultery's a mortal sin. That's in the Commandments. Materia prayed that God might overlook the impurity in her heart. For after all, her actions were correct.

Mercedes is born late in 1912. Materia loves her. She doesn't have to try, she just does, it's a Joyful Mystery. Thank you Jesus, Mary and Joseph and all the saints. And God too.

Materia doesn't begrudge Mrs. Luvovitz a third son, Ralph, two months younger than Mercedes; maybe they'll grow up to marry each other.

James doesn't object or even comment when Materia gets Mercedes baptized by the priest at the Catholic church in nearby Lingan. She starts going to mass again, not just Sunday but every day. Holy water in the desert, she hadn't known how thirsty she'd been. Materia lights candles and kneels to pray with Mercedes in her arms at the base of the beautiful eight-foot Mary. But Materia doesn't look up. She looks straight into the ruby eyes of the grinning serpent dying under the Virgin's foot.

Materia offers it a sacrifice. She will play only at church, and only from the hymnal. Her one concession is Mrs. Luvovitz's Yiddish songbook, which is the least she can do for a friend who has given so much. It's the same God, after all.

Eleven months later, Mrs. Luvovitz is on the spot again when Materia gives birth to Frances. Lucky thing, because Frances is set to walk out feet first. Mrs. Luvovitz reaches in and turns her around. Not so much difference between a calf and a child. Frances is born with the caul. An especially good omen for an island child, being a charm against drowning.

Frances looks a little starveling and she's bald as a post. Materia figures it's because she conceived too soon after Mercedes, the goodness in her womb hadn't yet been replenished. And her milk isn't as bountiful. All the more reason to love this one too.

Frances is baptized at the Empire Theatre on Plummer Avenue. The temporary digs of the new Our Lady of Mount Carmel Catholic Church.

Mercedes is a good baby, following everything closely with her brown eyes, sleeping when she ought, wanting to hold the cup and not spill a drop. Frances laughs at seven weeks.

Along with Frances, the town is officially born in 1913. The boom town has a name now: New Waterford.

James feels the normal pride of a man with a growing family. He works double shifts but that's a small price to pay. Those two babies are the proof. His demon is so far behind him now, he can reflect upon it: he was overworked. He hit his daughter by mistake and got terribly upset. In the ensuing panic there was a physical accident. Meaningless. Hanged men get hard-ons, for heaven's sake.

* * *

Materia's pregnant again.

James is glad to see that his wife has recovered her senses. No more roaming the shore, babbling. No more unnerving sights like that of his wife in the attic with her head in the hope chest, sound asleep or entranced. Never now does he hear her tormenting the piano as he comes up the walk from work. Crazy for religion, yes, but women are. And she'll get her shape back after the baby.

The two little ones seem fine, Mercedes breastfeeding a dolly and cooing to Frances. Frances has hair now. Curly golden locks, hazel eyes with glints of laughing green, first word: "Boo!"

It rains all winter. Plummer Avenue is aptly named and runs with mud but the Pipers have plenty of coal to burn off the damp. The fire is lit and the radiators clank to life the moment Kathleen gets home from school.

Materia watches Kathleen mount the stairs to her room, then returns to the kitchen and mixes flour and water for doughboys while James washes up at the kitchen pump. She watches him head to the front room, already absorbed in his *HALIFAX HERALD: News from merry old England: the Union Jack has unfolded itself over two acres of new territory every time the clock has ticked since 1880. . . .*

Five minutes later Materia wipes her hands on her apron and spot-checks James from the shadows of the front hall. Yes, he's safely settled in the wingback chair beneath the reading lamp—*Sozodont: Good for Bad Teeth, Not Bad for Good Teeth. . . .*

Materia returns to the kitchen, where supper simmers and Mercedes rocks Frances in the cradle. She sets the table. Twelve minutes later, she climbs the stairs to peer through the inch of doorway Kathleen has left open—the girl has a bad habit of lounging about in her underthings, draping herself over the side of her bed reading, wearing toe marks into the flocked wallpaper while brushing her hair, practicing different accents— yes, she's alone. Materia silently pulls the door to, turns and descends all the way to the cellar to stoke the furnace. The house can never be hot enough for the orchid on the second floor.

Once back in the kitchen, Materia fixes a honey lemon toddy and crosses again to the front hall—James now dozing in his chair, the paper slipped to the floor, *Disgruntled Serbia . . .* —continues upstairs, opens

Kathleen's door—"Mother! Can't you knock?"—hands the young lady her preprandial tonic and watches her sip from the steaming cup. A green vein shimmers beneath the surface of Kathleen's lily-white neck, summoned by the heat. Another glides from the crease at her armpit, to disappear behind the genuine silk camisole. A flush spreads from her cheeks down her throat, splashing her chest.

Materia lumbers back down to the kitchen, stirs the pot and hollers, "Supper!"

James shakes off his nap and arrives at the table rubbing his hands— "Something sure smells good."

Materia yells again for Kathleen, who saunters in loosely wrapped in a kimono—"Must you bellow? I'm right here"—slouches into a chair; "What are we having?"

Materia replies, "Boiled dinner."

"Oh boy," says James.

Kathleen groans, he laughs. "It's good for ya, old buddy, put hair on your chest."

Kathleen winces, he's so corny.

Real Cape Breton cuisine. Potatoes, turnips, cabbage, carrots and, if you're prosperous, plenty of pork hocks. If you've ever had it cooked right, your mouth waters at the thought. Materia continues to surpass herself in the kitchen, everything she touches turns to juices. She hauls the pot to the table and ladles out big portions. Kathleen is English for the moment. "No cabbage for me, thank you, Mother dear, *je refuse.*"

James is amused. He watches Kathleen rearrange the food on her plate and, after a token interval, gets up and makes her a toasted cheese.

Materia eats her own supper, then she eats Kathleen's, sopping up the broth with bread. James avoids looking at her—stooped over her plate, masticating slowly—he tries not to think it but there it is: bovine. Kathleen nibbles her cheese toast and leaves the crusts. The princess and the pea.

If James has forgotten the demon, Materia hasn't. She saw it. It looked at her. She knows it's coming back. Materia has two real daughters now, she loves them, so it's all very clear. One novena gives way to another, she logs miles along the Stations of the Cross, meditates upon the Mysteries— Joyful, Sorrowful and Glorious—of the rosary. Gains partial indulgences, does not hope to gain a plenary indulgence, being never free from attachment to sin despite frequent confessions.

The beautiful eight-foot Mary with her blue robe and sweet sorrow-ful face has been moved from Lingan to New Waterford's newly built Our Lady of Mount Carmel Church, and there, in her own grotto, she presides with her Holy Infant and serpent.

In the cool darkness, sweet chafing incense faint upon the air, Materia kneels at Our Lady's feet and prays that James be kept free of his demon for as long as possible. She prays to the demon. And lights another candle for it.

It's a freak spring, so hot Materia can hardly move; she's huge. What can be in there, wonders James. Looks like she's incubating a twelve-inch can-nonball. Nonetheless, she walks to church every morning with her two children in Kathleen's old English pram. Mrs. MacIsaac watches her inch by the drugstore window and worries for her: no one should be that close to God. Mr. MacIsaac beckons her in for raspberry soda. Materia declines, everything makes her queasy, but the little ones drink till they sport pink mustaches.

The bigger she gets, the harder she prays, for James has once again ceased to come near her, and Kathleen grows lovelier and more careless every day. Materia watches their heads mutually inclined over a sum on a slate; sees Kathleen prance before him in her newest frock. Watches his face when the girl sings just for him.

Swamped in flesh, Materia can't seem to get a clear deep breath. By June she's sleeping on the kitchen cot, no more stairs. This baby is sapping the life out of her—no more spot-checks on her husband and daughter, not at this rate.

She hasn't a thing to fit her anymore so she takes three old dresses and cuts them into one: rosebud print in front, green taffeta sides and plaid back. She spends a comfortable day but when James comes home it's "What in the name of God have you got on?"

She asks him for money. She buys a remaindered bolt of crazy floral calico and, with the help of Mrs. Luvovitz, fashions three roomy dresses. Mrs. Luvovitz offers her several yards of pale blue muslin instead but Materia declines. She likes the flowers. James shakes his head but doesn't comment.

Materia's always murmuring these days, her lips constantly moving whether she's mending a sock or changing a nappy. Worst, while making her glacial way through town to church.

"Don't be traipsing up Plummer Avenue nattering to yourself, woman."

"I not talking to myself."

"Then who're you talking to?"

"Mary."

Jesus Murphy.

Materia sees the demon grinning at her again from the mouth of its furnace. Night and day she secretes and spins a gauzy shroud of prayer in which she swaddles Kathleen. She sees the body of her daughter co-cooned, suspended, green eyes open. But no one can spin forever, and cocoons must yield, whether to release a butterfly or a meal. What has she left to sacrifice? She offered up her music long ago. She would mortify her flesh, but that might harm her unborn child. She has no vanity left to mortify, so she offers up her fat, her shabby shifts, her curly hair gone thin. But the demon isn't satisfied.

In the cool dark of Mount Carmel Church, Materia looks into the narrow green face of the serpent and makes the sign of the cross. Beside her kneels tiny Mercedes, little white-gloved hands folded around her very own rosary beads. Behind them baby Frances crawls beneath the pews, trailing her dress in the dust, finding shiny things. Materia fixes on the serpent's red eyes and bargains: if the demon will limit itself to one daughter, Materia will allow it to have Kathleen when the time comes. The demon grins. Agrees.

Then Materia looks up into the serene alabaster face of Our Lady and asks her to slow the demon down. Materia recites the Memorare: "Remember, O most gracious Virgin Mary, that never was it known that anyone who fled to your protection, implored your help or sought your intercession was left unaided. Inspired with this confidence, I fly unto you, O Virgin of virgins, my Mother; to you I come, before you I stand, sinful and sorrowful; O Mother of the Word Incarnate, despise not my petitions, but in your mercy hear and answer me. Amen."

Our Lady will think of something. Merciful are her ways.

The Third Secret of Fatima

*"I wonder," observed Emma, "whether well educated
Romanists really believe in all the strange miracles
which are said to have been worked by their saints."*

CLAUDIA, BY A.L.O.E.

JULY IS SWELTERING. THEY'VE vegetables enough to feed an army. The
scarecrow simmers in James's old pit boots and Materia's motley dress of
rosebuds, taffeta and plaid, the fedora angled on its blank head as always. If
you've ever stuck your hand inside a haystack and pulled it out again as
though from a hot oven, then you know what straw can do. Pete heats up
quietly. James waters the garden from the creek. Materia fills jar upon jar
with preserves, labeling them "Summer 1914."

James doesn't go to the baseball game on August 3, so he misses all the
excitement of New Waterford's victory over Sydney, but he'll read about
it on the front page of the *Post* next day. James has enough to keep himself
busy, what with his job, the garden and his daughter. That's why he
doesn't go to ball games, or sit down to politics in front of MacIsaac's store
or a deck of cards in back. In this way, he foils the efforts of most of New
Waterford never to let him forget that once a scab, always a scab.

James strolls up Plummer Avenue on his way to buy the paper. He no
longer takes the cart, for why shouldn't he walk through this town? He
lived here before there even was a town, before there was a coal company
or a single miner.

From a block away you might think James was walking on water, but it's just the shimmer of the cinders. Nothing is stirring this afternoon, certainly not a breeze. Those who have not taken refuge at the shore sit motionless on their front stoops, feet in buckets of ice water. For once it's a good day to be underground.

James is dressed, as usual, like a gentleman. Only a beast or an imperfectly civilized man reacts blindly to the vicissitudes of nature. Let the semiliterate masses strip to their undershirts, and behold the crux of their problem right there. So he strolls coolly into town. Cucumber in a woollen suit.

He buys the *Post* at MacIsaac's, where a couple of old-timers sit blinking occasionally. MacIsaac is sound asleep behind the cash. James drops his coins on the counter and, glancing at the headline as he leaves the store, can't suppress a pang of civic pride at his town's big baseball win. The old fellers watch him go, then break their wilted silence to speculate as to what qualifications might render a man insensible to scorching heat.

At the corner of Seventh Street an old West Indian woman rings a bell, selling oranges from a handcart. Atop her pyramid of fruit is set a sample of her wares split open. Blood-red juices. James buys one.

The sun has begun to set, the cool balm of evening coming on. Lilacs relax and the air is full of blue perfume. A dog barks, resurrected from the heat, and someone has struck up a strathspey on the fiddle, it being still too warm for a reel. James turns onto Water Street in time to see Leo Taylor pull up in front of the house in his buggy. Kathleen is home from her rehearsal. She waits while Taylor hops out and lets down the step for her. She descends from the buggy with the ease of a born aristocrat. Taylor says not a word and neither does Kathleen, nor does she look at him. It's moments like this that James savors. The sun basking in the west, blessing this island with rare rose and amber hues—it's all of life in a moment like this. God in His Heaven, and I in mine.

Kathleen sees James and runs to him as though she were suddenly seven years old again, breaking one spell to cast another. She's so excited, so nervous, "I could puke!"

"Some of the best singers puke before every show," James tells her.

She laughs, delighted and disgusted, frisking him for the treat she knows he'll have. Got it!—an orange hidden in the newspaper.

She's been practicing for weeks. Tonight she will sing publicly before a paying audience for the first time. Just at the Lyceum in Sydney. Just with amateurs and an audience of locals. But all the same. A performance is a performance.

"Always sing like you're at the Metropolitan Opera," says James. "Sing like you're at La Scala and never forget your public."

They're not calling it a debut. But it is a first, in its way. And they're both beside themselves with nerves.

That night:

THE ORPHEUS SOCIETY OF SYDNEY PRESENTS

Elegant Special Scenery
Wonderful Mechanical Devices
Mysterious Electrical Effects
In a very meritorious production of

Great Moments from Grand Opera

Don Juan disappears in a blaze of flashpots, dragged to hell by a statue. Silence. Applause. "Bravo!" "Encore!" "Blow 'er sky high, b'y!" The Lyceum is packed, standing room only. They've seen Tosca skewer Scarpia, then immediately leap into a void upstage. Seville has given way to Nagasaki, women have sleepwalked, been entombed in Egypt and brown body paint, stabbed themselves on their wedding day, and gone mad. Just the high points. INTERMISSION. Fans revolve in the vaulted ceiling, where leafy bowers and painted youths droop beside nymph-infested ponds. Below, spectators are happily abuzz as they unstick themselves from wooden seats and head for the lobby, where tea is served with date squares and little Union Jacks.

James stays put, his face shiny with impatience and anxiety, his stomach half turned by the past hour of grotesque huffing and straining on the tiny stage. Sister Saint Cecilia places a hand on his sleeve, but he doesn't notice. She rises and rustles off for a cuppa, thinking it's too bad and even a little odd that the girl's mother can't be here tonight—she had looked forward to meeting Mrs. Piper at last, and congratulating her on such a talented daughter. James is feeling badly in need of air but he's frozen in his seat. He has no wish to mingle and hear the effusions of the benighted throng. Kathleen is on after the intermission.

Unseen by James, a dark little round woman with a gray bun slips into the back of the hall with a tall young black woman. Mrs. Mahmoud is here because Benny made a delivery this morning. All these years, she has been able to resist waiting outside Holy Angels to get a look at Kathleen. She has managed never to send a note or a word via Benny to her daughter. But Mrs. Mahmoud has come here tonight because she needs to hear her granddaughter sing. And Teresa, her maid, was happy to accompany her, enjoying as she does, refined entertainment.

"Ladies and gentlemen, please take your seats for the second act." The audience rhubarbs back in—the upper crust of Sydney plus quite a few music lovers. The Sydney Symphonette tunes up. The house lights come down. The stage manager puts a taper to the footlights. The curtain rises. A courtyard. A midnight moon. A fountain. Ivy and climbing roses. A cardboard cat with eyes that open and shut, and one working paw— James is irritated, we're here for the music, not cheap theatrics. A man with a hump and a jester's hat of bells limps importantly onto the stage. The blood recedes from James's hands as he waits, every sinew in his body rapt and wrought like the strings on the first violin.

The orchestra sees her first. Then she appears from behind the painted jet of water. Incandescent. Kathleen. In a flowing white gown, her undone hair a halo of fire. James sits forward slightly—stop, stop, stop everyone and just look. Before you listen. You up there in the jingling hat, be still.

Rigoletto cries, *"Figlia!"* She flies into his arms; *"Mio padre!"* Father and daughter embrace. They weep, pledge their love, she asks what his real name is—"I am your father, let that suffice."

She asks who her mother was and what became of her.

(Con effusione) "She died."

"Oh Father, what great sorrow—*quanto dolor*—can cause such bitter tears?" But he can't tell her anything, he loves her too much. So much that he keeps her locked up here—

"You must never go out."

"I go out only to church."

"Good."

—so much that he'll put her in a bag and stab her by mistake *(Orror!)*—but that comes later. For now:

> *"Quanto affetto! Quali cure!*
> *che temete, padre mio?*

Lassù in cielo presso Dio,
veglia un angiol protettor. . . ."

With the first notes a frisson runs through the house; hairs spring to attention on napes of necks; erectile tissues stir unbidden beneath pearl-studded shirt fronts and matronly bodices, and within the farthest folds of nuns' habits. Two things can inspire such a shiver: a beautiful voice, and someone walking on your grave. But only the former can allow you to share the shiver with a packed house.

As the song takes wing, the Lyceum disappears and the heat melts away. James cannot suppress his tears. At first he's self-conscious, then he notices other people are wiping their eyes. It's nothing to do with the words, which are in a foreign language, or the story, which most people don't know. It's because a real and beautiful voice delicately rends the chest, discovers the heart, and holds it beating against a stainless edge until you long to be pierced utterly. For the voice is everything you do not remember. Everything you should not be able to live without and yet, tragically, do.

". . . Da noi toglie le sventure
di mia madre il priego santo;
non fia mai divelto o franto
questo a voi diletto fior."

The cavatina comes to an end, a simple song. There is a silence in the hall, full of the peace that can follow music and allow you to forget for a moment your mortal enemies, flesh and time.

The curtain falls. Applause. James releases Sister Saint Cecilia's hand. "I'm sorry, sister."

She smiles, testing discreetly the harmony of twenty-seven compressed bones.

The baritone in the hunchback suit waddles out and bows deeply with all the humility of haute ham but James pays him no mind—here she comes! The applause soars. "Brava!" cries the crowd, "Bravissima!" "Atta girl!" The audience rises to its feet. She curtsies, poised, dignified. James has never been so proud. For all his boyhood ambitions he never could have dreamed of this, of her, a gift of such magnificence. She belongs to the world, she's almost gone, he knows that and does not

begrudge it, he applauds with the rest. The baritone takes her hand,
kisses it—foolish lardass, get out of the way—any second the stagehand
will bring out the roses James has arranged, he can't wait to see her
face—she's being pelted with daisies—James swivels in his chair, intending to spot the culprit, and instead looks straight into the eyes of his
estranged mother-in-law. Teresa, the maid, sees the avid white face with
the boy-blue eyes and bird-of-prey bones and wonders, who is he to be
staring at Mrs. Mahmoud?

Meantime, the boy who fired the daisies is running toward the stage,
a black haired scallywag barely out of knickerbockers. The house is still
applauding. James turns to the front to see the boy vault onto the stage and
kiss his daughter on the cheek. An uproar, a laugh, more applause; the
youth turns pink, drops to his knees, laughing, worshipping. She knights
him with a daisy, James is on his way down the aisle, going to put a stop to
this, when "Ladies and gentlemen, may I have your urgent attention,
please!"

Clanging a handbell at the back of the hall, it's gray Mr. Foss, head of
the Orpheus Society. James stops in his tracks halfway through the brass
section. The roar of the crowd dies. All eyes are on Foss, who clears his
narrow throat and, with a reedy dignity befitting hope and glory, announces, "The offices of the *Sydney Post* have just received a cable from
the provincial parliament in Halifax. Today, Great Britain declared war on
Germany. Canada will heed the call of the Mother Country in her hour of
need. Ladies and gentlemen. We are at war."

Two minutes of silence will come four years later, but for now it's a
dotted-quarter-note rest broken by the boy on stage, who springs to his
feet *con spirito,* hurls three cheers into the air followed by a handful of
petals. The Sydney Symphonette strikes up "God Save the King." The
audience sings. James reaches for the lip of the stage to steady it, for it's
suddenly gone a little lopsided.

Late that night, twelve hours into The War, Kathleen sits at her vanity,
brushing her hair before the big oval looking-glass. She is not sleepy, how
could she be? Tonight she sang. The world will never be the same.

Who is that in the glass? She sees herself for the first time. She doesn't
require soft light, not at her age, not with her looks, so the effect of three
candles is excessively ravishing. Her hair sparks at every brush stroke. The
candlelight carves a grotto in the gloom around her. The mirror is a sacred

pool, in it she sees the future: her lips swollen with kissing, eyes caressing, come with me to my home beneath the sea and I will love you.

She unbuttons her nightgown. My beautiful throat. Bares a white shoulder, ohh. Parts the fabric to reveal her breasts, sailor take warning. Her image floating just beneath the twilight surface, tempting herself overboard.

She hovers her hand above a nipple that gathers and pleats to a point seeking heat. Kisses her palm with one eye on the mirror. Again, this time with her tongue. Experiments with the creation of cleavage. Arranges her hair: Gibson girl, milkmaid, madwoman, dryad. And leaves it there, spilling over her shoulders.

It's a self-portrait and the artist is in love.

Her mother has warned her against gazing too long into a mirror. If you like too well what you see there, the devil will appear behind you. This has always worried Kathleen in spite of the fact she knows it to be nonsense, so she has never lingered. But tonight she feels brazen. Prepared to test the theory.

She smiles at herself. And gets stuck. Can't move. Can't look away or break the smile tightening to a grin on her face until she seems to be mocking herself. That's when she sees him. Pete. In the shadows behind her. His smooth stuffed head. His hat. His no ears. His no face. She whimpers. Pete watches, *Hello there*. She can't find her voice, is this a dream? In a wistful tone, *Hello little girl*. His no mouth, *Hello*.

She explodes from the sateen stool with a cry, flies blindly through the room, through Pete for all she knows, crashes out her door, across the hall, screaming like an incoming shell to the room where her father sleeps alone. She lands heavily on his bed sobbing, "I want to sleep with you tonight!"

He's bolt upright, prepared to kill an intruder, but his fists turn to hands just in time to seize her shoulders. She's shaking.

"Shshsh," he says.

Carefully, through the darkness, he strokes her face. His thumb grazes her lips. "Hush now." His hand slips round the warm back of her neck, "Hush my darling." He kisses her cheek, the warm scent of her—he gets out of bed. Takes her briskly by the hand, "Come on, me old son," quick march down to the kitchen, on with the electric light. In her cot, Materia is already awake. "A bad dream, that's all, go back to sleep, missus." Hot milk with honey, "That'll fix you up, old buddy."

Kathleen sips and calms down while he reads the paper and Materia stares at the yellowing linoleum. She'll strip the wax tomorrow.

Back upstairs, he drags her mattress into the nursery room, where Frances and Mercedes sleep curled in their crib. Kathleen looks down at her sisters and feels her first rush of love for them, sweet bundles of babies' breath and milky dreams. She leans down to kiss them. When she rises, a lock of her hair is twined in Frances's fist. Gently she opens the tiny hand and tucks it under the covers.

Kathleen snuggles into her own bed on the floor and says to her father, "Don't go."

James says, "I'll be right here," and places his chair near the door, where he watches her till she falls asleep. Then he goes back to his own room and locks the door.

The next day, James outsmarts the demon for the second time. He enlists.

When James tells Materia that he has enlisted, she makes the sign of the cross. Oh no, he thinks, and tells her firmly, "It's no good asking me not to go, I've already joined up." She goes straight to church. James shakes his head. She might as well pray to the Kaiser for all the good it'll do. He's going, it's done.

Materia arrives at Mount Carmel and hurries over to Mary's grotto. There she prostrates herself as best she can, what with her unborn cargo, and gives thanks to Our Lady for sending The War.

Moving Picture

JAMES DECIDES IT CAN'T do any harm to carry a photo of Kathleen with him to the war. He gets one of Wheeler's boys to come out to New Waterford. He wants to remember her in her own home setting, not in a corpselike tableau against a backdrop of *faux* antiquity. Lifelike. Like her.

After school on August 7, Wheeler's assistant arrives with his contraption piled in Leo Taylor's buggy, between himself and Kathleen.

"Set 'er up out here," says James, "in front of the house, it's such a beautiful day."

The photographer peers through the circle of his thumb and forefinger at Kathleen standing motionless on the veranda with her hands folded and her feet in fifth position.

"That's lovely, Miss Piper, just lovely."

As Taylor unloads the buggy, James comes up and tells him quietly, "From now on, Taylor, any male passengers ride up front with you."

"Yes sir."

Taylor carries the boxy camera across the yard, its long hood trailing "like the severed head of a nun," thinks Kathleen, pleased with her own ghoulishness. The photographer arcs around her, finding just the right angle, as Taylor follows with the equipment. Kathleen is still in her Holy Angels uniform. James has told her not to bother changing.

"Beautiful, now just hold that pose, Miss Piper."

The photographer spears the tripod into the earth and disappears under the camera skirts. Taylor tilts a large black card above the lens. Everyone waits. Kathleen doesn't move a muscle until *snap*.

"Miss Piper, I'm afraid I must ask you to remain still."

"Sorry, I didn't know you were going to take it."

"Do you need to stretch again?"

"No."

Kathleen folds her hands once more and smiles. The photographer cranks the lens for what seems like forever. Kathleen mutters out the corner of her mouth, "Take the picture," just as *snap*—

"Miss Piper, please."

"Sorry, I'm sorry, I won't move this time."

Demure smile, eyes turning glassy, an eternity passes; her mind wanders, she pictures the geography teacher, Sister Saint Monica, without her veil, is she bald underneath? Do nuns go to the toilet? Kathleen scratches her nose just as *snap*.

The photographer pops his head out from under the hood, "It's not a motion camera, Miss Piper."

James catches Kathleen's eye and winks. She grins. The photographer huddles once more behind the camera, "That's nice, Miss Piper, that's lovely, one . . . two . . . three . . ."

James sneaks up behind the camera and pulls a cross-eyed face at Kathleen. She flops forward, hands on her knees, laughing into the camera, "Daddy!"—while at the same instant Materia appears in the window behind her and waves—*snap*. Through the lens, Materia's hand fractures into light, framing Kathleen's blur of hair. Materia must be holding something shiny.

"I give up!" The photographer collapses his tripod. "You don't have to pay me, Mr. Piper, except for the fillum, I got exactly nothing."

"Print up the last one, b'y, I'll pay you."

Leo Taylor packs the equipment back into his buggy. He's a bit surprised. He has never seen Mr. Piper anything but stern. Leo has always sensed something about Mr. Piper—the thing you sense about certain dogs. Best to avoid their eye, don't make them nervous with sudden moves. And yet here's Mr. Piper, high-jinksing with his daughter just as though he were her brother or her beau.

James and Kathleen are still laughing as the buggy rolls off in a cloud of sepia and Materia raps on the window with the scissors.

"Supper," says James.

"What're we having?" Kathleen asks.

"Steak and kidney pie."

"Yuck."

He ruffles her head and they go inside.

Limbo

THE CHILD WAS NOT right from the start. First of all, it hardly cried. Made a sound like a little wet kitten. So maybe it was just as well. The tragic part was that neither Materia nor James nor even Mrs. Luvovitz knew to baptize it in time; how could they? There was nothing out and out wrong with it, it was even a big child. Full term, born the day after Kathleen got her picture taken. Did Materia weaken it when she prostrated herself at the plaster feet of Mary a few days ago? Seems fanciful to think so. And a tad blasphemous. No, it was a big child with a good strong heartbeat and it lived three days, then died, no one knows why. Crib death. It just happens, children stop, why? It's a mystery. As though they arrive, look around with their little blind eyes and decide not to stay.

Materia had called it Lily but it can't be said to have been truly named; it was unbaptized and therefore no one, and therefore incinerated. James took it, wrapped in a sheet inside an orange crate—he was a little dazed—to the double company house on King Street that served as a hospital.

Burial was not an option. Mourning was not an option. This was the other Lily, before the Lily who would live to be twice baptized, as though to make up for the first. Other Lily.

What you do after a baby like this is get over it. Don't mope, it wasn't meant to be. Don't pray, prayers don't reach limbo. Have faith, God had a reason. To test you, most likely. God never sends us more than we can bear. Offer it up. Keep in mind it was another girl.

Materia gets on with it. Cleans the house in the night, bumping and scouring from pool to pool of kerosene light till the dawn reeks of lye and

she begins to bake and bake and bake. Who's going to eat all this? She takes
it over to the Luvovitzes; Abe and Rudy are teenagers now, big boys with
bottomless stomachs. Materia loves to watch them eat—beautiful healthy
boys, winking at their mother, towering over her, devoted to her. Good
sons.

Mercedes and Frances are disappointed. Bewildered. Their new sister
was there and then she wasn't. Kathleen is angry; babies shouldn't die.

"Well, what was wrong with it?"

"We don't know," says James.

"That's a stupid rotten answer."

"Life is sometimes rotten and stupid." James prides himself on always
telling her the truth.

"Not for me it won't be."

"No, not for you."

What upsets Kathleen most is the blank face on her mother. A baby
factory. Insensate. My life will not be like that.

James doesn't dwell on it. He feels sorry for the thing, but it's just as
well not to have another mouth to feed. And Materia has bounced back
remarkably. Like a heifer. He tries not to think it. Trouble is, she still looks
pregnant. She'll be slim again by the time I get back from the war.

But Materia will look pregnant from now on. People will always
assume she's six or seven months. This will come in handy.

James joins the 94th Victoria Regiment Argyll Highlanders. His captain
speaks Gaelic, as does eighty percent of the unit. James volunteers immediately for overseas duty, glad of any training that gets him away from
home. Bayonet fighting at the Wellington Barracks in Halifax: rushing at
bags bleeding sand, "under and up, ladies, under and up! You're caught in
his ribcage!" A British sergeant teaches them how to dig immaculate
trenches, neatly sandbagged: "Not too deep, lads, we ain't stopping
long!"—just long enough for a bit of a kip, then it's over the top with the
Hun on the run. James is among the older men there. He doesn't frater-
nize, he doesn't care about King George nor does he have anything against
the Kaiser. He counts the days till he's overseas. "Under and up, ladies,
under and up!"

Fifty years of European peace have generated exuberance on all sides.
A lot of horses stand ready to gallop across Europe in two directions. Cape
Breton has joined up in droves, despite the fact that over the past twenty-

five years the Canadian army has spent more time guarding the property of the Dominion Coal Company than it has fighting. But the recruiters have been eloquent—"poor little Belgium, the bloodthirsty Boche"—the mines have been slow and what boy doesn't long to be a soldier? The fact that friends will get to serve side by side is also very persuasive—whole towns in the same stretch of trench. Everyone is afraid that "she'll be all over by Christmas." James hopes the war will last two years. That way Kathleen will be old enough to leave home when he returns. If he returns.

James finishes basic training and takes up home defense duties. All through the fall, he and the rest of the 94th patrol the coast in a state of frustrated suspense, terribly worried lest the war should end before they get over there. They become known as the blueberry soldiers, because there's not a lot else for them to do besides pick blueberries and keep their eyes peeled for a German ghost ship. James eats at home, but sleeps with two other soldiers in a shack on the beach at Lingan. Ready, Aye, Ready.

Eventually, James is transferred to the Cape Breton Highlanders 85th Overseas Battalion of the Canadian Expeditionary Force. He is issued a Ross rifle. It's a good thing there's a knife attached to its barrel—no one knows yet just how far the Ross rifle's efficiency in a field of North American rabbits outstrips its performance in European mud. Along with sixty-five pounds of kit, James is also issued a khaki tunic, a leather battle kilt, a blond and black horsehair sporran, a dress kilt of bright Macdonald tartan and a beret with a red tassel. The Germans will be sure to see him coming. And with the regimental pipers first over the top, the Germans will be sure to hear them. Bagpipes have a liquefying effect on the bowels of the enemy, and bare knees in battle strike the fear of the fanatical. The Germans will come to call the Highland regiments *"die Damen von Hölle"*—the ladies from hell.

Finally, one day in December 1914, James stands in the drive while Taylor heaves his duffel bag into the buggy waiting to take him to the docks in Sydney. It's snowing and James feels the unaccustomed bite of winter on his knees. He knows he is in the proud dress of his ancestors but he sorely misses his trousers. Materia can't help but think how handsome he looks. James pats them all on the head. Frances tickles his knee, Mercedes offers him her soggy cookie, Kathleen throws her arms around him, can't stop herself crying, she never cries, she's not a sissy. She clings, he tries to disengage.

"Be a good soldier now, look after your mother."

"No!"

"That's enough now, shshsh. . . ."

But she runs to the house, ramming open the door—Daddy, my daddy is going away, he might be killed, or drowned before he even gets there—up the stairs two at a time—and he's leaving me here with this horrible woman! Into her room, avoiding the mirror, slamming the door, locking it.

"G'bye fellas, say a prayer for your old dad."

He knows Materia will pray, she'll pray her fool head off.

He's right, she does. She prays so hard that her head really does seem to get a little wobbly. She prays he'll be killed quickly and painlessly in Flanders.

Over Here

WITH JAMES GONE, MATERIA comes to life. She takes pleasure in her little ones—Mercedes is such a good girl and Frances is a clown. Kathleen keeps up a life of her own, staying late at school to train with Sister Saint Cecilia or to practice with the choir, solos of course. When she's home she's impossible, but at least she's out of harm's way, *inshallah*.

What to feed her is a constant conundrum. Nothing satisfies. She rolls her eyes, sighs ostentatiously, flounces from the room. Materia falls back on James's old standby of toasted cheese, slicing it daintily into four, placing it before her, *"SaHteyn."*

"Mother! English, please."

Kathleen, Mercedes and Frances share the impression that their mother doesn't speak much English. This didn't used to be true, but it has come somewhat to pass simply because Materia doesn't speak English much. For with whom would she converse in English? Not her husband. And Mrs. Luvovitz has always been mercifully undemanding of Materia in that regard, their friendship having revolved around food, children, the old Yiddish songbook. Materia has been content just to sit at Mrs. Luvovitz's kitchen table and listen to the older woman hold forth on what's what.

Prepositions were the first to fall away, then adverbs crumbled, along with whole clauses, until Materia was left with only the most stolid verbs and nouns.

The difference between Kathleen and the younger girls is that Materia speaks plenty with Mercedes and Frances—although she has lost some of her mother tongue too, through disuse, all but the indelible language of her own earliest memories. Thus Materia and her two younger daughters speak the Arabic of children—of food, endearments and storytelling. *Ya aa'yni, te'berini.*

Mercedes and Frances understand that Arabic is something just between them and Mumma. There are many Arabic-speakers in Cape Breton by now, but the little sisters think they and their mother are the only ones, outside the mysterious population of that far-off place called the Old Country. A place better than any on earth, but a place you are nonetheless lucky to have escaped,

"Why?"

"Because of the Turks."

"Oh."

A place where everyone speaks the Piper girls' private at-home language right out in the open, and everyone looks like their mother.

"Tell us about the Old Country again, Mumma."

On the kitchen cot, before Kathleen gets home, they sink into Materia's soft body, which provides a pillow for each head, her plushy smell of fresh wet bread and oil, a pot of *bezzella* and *roz* with lamb on the stove, the lid buzzing sleepily. Outside, the winter drizzle blurs the window.

"Lebanon is the most beautiful place in the world. There are gentle breezes, it's always warm there. The buildings are white, they sparkle in the sun like diamonds and the sea is crystal-blue. Lebanon is the Pearl of the Orient. And Beirut, where I was born, is the Paris of the Middle East."

"Can we go live there?"

"No." You were lucky to be born on this damp gray rock in the Atlantic, beautiful in its own mournful way.

"Because of the Turks?"

"Yes."

This island, familiar to famished Irish and gnarly-kneed Scots who had been replaced by sheep in their Old Country.

"Mumma, what's Turkish delight?"

"It's nasty."

"Oh."

Cape Breton Island is not a pearl—scratch anywhere and you'll find coal—but someday, millions of years from now, it may be a diamond. Cape Breton Diamond.

"Mumma, tell us about Jitdy and Sitdy again."

"Your *jitdy* was my daddy. He and my mother, your *sitdy,* came here with nothing and they worked very hard. They had many children and they prospered."

"Why didn't they stay?"

"They missed the Old Country."

"Someday we'll go see them, eh."

"When you're a grown woman with children of your own, you can go there."

"Mumma, tell us about the good Muslin lady again."

"Muslim."

"Muslim."

"She was a good woman. Her name was Mahmoud. Many years ago, when your *jitdy* was a baby, the Turks came to his village in the Old Country. They were looking for Christian babies to kill. The Mahmoud woman took your *jitdy* and put him among her own children. When the Turks came to the door and said, 'Are there any Christian babies here?' she said, 'No! All these children are my own.' And to convince them, she put your *jitdy* to her own breast and suckled him. The Turks went away. When he grew up, your *jitdy* took the Muslim lady's name out of gratitude. Even though he was really a Christian."

"Oh . . . Mumma, can we see the picture?"

And Materia gets out the picture of her and James in front of the painted Roman arch from that long-ago day at Wheeler's Photographic. Mercedes and Frances pore over the photo: when Mumma and Daddy were young. In Frances's mind, the arch leads sometimes to the Old Country, sometimes to The War.

"When's Daddy coming home?"

"Soon. We must pray."

Materia has heard from her sister Camille. Camille waited outside the Mahmoud kitchen door for the Jewish butcher to finish his weekly cup of tea with her mother. When he came out, Camille handed him a flat square parcel. She asked him to give it to Materia and, without waiting for a reply, hurried away. Benny passed it on to Mrs. Luvovitz, who gave it to Materia. Materia cried when she opened the gift. An Arabic record. Its paper cover bore a watercolor of Beirut by night. She looked inside eagerly for a note—half-expecting the childish printing of years ago, smiling at the memory even as it hurt her heart; my little Camille, "you're the prettiest of all of us, *ya Helwi.*" But there was only a scrap of brown paper and the words, "I'm married now."

At least once a week, Materia takes the record from the hope chest, carries Kathleen's gramophone down to the kitchen and winds it up. She aims the brass bloom and places the needle on the spinning wax:

First the antechamber of snowy static, airlock to another world, then . . . open sesame: The *deerbeki* beats rhythm, ankle bells and finger cymbals prance in, the *oud* alights and tiptoes, a woodwind uncoils, legless ancestor of the Highland bagpipe, rising reedy to undulate over thick strings thrumming now in unison. It all weaves and pulses into a spongy mesh for the female voice to penetrate—no words yet, a moan between joy and lament; the orchestra suspends itself below, trembling up at the voice, licorice, liquid, luring, "dance with me before I make love to you later, later, soon."

Materia gets up and dances the *dabke*. Her mother taught her this dance, and Materia has taught Frances and Mercedes. The *dabke* is a continuous series of small lilting steps in quarter-swirls which sway your hips, laze your shoulders back and forth and breeze your arms like treetops over your head. Your hands are supple seaweed, waving on unresisting wrists, encircling, grazing, flirting with each other.

This dance works best if you are buxom but anyone can do it, it's that kind of dance. And although officially a man is supposed to lead a line of pretty girls, the *dabke* is for everyone. At weddings, at baptisms, with children, grandmothers, anyone. That's why the eyes are so important. Because the whole point of the *dabke* is to get up and do it in the center of the gathering, where you acknowledge everyone until you pick out the person you will invite into the dance. Then you lower your arms towards them, hands still weaving to the music, and you lure that person until they get up and join you because they can't refuse. Then they become the center.

The *dabke* is all about hips and breeze whereas, if you find yourself at a *ceilidh,* Celtic step-dancing is all about feet and knees. Both can be danced in a kitchen by anyone.

The *dabke* is a big favorite with Frances and Mercedes. They'll do it as long as Materia can hold up, which, in these early days, is a long time. She teaches them a whole bunch of Arabic songs, as well as the way to wail them while dancing. The trick is that the dancing and singing are unrepeatable. Once you know this, you're ready to start learning.

When the precious record wears out, Frances innovates with a comb and wax paper to approximate the reeds and strings. Far from thinking it a sacrilege, Materia considers it ingenious, and it is.

Put the shell to your ear. You can hear the Mediterranean. Open the hope chest. You can smell the Old Country.

Holy Angels

Perhaps her requirements were too great,
or her indulgence for human weakness too small,
for her attempts to form a friendship had always
ended in disappointment.

CLAUDIA, BY A.L.O.E.

SISTER SAINT MONICA'S CLASS is decorated with a map of the world, a chart of a volcano in cross-section, a collection of fossils and a color print of her namesake. It hangs above the blackboard. In it, Saint Monica holds a book open on her lap, but she is not reading; she is gazing off, seemingly unaware of another pair of eyes peering up from the book itself, one on each page.

When she is overcome by boredom, Kathleen's eyes often stray to this picture, it being the one focal point for covert daydreaming not disapproved of by Sister Saint Monica, who is given to impromptu anecdotes on the lives of the saints in amongst lessons on the earth's crust and its chief capitals. The girls all know that the Prairies are the breadbasket of Canada and that Saint Monica was the mother of the greatest of all Church fathers, Saint Augustine. In his youth, Augustine lived in sin with a heathen African woman. His mother prayed for his redemption and one day, when Augustine was strolling in a garden, he heard a child's voice sing out, "Take it, read it!" It was the Bible talking. Augustine deserted his African concubine, converted to Christianity and became the scourge of fornicators. And Rangoon is the capital of Burma.

This afternoon, however, Kathleen's eyes are not on Saint Monica's picture. Kathleen is far far away in the English countryside, where she lives with her widowed father in a manor house—

"Kathleen!"

Kathleen jolts at her desk and looks up into Sister Saint Monica's towering wimple.

"Yes, sister?"

"What could possibly be more engrossing than the formation of glacial moraine?" Sister Saint Monica does not wait for an answer, but seizes Kathleen's novel from behind its camouflage *Geography of the British Empire*.

"Claudia, by A.L.O.E. Who"—scathing tones—"is A.L.O.E.?"

Kathleen feels herself blush. She looks down. ". . . A Lady of England."

"I beg your pardon? You have a voice, don't you?"—titters from the class—"Use it."

Kathleen looks up,

"A Lady of England."

"A Lady of England, what?"

"A Lady of England, sister."

Kathleen swallows as Sister Saint Monica scans the page. The other girls start whispering. "Silence!" Silence. Sister dangles the book before Kathleen and commands, "Share a few gems with the class."

Kathleen takes the book and bites her lip.

"Loudly and clearly. I for one do not wish to miss a single charming word."

Kathleen starts anywhere, reads, " 'I often catch a glimpse—' "

Singsong: "I can't hear you, Kathleen."

" '—of dark robes—' "

"Louder."

" '—passing across the little open space yonder—' "

"Good, continue."

" '—with something of the longing for forbidden fruit.' "

Giggles on all sides. Kathleen takes a breath, blinks. Continues, " 'Doubtless one would get a knowledge of good and evil by being better acquainted with convent life. I suspect more of the evil than of the good . . .' " Gasps from the other girls. Kathleen waits, her eyes on the book, please don't make me continue.

"Continue."

" '. . . but Papa forbade me to hold any intercourse whatsoever with the Romanist ladies.' "

Silence, shocked and appalled. Sorrowful sister. "Girls, profit and perpend. This is a piece of unalloyed trash, a libel hatched by a low type of woman whose refusal to publish under her true name testifies to the evil of her intentions. No one but an idiot or a fiend could derive pleasure between its covers; which, Kathleen, are you?"

Kathleen can't look up. All around her, petty triumph.

She forces herself to answer, which is, in itself, a defiance. "Neither."

Sister Saint Monica confiscates the book and swishes away to her desk.

Sister Saint Monica is the one teacher who does not subscribe to the untouchability of Kathleen Piper. She has been looking for an opportunity to give the girl the gift of mortification, but it hasn't been easy; Kathleen is a model student and it is well nigh impossible to put one's finger on the insolent pride that colors her flawless manners—not to mention the unsubstantiated but unmistakable whiff of immodesty. "I'll teach her," thinks Sister Saint Monica, locking the offending book in her desk.

"She'll learn," thinks Kathleen, staring at the inkwell, hot with humiliation. "She'll be sorry, I'll kill her with a stake in her heart, I'll be famous and she'll be ugly and dead, I'd like to poke out her eye, I'll show her. She's not worth showing." Kathleen bites her lip. Hard. "I'll show them all." She feels her eyes brim up. Don't cry. Don't. Stare. Harder.

Kathleen glares out the window at the blast furnaces of Dominion Iron and Steel; imagines herself bursting in flames from the stack and soaring all the way to La Scala. Or anywhere, so long as it's far from this one-horse burg, this wretched rock, these horrible girls—

"I said! Advance to the front."

Kathleen starts and looks up. Sister is waiting on her high platform in front of the blackboard—*Ice Age, Cretaceous, mass extinction*—what now? Kathleen slides from her desk, leaving palm prints on its surface, snagging her woolen stocking on a splinter, and walks the gauntlet of female eyes.

"Face the class."

Kathleen obeys. The next thing she knows, she is showered with scrap paper and pencil shavings, and the lights have gone out.

"Since you're so eager to fill your head with garbage," says Sister Saint Monica, "you may as well have a garbage can on your shoulders."

Shrieks of laughter.

"That's enough, girls. Now, Kathleen. Sing for us."

Kathleen is paralyzed. Blinking into the darkness of the metal can, she feels sweat trickling under her arms, between her legs.

"You're a 'songstress,' aren't you?"—*whack!*—the yardstick against the side of the can.

Kathleen is spared the sight of row after row of girls with their hands clamped over their mouths, plugging their noses against hilarity, crossing their legs—"I said sing!"

Only one song presents itself, perversely, to her mind, and she begins, muffled and echoey: " 'I'll take you home again, Kathleen . . .' "—hysterical laughter, sister gives them free rein—" 'Across the ocean wild and wide—' "

"Louder."

" 'To where your heart has ever been—Since first you were my bonny bride' "—a bare thread of a voice is all that's available to Kathleen, and it breaks.

"Continue."

" 'The roses all have left your cheek—I've watched them fade away and die—Your voice is sad whene'er you speak. And tears bedim your loving eyes. . . .' "

Kathleen is finally crying. Helpless, enraged. What's worse is that she hates this song—old-fashioned, sickly sweet, nothing to do with her but her name: " 'Oh I will take you back, Kathleen, To where your heart will feel no pain—And when the fields are fresh and green, I'll take you to your home again.' "

The song finished, Kathleen waits in dread to be dismissed—how can she possibly remove this can from her head in front of everyone? She knows she must, eventually. Some day. She has to go to the loo. She feels as though she's wet her pants with shame. Surely that's not possible, surely she would know if she had. . . . Kathleen realizes that she's been standing there for some time. And that Sister Saint Monica has resumed the lesson.

". . . And what occasioned the putting aside of Saint Augustine's African concubine?"

"Oh, sister, sister, I know—"

"One at a time, girls."

Kathleen stands motionless until the bell signals lunch and she hears Sister Saint Monica swish out after the last pupil.

★   ★   ★

Kathleen has no friends. She has her work and she's grateful for that because friends are simply not to be had at Holy Angels. Not that Kathleen goes out of her way: "Snob." Seeing her up there, anonymous, with a green metal garbage can for a head, hiding that conceited face—why do people think she's so pretty, her hair is horrible, it's *red*. That's all it is. Not "auburn," not "strawberry blond," red. Like a demon, like a floozie. Kathleen's ordeal at the hands of Sister Saint Monica soothes a lot of badly ruffled feathers.

The truth is, Kathleen has no idea how to go about making a friend. She has been trained to live for that glorious place, the Future. Friends are superfluous. This is reinforced by the tacit understanding that she is not to bring anyone home. Something to do with Mumma. She and Daddy would never say it, but they both know it.

Other girls spend nights at each other's homes, tucked in together talking till dawn. Kathleen overhears them whispering in the lavatory. She never finds out that Daddy would not let her spend a night at a friend's house, because she is never invited. James is planning to send her all the way to Italy by herself, but that's different. That's Life. The other is Nonsense. And who knows what another girl's father might get into his head? Kathleen is chaperoned every moment but she does not see it that way. Freedom consists of being insulated from the envy and ignorance of the unimportant people who temporarily surround her.

Now, after five years at Holy Angels, Kathleen would not know a friend if one sank its teeth into her wrist—which is more or less what she expects from the mass of other girls. She skirts them cautiously, as if they were dangerous wild animals loitering about a common watering hole ready to pounce, you'd never know why or what hit you. She fears them, sharp glinting creatures, and hasn't a clue what they talk about or how they do it. How they merge into gregarious packs. Kathleen is in fact horribly shy, but no one would ever suspect it—after all, she gets up and sings in front of halls full of people.

What seals Kathleen's fate, however, is the presence of several Mahmoud cousins at Holy Angels. One of them has even been in her class for the past six years. Though Materia hasn't wanted the girls to know anything at all about the shame of family exile, and has concocted her story about "the Old Country," James has told Kathleen the truth: Your mother and I were very young. We eloped. It was wrong, but what was worse was the behavior of the Mahmouds. Barbaric. They are from a part of the world that hasn't seen a moment's peace in hundreds of years, little wonder. You have cousins at Holy Angels. Ignore them. Don't give them the opportunity to snub you. Carry yourself like you own the place.

The Mahmouds are rich and civic-minded. The Mahmoud girls are popular, each of them a gleaming clear-eyed olive in plaid and perfect English. They have been told that Kathleen is the daughter of the Devil, and have duly accorded her a wide berth. To befriend Kathleen is to offend the Mahmoud girls. You can't have it both ways.

But is there not one potential friend among the horde, one bookish girl, plain as a rainy Tuesday, or so beautiful as to be unafraid? One who does not travel with the pack, who might come forward as a friend for Kathleen? No. Kathleen's fortress, her tower of creamy white, is steep and terrible. No one comes in or out. Except for her father, Sister Saint Cecilia and a select few minions necessary to support life. Such as her mother. Such as the buggy driver.

The other girls salve their corrosive envy and allay their fear of Kathleen, the antisocial prodigy, with an invigorating dose of racial hatred:

"She may be peaches and cream but you should see her mother . . . black as the ace of spades, my dear."

"You know that sort of thing stays in the blood. Evangeline Campbell's mother's cousin knows a girl had a baby in Louisburg? Black as coal, my dear, and the both their families white as snow and blond blond."

"We should've never let the coloreds into this country in the first place."

"My uncle saw a colored woman driving a cart with a load of coal, the next morning he was dead."

"They have a smell, they do."

"Kathleen Piper belongs in The Coke Ovens!"

And they laugh.

Naturally, this remedy is never indulged when the Mahmoud girls are around. That wouldn't do, they're nice girls and rich rich. The brothers of Holy Angels have already begun lining up.

No girlfriend has ever made it up to the tower chamber.

Three Sisters

FRANCES HAS DISCOVERED A new game: exploring the mysteries of the teenager, Kathleen. Unfortunately, she is too young to know how to investigate thoroughly without leaving a trace.

"Come here, you little brat."

Frances peeks out from behind Mercedes with a guilty twinkle in her eye, her hands folded innocently behind her back, and enters Kathleen's boudoir.

"If you come in here again I'll tell Pete to get after you," says Kathleen, enthroned at her vanity, where she has just discovered the comb where the brush should be and a candy heart gumming up one of her good lace hankies.

"Who's Pete?" asks Frances.

"He's the *bodechean* and he's going to drag you to hell!"

Frances laughs. Mercedes's eyes grow round as saucers and she says, "That's not nice."

"Not you, sweetie." Kathleen holds out her arms and Mercedes approaches. Kathleen pops her onto her knee. "He doesn't get after good little girls. What shall we read?"

"Water Babies." Mercedes chooses Frances's favorite out of love for her little sister, who doesn't mean to be naughty.

Kathleen eyes Frances's crooked grin. "Come here, you rascal, you can listen too."

Frances climbs onto the other knee. The two little girls look at each other and squirm, hands clamped over their mouths, cheeks ballooning with suppressed rapture.

"Quit wriggling or I'll stick you on a pin and use you for bait in the creek."

Mercedes composes herself; Frances shrieks with laughter and asks, "Can I play with your hair?"

"What do you say?"

"Please."

"What else?"

"With a whole bunch of cream and a cherry and fruit and candy."

"What else?"

"And a sword and a bug and a worm. And a bare bum!"

Mercedes says to herself on behalf of Frances, "Sorry dear God." Kathleen laughs and Frances giggles passionately, poised to plunge both hands into the red sea, but Kathleen holds out,

"What word am I thinking of?"

"Lantern."

"Nope."

"Stick."

"Nope."

"Matchbox."

"No."

"Teapot."

"Right."

"Yay!"

"Don't pull it or I'll skin you. 'Once upon a time there was a little chimney sweep. . . .' "

Kathleen has taken to spending time with her little sisters. At first she does this for Daddy's sake, because she knows that otherwise they get nothing but their mother's barbaric yammer during the day while she's at school—she can smell it hanging in the air when she gets home. But as the schooldays and the war drag along and Kathleen becomes lonelier, she grows to cherish the time with her little sisters every bit as much as they do. Sunday mornings, she allows them to sit on two stools at the threshold of her room—"If I'm in the mood"—and witness her toilette. They sit as still as they can, enthralled, while Kathleen sings the world's greatest songs in her opera voice, and slips on a white cotton blouse over her lace-embroidered petticoat. She turns the cuffs, fashions a Windsor knot in her striped silk tie, and pulls on her tan linen skirt, flared at the ankle—"My bicycling costume," she calls it, although she does not possess a bicycle.

Evenings after school, she stands with her arms akimbo at the door to the forbidden chamber, and groans, "Oh all right, you can come in. But not a peep! I'm studying."

The little girls always cross the threshold with a sense of awe, for Kathleen's room is a temple of sophistication. Its shelves are lined with every girls' book you could ever think of, from *Little Women* to *Anne of Green Gables*. Its walls are plastered with pictures of great artists and beautiful underthings cut from magazines.

There is a picture of a man with wild hair and a flying necktie, pouncing upon the keys of a piano. This is Liszt. Kathleen is in love with Liszt. Kathleen says even his name sounds like a romantic sigh. Mercedes and Frances breathe the name to each other as a kind of all-purpose adjective for everything divine: Jell-O, fresh bed linen, Mumma's molasses cookies, all are wonderfully "Liszt!"

There is a picture of a beautiful dark woman in a wide hat and an old-fashioned dress cut low, with a rose in her lap. This is Maria Malibran. "La Malibran," Kathleen says dramatically, "the greatest singer who ever lived." Kathleen has told Frances and Mercedes the tragic story of how Malibran went out riding on the wildest horse in the stable. She fell, caught her foot in the stirrup and was dragged over stones for a mile. She got up, powdered her cuts and bruises and sang that very night—beautifully, as usual. Then she died of a swollen brain and "she was only twenty-eight." Mercedes always says a little prayer to herself for Malibran, while Frances tries to put the pretty lady in the picture together with the idea of her being dragged with her head bonking along. It's terrible.

There is a big poster of "the woman of a thousand faces"—although in the poster she has only one. Her name is Eleonora Duse. She has burning dark eyes and piles of black hair. Daddy sent it to Kathleen from England before he went to the Front. Duse is "the greatest actress who ever lived." In the poster, she stands inside the front hall of a nice house. She is wearing an overcoat and her hand is reaching for the doorknob. The poster is for a scandalous play called *A Doll's House*. Daddy sent it with a letter, "to remind me not to get married and wreck my career," Kathleen has explained. Mercedes can't understand why Kathleen would not want to get married and have babies like Mumma, but Kathleen just snorts, "Marriage is a trap, kiddo. A great big lobster trap."

Every evening when Kathleen opens her door and grudgingly admits them, Mercedes and Frances wait in obedient silence for five endless minutes, after which Kathleen proclaims her homework finished. Then there are just too many treats to choose from.

Often all three of them wind up lying on their stomachs on Kathleen's bed, chin in hand, going through a priceless issue of *Harper's Bazaar,* picking out fashions and accessories "for those in the know."

"That's me," says Mercedes, and Kathleen reads the description. " 'A saucy confection of pale mauve crêpe de Chine touched up with rosettes of pussy-willow silk.' "

"Chic," says Mercedes wisely.

"Très chic," says Kathleen.

"I'm that one." Frances points and Kathleen obliges. " 'She lost her head over this good-looking and comfortable pair of corsets from La Resista. The lacy brassiere has the unmistakable Paris hallmark.' "

Frances giggles and echoes, "Brassiere!"

Even though there's a war on, there's still plenty of fashion pouring out of Paris—although according to the magazine the designers only keep it up for the sake of their poor seamstresses, who would otherwise be out of a job.

Kathleen teaches her sisters to mimic the effects of rouge by pinching their cheeks, and of lipstick by mercilessly biting their lips. " 'Beauty is a powerful weapon,' " she reads, at once sarcastic and enthralled. " 'To Fashion's Throne must the free untrammelled girl be brought for sacrifice.' "

The sisters invariably dine at Sherry's on Fifth Avenue, where Kathleen greets them in a French accent, "Good evening, *mesdemoiselles,* what would you like? We have Caviar on Toast, Vol au Vent of Sweetbreads, Brandied Peach Tarts and Green Turtle Soup. Or would you prefer Jellied Tongue?"

It's not all frivolity, however. Kathleen is religious about reading Lady Randolph Churchill's series on the war, *By the Simmering Samovar.* The sisters all hold their breath when they come upon a picture of a French casino that's been converted to a hospital. No . . . Daddy is not there.

And Kathleen always reads aloud the latest installment of a racy story while the little girls listen, mystified, and gaze at the illustrations over her shoulder: " '*Go!* You are nothing but a brute!' "

Kathleen eagerly awaits every issue of *Harper's Bazaar* that Mrs. Foss of the Orpheus Society passes on to her, and she savors them with a combination of delight and disgust. For example, there is one picture that

Kathleen has cut out for her wall just in order to remind herself that philistines are not confined to her own hometown—they can even be found amid high society: the photograph is supposedly of the great Geraldine Farrar singing *Carmen* at the Metropolitan Opera House of New York. Yet in the foreground sits a boxful of Astors admiring each other's jewelry. It had never before crossed Kathleen's mind that people might go to the Opera out of anything but a passion for opera. "Let that be a lesson," she thinks, vowing, "When I sing, no one will be allowed to look anywhere but at the stage!"

There always comes a point when Kathleen flings the *Harper's Bazaar* across the room and declares herself "fed up with frippery and foppery and the silly chits who fill their heads with all that rot!"

"Rubbish!" Mercedes agrees.

"Foolish burn bottoms!" seconds Frances.

"Frances!"

Mercedes is always shocked and Kathleen always laughs.

Then they return hungrily to fairy tales and *The Bobbsey Twins*.

Women of Canada Say, "Go!"

I used to walk the sidewalks in Nova Scotia town,
There was a man came down, his face was bronzed and brown,
He told us how King George was calling each to do his share,
He offered us a khaki coat to wear.
He told us how the call had gone far over land and sea,
And when I heard that speaker's word,
I said, "Why, that means me."

MARCHING SONG OF THE 85TH OVERSEAS BATTALION,
CANADIAN EXPEDITIONARY FORCE

HIS NOTES ARRIVE QUITE regularly, on standard military postcards.

Dear Missus,

All is well. Do not worry. Love to the girls.

James.

Nothing is ever blacked out—James never writes enough to give anything away. Materia's heart leaps at the mail because His Majesty's gratitude and regret come on a card of the same size. She tears open the envelope, looking for the black border, but it's never there.

In spring of '16, Mrs. Luvovitz shows up at Materia's kitchen door with little Ralph in tow. The tables are turned, Mrs. Luvovitz is crying. Here, here, come in, sit down, cuppa tea. She slumps over the kitchen table, Materia shoos Ralph away—he hovers in the door with Mercedes and

Frances, who wonder what's wrong with Mrs. Luv. Mrs. Luvovitz reaches out without looking up and clasps Materia's hand. Her boys are going, Abe and Rudy. They thought she'd be proud, they're real Canadians.

"Don't worry, they gonna be back soon," says Materia.

For all the papers say there's bound to be a breakthrough any day; the stalemate can't last forever.

Mrs. Luvovitz blows her nose, scrapes her face with her hanky. "I know, I know, you don't understand, we have"—and crumples once more—"we have family there," her voice creaking upward. "My mother is there—"

"Your people in Poland, they got no fighting in Poland."

"Benny's are in Poland, my people are German."

Materia hugs her while she cries just like a child. Her boys will be fighting their own flesh and blood. The Luvovitzes are real Canadians, and the Feingolds are real Germans.

Near the River Somme in summer 1916, there are several innovations: Canadians have helmets, and rifles that fire most of the time. Germans have machine guns. July 1 the British plan is this: a million shells to cut the Boche wire. Shoulder your seventy-pound pack as usual. Go over the top. Walk toward the German lines, they'll all be dead by now. Keep walking till you hit Berlin.

In four and a half hours, fifty thousand Britons and Canadians are shot. That afternoon, the British plan is revised: do everything as before. But this time, run.

Abe is killed walking. Rudy is killed running.

Neither of them killed any Germans. *Aleihem Ha'Shalom.*

July 2, 1916
Dear Missus,

     All is well. . . .

Mrs. Luvovitz never recovers. She functions, has to, she has her youngest son, she has Benny. And there's Materia, a child still really, I remember when I found her on the cliff, what would she do without me? She took the news about the boys very hard. Materia's husband will probably be killed, a blessing, God forgive me, I don't know why but he scares me. Benny says that's prejudice. It isn't. It's superstition. There's something not right, I can't prove it, I can feel it. I may be *meshuga,* one thing I know, I'll maim my son Ralph before I let him go to a war, I'll nail his feet to the floor.

It's begun to sink in on two continents. Younger sons are being dragged away from recruiting stations before they can say, "Sixteen, sir, honest." Everywhere, the youngest have suddenly become the eldest.

None of this is what Materia intended.

Ypres: gas—at least it kills rats too. Passchendaele: it doesn't matter if you can swim.

Dear Missus,

I am fine. . . .

Summer of '17, Number 12 Mine, where James worked, explodes. Sixty-five dead. The war has created a boom in the Sydney coalfields. Full employment, lower wages, and strikes forbidden by law, coal being vital to the war effort. Production has been stepped up, airways left shut, gas building up. Number 12 was always bad that way. Materia plays at many funerals, and ponders James's luck and her own stupefying sins.

To whom can she confess? Not to her dear friend, Mrs. Luvovitz. She tries to tell the priest. "Father forgive me for I have sinned, I brought the war." But he tells her she's guilty only of the sin of pride; "Say the rosary three times and ask God for humility." So Materia goes unabsolved. She visits the cliff every day in her mind and every day she swan-dives off it, weightless for a moment, feeling the slim girl she used to be, then the sudden satisfying impact of the rocks. It's where she belongs, she craves the caress of the violent shore, to come alive like that once more in a clash of stone and then to die. Peace. But she has her little girls, and suicide is the unforgivable sin.

In the fall of 1917, Our Lady appears to three children in Fátima, Portugal, and tells them three secrets, the third of which remains a Vatican secret to this day. But Materia knows what the third secret was. It was this: "Dear children; I sent the Great War in order to shield, a little longer, the body and soul of Kathleen Piper."

Dulce et Decorum

Now we wear the feather, the 85th feather,
We wear it with pride and joy.
That fake Advertiser, Old Billy the Kaiser,
Shall hear from each Bluenose boy.
Where trouble is brewing, our bit we'll be doing,
To hammer down Briton's foes,
With the bagpipes a-humming, the 85th coming,
From the land where the maple leaf grows.

85TH OVERSEAS BATTALION, CEF

IT MUST MEAN SOMETHING, there are so many of us—never have so many sacrificed so much for so little. It must mean something, otherwise there would not be this parade; there would not be this royal inspection, these brassy buttons, these slender wounds in the earth across Europe, these sturdy beams holding back the tide of mud and human tissue, this meticulous network of miniature mines, these lice, these rats, these boots returning unto dust, these toes lying scattered about my feet, like leaves, like fallen teeth.

James has spent three years in a narrow strip of France and Flanders, dodging snipers in order to collect the dead and comfort the dying. He is not a medic, he just volunteers a lot. Wiring parties, digging parties, reconnaissance parties, one big party. The streamers, fireworks and ticker tape that sent them off are nothing compared to the bright bits of men that sail through the air and festoon the remaining trees here in the land of permanent November. These decorations will stay up for years.

Chloride of lime to kill the stench, cordite to kill the lice, whale oil to keep the feet from rotting. Fifty-four days at a stretch in the flooded mass grave of the living but he never complains. James has prolonged the lives of so many men that he has been mentioned in dispatches several times. Originally he was recommended for the Victoria Cross, but as the Great Adventure dragged on his brand of "conspicuous gallantry" reflected poorly on the war.

Once, a wrecked man called him Mummy and clutched at the buttons on James's chest. Nothing was surprising. James let the boy from Saskatchewan suck on one of his brass buttons before dying. The Mother Country.

The mud between the opposing trenches is known as No Man's Land. This is a reasonable name for a stretch of contested ground that has yet to be won by either side. But James and possibly a number of others along the line have forgotten that this is the origin of the name. The name has come to mean a haunted foggy expanse of silent slime. A limbo—gray, yellow, green, mostly gray, and empty except for the dead. Rats may scamper across it and remain rats. Birds may fly above it and remain birds; they may alight and tear and eat and prick up their heads to stare motionless and beady for a moment before pecking and eating again, and remain birds. But no man may venture into this space between the lines and remain a man. That is the difference. No man may enter, either stealthily on his belly alone, or noisily on two feet racing through glue with a thousand versions of himself firing, falling, on either side as far as the eye can see, and remain a man. It is possible to become a man once more if you make it back behind your line again, but you suspend your humanity for your sojourn in between. That is why the place is called No Man's Land.

By 1916 James had volunteered so often that other men assumed he had a death wish. Either that or he was protected—by an Angel of Mons, perhaps, or Old Nick. They didn't know whether it was lucky to stick close to James, or if that was asking for the next bullet that missed him by an inch. Before a night raid or a dawn attack, when other men were tucking Bibles into their left breast pockets, kissing love letters or a lucky rat's paw, James was relaxed against a reeky sandbag full of mud and pieces of former men, reading.

James's first act of "total disregard for his own safety" was in the fall of 1915. Five men had gone out after dark with their bouquets of barbed wire, and four came back, but no one had heard a shot or a shout. That meant the fifth man was out there lost, wandering around in the place of no reference points. German Very lights bloomed in the sky from three directions, adding confusion to danger. Briefly lit, a shattered tree, a sea of craters, corpses interchangeable, now pink, now bronze, now blue. On the western front there is nothing so colorful as the night. James went out after the fifth man. He wasn't a friend, he was just some fella.

After two hours he found the man walking toward the German line. James brought him in, but he didn't make friends with him or anyone else.

On Christmas Day 1914, the British and the Germans had laid down their arms, climbed out of their trenches, and walked into No Man's Land. They met halfway between the lines, and exchanged gifts. Not so strange, considering that never before had so many nice men with families and decent jobs volunteered to face each other under arms across distances as brief and static as twenty yards. Such chocolate. Such bully beef. The truce was completely spontaneous and not repeated in anything like those numbers again—somehow people can still get into the Christmas spirit when they've only been mowing each other down with ordinary bullets, but the festivity goes right out of the season once they've gassed each other. Nonetheless, James brought over a gift on the Christmas of 1916.

At night you tell yourself that the howls and whimpers out there are wild dogs. This gets difficult if one of the dogs starts praying. The night before Christmas, James had already brought in two wounded and he was out looking for another. By the light of a flare he saw two dead stretcher-bearers lying at either end of a stretcher containing a bandaged man—an unusual sight in that the dead were whole. As the flare died, James saw the man on the stretcher stir. He approached but found the man was dead after all—a feast for the rats that had turned him over in the course of their meal. James carried on, blind-man's-buff, listening for any sound that was not a rustling or a gnawing. He stopped and crouched over a whimper. He felt for arms, legs, and guts (if the guts are merely exposed, it's worth picking him up; otherwise, finish him off quietly). This man was in pretty good shape, though unable to walk, and when he answered James's "How ya doin, buddy?" with *"Ich will nicht sterben, bitte,"* James picked him up and walked east. When they got close to the German trench, the man cried out to his comrades, *"Nicht schiessen, nicht schiessen!"* James laid him down within arm's reach of the parapet, turned around and walked back to his own side.

James could do all this because he had made a bargain with himself: he wouldn't try to get killed, nor would he try to survive. He could do all this because he felt terribly sorry for the men he rescued. They harbored the saddest and most foolish desire of all. The desire to go on living.

The Bobbseys at Home

ONE EVENING, KATHLEEN HAS instructed Mercedes and Frances to play on their own while she finishes a letter to Daddy—". . . school is great . . . lots of fun. . . ." By now she finds their chatter less distracting than their eager silence.

Frances is at the reins of the covered wagon they've made from Kathleen's bedspread. "When I grow up I'm going to have so much hair and be the boss of everything and I'll be singing and eating candy."

Mercedes is the pioneer mother with the babies. "Me too, and when I grow up I'm going to the Old Country and visit Sitdy and Jitdy."

"Me too."

Kathleen looks up from her letter. "They're not in 'the Old Country.' What are you talking about?"

Frances clicks her tongue at the horses, Mercedes comforts the monkey baby and answers, "Yes, because they prospered—"

"But then they missed the fruits and diamonds—"

"They darn well live in Sydney," says Kathleen.

Frances blinks and the horses disappear. The babies cool to porcelain and rubber in Mercedes' arms. ". . . Mumma said—"

"I don't care what she said, they live in Sydney and they hate us, they're stupid rotten idiots and we're better off without them." Kathleen tosses her pencil onto the desk and stands up. "What shall we read?"

Frances looks to Mercedes. Mercedes says, "The magazine."

"No," Kathleen decrees.

"The Red Shoes."

Frances enthuses, "Oh yes, and she gets her feet chopped off."

Mercedes bursts into tears. Then so does Frances.

"She does not get her feet chopped off," says Kathleen.

Frances sobs, "She does, she does."

Mercedes wails, "She does."

"Not if I say she doesn't."

But they are inconsolable, clinging to each other and crying for Mumma.

"What a couple of sissies, come on, we'll read something else."

She wipes their noses, hands Frances her hairbrush and settles Mercedes in her lap.

"Can we sleep with you tonight?"

"Oh all right, get in—"

"Yay!"

And when they've snuggled down, "Now clam up and listen. *The Bobbsey Twins at the Seashore—*"

It's wonderful when Kathleen reads because she does all different voices and accents. " 'Suah's yo' lib, we do keep a-movin'!' cried Dinah, as she climbed into the big depot wagon. Dinah, the colored maid, had been with the family so long the children called her Dinah Bobbsey, although her real name was Mrs. Sam Johnston.' "

Downstairs, Materia wrings her hands before a big bout of cleaning and baking. She received a telegram today. James is coming home.

Boots

ON A COLD APRIL afternoon in 1917, James got the inspiration for his boot business from a French soldier near Vimy.

The Frenchman wandered skeletal from the fog, his bare feet sucking the yellow muck where James was looking for wounded. The Frenchman drove his thumbs into either side of James's windpipe, slamming him into the slime, holding his head under. Then he went to work on James's boots, slicing the laces. James wrenched up and stuck the man. Luckily no one saw for the fog—the French were our allies.

From that moment, boots are all James can think about. It's the only thing that will drown the sound of his bayonet scraping between Frenchie's peekaboo ribs, and the sight of him scarecrowing off the end when James managed to shoot free—under and up, ladies, under and up. Boots are what count. More than weapons, food or strategy. We will win because we have more and better boots, boots determine history. Warm dry feet will allow us to go on being killed longer than the enemy. When the enemy's boots wear out, they will no longer be able to run in waves into our machine-gun fire, and they will surrender. I'm going to be ready for the next war by making boots. I'll be rich enough to send my daughter to the conservatory in Halifax for a year, then to anywhere in the world. But not Milan or Salzburg or even London. The Old World is a graveyard. " 'Is't not fine to dance and sing, When the bells of death do ring?' " No, it isn't. The great music will immigrate to the New World. New York. James can smell it. He has a distant cousin there—an old maid with an odd first name . . . Giles—that's it—she works with the nuns. Everything is turning out beautifully. Everything's going to be fine. Spit and polish, rise and shine.

James starts polishing his boots every day, sometimes all day, because often all day is all there is. Between the rips and rotten bits, around his exposed toes, the remains of James's boots positively glow through the perpetual fog. The other men call him "Rudolph."

It is this habit of the boots that prevents James from yet another tour of duty, although he's volunteered. His superiors determine that he is no longer fit for combat conditions. Sticking someone is perfectly normal in the mud culture. Obsessively polishing a pair of disintegrating boots is not. It's shell-shock. James's superiors do not refer to him as "Rudolph"; they call him "Lady Macbeth."

Along with an invisible part of himself, James loses a toe. It falls off, painlessly. And is seized and carried away by a rat right before his eyes. If the shell-shock hadn't got him, this thing with the toe would have. So, out of consideration for a man's pride, "shell shock" is not what James's superiors write on his discharge. Officially he is invalided out because of the injury to his foot.

James is taken out of the drowning pools of Passchendaele and across the Channel to Buckingham Palace, where he is awarded the Distinguished Service Order "for extreme devotion to duty in the presence of the enemy." During the ceremony he looks from people's footwear to their faces and decides whether or not they match.

He is shipped home to be honorably discharged. No one can know how tired he is. He will be tired for the rest of his life.

When James sees Halifax Harbour from the deck of the troopship in December 1917, he revises his plans for Kathleen. He'll have to send her straight to New York City. Halifax has been blown up. He doesn't wonder how or why. The war has grazed the edge of Canada, is all.

The Candy of Strangers

A WAR CHANGES PEOPLE IN a number of ways. It either shortcuts you to your very self; or it triggers such variations that you might as well have been a larva, pupating in dampness, darkness and tightly wrapped puttees. Then, providing you don't take flight from a burst shell, you emerge from your khaki cocoon so changed from what you were that you fear you've gone mad, because people at home treat you as though you were someone else. Someone who, through a bizarre coincidence, had the same name, address and blood ties as you, but who must have died in the war. And you have no choice but to live as an impostor because you can't remember who you were before the war. There's a simple but horrible explanation for this: you were born in the war. You slid, slick, bloody and fully formed, out of a trench.

The Great War was the greatest changer of them all.

James has one thing in common with the man who marched off to the wars three years before: their daughter, Kathleen. On December 10, 1917, he steps off the train in Sydney, an unexploded shell.

He has had a few years' practice being present and absent at the same time so he is able to find his way from Sydney to New Waterford. He walks the nine miles of frosted dirt road in his civvies, his duffel bag over his shoulder, and with each step his mind says, "Sydney, New Waterford. Sydney, New Waterford." To his left is Europe.

Several people see him enter town and walk down Plummer Avenue. They don't know he is a hero, they just know he has survived when most died—are still dying. James walks up the steps onto his veranda and is able to say hello to his wife as though she were someone he once knew, pat two little girls who squeal and call him Daddy, and avoid the eyes of the one person who is all too real.

He walks past her into the house and up to the attic. He puts his bayonet in the hope chest. He ignores the military doctor's orders and gets straight to work. He must banish her before he gets used to being alive again.

Kathleen is worried but tries to be grown up about it: it's not that Daddy doesn't love me anymore, it's that the war was so terrible.

James builds a shed off to the side of the house, and a workbench to go in it. Christmas comes and goes but he takes no notice, despite the excitement of the little ones, and the smell of baking from the kitchen. Without a word to his wife, and bold as brass, he writes to old Mahmoud and cuts a deal. Mahmoud supplies the Dominion Coal and Steel Company and James will supply Mahmoud. With boots only, but that's a significant product where mines and mills are concerned. Mahmoud will lend James the start-up money and then buy the boots below the wholesale rate he currently pays to ship them from Halifax into his Sydney store. James starts making boots.

"Daddy?"

"Yes, Kathleen?"

"Are you all right?"

"I'm right as rain."

". . . It's my birthday today."

"Happy Birthday, old buddy."

"Thank you. Daddy?"

"Yes?"

"Would you like me to sing to you?"

"I'd love that, my dear, but I've work to do."

Mahmoud develops a grudging respect for his good-for-nothing son-in-law but draws the line at direct contact with James or the family. Fine with James. They exchange messages via Leo Taylor. James starts to make money.

He digs out the business cards he collected at Kathleen's recital in Halifax years ago. Makes inquiries. He writes to the chief administrator of the Metropolitan Opera of New York, "Dear Sir: Who, in your expert opinion, would you say is the pre-eminent practitioner in the field of vocal training?" He receives the answer, and sends a lengthy telegram to a man with a German-sounding name in New York City. Receives a reply: "Yes, Herr —— will see Kathleen in his studio at 64th Street and Central Park West, 10:00 A.M., March 1, 1918." James writes to his spinster cousin, Giles, in New York, ". . . and as my mother always spoke highly of you . . . Naturally I am prepared to reimburse you for any and all . . ."

The time has come. Kathleen is barely eighteen, but her voice is ready. And cousin Giles has agreed to act as chaperone. Moreover, James no longer deludes himself as to where the girl is likely to be safest.

Even with the boots, it becomes apparent that this step will be crushing to the family finances. James does not hesitate. He writes to Mahmoud and asks him straight out for money to send the girl to New York.

The directness of the request startles Mahmoud even more than James's initial business overture. Ensconced in a mauve satin armchair, his slippered feet resting on a cushioned ottoman, Mahmoud squints and reads the note a second time.

Surrounded as he is by comfortable curves, it is easy to see how angular Mahmoud has become with the years. Business has eroded flesh and sharpened bones; vigilance has contracted the eyes, which are as keen as ever. His hair has thinned to a meticulous steel-gray and two deep lines crease either side of his leather face from cheekbones to jaw. He has grown to resemble his spare wooden chair in the back room of his shop. Only Mrs. Mahmoud looks at him now and sees the tall dark and handsome he used to be.

Mahmoud glances up from James's letter over to the old accursed piano. The voice comes from the Mahmoud side, of course. All the men and women of his family sing. Born singing. It is a gift from God and apparently God and Mr. Mahmoud have transmitted this gift through Materia—dead to me, she is dead—to the eldest daughter of the *enklese* bastard. Too bad. She is no granddaughter of mine.

Mahmoud raises the forefinger of his left hand slightly, and his wife replenishes his teacup.

In the kitchen, Teresa Taylor chops parsley for *tabooleh* and wonders why Mr. Mahmoud treats his wife like a maid now that he can afford several real ones. The old standby about the strangeness of white people doesn't really apply here because, although you'd take your life in your hands if you said it, the Mahmouds aren't really white, are they? They're something else. They are somewhat colored. What this means in Nova Scotia at this time is that, for the Mahmouds, the color bar that guards access to most aspects of society tends to be negotiable. It helps that they have money.

Teresa is a beauty. Although most people in these parts might not think so unless they saw a picture of her in a book about Africa. Everything about Teresa is tall—her face, her eyes especially. Everything about her is fine—her hands dicing tomatoes, her ankles standing, striding between counter, table and sink nine hours a day. Her voice with its trace of Barbados. And beneath her dress, the silver cross she wears that Hector gave her.

Teresa won't be a maid forever. She is engaged to be married. She squeezes the juice of three lemons and says a little prayer of thanks to Jesus for keeping Hector safe. In 1914 he volunteered to go overseas and fight but the army wouldn't have him: this was a white man's war, they didn't want "a checkerboard army." Hector went into the steel plant instead and swore off wars altogether. Now they can't conscript him because he is in a vital industry. Teresa and Hector are both saving money so that he can go to the United States and study to become an Anglican minister.

Teresa has known Hector all her life. When she was ten, their families came here at the same time, moving from a lush island to a stark one, so their daddies could work, first in the mines, then at the mill. Teresa has grown up in The Coke Ovens section of Sydney's Whitney Pier and, despite the ongoing battle with grime from the trains and smokestacks, she wouldn't want to live anywhere else, except New York City. That's where she and Hector will move once they're married.

Thus, Teresa does not begrudge a single working hour at the Mahmouds'. And it really isn't a bad job. She likes the food she's learned to prepare for them—this *tabooleh,* for instance. It makes a nice change from the Anglos and Scotch she has worked for, with their endless meat and potatoes and not a spice in sight. Most of the Mahmouds are very friendly and they know how to throw a party—always singing, with no need of liquor to let go, not like the meat-and-potato set. And Mr. Mahmoud pays well. Teresa has already started buying her trousseau. He expects the best but, unlike most, he's prepared to pay for it—he hasn't forgotten where he came from. Nor has he ever made an improper advance, though he does have a temper. Ask his daughters. In the meantime, Teresa works hard, stays out of his way, and feels sorry for her. Mrs. Mahmoud has everything

money can buy—not to mention a devoted family and lots of grandchildren. But she has a private sorrow, too, Teresa can tell. Teresa drains
the water from the cracked wheat the Lebanese call *burghul,* and folds it
into the spiced meat—they're having *kibbeh* tonight.

In the big front room, Mr. Mahmoud dozes while his wife, Giselle,
looks on. Except for her gray bun, she seems not to have changed at all
over the years. The same smooth round face, round arms, soft eyes. She is
wearing her moonstone ring and strand of genuine pearls to please her
husband. Carefully, she removes the note from his hand and takes it into
the kitchen.

"Teresa. Read please."

Mrs. Mahmoud has never learned to read English. Teresa reads the
letter aloud, then says, "Kathleen Piper. That's the young lady we heard
sing at the Lyceum before the war."

Mrs. Mahmoud nods. "My granddaughter."

Teresa raises an eyebrow. The girl my little brother ferries to and
from school. The princess who has never spoken a single word to him.
The one with the voice. Well. "That's your granddaughter, Mrs. Mahmoud?"

Giselle nods.

That night in bed, Giselle skillfully enlightens her husband as to his
own intentions. In the morning he writes a check. He tells himself that he
does it for Giselle. But as he writes the third zero, he reflects upon the
future of the family voice. Universally acclaimed. The crowning glory of
his success in the New World.

Only Teresa will do for an errand of such importance, and Mahmoud puts
the envelope into her hand, saying, "Get a receipt." Teresa sets out for
New Waterford, where she anticipates a rare look at the severed branch of
the Mahmoud family tree.

Materia answers the door. She is wearing a smock. She has a pair of
stained scissors in her hand. She's been cutting kidneys for a pie. Little
Frances stands peeking out from behind the foliage of her mother's crazy
floral print. Materia's gaze has widened over the years, as though she sees
more of the world at once than other people do. But although she seems to
see more, she does not have the expression of someone who is processing
what she sees. She doesn't look, she stares. Now she's staring up at Teresa.

Teresa recognizes the look of someone who's not all there. Teresa would have assumed that the big sad woman in the doorway was the hired help had she not been prepared to spot the Mahmoud family resemblance—discernible in the shade and smoothness of the skin, in Mrs. Mahmoud's eyes veiled in a vague face.

"Mrs. Piper?"

Materia nods. Teresa inquires politely, "Is Mr. Piper home, ma'am?"

Wee Frances has never seen a black person before. Everyone around her is chalk-white except for her own tan mother. She reaches out to Teresa and touches one of her hands. The one holding the envelope. Teresa smiles down at her. Frances collects the moment and puts it in a safe place with two or three others.

Meanwhile, Materia has muttered something and waved her scissors in the general direction of the shed at the side of the house. Teresa heads for the shed and Frances follows her. Materia returns to her kidneys, *snip, snap.*

Through the crack in the door, Frances sees Teresa hand an envelope to Daddy. Daddy opens the envelope and looks at the contents for quite a while. Then Teresa gets him to write something on a piece of paper that she puts back into her purse. When Teresa comes out of the shed, Frances is lingering nearby.

"What do you want, darlin, hmm? Where'd you get all that pretty yellow hair?"

Frances gazes up by way of an answer. What she wants is everything about this fabulous woman, who is surely a queen from some far-off place. Teresa would laugh if she knew: the Queen of Whitney Pier, dear.

"Here you go, honey." Teresa hands Frances a piece of rock candy just as—

"Frances!"

The child and the woman look up to see the golden girl step from the taxicab that has pulled up in front of the house. Leo Taylor has an actual automobile now, a Model T Ford with his name stenciled on the side, Leo Taylor Transport. He holds the door open and Kathleen walks past him without a glance. It was she who called out and interrupted the sweet transaction. Now she walks stately toward them and, in cultivated tones, inquires of Teresa, "Can I help you, miss?"

To heck with you, thinks Teresa, "No, Miss Piper, I just dropped something off for your father."

"Hey, Trese, come on, girl!"

Leo Taylor doesn't like to linger here. Teresa shakes her head as she climbs into her brother's cab. The Pipers—living like hillbillies, acting like royalty. They drive away.

"Show me your hand, Frances."

Frances opens her little hand and reveals the black and white licorice peppermint. A prize. Kathleen takes the sweet and throws it in a high arc across the yard till it lands in the creek with a small plop.

"You know you shouldn't take candy from strangers, Frances. Especially colored strangers."

Lady Liberty

Girl as she was, Claudia looked upon the world
before her like some young untried knight.

CLAUDIA, BY A.L.O.E.

KATHLEEN IS TRULY AND utterly and completely Kathleen in New York. That's what the city does for you if it's meant for you. She's got plenty of personality and no history, and she has never breathed so much air in her life. She comes from an Atlantic island surrounded by nothing but sea air, yet in the man-made outdoor corridors of this fantastic city she can finally breathe. This air is what the gods live upon. The gods who get things done. Not the gods who mope on ancient promontories and exhale fossil vapors, waiting for someone to fill in the fragments of forgotten sagas that have come unraveled with age. Those gods have sagged so long on their rocks, they are well on the way to turning to stone themselves.

But the new gods. That bright baritone chorus. They inhabit every steel support, every suspension bridge, every gleaming silver train, all things vertical and horizontal, all glass, gravel and sand. They take big breaths and they make big sounds and with every breath and sound they open up more sky.

When Kathleen steps onto Pier 54, she starts writing the book of her life in her head: *And then she arrived in the New World. She heard the heels of her sensible shoes ring out on the gangplank, and resolved never to be sensible.*

There are a bewildering number of uniformed porters and un-uniformed scamps ready to seize her trunk and make off with it, but

Kathleen hauls it to the center of the terminal and sits on it beneath the big clock, an eye out for her distant cousin, not minding the wait, serenaded by the crowds. It's clear: the whole world comes to New York City.

Kathleen intends to be the Eleonora Duse of the operatic stage. If anyone can do this, she can: a classically trained girl with modern ideas about holding the mirror up to nature. The born performer's zeal to leave no heart intact. An engine in her stoked so high it turned her hair red in the womb. Her mixed Celtic-Arab blood and her origins on a scraggly island off the east coast of a country popularly supposed to consist of a polar ice cap are enough, by American standards, both to cloak her in sufficient diva mystery and to temper the exotic with a dash of windswept North American charm. She'll refer to pickled moose meat and kippered cod tongues and occasionally swear in Arabic just to get the legend rolling, but she is of the New World, the golden West. She is no Sicilian or Castilian castaway bound for glory, then early ruin. Like them she is going to be great but, unlike them, she is going to survive. She has decided never to stop singing. She will be singing at seventy-five.

She eats a frankfurter in a bun she bought from a fat man with a black mustache who told her the story of his life in broken English. Her life has finally started.

"Kathleen?" Kathleen turns and sees a little spinster lady.

"I'm Giles. Welcome to New York City, dear."

Giles, to whom Kathleen has been entrusted, has unfaded blue eyes and a genteel apartment in Greenwich Village. Kathleen estimates Giles's age to be in the vicinity of a hundred and two. In fact Giles is a young sixty. Perhaps, Kathleen speculates, Giles was once a schoolteacher or— better—perhaps Giles is a beneficiary of that vague yet respectable means of support known among English literary heroines as "an annuity."

Being retired, Giles volunteers at a convent infirmary, where she helps old nuns to die. Her highest qualification for this calling is not her compassion, or her surprisingly strong stomach, or even her piety. It is her unshockability. Giles has lowered her ear to many a withered mouth and heard confessions no priest ever has—for toward the end there is often confusion; a sudden disquiet lest one has after all confessed and repented of the wrong things in life. Ancient sins bloom afresh, fragrant with the purity they possessed a moment before they were named and nipped in the bud. And having listened, Giles may remark, "I know, dear." Sometimes the dying words come in the form of a question to which Giles may reply, upon reflection, "I wonder that myself, dear, from time to time, truly I do." But Giles never asks any questions herself.

All of which makes Giles a pretty poor chaperone for a young champion like Kathleen.

That first night in Giles's guest room, which overlooks the roofs of the Village and affords a view of the tallest buildings on earth, Kathleen opens a fresh new Holy Angels notebook and writes on the virgin page:

8 pm, February 29, 1918, New York City
Dear Diary . . .

She keeps her appointment the next day, at the corner of 64th Street and Central Park West in a fifth-floor studio. It is a room of excellent posture. There is a Frenchified sofa that is apparently not for sitting. To the right of the door stands a bust of Verdi atop a marble column. To the left is Mozart. On the gleaming parquet floor, a Persian carpet. A high coffered ceiling in mahogany, a giant window onto the park, a grand piano. An immaculate wheat-colored man with a goatee, morning coat, tapered trousers and striped cravat. The maestro. From somewhere in Europe. Brief introductions, she is not invited to be seated, she is instructed to sing something.

She does.

It's a small room. It's a big voice.

The maestro's gaze alights on a corner of the carpet, disinterested as an insect, and stays there for the duration of the song. Kathleen finishes. The maestro glances up and perceives the flush on her face, the moist glistening of her eye, the pulse at her neck, her lips still parted. And he says in a wafer-thin voice, "We have a lot of work to do."

Corruption hangs in the air around a great talent. Such a gift is unstable by nature, apt to embarrass its handlers. About her there is the whiff of the entertainer. Like vaudeville nipping the heels of grand opera. The maestro smells all this on Kathleen and cools his blood to a temperature undetectable by wild animals. Before him lies a grueling task. It is so much easier to shape competence. Yet, in a small spot beneath the hardest part of his skull, the maestro is feverish with excitement. You don't get a student like this every day—perhaps two in a lifetime. He prepares to show her no mercy.

As Kathleen works harder and harder, she walks farther and farther. Between sadistic singing lessons with the maestro and suffocatingly sedate suppers with Giles, Kathleen walks the length and breadth of the Island of Manhattan. From the East River to the Hudson; from Battery Park to the Haarlem River.

One day, a girl is sitting at the maestro's grand piano when Kathleen drags herself up to the studio. She is Rose, in a pale pink dress perfect for a dear little thing with an open face and a trusting nature, and therefore all wrong on Rose.

Rose is an extremely good pianist, but Kathleen doesn't notice that at first, for two reasons. First, because when you're training with a famous bastard in New York City, with one eye on the Met and the other on obscurity, you don't notice the quality of the piano accompaniment during your lesson unless it is incompetent. But this pianist is doubly inaudible because she is black and therefore outside any system that nurtures and advances a classical virtuosa. So Kathleen thinks of Rose not as a pianist but as an accompanist.

When Rose looks at Kathleen the first time, she sees a daughter of fortune and looks back down at her piano keys. When she looks the second time it is to verify that the sound that just filled the room really came from that milk-fed thing standing on the carpet. The voice is worth considering. The singer can go to hell.

"The piano is out of tune," says Kathleen.

Ordinarily, Kathleen says nothing during her lessons. She makes the sounds the maestro orders her to make and, in the privacy of her own mind, thinks up a thousand devastating retorts with which to slay him. But today she is impelled to speak, because what's the good of an accompanist if she can't even hear when the piano is off key? Kathleen has addressed her observation to the maestro, but Rose addresses Kathleen, "The piano is perfectly in tune. You're flat."

Kathleen glares at the accompanist, with equal parts fury and disbelief. And the accompanist looks back—calm, level gaze. Insolent, more like it, how dare she? Handsome features cut like sculpture into her face, so at odds with the puffed sleeves and schoolgirl braids. Kathleen looks away dismissively from the beanpole in a hand-me-down dress. She expects the maestro to scold the accompanist or, preferably, fire her. But instead he turns to Kathleen. "Perhaps if you were less intent upon making noise, and more intent upon listening, you might learn to hear the difference between that"—the maestro jabs at a piano key—"and this"—the maestro makes a horrible honking sound through his nose, supposedly in imitation of Kathleen.

Kathleen floods crimson. The maestro instructs her coolly, *"Lesson One:* The Scale." Lesson One! Kathleen takes a breath and steadies herself for the giant step backward. She pictures a shining sword sharp at both edges, and sings the scale, pondering all the while who is worse: Sister Saint Monica, or this singing teacher whom she has come to think of as the Kaiser. And before she is halfway through the scale, she decides: the accompanist is worse.

Rose plays the scale and watches the singer. Decides she is not white, not even red. But green. Faintly visible, called up by outrage, are the veins at her wrists, neck, temple. This is the only physical detail that corroborates the voice, which Rose knows to be not of human origin. The green must be seaweed. Rose allows her mind to wander in this way whenever she is required to play in harness. It helps take the sting from the bit. Rose has no need of fancy when she plays her own music, because there is no difference between her own music and her mind. All alone after hours in a second-story church in Harlem, far north of this studio. Free rein.

But for now: Lesson One—*La Scala.* Kathleen glowers at the accompanist. Rose blinks at the singer and allows the slightest bit of curiosity to mingle with scorn.

It's 1918. New York City is inching toward the center of the universe. Its streets throng with working girls and doughboys and the gumption of immigrants from the four corners of the earth. Kathleen is sorely tempted to cut her classes, her hair and her hems. She has forgotten all about the "fashionable New York" of *Harper's Bazaar.* She is consumed by the new New York, which is more various and fabulous at two in the afternoon on Mulberry Street than come midnight at the Ziegfeld Follies. In Manhattan's north end Rose plays her own music, while outside her church window Haarlem is turning into Harlem. Rose's mother has raised her to be an example to The Race, and every day the list of places Rose must never set foot in grows longer. But Kathleen is subject to no such restrictions. Her father is far away, and Giles asks no questions except to inquire, "How are you enjoying New York, dear?"

First Kathleen fell in love with New York. Then she fell in love with a New Yorker. It happened very quickly, the way things are supposed to happen when you move from New Waterford to New York at eighteen.

The Children's Hour

AT HOME, JAMES SLOWS down a bit. With Kathleen gone, it's safe for him to spend an after–supper hour in the wingback chair again. In the corner of the front room sit two unopened crates of books, but there are still so many unread in the glass cabinet that James leaves the crates untouched. There will be time enough later, when Kathleen is launched in her career and he doesn't have to work so hard. Fifty-two books, not counting the *Encyclopaedia Britannica*. One day, I'll sit down with all my books around me, and just start reading.

Right now, however, there's still too much work to do. What's more, James has taken to devoting his precious evening hour to his two little girls, whom he has noticed for the first time. He is pleased to find they're bright, the both of them, and he reproves himself for having simply handed them over to Materia until now. He intends to make it up to them. To this end, one evening soon after Kathleen's departure James calls the two wee ones over to the wingback chair, tucks them in one on either side, opens a big book and reads, " 'In the second century of the Christian era the empire of Rome comprehended the fairest part of the earth and the most civilized portion of mankind.' " And the little girls listen, bewildered by the strange names and long words but enchanted by Daddy's careful voice, by glimpses of wonderful worlds that unfold at his command and, most of all, by his special attention.

It is different from the thrill they experienced with Kathleen. With Daddy they are aware of something rare and solemn. They understand that he is teaching them. And they respond with as much reverence as they can muster.

Mercedes is almost six. She never fails to bring Daddy his tea, balancing it carefully along with the evening's book. She is a good child who takes her role as Mumma's helper and Frances's big sister very seriously—although it looks likely she'll turn out on the plain side, her hair a bit mousy. Nonetheless she has nice brown eyes and a good disposition. But James can't help being particularly taken with Frances. She's a live one, going on five, with her burnished gold ringlets and mischievous grin, green lights dancing in her hazel eyes. Always ready with a joke for Daddy: "I've got your nose!" And full of good ideas for games that she and Mercedes can play. "Mercedes, let's shave!" "Mercedes, know what? These buttons can fit in our noses." Mercedes has learned by trial and error when to say, "Okay," and when to say, "Let's pretend."

James doesn't like the sound of Materia and the children chattering in Arabic but he doesn't object. He simply counters with the special time they spend together after supper. He leavens the weight of classics with fairy tales and rhymes. The girls love poems and learn them easily. Standing at the foot of his chair holding hands, neat as two pins in Kathleen's old frocks—blue for Mercedes, red for Frances—their button boots so nicely shined, they recite in piping singsong voices: " 'I have a little shadow that goes in and out with me, And what can be the use of him is more than I can see. He is very, very like me from the heels up to the head; And I see him jump before me, when I jump into my bed.' "

Then Frances squeals with glee and Mercedes curtsies. James smiles and claps. Frances scrambles onto his knee, Mercedes lays her cheek against his hand and James feels the ice in his chest breaking up. The war is finally over. He is home again, and everything is turning out all right after all.

> I have you fast in my fortress
> And will not let you depart,
> But put you down into the dungeon
> In the round-tower of my heart.
>
> And there will I keep you for ever,
> Yes for ever and a day
> Till the walls shall crumble to ruin
> And moulder in dust away.

There are fewer letters from Kathleen than James would like, but now and then Giles sends a card assuring him that all is well. In June, a package arrives from Kathleen containing twin sailor-boy dolls, one for Frances and one for Mercedes. They are thrilled and immediately take the new additions to meet the rest of their doll family, "Look, children, these are your new American cousins." There is also a letter and James calls his girls to the wingback chair and reads it aloud.

" 'Dear Daddy and Mumma and young ladies,

I am making wonderful progress under the expert tutelage of my voice teacher. He could not be better pleased, and neither could I. Giles is a wonderful companion and she has introduced me to a number of quite inspiring cultural experiences. To date, I have enjoyed excursions to the Museum of Natural History, as well as theatrical evenings of modern dance. There is also a good deal of modern music being premièred in Manhattan, and it is a privilege to be among the first to hear such ground-breaking compositions. There are also numerous soldiers passing through on their way to the Front, and I plan to assist Giles in wrapping bandages—although I cannot claim any great skill with knitting-needles and would pity the poor soldier who received a pair of socks from me! These diversions aside, my time is almost entirely caught up with lessons and practice, practice, practice. Please say hello to Sister Saint Cecilia if you happen to see her in town. I will write again soon.

Love, Kathleen' "

Content, James folds the letter and tucks it into his breast pocket. Then he tells Frances and Mercedes once again about how, when Kathleen finishes her schooling, they will take the train to New York City and hear her sing at the Metropolitan Opera House. Mercedes pictures a white palace, and Kathleen sitting on a throne next to a handsome prince. Frances sees a castle with mermaids swimming in a moat full of ginger beer, and Kathleen holding a sword, singing on a balcony.

The summer flies past. Materia cooks, James works, the little girls thrive. By fall, they can read. It has happened by osmosis, the way it ought to: after they have spent several months on Daddy's lap, following his spoken words with their eyes and pretending to read, there comes a day when they no longer have to pretend. The glass of the mirror has simply melted away and now they are free to enter as many worlds as they like, together or alone. Thank you, Daddy.

On November 7, James walks to the post office with his girls to find a letter from New York waiting for him. There is his usual pleasure at the sight of the postmark, but it is followed today by slight surprise, for there is no return address and his own name and address are written in a ladylike but unknown hand. While Frances and Mercedes scrupulously divide a shoestring of licorice, James opens the letter and reads. . . .

Its contents are a cruel contrast to its refined penmanship. It is signed "An Anonymous Well-Wisher." James folds the letter over and over until it is minute, and considers: Either it is a malicious joke. Or it is true. He leaves that night.

Three and a half days later, at 6:05 A.M. on November 11, 1918, he walks out of Grand Central Station.

He finds Kathleen. And takes her home again.

Book 2

NO MAN'S
LAND

O Holy Night

ON THE FIRST NIGHT of summer 1919, in the attic of the house on Water Street, as Kathleen lies dying—and unable to appreciate that fact due to the heaving and excessive pain, due to the blood that's all a result of the bomb jammed in the antechamber of her belly, threatening to explode before it can be dropped to earth—she has a moment's respite: a calm descends and the pain dissolves and disappears, along with the siren wail of her mother's incessant prayer warning of an air raid, *God is coming,* wailing in supplication, *Come O Lord,* begging God to pass over and to bless, not touch, this house. O Lord hear our prayer. O Lord be with us at a safe distance now and at the hour of our death—

This is a breech birth; the child is stuck feet first. Someone will not get out of this room alive. There was a choice to be made. It has been made. Or at least the choice has been allowed to occur. Everything disappears from sound for Kathleen: her mother's voice—by now perhaps speaking in tongues or at least the mother tongue—the pounding of her father's fists on the door—he'll break it down in a moment. She levitates in a profound and complete relief, peace, floating absence of pain. It's all over for her now, anyone can see that.

Materia sees it. Has been expecting it, accepts it, unlike James on the other side of the door. She gently closes her daughter's eyes, then takes a pair of scissors—the old kitchen scissors, freshly sharp and sterilized to cut the cord—and plunges the pointier blade into Kathleen's abdomen just above the topography of buried head. She makes a horizontal incision and reaches in; there's not much time, the infant will suffocate in a moment, in a moment James will be through the door, one cut is not enough. Materia sculpts panic into a slow march, reining it in, *now and at the hour of our*—she makes another cut, a vertical one bisecting the first. She prayer-dives both hands through the center of the cross-cut into the warm swamp slippery with life, past mysterious ferns and swaying fibers, searching for a handhold on sunken treasure, there an ankle, there an arm, the living treasure caught in a net of fingers. With a series of precise and dire yanks the catch is dragged from where it lay lodged halfway down the canal that locked despite the battering of the seismic tides that were set off by those first gravitational yearnings. The bundle of tiny limbs and vestigial gills and unique fingerprints is hauled toward the torn surface of its small swollen sea. Its four eyes are scorched by the sudden light that jags in through the flapping entrance to the outside world, and in an instant it is borne up and through the wound in Kathleen's belly.

The air splashes and spumes against it, threatening to drown it—*them*—for there are two but they have yet to be cut in half, they are still one creature, really, male and female segments joined at the belly by a common root system. It-they is a blood breather and could drown in this fatal spray of oxygen, will drown if they remain silent much longer, will become bright blue fishes in a moment. But the cords are cut, *snip-snap,* and tied just in time, and in an instant the shocking air is gulped and strafed into the lungs. They become babies just in time; slick, bloody, new, wailing, squinting, furious, two.

One of them, the male child, bleeds a little from a cut on his ankle. His feet were nestled next to his sister's head when the scissors descended. He was all set to arrive head first like a good mammal. Technically, therefore, the female twin is responsible for the death of the mother, for it is she who was breech. But this was pure roulette. The pair had been revolving counterclockwise in the chamber for weeks before their birth was triggered.

Kathleen is an abandoned mine. A bootleg mine, plundered, flooded; a ruined and dangerous shaft, stripped of fuel, of coal, of fossil ferns and sea anemones and bones, of creatures half plant, half animal, and any chance that any of it might end up a diamond.

James has supposedly seen worse. He was in the war after all. Now he finally sees something from which he will not recover. Beyond shell shock. Beyond No Man's Land.

In a cavern in a canyon,
excavating for a mine,
dwelt a miner, forty-niner,
and his daughter Clementine.
Light she was and like a fairy,
and her shoes were number nine,
herring boxes without topses,
shoes they were for Clementine.
Oh m'darlin, oh m'darlin, oh m'darlin Clementine;
you are lost and gone forever,
dreadful sorry, Clementine.

Here's what Kathleen saw just before the moment of respite. Between agony and release, she saw—framed by the door which is thumping like a heart attack—Pete. With his head off *Hello little girl*. This time he's not behind her in the mirror. He is out in the open. It's safe for him now. And after all, he just wants to get a look at her, just one good look *Hello there*. His no face tucked beneath his arm *Hello*.

And when he has looked his fill, he politely nods his stump of neck and leaves. She whimpers briefly. There is the blissful release from pain. Nothing has ever been better than this moment. It is enough. And then all we can do is see her through her mother's eyes, because her own are extinguished.

Materia's dilemma was this: Do I let the mother live by removing the infants limb by limb, finally crushing the heads to allow for complete expulsion from the mother's body? It is hard to imagine a worse sin for a Catholic. The sin resides not in the gory details of the operation, because the details of doing the right thing are equally gory. The sin resides in preferring the life of the mother to those of the children. For this you are eternally damned. Materia does the right thing by allowing the mother to die and the children to live.

So why does Materia die a few days later of a guilty conscience? Because she did the right thing for the wrong reason. For a reason which was itself a mortal sin. For two days she wrestles with her conscience. But God is everywhere. It takes Materia forty-eight hours to face that what she did, although correct in the eyes of the Church, was murder in His all-seeing eyes: the real reason I let my daughter die is because I knew she was better off that way. I didn't know her well, but I knew she didn't want to live anymore. She preferred to die and I allowed her to do so.

Looked at from this angle, Materia has not saved two babies, she has mercy-killed one young woman, and therein lies the mortal sin. For Materia cannot swear that, had her daughter been clamoring for life, she might not have used the scissors to dismember the infants rather than open the sky for them. In her heart of hearts she suspects this might have been so. And in this suspicion Materia discovers the chill comfort that, in the end, she managed to love her daughter after all.

God sees an opening and rushes in. He makes himself comfortable in the back of Materia's mind for a couple of days, during which time she cleans obsessively.

On the third day she cleans the oven, first turning on the gas to soften up the grit inside, it'll only take a moment. She is so tired. She hasn't slept in three nights, not so much as a tiny zizz, and she has never worked harder. She kneels in front of the oven, peering in, waiting for the gas to do its work, her arms folded on the rack. It'll only take a moment—she rests her head upon her arms. She is so tired. She will start scrubbing in just a moment, just one more moment. . . .

For the umpteenth time that week James has to improvise a criminal mind, for he doesn't naturally have one. He turns off the gas, hauls his late wife upstairs and onto their bed, scrunches her rosary into her hands, then calls the doctor and the priest. This allows Materia to be buried next to Kathleen in the churchyard instead of in an unsanctified field somewhere—in the type of place where soldiers and suicides and unbaptized babies sit out eternity, some unholy No Man's Land.

The Mass Card

MAY JESUS HAVE MERCY ON THE SOUL OF

Mrs. James (Materia) Piper (née Mahmoud)
Died June 23, 1919
Age 33

"We have loved her in life. Let us not abandon her, until we have conducted her by our prayers into the house of the Lord." ST. AMBROSE

Solace Art. Co.—202 E. 44th St. N.Y.

FRANCES IS GOING ON six now. She has a number of questions regarding the mass card, but this is clearly not the time or place to raise them. Mercedes kneels next to her, crying and crying into her little white gloves, her hanky already drenched. Daddy's face is frozen. If the wind changes it will stay that way for ever. Mrs. Luvovitz, in a pew across the aisle, is crying behind her black veil. This is the first time Mrs. Luvovitz has ever been inside a church. Mrs. MacIsaac is there too, with dusty grapes on her hat. Frances decides the wind must have changed for her long ago. Filling in for Materia at the organ is Sister Saint Cecilia. Or at least it must be she within the flowing black robe beneath the Gothic skyline of starched white wimple. Frances thinks it logical that nuns wear cathedrals on their heads.

At the back of the church there is a phalanx of strangers. People with black curly hair, full features and smooth olive faces. These are some of Frances's unknown relatives. Frances's unknown Grandfather Mahmoud is not present. For him this funeral is redundant. Right now he's locked in the back of his store, hunched on a plain wooden chair, apparently poring over a ledger.

Mr. Benny-the-Butcher Luvovitz, Daddy and Mr. MacIsaac are the pallbearers. It's all very much like Kathleen's funeral a few days ago except for three things: Mumma was sitting at the church organ that day instead of lying in the box. And the scary old man who peered into Kathleen's casket and muttered bad words in Mumma's language, he's not here. But most important, Frances has noticed at the very back, standing next to the dark little round woman with the gray bun, one tall lean figure: the dark lady who came with an envelope for Daddy and a candy for Frances a whole year and a bit ago. Teresa is here for some reason. Teresa the maid. Queen Teresa. Frances doesn't listen when told to keep her eyes front, and has to be yanked around by Daddy, who will reserve proper punishment for home later on. If she hurries, perhaps Frances will be able to make it out of the church in time to run after the lady and hop into the taxi with her, never to return. They will drive off together into the land of black and white licorice peppermint rock candy.

"Eyes front!"

Frances is really going to get it after the funeral. She dares not sneak another look behind her at the woman of her dreams. So she concentrates on the mass card instead: *ST. AMBROSE*. The name detaches itself from the card, leaving its holy prefix behind like a tail, and floats up into her mind, where it wafts about gently until it settles via some mysterious associative route upon the infant boy who died a few nights ago in her arms. Ambrose. Yes. That will be his name. Ambrose.

There have been three deaths in the space of one week at 191 Water Street. And two funerals. And three baptisms. And three burials. And two mass cards, identical, fill in the blanks. What a week. Enough to make you feel as though you've breathed laughing gas. And right now Frances wants very badly to laugh, she can't tell why, except that it's the single worst thing a person could do right about now. Oh no. Now that she has thought of laughing she can't unthink it. She covers her face with her hands and grins. She tries to grin out the laughter. To exhale it silently, smoothly. But she starts to convulse and shake. She clamps her hands tighter against her face and gives in. She can no longer resist. It's like the tide of pee when you're outside playing and refuse to go inside and use the toilet—your water breaks and it's both a blessed relief and the ultimate mortification.

Frances is spared the pee. But what could be worse than this outrageous hilarity at her mother's funeral which comes two days after her sister's funeral which came two days after all the baptisms and the death of—oh no, tears of laughter are darkening her white cotton gloves. Frances expects her father's hand to grip the back of her neck, expects to be dragged in disgrace from the church. But what happens instead is a gentle pat upon her head—her father's sympathetic hand, her sister's offer of a sodden hanky. Frances is amazed. *They think I'm crying.*

Frances learns something in this moment that will allow her to survive and function for the rest of her life. She finds out that one thing can look like another. That the facts of a situation don't necessarily indicate anything about the truth of a situation. In this moment, fact and truth become separated and commence to wander like twins in a fairy tale, waiting to be reunited by that special someone who possesses the secret of telling them apart.

Some would simply say that Frances learned how to lie.

Of all her secrets, Ambrose was Frances's biggest. He was also her greatest gift to Lily.

Cave Paintings

WHEN THE ATTIC DOOR finally gave way, James saw this silent portrait: *Death and the Young Mother.* It's an overdone, tasteless, melodramatic painting. A folk painting from a hot culture. Naive. Grotesque. Authentic.

This is not a gauzy Victorian death scene. No fetishized feminine pallor, no agnostic slant of celestial light, no decorously distraught husband. This portrait is in livid color. A crucified Christ hangs over a metal-frame single bed. On either side of the crucifix are two small pictures: one is of the Virgin Mary exposing her sacred heart aflame, the other is of her son Jesus, his heart likewise exposed and pierced to precious blood by a chain of thorns. They look utterly complaisant, Mother and Son. They have achieved a mutual plateau of exquisite suffering.

On the bed lies the Young Mother. Her eyes are closed. Her blond-red hair is damp and ratty on the pillow. The sheets are black with blood. The center of her body is ravaged. A plump dark woman who looks much older than thirty-three stands over her. This is the Grandmother. She holds two dripping infants trussed by the ankles, one in each hand, like a canny shopper guesstimating the weight of a brace of chickens. The Grandmother's face looks straight out from the picture at the viewer.

If this were really a painting, there would also be a demon peering out from under the lid of the hope chest at the foot of the bed, looking to steal the Young Mother's Soul. But he'd be preempted by her Guardian Angel waiting in the wings to guide her already departing Soul up to God. The Soul, half in, half out of the tomb of her body, is in very good condition, the hair freshly combed, the nightgown spotless, the face expressionless— the first divine divestiture has taken place, she has sloughed off her personality like an old skin. She won't need it where she's going. Above the crucifix, the wall has dematerialized. Clouds hover. Somewhere within is God, waiting.

But since this is not really a painting but a moment freeze-framed by James's eye, the supernatural elements are, if present, invisible. There is the dead Young Mother, the Grandmother, the Infants, the Icons, the hope chest. What can you do with such a picture? You never want to see it again yet you can't bring yourself to burn it or slash it to dust. You have to keep it.

Put it in the hope chest, James. Yes. That's a good place for it. No one ever rummages in there. This is crazy, of course. You can't stuff a memory of a moment into a real-life hope chest as if it were a family heirloom. But for a second James feels as though that's what he's looking at—an old portrait that he hid in the hope chest many years ago and just stumbled upon again. This temporary confusion is a premonition; it tells him that he will never get over this sight. That it will be as fresh fourteen years from now, the colors not quite dry, just as it is today.

James goes out of the room, but not far. His legs give way and he collapses outside the fallen door, unconscious. He doesn't hear the first cries of the babies inside. The involuntary part of his mind does, though. It is just not conveying the message. It is keeping it on a crumpled piece of paper on the floor of its cave. It is taking a break, admiring its cave painting by the light of the dark.

A few moments later, James's hand shoots out and fastens on Materia's ankle, almost toppling her down the narrow staircase as she leaves the room. James's mouth opens a split second before his eyes. "Where the hell are you going?"

"I'm gonna get the priest."

"No you're not." He's awake now.

"They gonna be baptized."

"No they're not."

"They gotta be baptized."

"No!" James roars.

"You gonna kill them, you gonna kill their souls, you're the devil—"

She's hitting him. Closed fists in his face. If the scissors were handy she wouldn't bother to shut his eyes first— *"Ebn sharmoota, kes emmak! Ya khereb bEytak, ya Hara' deenak!"* If the bayonet were near she would not hesitate. And God would understand. Why didn't she think of this before?

Materia too is awake now, after a nineteen-year slumber. She will kill him if she can.

James gets her wrists in a vise grip. His other hand clamps across her mouth. Her eyes roll back. James tells her, "Who's the killer eh?! Who's the killer?! God damn you, God damn you, damn you—" He begins to punctuate the curses by slowly slamming her head into the wall. Her eyes are trying to reason with him, but without the help of words her eyes become a horse's eyes, as mute, as panicked. His tears are flowing now. His lips tripping on salt and snot, his nose bleeding, he's retching out the most agonizing man-sobs, the wall is starting to conform to her skull. This time, however, he hears the tiny cries from inside. Like kittens. He picks up Materia and carries her three flights down to the coal cellar and locks her in. Then he goes for a walk. And many fast drinks, of course. Some of us are just not equipped for suicide. When we're at the bottom, suicide is too creative an act to initiate.

Which leaves little Frances. At the bottom of the attic stairs. Based on her upbringing, and from what she has heard and seen tonight, one thing is clear: the babies up there must be baptized. But she has to be careful. She has to hurry. She mustn't get caught. She stands at the bottom looking up.

The attic room has been a place of absolute peace and quiet for the past many months. Until tonight. Her oldest sister has lain up there not saying anything. Frances and Mercedes have been allowed in to read to her and to bring her trays of food. They have read *Black Beauty, Treasure Island, Bleak House, Jane Eyre, What Katy Did, Little Women* and every story in *The Children's Treasury of Saints and Martyrs*. The two of them decided to look up the hard words next time around, rather than break up the reading aloud. They also got their mother to search out recipes for the invalid food found in *What Katy Did* and *Little Women*. "Blancmange" seems to be the favorite of languishing girls. They never do find out what it is. "White eat." What would that taste like?

Frances knew Kathleen must be very ill because of the huge lump in her stomach. Mercedes told her it was a tumor. "We must pray for her." Together Frances and Mercedes have prayed for Kathleen. They have made a little shrine and given up sweets for as long as it takes her to get well.

So here's Frances at the bottom of the narrow attic staircase. She is almost six. She is not afraid of the dark. Besides, there's a little light coming from that room. And she's not alone. Her big sister, Kathleen, is up there.

And so are the babies. The babies, which sound exactly like kittens. Frances is very fond of kittens. She's in her bare feet. She's got her white nightgown on and her hair is in two long french braids. She gets to the landing. She's too small to be on eye level with the new depression in the wall; just as well. But what does it matter, she saw how it got there, and now the child is entering the room and she's going to see everything. She's stepping over the splintered caved-in door with her bare feet.

The difference between Frances and James is that, although she sees a version of the same horrible picture, Frances is young enough still to be under the greater influence of the cave mind. It will never forget. But it steals the picture from her voluntary mind—grand theft art—and stows it, canvas side to the cave wall. It has decided, "If we are to continue functioning, we can't have this picture lying around." So Frances sees her sister and, unlike her father, will forget almost immediately, but, like her father, will not get over it.

What Frances sees: the gore. The pictures over the bed. The scissors. And the babies, squirming slightly and mewing between Kathleen's legs, where they have been wedged for safekeeping until the priest can be dug up. So . . . the secret contents of Kathleen's tumor, revealed; this gets filed under "Normal" in Frances's mind.

Frances devises a way of carrying both babies: she spreads the front of her white nightie on the bed and places the slippery babies on it. She folds them into the fabric, making a cozy bundle. She cradles her bundle of babies and walks carefully all the way down two flights of stairs with her underpants showing, through the kitchen, out the back door, across the pitch-dark coal clinkers in the backyard, until she comes to the bank of the creek. There is one scary thing: the scarecrow in the center of the garden on the other side of the creek. If toys come alive at midnight, what happens to scarecrows? Frances avoids looking at it. "It's just a thing." But she doesn't want to offend it. She lovingly empties the tiny children onto the grass. It's a nice warm evening.

Frances regrets that she didn't think to rifle the hope chest for the white lace gown and bonnet—the outfit that she, Mercedes and Kathleen were all baptized in. Too late now, there's no time, *I have to get this done before Daddy comes home.*

Frances loves her little niece and nephew already. There is nothing she would not do to make sure their souls are safe. She knows that otherwise they die with Original Sin on them and go to that non-place,

Limbo, and become no one for all eternity. Frances has never been up close at a baptism, but she's heard the priest mumble, barely moving his lips, she's seen him dip the baby's head into the water. The priest is praying, that's for certain, so Frances must pray too. *Hurry Frances.* Frances makes the sign of the cross, *In nomine padre . . .* In the name of the Father, the Son and the Holy Ghost. She looks at the wee babies in the skimpy moonlight; "Ladies first." She picks up the girl baby, and shimmies on her bum down the embankment to the creek. She wades to the center. The water is waist-deep. On wee Frances, that is. Her nightgown puffs and floats on the surface before taking on water and silting down around her legs. She makes the sign of the cross with her thumb on the baby's forehead.

Now's the part where you pray. Frances takes a stab at it: "Dear God, please baptize this baby." And then her favorite prayer from bedtime, "Angel of God, my guardian dear, to whom God's love commits me here, ever this day be at my side, to light, to guard, to rule and guide. Amen." Now's the part where you dip the head in the water. Frances tips the baby carefully toward the water. The little thing is still slick and slips through her hands and sinks. Oh no. Quick! *Hen, rooster, chicken, duck!* Frances plunges down, grabs the baby before it hits the bottom, then breaks the surface clutching it to her body. It's okay. Frances's little heart is beating like a bird in the jaws of a cat, she catches her breath, the baby lets out a tiny holler and the sweetest little sputtering coughs. It's okay, it just swallowed a bit of water, it's okay. It's okay. Frances rocks it gently and sings to it a small song composed then and there, "Baby, baby . . . baby, baby . . . baby baby." There. At least it's nice and clean now.

Frances crawls up the bank again, lays the girl baby down on the grass, kisses her little hands and head and picks up the boy. She knows that you have to be extra careful with new babies because their heads aren't closed yet. Like a ditch or something along the top of their skulls. It's called a "soft spot" even though it's in the shape of a line. You can see it stretching along beneath the layer of bluish skin that's draped across it. Frances didn't see it on the girl baby's head because the girl baby has a weirdly dense thatch of black hair. But there it is on the boy baby's feathery pate: a shallow trench dividing his head in half. Frances enters once more the waters of the creek and lightly traces the pale blue fault line in the infant's skull. What if someone just came along and poked their fingers in there, what would happen? He would die. Frances squirms at the thought that just anyone could come along and do that. What if her fingers just went ahead and did that? *Oh no, hurry, you have to get him baptized before it's too late. Before Daddy comes home, or before anyone's fingers can press in his head.*

Frances drops the second baby. Oh no. Quick! *Hen, rooster, chicken—*

"What in God's name are you doing?"

Frances's head jerks up, arresting her plunge. It's Daddy. There's the great upside-down V of his legs towering at the top of the creek embankment. He's got the girl baby in one arm.

"Get the hell out of there!"

He's drunk, otherwise he would never curse in the presence of a child. He reaches down and gets Frances by one arm, easily swinging her up out of the water, her soaked nightgown hanging down past her toes, she could be the Little Mermaid invited at long last onto the good ship *Homo Sapiens,* ready to try out her new feet. Except for the bloodstains.

The water is dark. James doesn't see the child on the creek bed. "No!" Frances screams as he sets her down on the grass. She can't find the words. She can't tell him, telling is not an option, this is like a dream, she's forgotten how to say in waking English, "The other baby is in there, he's going to drown, we have to get him out!" James tosses her ahead, herding her in jerks back towards the house. Frances breaks and runs back. He lurches after her. She reaches the edge of the creek and leaps. Over the top. Splash and plunge. She scrabbles about on the bottom for the baby, her lungs are stinging, in this water she's as blind as the newborn she can't find, she finds him. She breaks the surface for the second time as James arrives back, swaying a little, at the creek's edge. She bundles the baby to her chest; it stirs once and is silent. She stares up at her father and the girl baby. She starts to shiver.

James either says or thinks, "Jesus Christ, Jesus Christ, Jesus Christ." He slides down the bank, takes the child and goes through the motions of resuscitation. But it's no use. The boy baby was in the water a good twenty seconds too long. Frances's teeth start to chatter, and she wonders if her black and white candy is still at the bottom of the creek or if it has been washed out to sea.

Blancmange

FRANCES SPENDS THE NEXT day in bed, shivering. Her teeth are chattering. She can't get warm. Outside it's June. Her lips are blue.

Mercedes wraps her in several blankets and feeds her pretend blancmange. "Pretend" because the dish is unavailable to them outside the realm of fiction, and because all Frances can manage to eat for the next couple of days is pretend food.

Where's Mumma? What with a freezing child in one bedroom and a burning hot infant in another? She's downstairs cleaning. The house is spotless.

MAY JESUS HAVE MERCY ON THE SOUL OF

Kathleen Cecilia Piper
Died June 20, 1919
Age 19

"We have loved her in life. Let us not abandon her, until we have conducted her by our prayers into the house of the Lord." St. Ambrose

Solace Art. Co.—202 E. 44th St. N.Y.

★   ★   ★

Frances stops shivering in time to attend Kathleen's funeral but she still hasn't eaten any real-life food. By now she has already lost her conscious grip on the events of two nights ago, when the babies were born. She has shivered them away. The cave mind has entered into a creative collaboration with the voluntary mind, and soon the two of them will cocoon memory in a spinning wealth of dreams and yarns and fingerpaintings. Fact and truth, fact and truth . . . "Where's my nightgown, the one with the— I spilled something, I have to wash it, remember that fish I caught in the creek that time?—I did, I did, there are *so* fish in there—it had a thin blue stripe but I let it go, it was just a baby fish, too small to eat, I threw it back, it swam away, back to the ocean. . . ."

But the nightgown is long gone—committed to earth by James, who made of it a shroud for an infant boy.

And as for the fish, everyone knows there have never been any fish to be caught in the creek. The only thing anyone's ever going to catch in that creek is polio.

On the day after Kathleen's funeral, on the third day following Kathleen's death, Frances is still fasting when she is overcome by a powerful craving. She goes to the kitchen, where Mumma is getting ready to clean the oven. She opens a long cupboard and takes the lid off the flour bin. She fills her hands with the white dust and carries it carefully across the kitchen and upstairs to her room. Materia sweeps up the thin white trail behind Frances without a word, without looking up, without following it beyond the border of the kitchen linoleum.

Once in her bedroom—the one she shares with Mercedes—Frances releases the flour from her hands into the empty porcelain washbasin on her dresser. She adds water from the pitcher and mixes it with her hands until she has a soft sticky dough. She takes the dough in both hands, curls up on her bed and begins to suck on it. At first she sucks rapidly, making little sounds, then more slowly as the craving subsides. Her eyelids get heavy and she falls asleep, her mouth filled with the soft moist mass.

Mercedes enters carrying a tray heaped with invisible delicacies. Frances's lips still suck a little intermittently in her sleep. Mercedes puts down the tray, careful not to upset the flagon of port and send it streaming into the blancmange. She bends over Frances and feels her forehead, then gently pries the glutinous white blob from her mouth. She carries it downstairs, following the trail of white powder back to where it ends at the kitchen linoleum, and stops. Not because the trail stops. But because of what she sees. Mumma. Mercedes stands staring, the raw dough cupped in her hands like an offering. She was going to bake it for Frances. It's not good to eat raw dough, you might get worms. Mercedes was going to bake it in the oven. But her mother is using the oven. Mercedes stands there for a long time, with her hands full of wet white dust.

See No Evil

ON THE NIGHT WHEN Lily and Ambrose were born, Mercedes was awakened by the same racket that woke Frances. But Mercedes stayed in bed, while Frances crept out to the attic stairs. Mercedes held onto the blankets just under her chin and said the rosary, even though she was too scared to turn and reach for the beads where they lay under her pillow. It was after this night that Mercedes started actually to wear a rosary on her person, because sometimes even under the pillow is too far away when it comes to a rosary. So Mercedes said the rosary with the tufted nubs of the chenille bedspread instead:

Mercedes stares hard at a row of white tufts but she has trouble getting the rosary going, not because it's just a bedspread, but because of the Devil. Only the Devil would block her mind with a picture of the wooden backscratcher that leans against the mirror on her bureau. You can't see it now, it's too dark, but it's there. A long wooden backscratcher carved with three monkeys doing "see no evil, hear no evil, speak no evil," and at the tip of it are three prongs curved like claws for scratching. It was a joke gift from a friend of Mumma's at the Empire. Mercedes has just realized that it is an evil thing, and in the morning she will put it in the garbage. No, the furnace. In the morning. When it's light and the sounds from up in the attic have stopped. Someone just started hammering the wall up there. Maybe they're hanging a picture.

Mercedes fights the Devil and wins. She manages to make the backscratcher disappear from her mind, she banishes it with the first prayer that's able to break through—"Angel of God, my guardian dear, to whom God's love commits me here, ever this day be at my side, to light, to guard, to rule and guide. Amen." Quick, before the evil picture comes back, quick, "Hail Mary, Mother of God, the Lord is with thee, blessed art thou among women and blessed is the fruit of thy womb, Jesus. . . ." and the rosary is safely started. And once it's started, you can just keep going around and around for as long as you want or need, following the stepping-stones of the bedspread. Yes, in an emergency you can say the rosary anywhere, provided you have faith.

Finally the house is quiet. Where's Frances? Mercedes creeps softly into the hallway. She looks up the attic stairs. There's a little light up there, but silence. Mercedes has no desire to go up there. Perhaps the thing in the back of her mind takes better care of her than the thing in the back of Frances's mind. Perhaps. Mercedes turns away from the attic door and walks towards her parents' bedroom. On her way she steps in something sticky. She gives herself a gentle reprimand for not putting her slippers on, and in fact gropes her way back to her room, finds her slippers and her green tartan housecoat and puts them on, tying the flannel belt snugly around her waist and smoothing down her hair before venturing back out into the hallway. She reaches the door of her parents' room. It's half open. She stands very still and listens. Nothing. No breathing. Her heart leaps for a moment, *no breathing!* She is young enough to fear that both her parents may simply have died in their sleep. She moves softly toward their bed and reaches out her hands like a sleepwalker, still listening. Will they be there? Will it be their bodies? Will they wake up and be annoyed with her? It's a sin to doubt so much. If you really have faith in God you won't go around expecting to find your parents dead in their bed for no reason. Say a little prayer. "I'm sorry, dear God." Now let your hands descend gently towards the bed and—nothing—empty sheets. What a relief, they're not lying there dead, they're just not there at all. *Oh no!* Where are they? It's the middle of the night, where are my parents? Where is Mumma, where is Daddy? Stop it, you're going to make God angry, you deserve to find them dead downstairs, murdered by a tramp.

Mercedes' almost-seven-year-old nerves are still tender but tonight begins a process that will eventually turn them into steel. Her little nerve fibers are being heated up. Tonight is the smelter. When her nerves have been heated up enough, when they are white-hot, they'll be plunged into cold water, tempered and strong forever. Strong enough to support a building or a family, strong enough to prevent the house at 191 Water

Street from caving in on itself in the years to come. It will stand. *It will stand*. But for now: *go downstairs. . . .*

Mercedes' search carries on in this way. Listening, listening. Looking, looking. She finds no one downstairs. Apparently she is all alone in the house. Oh, except for Kathleen. Or maybe Kathleen is gone too. Maybe they've all gone and left her. *You could go check, Mercedes. Check in the attic.* No. "And besides," Mercedes answers, "Kathleen doesn't speak anymore, she couldn't tell me where they've gone." *You haven't checked the cellar.* "There's nothing in the cellar but coal and the furnace."

It would take a less rational sort of person to conduct the type of search that would result in real information—the type of search that turns up the reading glasses in the icebox and the car keys in the medicine cabinet. But then, it takes a less rational sort of person to misplace things so spectacularly. Or to speculate, "Hmmm, perhaps my mother is locked in the coal cellar, I'll just have a little look-see." And it would take the sort of person who can't resist trouble to actually climb those attic steps after the wailing and rampaging that have issued from that direction. Mercedes can resist. She can hold out against trouble, against curiosity, someone has to.

She returns to her bedroom. She makes the blankets into a cloak around her and sits on her knees on her bed, staring out the window at the moon over the backyard. Our Lady is in the moon. The cool white light is her love. Everything's going to be all right. And finally Mercedes sees something which is not an absence. It's Frances, down there in the creek. She's holding something, cradling it—a bundle. And on the embankment there's something moving. A small animal. A kitten. That must also be a kitten she's holding. Frances dunks the bundle, then dives after it. What's she doing? No! No, Frances loves kittens, she wouldn't be drowning them. She's giving them a bath. That's what she's doing. She puts the one kitten down and picks up the other one, but Mercedes doesn't see what happens next because Daddy comes into the yard and up to the creek, blocking her view. Uh oh, Frances is really going to get it now. Well, she shouldn't be up playing in the creek at this hour anyhow. In fact, no one's allowed playing in the creek ever. It's not a beach. Mercedes sees the struggle, the extent of Frances's disobedience in running back to the creek, leaping in. Why is she so bad? Some people are just made that way.

When Frances comes to bed she is ice cold. Mercedes pretends to be fast asleep, and in her pretend sleep she snuggles over to Frances and folds her into her tartan housecoat. Frances is bare naked. This too is unusual. But no matter how Mercedes snuggles Frances, Frances goes on shivering.

Mercedes will never again sleep through a night. From now on she will be listening even in her sleep. Someone has to.

In the morning, Mercedes notices the blood in her slipper. She washes it out. The only other thing different about this morning is that, if you look out at the garden, you'll notice that the scarecrow is gone and in its place there's a big rock.

The Adoration of the Body

James, knee-deep in water, reached up and placed the dead infant on the ground on the far side of the creek, then climbed out after it. Frances was holding the girl baby close against her stained and soaking nightgown and she made a move to head back to the house.

"Stay right where you are!"

Frances watches as Daddy squishes in his wet shoes over to the scarecrow. He takes hold of its legs and yanks at it as if he were uprooting a small tree. Its head wobbles and falls off and rolls down the slope into the creek with a splash. The creek begins to carry it away. Frances watches the head bobbing along on the water and thinks, "He's going to find my black and white candy, he's going to eat it, he's going to tell someone in a far-off land what I did." The head is carried off and out of sight toward the sea. But the hat remains. The crunched fedora.

James tears the scarecrow free of the earth. Its body was impaled on a stake and that stake must have been green wood, because now that Daddy has yanked the pointed end from the ground you can see it is alive with pale sprouting roots. Eventually a tree would have grown right up through the scarecrow. Maybe with fruit too. A branch would have grown straight out through his mouth, and on the end of the branch a big red apple. "Imagine," thinks Frances. "Imagine if you had a tree growing inside you." Imagine seeing the green leaves everywhere, trapped just under your skin and growing, imagine seeing the thin roots swirling under the surface of the soles of your feet, their white ends looking for a place to poke through. The earth is a magnet for roots.

James tosses the scarecrow across the creek. It lands with a thud next to Frances, its neck bleeding straw, its legs splayed crazy on either side of the teeming wooden stake. Frances can feel the scarecrow looking up at her. It has no head but she can see its expression anyway, pathetic and sad: "Why did you do this to me?" Lying there like a dying soldier wanting to give her a message from his dying throat: the location of the enemy, a message for a loved one back home, a piece of a joke, a piece of a poem, the address of his childhood home crystal clear, the memory of a boy drinking from a summer stream in a painting *or did that really happen, was that me?* Frances doesn't answer. She looks away from the scarecrow even though she knows it may move if she doesn't keep an eye on it. Her arms have congealed around the clammy little baby. She fastens her eyes on the scarecrow's hat. The hat is lying next to Daddy. And Daddy is digging in the garden. With his bare hands.

James stops. It's ridiculous to dig anywhere but in a sandbox with your bare hands, but in a New Waterford backyard it's even more ridiculous, because there's coal not far under the ground, even coal right at the surface in places. And rock. James is crying. He covers his face with his hands, streaking it with mud and soot and blood. He has never cried like this before, not counting early childhood. He's in the war. Not that he is hallucinating himself back to the Front or hearing shells explode in his head or seeing chopped-up men, it's not that conscious. It's just that if you asked the layer of his self that's in charge of assumptions, "Where are we now?" it would reply, "In the war, of course." There is a water-filled trench. There is an unhappy man with bleeding hands. There is the body of a boy. Of course.

"Daddy."

"No-o-o-o-o-o. No-o-o-o-ho-ho-ho-ho-ho." Like Santa Claus, only sad.

"Daddy, I'm sorry."

James quiets down a bit and rocks on his heels for a while, making only very small sounds, with his hands still covering his face.

"The baby's cold, Daddy."

James gets up, gasping, swaying a bit, every breath touching off a little moan. But they're just the aftershocks of grief. He can function now, the chest-heaving will run its course like a case of hiccups. He looks across at Frances. He splashes through the creek and takes the live baby from her. Her elbow joints unsquinge like damp springs, and her arms levitate in giving up the child's weight, while retaining its warm impression—a phantom baby she will feel in her arms for days to come. James gives her a light shove toward the house.

"Go to bed now, go on."

"Don't hurt her."

"I won't hurt the baby, go."

Frances goes.

"Wait. Take off your nightgown."

She peels it from her body and James takes it from her. She watches Daddy return to the garden, where he swaddles the infant boy in her nightgown and tucks him into the shallow earth.

Frances walks across the yard back to the house, savoring the novelty of the night air on her bare chest. Boys are the only ones who ever get to feel this. There's a bright moon, her underpants glow white and she pretends to herself that she's really a boy stripped down for a swim at Lingan. She skips across the backyard feeling light and free, and it's not until she steps out of her damp underpants and snuggles down in bed next to toasty-warm Mercedes that Frances starts to feel cold and to shiver.

Down in the cellar, Materia is curled asleep on a pillow of ashes behind the coal furnace. She dreams of an expanse of quiet earth embroidered by drought, then a calm sea of sand. In her dream she is aware that kings and queens are buried in the sand. A wide blue river blinks in the distance. In the river there is something she needs. But the sand makes her sleepy. Sleepy like Arctic snow. It's not the cold that makes you sleep yourself to death in the Arctic, it's the smooth pallor of the landscape, and the desert has that same smooth pallor, though Arabic. It's the whiteness, the sameness of everything, that makes you fall asleep out of life, parched or frozen and so so comfortable when you finally let it roll over your mind, like a rolling-pin over dough.

The latch on the cellar door thwacks open and the airborne part of Materia slams back into her body, her eyes opening on impact; she has fallen awake. His shoes squish heavily down the steep wooden stair slats. He stumbles a bit at the bottom because there's no light down here and he hasn't brought a lantern. Materia doesn't move a muscle. She is a pair of eyes now, that's all she is. A desert with eyes.

James has either forgotten she's there or doesn't consider it of any importance. He yanks open the door of the cold furnace and tosses in a

load of bloody sheets, douses it with kerosene and lights it. The sudden
glow across his face startles even Materia and tears spring to her eyes, there
is nothing sadder than the Devil. Tears spring to her eyes because in this
light, in firelight as in candlelight, the essential beauty of a person is
evident. Candlelight is kind and caressing and therefore a natural companion to romance. The essential James is what the flames illuminate and it's
splintering what's left of her heart, the sight of him as he was so long ago,
the two of them alone in the hunting cabin out of season with his gift of his
mother's tartan blanket and the song and his bliss at the sound of her
mother tongue, he loved her but she didn't know she was supposed to save
him, she didn't know, she didn't know, he must have fallen down and hurt
himself just now because his face is dirty, he's been crying and his cheeks
are striped with blood.

He sprinkles a little more fuel onto the flames. Materia can't stay by
the furnace much longer what with it heating up like this. If he doesn't
leave soon she will have to move and betray her presence. But he shuts the
potbelly door and the glow dies down, his sweet agony disappears and is
replaced by the shadows of the face she has come to know and Materia
ceases to feel the lump in her throat.

As he heaves and shifts the weight of himself from one foot to another
up the steps, Materia wipes the tears from her face with her sooty hands.
She unwedges her body and drags it along the cinder floor behind her until
she can stand up in it again, and goes back to being nothing but a pair of
traveling eyes.

Before dawn, with Mercedes still sound asleep beside her, Frances opens
her eyes and sees a black woman staring down at her. The woman reaches
out and lightly strokes Frances's forehead. She does the same to Mercedes,
and then leaves. Frances falls back asleep. Candy. She dreams of candy.

The night is bright with the moon. Look down over Water Street. On the
lonely stretch between where the houses end and where the sea bites into
the land, a tree casts a network of shadow that stirs and bloats in one spot, as
though putting forth dark fruit that droops, then drops from the bough.
It's a figure come out from under the branches and onto the street. It stops,
drifting in place like a plant on the ocean floor. Then it travels again all the
way down the street to the graveyard. It passes among the headstones that
have flourished with the town, but it does not linger at the freshest mound.

It continues to the edge of the cliff. There, it lies down on its stomach and places its neck upon the lip of the precipice, as though the earth were a giant guillotine. It looks straight out to the sea that stretches four thousand miles due east, and sings.

Is it possible that the Atlantic conducts the song across its waters until, thirsty and ragged, the song reaches the Strait of Gibraltar, revives a little with the refreshment of its own echo off the rock of ages and continues its journey, turning on its tattered axis all the way to Lebanon, where it finally loses momentum and rests in air for a moment before descending in soft arcs to the sandy shore below, to sleep there in peace and forever, at last?

When Mrs. Luvovitz opens her back door at three that morning she gets a fright. There's someone in her garden. Just standing there at a slight tilt, as though blown that way by a wind that's since died down.

Mrs. Luvovitz woke up because she heard something. A woman singing, of all things. She couldn't make out the words. It didn't wake Benny. Hard not to think *"banshee"*—sometimes they wail, sometimes they weep or just sing softly, but their message is always the same: someone will cross over. By the time Mrs. Luvovitz got her eyes properly open the singing had ended. But she looked out the front window anyhow—nothing. Just to be sure, she went downstairs and opened the back door, and that's when she got the fright—a figure stood in her garden, with its back to her.

Fear turned to surprise the next instant when Mrs. Luvovitz recognized the shape.

"Materia?"

Materia does not turn around, she does not stir. She is a ripe stalk planted in shallow soil, top-heavy, about to fall over roots-up. Just a baby's breath will do it now.

Mrs. Luvovitz walks between the beans and tomatoes until she is close enough to touch Materia's arm. It is cool and smooth and plump. Materia's hair is loose. It hangs in wiry black waves that just touch her shoulders. She's wearing one of the loose cotton dresses that Mrs. Luvovitz helped her sew, soft and favorite now with age, covered in faded wild flowers.

Materia turns at the touch and Mrs. Luvovitz sees the front of her. *"Gott in Himmel."*

Materia stands in Mrs. Luvovitz's tub while Mrs. Luvovitz washes

her. They're in the kitchen with the fire going. The water is black with
coal dust and blood. Materia's dress is on the floor, the front of it is a scab, it
will be thrown out. Mrs. Luvovitz washes her gently, no scrubbing, no
cloth, with her soap-sliding hands only, as though Materia were a newborn. It's a milky skin Materia has, not in color but in texture, all curves,
compact muscle under a soft sheath. Materia doesn't say anything. All the
effort and anxiety of distinguishing one thing from another drained away
forever, all distances now equal—Mrs. Luvovitz's face and the Cape of
Good Hope, Materia's own warm body and the rest of the world.

Mrs. Luvovitz has sent Benny to the Piper house to find out what in
God's name is going on over there. When he arrives he finds James in a
clean white shirt making tea, at 3:30 A.M. The house is very warm, hot.
Kathleen is dead upstairs under fresh linen. There's an infant girl asleep in a
crib by the stove.

"I'm sorry for your trouble, James."

"Thank you, Ben. Will you have a drink?"

"Cuppa tea."

In the morning, Mercedes awakens next to Frances and sees a black
smudge on her little sister's forehead. It looks like ashes from the fireplace.
Mercedes licks her finger and cleans it off. Frances sleeps on. While
dressing, Mercedes notices a similar smudge on her own forehead. She
wipes it away. Frances wakes up.

"Mercedes, I dreamed that the lady who gave me the candy came
into our room last night."

"What lady?"

"The dark lady. She touched me."

Mercedes knows that it was the Devil and that they were protected
by the rosary. The Devil would leave a coal smudge on your forehead. It
would be like him to mock what the priest does on Ash Wednesday. And
it couldn't have been Our Lady. Everyone knows Our Lady is pure white
in a blue dress.

"It was just a dream, Frances."

"She was beautiful."

Mercedes says a silent prayer for her sister.

"She's my fairy godmother," says Frances.

Mercedes puts the rosary around Frances's neck and goes downstairs
to help Mumma make breakfast. Frances curls up on her side and shivers.

Daddy is waiting for Mercedes in the kitchen. He has made porridge for her. She sits down at the table.

"Good morning, Daddy."

"I need you to be a big girl, Mercedes."

He looks at her. They have the same eyes, though hers are brown. Their faces are of sandstone, though hers is tinged with olive. Mercedes understands that the worst is coming and unfolds her serviette, placing it neatly on her lap. She's glad she took special care with her braids this morning.

"Your sister Kathleen has been taken away from us."

"Has she gone to New York City?"

"She's gone to God."

A gap opens up in Mercedes' stomach. She bridges it by picking up her spoon. "Thank you for breakfast, Daddy."

"I need you to look after your mother."

"Is Mumma sick?"

"No. But she's very tired. She's just had a baby."

"Oh." Mercedes shows her teeth politely and gets her first permanent wrinkle. "A boy or a girl?"

"Another little sister for you."

"Oh." The second permanent wrinkle.

"Mumma is very sad about losing Kathleen. She's too tired to look after the new baby."

"I'll look after it."

"That's my girl."

"Don't worry, Daddy."

The Official Version

*She endured the most severe trials with a calmness,
fortitude and resignation which are the best proofs
of the innocence of her life.*

EPITAPH, HALIFAX CEMETERY

MATERIA HAD DONE THE Roman Catholic thing; the mother had died. And James, of course, had not been in attendance at the birth and had therefore been in no position to apprehend the danger or to intervene. So there was no inquest, and the examining doctor and the undertaker kept the details to themselves and their wives.

One child was born.

Kathleen looked lovely, God rest her soul, so young and lifelike. Just as though she were asleep. They buried her in white, it should have been her wedding dress. The influenza, you know, there's not a family on three continents hasn't been touched by it. And her with her God-given gift and her whole life ahead of her.

Everyone knew that Kathleen was pregnant and that she died of the child. You'd have to be an idiot not to have figured that out, what with the girl's hasty home-coming and incarceration in the house. But the thing you do in a case like this is go along with the idea that the child is the offspring of its grandparents. Everyone agrees to this fiction, and the only people who'd breathe a word of the actual facts to the illegitimate child are those who are so malicious to begin with that they are easily dismissed as liars. As in truth they are. For the beneficent lie tells the truth about the child, which is "you belong to this community," whereas the malicious truth-tellers use fact to convey a lie, which is "you don't belong." This is an imperfect system but it's the prevailing one. And as the years go by the facts get eroded and scattered by time, until there are more people who don't know than people who do.

Mahmoud Mourns

Mahmoud never wants to see Materia or her husband or her children or any evidence of them ever again. The only communication he's had with the Piper family for the past nineteen years has been the business arrangement with James, and they've both done well out of that while never once coming face to face. But that's over now.

Kathleen was the one Mahmoud invested in, was proud of, but he ought to have known that exposing the girl and her gift to the world was exactly prostitution. She went out and reaped the wages of her parents' vanity (in the case of James) and stupidity (in the case of Materia) and wound up a tramp. It's what happens. Where did she do it, who did she let do it to her and how often, who was it, some Anglo dog son-of-an-*enklese*-bitch with no respect for people's daughters, or worse, a Jew, New York is full with them, or worse, a colored man—likewise thronging in that city—and once that's in the blood it sleeps there for generations until you least expect it, where was her father when his daughter was being ruined in the worst city in the world, where people mate like mongrels? And now a bastard in the family, another girl to boot, my son-in-law is truly cursed. Bad from the beginning, bad in the end, I wash my hands.

Mahmoud is enraged to find himself choked with tears as he looks at the lily-white girl in the casket with her copper hair spread out around her. He's never seen her up close before. And he fumes that they would dare to send her to her grave in white, *in white* they would send her to God who sees all! "And there's my idiot daughter at the organ. I should have broken her fingers at birth. I should have dismantled the piano and shot the bastard, Piper. I was merciful and look at the result."

Mahmoud scans Mercedes and Frances sitting scrubbed and gleaming in the pew next to James, who looks positively bleached in his black suit, "If he's smart he'll have the older one in a convent and the younger one out of the house and married before her first period, damn them all to hell."

The Rocking Chair

James takes his last drink on the night of Kathleen's funeral. It's after midnight when he comes in from the shed, sits down at the piano in the front room and plays. The opening bars of "Moonlight Sonata" and many other pieces.

Upstairs, Mercedes awakens when the music stops. Frances is not in bed. Mercedes sits up and looks out the window, expecting to see Frances down at the creek again, but no. Mercedes leaves the room and pauses on the landing looking down. There's a light coming from the front room. And something else coming from the kitchen—a smell. It's late at night but Mumma's cooking kidneys for a pie. Daddy's favorite. Mercedes takes one step down. Two steps. Three. And stops to listen . . . a little sound like a puppy. Mercedes thinks of the kittens in the creek the other night and shudders. She doesn't like it when Frances goes roaming in the dark. She wishes everyone would just stay in bed at night. She wishes she were back in her own cozy bed too, but she is the eldest now. Mercedes places her hand lightly on the railing and descends toward the light spilling over the bottom of the stairs. She rounds the archway of the front room and stops.

It's all right. Frances is alive alive-o. She is in the rocking-chair with Daddy. It's funny that Frances seems already to have been looking at Mercedes even before Mercedes arrived in the doorway. It's Daddy making the puppy sound. He is sad because Kathleen died. He needs his other little girls all the more now. Frances is sitting nice and still, not squirming for a change. Mercedes waits until the rocking chair stops and Frances slides from Daddy's lap to join her in the doorway. As they walk upstairs hand in hand Frances says, "It doesn't hurt." Mercedes says, "I don't like that smell of kidneys cooking." And Frances says, "Me neither."

Back in bed with Frances cuddled once more at her side, Mercedes starts to feel afraid. And a bit sick to her stomach although she can't understand why. She rises, goes over to the washbasin and throws up. It must have been that smell of kidneys cooking that got her upset, because why was Mumma making meat pies in the night? And are there really places where people put children into pies and eat them? It's a sin to think that about Mumma. But Mercedes can't help it. She knows there couldn't really be a baby in the pie, but she also knows that whenever she loses track of Frances, bad things happen.

The First Holy Sacrament

"Daddy, where's Mumma?"

"I need you to be a big girl, Mercedes."

The first thing James did after dragging Materia's body up to the bedroom was run and get the priest—not for Materia, too late for her—for the baby girl. James has caught on: there is a God. There is a Devil—necessary evil. You may be cursed, but at least God has a plan for you.

The alternative to believing is buckling under the weight of irredeemable guilt and the meaninglessness that used to be your free will; ceasing to function; and that is not an option. He has a family of motherless children depending on him.

He sent the priest on ahead, then ran for the doctor.

The baby girl is on fire with poliomyelitis. Or "infantile paralysis." You don't have to be an infant to get it.

The house is quarantined. It doesn't make much difference, there never having been many comings or goings. But now it's official. The doctor has taken his pot of black paint and slapped an X on the front door as he has on so many others. Every day, people spit on their thresholds front and back, declaring, "No disease in my house!" but the charm has lost its power. There's disease everywhere.

Stealing center stage from the regular cast of diphtheria, TB, scarlet fever and typhus is Spanish influenza. You don't have to be Spanish to get it. In 1918 and '19 the flu kills millions more people worldwide than the war did. Many believe the disease spread from the rats that fed off the corpses in the trenches.

The graveyard has sprouted afresh with little white crosses carved with cuddlesome lambs. Children have been hit particularly hard. Mercedes has just finished first grade. She goes to Our Lady of Mount Carmel School and up until the summer holidays she had to wear a white surgical mask to class like all the other children, so as not to spread germs. "Miss Polly had a dolly who was sick, sick, sick, so she called up the doctor to be quick, quick, quick." All through town, groceries are left at the bottom of front yards along with the milk, no one wants to get near. Even doctors and nurses are dropping like flies. Coal deliveries are carefully monitored: if a coal cart delivers a load you never ordered, look out, someone's going to leave your house in a box. If a black horse stops in front of your house for no reason, start praying. If a white horse comes in the night, forget it.

The doctor stands on one side of James, looking into the crib. The priest stands on the other. He is wearing his vestments and holding cruets of holy water and oil. James has no idea that the infant has already been baptized. He doesn't know that's what Frances was doing out there in the creek, he just knows she's bad. As for the night of Kathleen's funeral— well, he won't be touching another drop of anything stronger than tea from now on.

The priest will baptize the baby without picking her up because to move her at this point in her illness would be very dangerous. He asks James, "Who will stand as godfather for the child?"

"I will," says James, since there's no one else but the doctor in the quarantined house, and he's a Protestant.

The Holy Roman Church has been waiting for James all along. He thinks back to his own forced baptism years ago when he married Materia. He stood defiantly with his head unbowed while a priest mumbled words over him, "The voice of the Lord is mighty. The voice of the Lord is majestic. The voice of the Lord breaks the cedars of Lebanon. . . ." He endured it as a sham. But now he knows there are no accidents, only tests. The Church is full of examples of men like him, who thought themselves damned and yet were saved. Men equal parts monster and martyr. And through one last act—perhaps occurring invisibly and deep within the heart at the hour of death—they were saved. Even sainted.

"And who will stand as godmother?" inquires the priest.

James opens the door to where Mercedes is waiting. He has her stay on the threshold, well back from the seething crib. Mercedes' hair is freshly though unevenly braided, she's not yet used to doing it herself. A blue gingham pinafore, stockings of red because blue and red match.

The priest doesn't flinch. In the eyes of the Church a child can stand as sponsor in an emergency, and besides, it is fairly clear this baby will soon be with God.

Godparents must promise that, should anything happen to the child's parents, they will bring the child up in the Roman Catholic faith. This is usually a hypothetical vow, but not for Mercedes because Mumma is already dead. "I'm the mother now," she tells herself. "And I've had my confirmation so I'm ready." Last May Mercedes put on an immaculate white dress and veil and, along with the rest of her shiny clean classmates, was ritually slapped by the bishop. Three of her classmates have since died. Dottie Duggan died, she sat next to Mercedes. Dottie had the disgusting habits of eating glue and picking her nose, but now she is one of God's angels. Mercedes chose Saint Catherine of Siena as her saint's name even though she badly wanted Bernadette, but Bernadette isn't a saint yet, when oh when? Frances told Mercedes to take Veronica as her saint's name because of Veronica's magic hanky. "Not magic, Frances. Miracle."

The priest leans over the crib where the infant lies on its little bed of coals and he asks it, *"Quo nomine vocaris?"*

In the doorway, Mercedes and James answer together on behalf of the baby, "Lily."

James hasn't thought of a middle name. There hasn't been time. He just prays that she'll grow up to use this one.

The priest continues, "Lily, *quid petis ab Ecclesia Dei?"*

Mercedes and James reply, "Faith." They have a special dispensation to reply in English because Mercedes is too young to have learned all that Latin—though she would have tried had there been time.

Mercedes is longing for a look at her new baby sister. She watches as the priest bends down and blows softly three times into the crib. He is blowing away the unclean spirit to make room for the Holy Spirit. The Consoler.

"Exorcizo te, immunde spiritus . . . maledicte diabole."

The priest spends a long time blessing Lily and praying over her. Mercedes and James say the Apostles' Creed and the Lord's Prayer. And then the priest resumes his questions. "Lily, *abrenuntias satanae?"*

"I do renounce him."

"Et omnibus operibus eius?"

"I do renounce them."

The priest anoints Lily's head with oil as the godparents attest to her faith in the Holy Ghost, the Holy Catholic Church, the communion of

saints, the forgiveness of sins, the resurrection of the body and life everlast-
ing. Finally, he sprinkles holy water onto the burning forehead. It beads
into the oil and simmers there as he baptizes her, *"in nomine Patris, et Filii,
et Spiritus Sancti."*

When the priest turns to Mercedes, she trembles with the gravity of
the moment and hands James the precious white satin bundle she has been
holding neatly folded in her arms. It is the family baptismal gown. James
takes the gown over to the priest. Lily is too sick to wear it, so the priest
merely lays it over her and tells her to accept this white garment, and never
to allow it to become stained.

Thus, along with her father, and at the age of almost seven, Mercedes
assumes responsibility for the soul of Lily Piper.

Now it's the doctor's turn. He peers into the crib, shakes his head,
gives James the it's-in-God's-hands-now look, pats Mercedes on the
shoulder and leaves with the priest.

Babes in the Wood

"Frances," said Mercedes, handing her a mug of cocoa, "Mumma's gone
away."

"Where?"

"To God."

The graveyard was scary even though it was a sunny day with a breeze off
the water. They watched Mumma's coffin go into the ground. They each
threw down some dirt. It made them feel a bit funny doing that—it didn't
seem like a very nice thing to do. Kathleen's grave was right next to
Mumma's. Kathleen is down there, thought Mercedes and Frances—
although Mercedes tried to remind herself that Kathleen was not down
there, she was with God. Frances was very worried about Kathleen—it's
dark down there. How can she breathe? Is she scared of the other dead
people? Most of them are skeletons by now. Are there worms?

Afterward they went home and Daddy took a steak-and-kidney pie
out of the icebox and heated it in the oven. How could it be that
Mumma's cooking was on the table when Mumma was in the ground?
James ate, but the little girls couldn't touch a bite. They tried to stop
breathing until they were allowed to leave the table. Frances tried not to

picture Mumma cutting raw kidneys with the scissors. The *snip-snap* sound.

That night of Mumma's funeral they couldn't sleep. They crept out of bed and knelt outside the door to Kathleen's old bedroom, where their new baby sister lay. How many Lilys can there be in one family, Mercedes asked herself. Frances was worried; babies called Lily lay perfectly still, then were taken away. Daddy called her Lily because of something I did, thought Frances. It's to remind me. Of something. They prayed.

"Angel of God, my guardian dear, please save our baby sister, amen."

They sang to her:

" 'Oh, playmate! Come out and play with me. And bring your dollies three, climb up my apple tree. Shout down my rain barrel, slide down my cellar door, and we'll be jolly friends for ever more. . . .' "

And they told her all the nice things they would do together when she got well.

"We'll have candy for breakfast," promised Frances.

"We'll join the choir," Mercedes pledged.

"We'll put on a beautiful ball gown."

"We'll cook lovely things for Daddy."

"We promise, Lily."

"We swear."

"On our graves."

"On our bones."

"On our kidneys." Which made them burst out laughing and Daddy called upstairs for them to go straight to bed, which made them both start whisper-singing at the very same time, " 'The doctor sighed and he shook his head, and he said, Miss Polly put her straight to bed!' "

Mercedes tucked Frances in with her favorite doll, a beautiful fla-menco dancer in a red dress. Frances made the doll dance quietly for a while. She made her go home and make molasses cookies for her children. "Now be good," said the dancer to her children, "I am going to study. And afterward, if I'm not too tired, maybe we will go to the Old Country. *Inshallah.*" After a while Frances said, "Mercedes?"

"What?"

"What if Daddy dies?"

"Daddy's not going to die, Frances."

"We would be orphans."

"Daddy's not going to die."

But Frances was crying, her twinkly face all crumpled, her tears hot like hot water from the kettle.

"Frances, I wouldn't let you be an orphan."

"I don't want Daddy to die," Frances sobbed, inconsolable because of poor Daddy, his two little girls lost in the woods with leaves for a blanket and no food. She cried because of the kind birds and the sad squirrels and poor Daddy can't save his dear children. It was the warmest she'd been in days.

"Frances, I wouldn't let you be an orphan."

Frances was crying so hard now that Mercedes got worried.

"I want my Mumma to come ba-a-a-a-ack."

Mercedes stroked Frances's fuzzy braids and whispered tenderly, "It's all right, baby, Mumma's here."

Frances stopped crying.

"I'm your mumma now," said Mercedes.

Frances lay still for a while, then she said, "No you're not."

"Yes I am, sweetheart."

Frances curled up into a tight ball.

"Mumma's here," Mercedes cooed, "Mumma's here."

Frances hugged her knees till her bones met one another. She turned her limbs into strong little tree branches. She made her spine into a springy switch and her skin into new bark. Not crying.

Frances never cried for Mumma after that night.

"It's a good thing Mumma's gone," Frances would say to herself, going over and over in her mind all the terrible things she couldn't quite recall—weaving the threads together into an ingenious cloak of motley. "Because if Mumma were here, she would know what a bad girl I've been."

Lily Who Lived

The morning after Materia's funeral dawns joyfully. James says to Mercedes, "Come and see your godchild." Frances follows. They walk into the sickroom, now stripped of everything but the glorious sunlight pouring through the open window, bathing the crib in a dazzle of dust sprites. Frances and Mercedes approach and look through the bars. Daddy beams. The little girls expect to see a plump and peachy version of their doll babies, but lying there is a thin-cheeked thing under a mass of black hair that looks like a fright wig. Dark eyes full of intense and watchful concern—they seem to have seen plenty already.

"What's wrong with her?" asks Frances.

"Nothing, she's perfect," says James.

She looks like a golliwog, thinks Mercedes, and Frances says, "There is so something wrong with her."

For which she gets a clip on the ear.

Mercedes says, "She's beautiful," and makes a mental note to confess the lie.

James picks the baby up. "She's a prizefighter."

Frances follows Daddy and the baby and Mercedes downstairs. They're going to feed her now. Coming from the kitchen is sweet tinkly music. They enter to see a six-inch porcelain girl revolving on the table. She wears kid button-boots and a lime-green silk dress over several petticoats, and holds a yellow and white parasol over her golden ringlets. On the base is an inscription, *An Old-Fashioned Girl*. It's for Mercedes, "For being such a good grown-up girl."

"Oh, Daddy, thank you."

Frances is pleased, happy that there is happiness in the house.

"It can be both of ours, Frances."

"No, it's your special thing, Mercedes."

Mercedes lets Frances wind it up, "Careful, not too tight."

Frances treats it reverently, but can't suppress a craving to know what makes the music.

The baby lies limp but alert in Mercedes' arms while James feeds her milk from a dropper. He says, "She's going to be fine. It's a miracle."

I am holding a miracle, thinks Mercedes.

"There is so something wrong with her," says Frances under her breath.

I'll take you home again, Kathleen . . .

Making love with the New Yorker is an experience which announces to Kathleen that the present tense has finally begun. It's summer now. For Kathleen the Present is a new country, unassailable by the old countries because the Goths and Vandals of the old countries don't even know the Present exists. But it is assailable. It will be breached. Kathleen is too young to know that. Right now, in summer, she is making love. She is just being born.

> My love
> I love you
> Oh
> Sweet honey
> I love you
> Sweet, oh
> Oh

It's a first-love conversation. Mouths can't kiss each other enough or find enough of the beloved to be kissed enough. The invisible ocean holds the room and the bed and the lovers suspended and treats them like aquatic plants, arms can never stop moving, fronds in the liquid breeze, hands never stop waving slowly side to side, caressing the loved one, *hello . . .* fingers never stop fanning, tendrils in a ceaseless bouquet, all parts sway and sway sometimes violently sometimes almost not at all. A small grazing gesture ignites the need for closer, and breaks the surface of the water, *never in you enough,* gulping air, *never contain you enough,*

on dry land now, *never hold you enough,* the desert heat, *drink you, oasis lover shimmering under a palm, I will burn to ashes here then blow away*—until that merciful peak is discovered, and once that is discovered, the slow tumble back down the hill, buckets of water spilling in slow motion, streaking the sand along their way until again the gentle sway, the ocean floor, the grazing touch that reignites the sea.

I want you
want you to
want you too
want to
oh you
so, so
sweet
Oh
Oh
like honey
I love you
taste like honey
my love

That fall James got a letter. He went down there and brought Kathleen home the day the war ended.

across the ocean wide and wild . . .

Book 3

THE SHOEMAKER AND HIS ELVES

Bootleg

1925. APRIL FOOL'S DAY—although Frances never needs an excuse. She and Lily are playing in the attic surrounded by a rabble of dolls. The room is otherwise empty except for the hope chest. Lily is going on six. Frances is eleven. She is Lily's self-appointed babysitter, playmate and tormentor. Lily wouldn't have it any other way.

Lily no longer resembles the strange baby she was. The only trace is in the particular attentiveness of her lovely green eyes, as though always prepared to take in a solemn truth. This is a quality that Frances especially enjoys. Lily's black hair has acquired an auburn sheen and, although nowadays a lot of little girls and boys have Buster Brown haircuts, Lily's hair falls down past her waist when loose. Her skin is peaches and cream and honey, she looks to have been kissed by the sun even in winter. She has lips like Rose Red, and an adorable little bump that appears in her forehead when she is perturbed. Frances has told her it is a horn that will soon grow out through the skin.

Today Lily is dolled up in a frilly knee-length dress of light green taffeta with a crinoline—no special occasion, just because she is our darling sweet Lily and Daddy likes to see her prettily turned out. Most girls, both little and big, have long since renounced crinolines and petticoats—women no longer need all that nonsense tripping them up, they've had far too much to do since the war. But Lily doesn't have to do anything but be happy.

Today, as usual, she wears a gleaming crown of french braids scraped so tight by Mercedes that the corners of her eyes are slightly stretched. Mercedes is in charge of Lily's hair, but Lily doesn't like anyone but

Frances to dress her or give her a bath. That's just the way it is. Even though Lily never knows when Frances will do or say something alarming—"Honest, Lily, you were adopted. We just found you in the garbage one day. You had potato peelings stuck all over you."

Frances is a wiry girl. And white as a sheet, usually. Except for the freckle on her Roman nose. And except for when she is laughing, or thinking up something really good. Then the bits of green glass in her hazel eyes light up, her nose goes pink and a little white stripe appears across its bridge. Lily watches Frances's nose as a sailor might watch for a lighthouse beam. When the stripe appears, it means Frances is about to go overboard.

And what has become of Frances's beautiful dark blond curls? They have given way to an invasion of wild undergrowth. "Naturally curly" is a euphemism. In brilliant sunlight it is possible to catch a hint of the blond halo she used to wear. Otherwise it has been obliterated by a riot of rust and brassy browns. Frances wears her hair in braids too, just like Lily and Mercedes, although hers writhe with escape-artist locks that by the end of the day bounce free. She cuts her own bangs.

Mercedes doesn't much care for dolls anymore, but Lily is passionate about them and so is Frances. She still has all her dolls from when she was little. When the dolls are not sleeping on the bed, they live in the attic. At the moment, they are all nicely lined up against the hope chest: there is Maurice, the organ-grinder's monkey; there is Scarlet Fever, the girl baby with the porcelain head; there is Diphtheria Rose, whose velvet dress Frances has shortened fashionably; there are the twin sailors, Typhoid and TB Ahoy, and the little boy doll, Small Pox. There used to be a lovely lady doll in a ball gown, Cholera La France, but she got lost somewhere. In pride of place is the flamenco dancer with her crimson dress and castanets. Spanish Influenza.

Lily reveres Frances's dolls, but the one she loves with all her heart is her very own Raggedy-Lily-of-the-Valley. Mrs. Luvovitz made her and Lily named her in honor of Frances's favorite perfume. She has lovely thick brown woolen locks, perfect for braiding, except where Frances gave her a bit of a haircut. Today, Lily takes Raggedy-Lily-of-the-Valley and picks the mouth off her for no reason. Regret is bitter and instantaneous. But what is to be done now?

"You've wrecked her," observes Frances.

"No I haven't."

"You sure have, here, give her to me."

"What are you going to do to her?"

"I'm going to fix her."

"Don't wreck her."

"She's already wrecked."

Lily hands over the rag doll.

"It's okay Lily, we can just pretend she had leprosy—"

"No!"

"—but then she meets Jesus and he heals her."

Frances takes a fountain pen from the pocket of her plaid jumper. Lily watches, poised to grab and rescue if need be. Frances calmly holds the doll just out of Lily's reach, but reassuringly tilted in such a way that Lily can watch the careful restoration of Raggedy's smile. Frances sings as she works, " 'Miss Polly had a dolly who was sick sick sick, so she called up the doctor to be quick quick quick. The doctor sighed and he shook his head, and he said Miss Polly, she is dead dead dead.' "

Lily howls, "No, Frances those aren't the words!"

Frances hands the doll back, "There."

"How come you gave her a blue mouth?"

"She stayed in the water too long and her lips turned blue."

"But what about when she gets warm?"

"She won't."

"Frances!"

"I can't help it, Lily," Frances points out reasonably. "You're the one who picked half her face off. I just fixed her, that's all, she looked stupid without a mouth. What an ungrateful little brat."

Lily stares at Raggedy.

"Thank you, Frances."

"You're lucky she didn't drown."

Lily finds the place within herself where love discovers that Raggedy is now more dear than ever. Frances watches Lily soothe the cruddy rag thing, and twines a finger round a stray coil of hair.

"Lily . . ." says Frances in a friendly confiding tone, "you know what Daddy has back there in his shed? A still. He's a bootlegger."

"He is not. He's a bootmaker."

"Why do you think they call it bootleg whiskey? Because Daddy makes it along with the boots."

"Frances."

"And I'm an alcoholic. I have been since I was six. Don't tell Mercedes. I took to the bottle the day you were born and I've been secretly drunk ever since. I'm drunk right now."

Lily doesn't like it when Frances's eyes start to glint green. It's the first sign. It means Frances is going to tell her something.

"No, you're not drunk, Frances, I can't smell it."

"It's so pure it doesn't even have a smell." Frances knows how to make her voice so calm and serious at the same time, the plain truth, like a doctor; "I'm afraid that head's going to have to come off, Mrs. Jones."

"Daddy wouldn't let you, Frances."

"Daddy gives it to me. I'm the taster."

"I'm asking him myself, that's not true, Frances."

"Lily, if you ask Daddy it will really hurt his feelings. He only makes the whiskey so we can afford a decent life. And I have to help him. It's too bad I got addicted but that's the sacrifice I made to help you and Mercedes. What if we couldn't have afforded a doctor? They'd've cut your leg off."

Lily starts to cry.

"Frances, I don't want you to be an alcoholic."

Lily's tears are pouring out and her throat is getting sore from sorrow. "I'm going to tell Daddy not to give you any more."

"Don't cry, Lily, it's okay, I don't mind. I've always known I would die young."

"No-o-o!" Lily covers her face and water streams through her fingers. Slowly, Frances puts her arms around Lily and begins gently to rock her as she cries.

"Daddy's not a bad man, Lily. He loves us very much."

Frances closes her eyes and soaks up Lily's warm grief for her predicament. It spreads like medicine through Frances's narrow chest. She experiences a precious moment of peace. Dear Lily. Frances breathes deeply, and her face undoes itself until it is as smooth as a young girl's skin.

"Frances, Lily . . . where are you?"

Mercedes doesn't like to raise her voice. Anything worth saying is worth saying in a civilized tone. This means she climbs a lot of stairs.

Mercedes' light brown braids are decently folded into a bun at the back of her neck. She wears a cameo fastened to the throat of her stand-up collar, and her blue serge skirt hangs three inches below her knees.

Modesty is always in style. Mercedes is a slim girl who is scrupulous about her posture. Mercedes is twelve going on forty.

Second floor. No sign of the girls, meantime the liver is getting cold in the pan downstairs. Loaded with iron, and economical, you can't go wrong with liver. Mr. Luvovitz has said so and he should know. Mercedes does most of the grocery shopping these days. Every Friday, Daddy entrusts her with housekeeping money, and on Saturday morning she makes the rounds. Lately she has begun doing most of the cooking too. After supper, she and Frances do the washing up. Then Mercedes does her homework. And then she does Frances's homework—although she tells herself that she is merely helping Frances, otherwise it would be cheating. And what does Frances do? Plays with Lily or fools around on the piano. Daddy taught Mercedes how to play up to grade seven according to the Toronto Conservatory, but he gave up on Frances early on. Frances prefers to play by ear, but only when Daddy's out working.

Mercedes peeps into Frances and Lily's bedroom. They're not there either. It always irks Mercedes when dinner is late, and it usually is, through no fault of hers. She sighs and looks forward to the end of day, when all her chores will be done and she can settle in with her book. These days she is achingly absorbed in *Jane Eyre* for the second time. Today is Thursday. Just two more days till glorious Saturday when, after she has done the shopping and the washing and ironing, Mercedes will go as usual to the home of Helen Frye, her best friend—best after Frances, that is. Helen Frye lives in a company house because her daddy is a miner, but the Fryes are not as poor as other mining families because Helen is that rarity, an only child. The others all died. So Helen has her own room and quite nice clothes. Maybe this Saturday Mercedes and Helen will take in a picture at the Bijou. Or work on one of several shared projects; they have a quilt on the go, along with baby clothes for their future children. And maybe, as they have been recently wont to do, they will discuss love. Helen is in love with Douglas Fairbanks. Mercedes is in love too, but she cannot yet bring herself to speak his holy name.

The door to the attic stairs is ajar. Mercedes stands at the bottom, a little put out. What's the attraction? Why do they play up there? For one thing, there's nothing up there but the old hope chest and she has the key, and for another thing Frances is rather too old for play. Frances could do with some friends her own age. Mercedes cups her hands around her mouth and speaks into the darkness of the stairwell.

"Frances, Lily, supper."

No answer. Then a low moan and a whistling sound like the wind, except it obviously isn't the wind.

"Frances, no nonsense now, supper's getting cold"—allowing herself a hint of genteel exasperation.

"Mercedes . . . give me back my liver."

"For gosh sake, Frances—"

"Mercedes . . . I'm on the first step." Metallic clomp.

"Supper's getting cold."

"Mercedes . . . I'm on the second step." Clank.

"Fine, starve."

Whispering, "Mercedes . . . BOO!"

"A-a-a!"

Why? Why does it always work?

Frances emerges into the hallway and dances the highland fling, the iron brace on her left leg swinging like a shillelagh.

"Frances, Daddy is right downstairs . . . Frances!"

Frances dances on, high kicking into Offenbach, singing in a Scottish accent, "Can, can you do the cancan, can you do the cancan"—accelerating—"canyoudothecancancanyoudothecancan—"

Lily has collapsed at the bottom of the attic stairs, beside herself with giggles, trying not to pee; Mercedes starts to succumb in spite of herself—

"What's all the commotion up there?" It's Daddy on the first step.

Mercedes snaps to the banister and calls down, "Nothing, Daddy, we're coming." She hurries down the stairs, heading him off, "Supper's ready when you are, Daddy," while Frances undoes the leather straps of the heavy steel brace and gives it back to Lily.

They say grace around the kitchen table, "Bless us O Lord and these Thy gifts which we are about to receive through Thy bounty through Christ our Lord, amen." Frances adds, *"Inshallah."*

James eyes her and shakes his head slightly. Lily grins behind her napkin. Mercedes serves.

"Mmmm," says Frances, "leather and onions."

Clip to the ear from Daddy, she earned that one. Let's all just ignore her.

"These carrots are from our own garden, Daddy," says Mercedes.

James had let the garden go to seed, but Mercedes resurrected it last year because she knows how much it meant to him at one time. Before all the sad things happened. She is very proud of the scrawny carrots and strange potatoes it produces and she always announces the fact that the family is being nourished by the bounty of their own backyard. James nods, gives her his faint distant smile and goes on eating. Frances, however, experiences difficulty.

Eat. Chew, chew, chew, offer it up for the poor souls in purgatory. Frances has difficulty getting through a whole meal at the best of times— maybe if I smuggle the liver into my pockets bite by bite—I know, tonight while everyone's asleep I'll glue a big envelope to the underside of my chair so that from now on—

"Eat," James tells her.

Lily's forehead has puckered, there are tears in her eyes, but she eats bravely on.

"It's all right, old buddy, you don't have to finish it," says James.

Lily looks to Mercedes, hating to hurt her feelings. "That's okay, it's delicious. Thank you, Mercedes."

James smiles mature complicity at Mercedes, who forms a smile in return and removes Lily's plate, saying in her kind voice, "Lily, would you like a toasted cheese?"

"Yes please, Mercedes."

"Atta girl," says James.

"I could use a filet mignon, personally," says Frances.

James shoots her a look—she'll feel the back of his hand in a minute.

He turns to Lily and tugs one of her braids. So like her mother, her mother's lovely mouth and perfect nose, her eyes. So like Kathleen but for the blight. That only makes her more precious to me. In the right way.

Lily doesn't know whom she looks like. She knows she had a sister who died, and Mumma died of a broken heart right after, and Daddy loves us very much.

James strokes Lily's sweet head and she caresses Daddy's hand with her cheek. The hand turns into a spider and tickles her under the ear; she wriggles and squeals and makes him stop with a little kiss. Lily senses that Mercedes disapproves, probably thinks she's too old for this game, but Lily can't imagine ever being too old to play with Daddy. She never wants to get that old.

On the whole James is satisfied with his life, and in some ways very happy. Mercedes is a pillar. And Lily is precious. They make up for Frances. "How was school today?" he asks her.

"Great, we looked at a bunch of fossils and spent the whole day on *Jane Eyre.*" Which is true, Frances did look at fossils; she spent the day at the shore, reading and skipping rocks.

James looks at her and in the silence Frances feels a little prickly, but takes another bite of liver. Mercedes waits by the stove. She will leave it till later to reprove Frances for borrowing her book without permission. For now she watches Daddy. Will he drop the subject? James opens his mouth but Mercedes chirps, "Daddy, you'll never guess what happened today," placing the toasted cheese before Lily and resuming her seat. "Ronald Chism's pet frog escaped from the pocket of his trousers."

"What happened?" asks Lily, all ears.

"Well, the errant frog was nowhere to be found until Sister Saint Agnes started from her chair and the creature leapt from behind the hem of her habit, to the great amusement of the class and the consternation of Sister Saint Agnes."

James chuckles politely, Frances yawns audibly.

James returns his attention to his plate and Mercedes breathes again. She ponders Daddy's love for Lily. And his anger at Frances. She picks up her fork and feels lonely.

That night, Mercedes creeps into the room Frances shares with Lily and into bed next to her sisters, and whispers, "Frances . . . are you awake?"

"No, I'm talking in my sleep."

"You have to come to school tomorrow."

" 'Oh, Daddy, 'twas so-o amusing, Mistah Froggy was moast impehtinent, methought he would leap right up the dingy crack of Sister Saint Agnarse.' "

"Frances!"

"You're laughing."

"I am not." Mercedes laughs silently into the pillow for a while. Finally she collects herself, wipes away tears and, "Frances?"

"What?"

"Promise me you'll come to school tomorrow."

"What for?"

"Sister Saint Eustace will have to get the truant officer after you and he'll tell Daddy."

"So what? We could use a little excitement around this joint."

"Frances, please."

"All right, all right." Frances rolls over and starts snoring.

"Frances, can I sleep here tonight?"

"I don't care."

"Thanks." Mercedes snuggles in, tucking Frances's always icy feet between her own.

"Aa'di aa'e'ley, Habibti."

"Don't worry, Mercedes."

"Te'berini."

"Yeah, yeah."

"Good night, Frances. I love you."

"Barf."

Mercedes giggles and falls asleep.

The Demon Rum

JAMES IS DOING WELL off the Nova Scotia Temperance Act. He's doing even better off the Eighteenth Amendment to the U.S. Constitution, otherwise known as Prohibition. Frances doesn't know it for a fact but she suspects. In Our Lady of Mount Carmel schoolyard, two brothers, both named Cornelius in case one dies, flung the truth at her. "Your old man's nothing but a bootlegger!" Frances retorted, "Oh yeah? Well your old man's a silly bitch!" They came after her but she ran, and no one can catch Frances on the run.

Frances has already learned that boys and fishermen have a richer vocabulary than girls and nuns—even if she's not always sure of the exact meaning of the powerful words she likes to use. She knew she wouldn't find "bootlegger" in the dictionary, any more than she had been able to find a satisfactory entry for "bugger," so she went to Mr. MacIsaac. His red face split in a grin, he wheezed out his laugh like a busted accordion and told her what it meant, quick to add, "But your daddy's not a bootlegger, lass, where'd you get that idea?"

Frances figured Mr. MacIsaac was just saying that to be nice. Either that or he's stupid. Why else does he fail to notice how sticky her fingers get whenever she passes the bin of cinnamon hearts and jellybeans? Frances let Mercedes in on her theory about the true nature of Daddy's work, but Mercedes just said "silly nonsense."

James is a bootlegger. When he works, he works at night. He leaves the house around eleven o'clock and locks the girls inside. He lights a lantern in the shed, where his cobbling tools sit gathering dust. Then he leaves the shed too and locks the door. He drives away, leaving the light to burn all night in the window.

He goes to the mouth of a certain stream and meets the dories that row in from the boats anchored offshore on "rum row." These boats are en route from the British colony of Newfoundland, where liquor is legal, to points down the coast as far as New York City. James carries barrel after barrel and case after case up the middle of the stream to a hiding place. He returns the next night, loads up his automobile and makes trips from the hiding place to his secret premises back in the woods. He is starting to feel too old for all this lifting and ferrying, however, and is considering hiring a couple of younger or poorer men. There are plenty of both kinds about these days.

One strike follows another: '22, '23, and just this past March of '25 the miners walked out again. It reminds James of New Waterford's bad old days before the war. Outside Cape Breton, the twenties are roaring. But the famous postwar boom never hit here. At least not for ordinary people. Things have gone from bad to worse. The politicians and the captains of industry blame it on that mysterious mechanism, "the world economy." But even James recognizes this as a euphemism for "God-forsaken sons-of-bitches who took everything out of here and never put a thing back." Many miners' children walk to school barefoot and eat lard sandwiches soaked in water to give them substance—this during times of full employment. No one knows it yet, but Cape Breton is a dress rehearsal for the Great Depression.

It's not surprising that bootlegging is tolerated. Who can blame a body for seeking to supplement his income a little? Or for just brewing some consolation to share with friends and family around a fiddle? And that's what most people do. It's unusual to find a local who sells home-made 'shine at more than cost. And it's unusual to find someone who doesn't have a jug stashed somewhere, if not a vat on the stove. The story goes that Father Nicholson opened Mount Carmel's rectory door to a stranger who inquired, "Where can a fella get a drop around here, father?" And the priest replied, "Well, my son, you've come to the only place in town where you can't get a drop, although I don't know, my curate might be selling." The few serious bootleggers tend to be good fellas—wild but not bad, and certainly not stingy or vindictive. Even the Mounties enjoy the game, no matter how often they're outwitted, and a mutual respect flourishes. Win some, lose some.

Naturally there is a Women's Christian Temperance League, but they are a Protestant bevy and New Waterford is a Catholic town. Even in Sydney, where there are more teetotal Protestants, the hotels serve strong drink with only the threat of now and then being charged a token fine for a first violation. A second violation shuts you down, but a proprietor would have to make himself very unpopular in order to have his twentieth violation designated a "second."

There is no shame in bootlegging. Not the way it is practiced by most people. James, however, is a professional. At his shack, in the middle of a secret clearing in the woods, he takes genuine scotch and gin, real rum, and cuts it all with his own lye-quickened concoction that bubbles day and night. He reseals the genuine liquor bottles and turns a handsome profit. It helps that he doesn't have friends to blab to. Otherwise one thing leads to another and, before you know it, the Mountie who has just turned up at your still to purchase a drop of Christmas cheer is duty-bound, come New Year's, to burn you down, no hard feelings.

Like the professional he is, James sells only to those most likely to pay: to several wealthy individuals who do their drinking at home and can afford a cut above the usual "recipe" of molasses, yeast and water. And to most of the hotels and blind pigs from Sydney Mines to Glace Bay—where the liquor gets diluted again. He no longer sells to miners because he has grown weary of collecting debts. James has read in the papers about spectacular outbreaks of violence down in the States, where gangs fight for control of their patch and men are shot over bad debts. But in James's experience, all that's usually required is a threat to tell the poor bastard's wife. James is sick of hearing their sob stories. If their children are so hard up, they shouldn't part with a penny for his poison. And they need look no further than James himself for a good example: he doesn't touch a drop.

All this helps to keep James well and truly hated. Why? Because I'm not disappearing down the same drain they are. Because I have the guts and the sense to support my family.

Not only does James's work keep meat on the table when most people are lucky to get porridge, and good clothes on his children's backs when many go about in made-over flour sacks—the hours allow him to devote himself to what matters: Lily.

James has stopped counting his books; there are too many. Mercedes and Frances have dipped into all the crates and he encourages them. But for his own part, he barely has time to glance at the newspaper before supper, and daytime is reserved for teaching Lily.

They do a different letter of the *Encyclopaedia Britannica* each day for two hours. James assigns passages for Lily to memorize and he quizzes her as to comprehension. She writes miniature essays on butterflies, boxcars, Bulgaria and Big Berthas. Lily loves to learn, but most of all she loves Daddy. After book-learning, James takes Lily for drives in the automobile. Sometimes they stay away all night; like the time they went to St. Ann's and saw the home of Angus McAskill, the Cape Breton Giant. Lily saw a picture of the big man holding Tom Thumb on the palm of his hand. She was awed by the tender bond between giant and midget—glad they had each other.

James has got permission to keep Lily out of school. She is crippled. It makes sense that she would be delicate. Everyone assumes she is— everyone but Frances. James doesn't entirely approve of the closeness that has developed between Lily and Frances, but he can't deny Lily anything. He just tries to keep track of them. Always at the back of his mind is the episode in the creek the night Lily was born and he caught Frances trying to drown her. Only James knows whom Lily has to thank for her withered leg, because surely Frances was too young to remember. Just as she was too young to remember the second infant. . . .

Now and then at dawn, on his way home from a night's work, James stops at the cemetery and visits Kathleen. He doesn't leave flowers. What's the point? He may pull a weed if it obscures her name. Her headstone is dignified and free of second-rate sentiment. It says simply, "Beloved Daughter." James does not tend Materia's grave because someone else does that. "Call'd from the cares of this world." Someone also leaves flowers, he doesn't know who. James stands as still as the stones, looks out at the water and feels how small the world has become. Europe is in front of him. Home is behind him. And at his feet . . .

At this hour there is always a mist about a mile out. James is a Catholic but he cannot believe in life hereafter. Not for himself, anyway. Sometimes, though, when he looks out at the fog on the water, he feels comforted.

Little Women

MERCEDES IS IN LOVE. He is tall—at least she thinks so—dark, that's for sure, and handsome, no question. His eyes burn into her very soul and seem to say, I need so much, so badly, for a good woman to love me and tame me. He wears a turban. He is most often to be found in his lavish striped tent, or galloping across the sands on a white Arabian charger. He is Rudolph Valentino. Mercedes does not know whether to hate Pola Negri with all her heart, or to pray for her since she has been entrusted with Mercedes' one true love. She prays for Valentino every night. She has never heard his voice, but somehow she has married his silent image to the rich baritone of Titta Ruffo, whose every recording she possesses.

"Rudy probably has a horrible plugged-nose voice and a lisp," says Frances, mercilessly. "He's probably a midget in real life." How did Frances guess her secret, anyway? Mercedes has been so careful not to betray her heart, but Frances is uncanny; tying a tea towel around her face as a veil, batting her eyelashes and swooning in an all-purpose exotic accent: " 'Someday you weel beat me with those str-r-rong hands. I should like to know what it fee-eels like.' "

Mercedes has told only Helen Frye, who is in love too, with Douglas Fairbanks. Mercedes indulges Helen's schoolgirl crush but can't sympathize; Fairbanks is somehow smug and self-sufficient. Valentino is haplessly fierce and hopelessly needy. Helen once said he was coarse—there almost went the friendship. But they made up the next day and took turns describing their future married life with their respective paramours.

Whenever Mercedes has had a particularly lovely time with Helen, she feels a bit guilty. It pains her that Frances doesn't seem to have any friends. Unless you can call those dirty sniggering boys at school "friends." Frances skulks off with them behind the boonies at recess sometimes. Mercedes knows they probably smoke and spit and swear. It's dreadful. And then, who knows what Frances does when she disappears from school altogether? Mercedes does her best, but it's difficult keeping Frances out of trouble. For example, Frances always seems to have the latest issue of that lurid rag *Weird Tales,* by H. P. Lovecraft. Daddy does not permit trash in the house and Mercedes is constantly hiding Frances's contraband under her pillow, or simply doing her the favor of tossing it into the furnace.

When Mercedes feels the prick of sisterly conscience, she invites Frances to tag along with her and Helen. Helen always purses her lips at the sight of Frances and Mercedes can't blame her. The last time they made a threesome, it was to see Douglas Fairbanks again, in *The Thief of Baghdad,* at the Bijou. Frances was terribly provoking, speaking aloud all the lines in the script the second before they came on the screen, but worst of all, she scandalized Helen with "Okay watch, here comes the part where he gets flogged 'n he escapes from the palace and you can see his pecker right through his pants."

Frances is a moving-picture fan too but she has different idols. Lillian Gish. Lillian Gish. Lillian Gish. Her hair is perfect, her eyes are perfect, her little mouth is perfect. She is so small and so brave. She can be bent, but never broken. Men are brutes, and if they are not, they are big galoots or else chivalrous princes who arrive too late. When Frances plays hooky, she can be found down at the shore, maybe chatting with the lobstermen—or, if she has the price of admission, slouched with her legs dangling over the seat in front of her in the ecstatic darkness of the Empire or the Bijou, taking in the matinee.

Having no funds of her own, Frances frequently manages to talk Mercedes out of a dime from the housekeeping money, then pilfers half as much again when Mercedes isn't looking. If Frances takes Lily along of a Saturday, then Lily pays out of her allowance. Otherwise Frances just helps herself from Lily's stash that she leaves right out in the open on top of the dresser they share. Frances only takes what she needs—"a mere bagatelle"—and she knows Lillian Gish would do the same. They have so much in common: forced to live in poverty; to stoop to shameful strata-gems and desperate measures just in order to survive. And they both know what it's like to live "way down east."

For her part, Lily has been slain by Mary Pickford. She cries through

Pollyanna every time. Frances tries to broaden Lily's horizons: "Look, Lily, don't you see that once she turned into a cripple she got boring and sucky?"

"No."

"That's 'cause you're a suck."

"I am not!"

They'll be walking home down Plummer Avenue sharing a fizzy Havelock Iron Brew that Lily has kindly sprung for.

"Just like in *What Katy Did,* she's a holy terror till she breaks her back, then she's a sooky baby just like you."

"I am not a sooky baby, Frances."

"Oh yeah? Prove it."

Then Lily may take a poke at Frances, who laughs, holds Lily's head just beyond arm's length and watches her swing. And when Lily is exhausted, "Lily. Say bastard."

Lily hesitates. Frances taunts, "See, I told you—baby."

"Bastard!"

Frances looks around, "Jeez, Lily, not so loud."

And Lily whispers, "Bastard."

"Say horse's arse."

"Horse's arse."

"Say Lily Piper is a horse's arse."

"Frances Piper is a stupid bum-ass."

"Lily." Frances stops in her tracks. "You have really hurt my feelings this time."

Lily's eyes fill up. "I'm sorry, Frances."

Then Frances smirks and says, "Suck."

While Frances can tolerate Lily's idiotic crush on America's Sweetheart, she has no patience with The Sheik because ever since Mercedes fell in love with Valentino she's been no fun. She won't play anymore, just patrols the house and makes the meals and acts like she's lost a cucumber sideways up a woman's most precious possession. Or works on her other obsession: the family tree. A dry diagram covered mostly with names of dead Scottish people. Frances knows that Mercedes has started her period. Maybe that explains it. Mrs. Luvovitz came over one afternoon in January and locked herself in the bathroom with Mercedes for over an hour. Then Mercedes emerged with a kindly yet superior smile on her face, because Mrs. Luvovitz had told her the wonderful news that she was a woman now. "And soon, Frances," Mercedes simpered, "the same miraculous thing will happen to you."

In the good old days, however, all three sisters used to play together. Lily was their doll, they could do anything with her. Until she started to scream. Then they'd let her be an active participant. She was great to play with because she would get so caught up.

"Let's play 'Little Women,' okay?"

"Okay, Mercedes."

"Lily, you be Beth, okay? And we all tell you how much we love you and you forgive us for ever teasing you and then you die, okay?"

"Okay, Frances."

Mercedes would be motherly Meg, and Frances would be tomboy Jo who cuts off her hair but gets married in the end, and Lily would be delicate Beth who was so nice and then she died.

Even though the Little Women in the book were Protestant, "Let's say they're really Catholic, okay?" and Frances and Mercedes would do extreme unction on Beth in her death-bed and apply a holy relic to her burning forehead, let's say it's a piece of the Shroud of Turin, okay? No, let's say it's Saint Anthony's tongue.

"Goodbye, dear sisters, I'll pray for you. Thank you for always being such dear sisters and for making cinnamon toast, and Jo for letting me play with your Spanish doll, and Meg for always being such a good cook. Good . . . bye." Lily's eyelids would flutter convincingly, then she would lie perfectly still not breathing. It was great. Mercedes would cry every time. In the early days so would Frances, but later on she would wreck it all by saying, "Now let's go and steal her pennies and divide up her clothes."

A year or so before Mercedes stopped playing, the game deepened. It darkened, time distended and they entered another world. They played "Little Women Doing the Stations of the Cross." Lily got to be Beth being Veronica wiping the face of Jesus with a cloth and the picture of his face goes perfectly onto her cloth as a gift for her kindness. Mercedes got to be Meg being Simon of Cyrene who helps Jesus carry the Cross, and Frances wanted to be Jo being Jesus but Mercedes said that would be blasphemous so Frances got to be the Good Thief hanging next to Jesus. That is, she got to be Jo being the Good Thief.

They descended another level and shed their intermediary Little Women personae. They entered the world of "The Children's Treasury of Saints and Martyrs." They went through the canon. They'd always start with Saint Lawrence, who got roasted alive on a grill and halfway through said, "You can turn me over, I'm done on this side," and became the patron saint of people who roast meat for a living. At which they'd laugh uncontrollably, even Mercedes. They all three felt hot and wicked, but as they played on the game grew grave and reverent and they reached heights of pious fervor.

They each had favorites. Sometimes Frances was Saint Barbara, whose father was a pagan and when she wanted to be a Christian he took her up a mountain and cut off her head while she was praying for him. Or else Saint Winnifred, who once knew a man who wanted to do wrong with her but she said no so he cut off her head but her kind uncle put it back on her leaving only a thin white scar. Or sometimes she was Saint Dymphna, who had a father who wanted to do wrong with her but she wouldn't so she escaped with the court jester, but her father found her in Belgium and cut her head off but she didn't have a kind uncle so she died and got to be the patron saint of crazy people.

Mercedes' favorite was Bernadette.

"That's no fair, Mercedes," said Frances, "Bernadette's not even a saint yet." True, Bernadette had only recently been beatified, but because Mercedes was the eldest they played the game of Bernadette being such a good daughter and having asthma and seeing Our Lady in the grotto at Lourdes where Our Lady told her three secrets.

Lily only ever wanted to be Saint Veronica wiping the face of Jesus, which got tedious after the nth time and Frances and Mercedes would try to persuade her to be someone else.

"Why don't you be the little boy saint who gets his hands and feet cut off but then he gets nice new silver ones?"

"Why don't you be Saint Giles, who was the patron saint of cripples, Lily?"

"Lily, do you want to be Saint Gemma, who had tuberculosis of the spine but Our Lady cured her?"

"No," said Lily, "I want to be Veronica."

All right, all right—if you don't let her, she'll scream and Daddy'll come running and that'll be it.

They always exited their passion plays of ecstatic faith and glorious martyrdom with the same story, in which they all starred simultaneously: that of Saint Brigid. She was the most beautiful girl in Ireland but she wanted to be a nun, but there were too many young men who wanted to marry her so she prayed to God, "Please, dear God, make me ugly."

And He did.

One by one, Frances, Mercedes and Lily would crumple and wither till they were wicked-witch ugly. Then, bent over and shriveled, they'd join the convent with cackling voices—"Hello, sister, how are you today, ya-ha-haa!"—where they'd kneel down at the altar rail and the miracle would happen: Saint Brigid turns beautiful again. "Why, sister, you are beautiful!" "So are you, sister!" "Oh, sisters, look at my beautiful golden hair!" "And look at my lovely lips!" "Oh, look at my ball gown!" "Look at mine!"

Many a long Saturday and Sunday afternoon, while Daddy slept off his night's work in the wingback chair downstairs . . .

It was short days ago, but it seems like forever since Mercedes got her period and fell in love and lost her mind. Oh well. At least Frances and Lily still know how to have fun.

Cat's Cradle

FRANCES AND LILY SHARE a room. James would have preferred that Lily share with Mercedes, but Lily insisted—to Mercedes' silent relief. Frances has set up their bedroom so that there's two of everything and Lily knows exactly which side of everything is hers and which is Frances's. You might think Frances would be a slob, but she isn't, she's very neat and organized. She has accommodated Lily with a framed magazine photograph of Mary Pickford in a stupid gingham apron. It hangs next to Lily's color print of Jesus with the lambs. Jesus looks sad, of course, "because he's thinking about how much he likes lamb chops," says Frances, but Lily is not fooled by that. The rest of the walls are covered in Frances's collection. She writes away for publicity photos. There is one of Lillian Gish trapped on an ice floe. There is Houdini naked and furious in a milk can. There is an actual poster that an usher at the Empire gave her of Theda Bara in Sin, holding her unbelievably long tresses at arm's length above her head like a mad-woman. Frances calls her Head of Haira. Mercedes thinks the picture is immoral.

One evening, Frances is seated at her side of the desk, pen in hand, doing her "homework":

Dear Miss Lillian Gish,

I am writing to you to respectfully request an autographed photograph of you in any picture. I have seen them all. It would mean so much to me because I am a crippled girl and have spent all my life in a wheelchair. I rode the wildest horse in the stable. I was dragged, but I did not die, thanks to my Guardian Angel. I wish I could run and play like the other children, but at least I am glad that Daddy dear can wheel me to the picture house so I can see you. Thank you.

Yours truly . . .

Frances muses for a moment and then it comes to her . . . who the letter is from, that is. She signs it, tucks it into the envelope and addresses it to Miss Gish's fan club in Hollywood, California. Then she looks up at Lily, who has been waiting obediently for playtime to begin, and says, "All right, Lily, come with me."

Lily follows Frances up to the attic.

"I was going to show you something but now I think maybe you're not old enough."

"I am, Frances. I'm old."

They are seated on the floor, cross-legged before the hope chest. "This was Kathleen's room, eh, Frances," always must be said, and the response, "That's right, Lily, this is where she died," before they can get on with whatever game Frances has in mind. This liturgy serves to honor the story that no longer needs repeating. The story that Frances told Lily so long ago and so often:

"Our beautiful older sister, Kathleen. She had red hair like an angel on fire. And she had the voice of an angel. God loved her so much, He took her. She was only nineteen when she died of the flu. I was there when she died and I closed her eyes."

There is always a pause here while they both picture it faithfully. Then Frances continues, "Her last words were . . . 'Dear Frances, you are my favorite sister. And you are also the most beautiful next to me. Please. Look after Lily.' " Frances's eyes start to glint green, but it is a serious glint. Scary. Lily's eyes grow round and wet. The bump appears in her forehead.

"Why did she say look after me?"

Frances doesn't take her eyes off Lily, she just says evenly, "Because she loved you, Lily."

". . . I love her too." Tears.

Frances puts out a hand and barely strokes Lily's long hair that's never been cut. Then . . . "Okay, quit blubbering, let's play."

It is understood that Kathleen is not to be mentioned around Daddy, "because, Lily, it would hurt him terribly if you even said her name."

On this particular evening, Frances has decided that the time has come to talk of other things. She reaches into her pocket and produces the key to the hope chest. Lily gasps.

"Don't be so melodramatic, Lily."

"What's melon dramatic?"

"It's stupid."

"Oh."

Frances repockets the key. "I made a mistake, you're too young."

"I am not!"

"Keep your voice down."

Whispering passionately, "I am not, Frances, I won't tell."

Frances raises an eyebrow, shakes her head, mutters, "I must be losing my marbles," and inserts the key into the lock. Raises the lid. The waft of cedar . . . Frances gets a lump in her throat, blinks past it. Lily knows better than to ask.

"Close your eyes, Lily."

"Okay."

"There are things in here that you're not ready to see."

Rustle, rustle.

"Put your hand out."

Lily does. "It feels silky."

"It's pure satin. Open your eyes."

Frances holds what looks like a miniature wedding gown, gone a little yellow with age.

"It's beautiful," Lily breathes.

"It's the christening gown. We were all baptized in it. Kathleen, Mercedes, me, you. And Ambrose."

Lily looks up. "Who's Ambrose?"

The thin white stripe appears across the bridge of Frances's nose. It usually only appears when she's laughing, but she's not laughing now.

"He's your brother, Lily."

Lily stays perfectly quiet, looking into Frances's eyes, waiting. Frances says, "Here. You can hold it."

Lily takes the gown from Frances and cradles it in her arms, such a precious thing, an heirloom.

Frances says, "Ambrose died."

Lily waits. Listens. Frances tells the story:

"On the day you both were born, a stray orange cat came in through the cellar door. It climbed the cellar steps. It climbed the front hall steps. It climbed all the way up to the attic without a sound. It came in here where you both were sleeping and it leaped into your crib. It put its mouth over Ambrose's face and sucked the breath out of him. He turned blue and died. Then the orange cat put its paws on your chest and it was about to do the same thing to you but I came in and I saved you. Daddy took the orange cat and drowned it in the creek. Then he buried it in the garden. In the spot where the scarecrow used to be but now there's a stone. I helped."

Lily doesn't move a muscle. Frances takes the gown carefully from her and calls, "Here, Trixie," making kissing sounds with her mouth, "Come on, Trixie, come on," until they hear the loping *pad pad* up the stairs and Trixie appears in the room, blink. You called?

"That's a good Trixie, c'mere."

Trixie comes. She always does when Frances calls. She found Frances three years ago. Trixie is pure black with yellow eyes. Although, who can say, maybe her missing front paw had a white slipper on it, we'll never know.

"Frances, Lily, supper."

"Coming, Mercedes."

Downstairs, Mercedes pops her head out the front door, looking for Daddy's Hupmobile. He had to do an emergency delivery to Glace Bay this afternoon. Someone needed twenty pairs of shoes right away. Mercedes is proud that Daddy works so hard, and always at night, just so he can look after Lily. Otherwise Mercedes would have had to leave school. Daddy drives all over the island delivering dry goods he picks up in Sydney. And often he makes boots all night in the shed. Mercedes has seen the reassuring glow of his lamp down there in the window, although she would never dream of disturbing him—Daddy doesn't like to be interrupted when he's working.

Mercedes is proud they have an automobile, although she knows she should only be grateful. Here it comes, right on schedule, long and boxy, bobbing over the ruts. And here come the girls down from the attic; it looks as though supper will be on time for once. Tonight it's an old Cape Breton recipe that Mercedes got from Mrs. MacIsaac: *ceann groppi*. That's Gaelic for "stuffed cod head." It's taken Mercedes all afternoon, she sincerely hopes Daddy will be thrilled: take a big cod head, take a lot of cod livers, scrape off the iffy bits, take rolled oats, cornmeal, flour and salt, stuff the head through the mouth, holding it with a finger in each eye. Boil.

James tosses his cap onto the halltree hook and says, "Come and hit the ivories, Mercedes, I feel like cutting the rug with my best girl."

Mercedes smiles at Daddy and proceeds obediently to the front room, forced to wait dinner after all. Tortured as though by tacit conspiracy involving her entire family. She sits at the piano and grits her teeth at the sound of Lily giggling and running to Daddy. Mercedes opens the old *Let Us Have Music for Piano* and plays.

Lily places her left foot on top of Daddy's right one, her right one on his left, and they dance to "Roses of Picardy."

Until finally "I'm starved," says Daddy. "What's for supper, Mercedes?"

Supper.

"You've got to be kidding," says Frances.

Even James. "I'm sure it's delicious, Mercedes, but I have a hard time eating with my dinner looking me straight in the eyes."

They all laugh except Mercedes, who gets up and leaves the room.

"What's the matter with her?" asks James.

Frances responds, "It's her period."

James winces, so sorry to have inquired that he fails to notice the inappropriateness of the answer. "Well . . . I'll apologize. Who wants tea biscuits and molasses?"

Up in her room, Mercedes consoles herself with the family tree. She has been working on it for almost a year. It is a painstaking process. Whenever she has a new entry—whenever she has had the precious time to dig a little deeper in the Sydney library, or on those rare occasions when she has received a long-awaited reply from the provincial archives in Halifax—she carefully unrolls the large scroll of special paper on her desk. She fastens down the corners, takes out a pencil and a ruler and neatly draws a short vertical line beneath one of several long horizontal ones, under which she inscribes the latest name. And there it hangs, quietly suspended like a piece of desiccated fruit.

Mercedes' patience for this task is unlimited. She plans to surprise Daddy with it. He never talks about his own family except to say they all died. Perhaps she can restore to Daddy a fragment of what he has lost.

After supper on this evening, Lily comes up to find Mercedes going over all the pencil lines in careful ink.

"Thank you for supper, Mercedes."

Mercedes looks up sharply to see if Lily is being mean. But Lily is never intentionally cruel; Mercedes knows that and repents of her suspicion. She returns to her work and says merely, "Hmm."

Lily approaches and looks over Mercedes' shoulder, fascinated.

"How come it doesn't look like a tree?"

" 'Tree' is only an expression, Lily. If it looked like a tree then it would be art. This is a chart."

"Like a map?"

"Kind of."

"Is there treasure?"

"Each name is a treasure."

"Where does it lead to?"

" 'Map' is just an expression too. It doesn't lead anywhere." Mercedes relaxes back in her chair. "Well, maybe in a way it does. It leads into the past. It tells us where we came from. But it doesn't tell us where we're going. Only God knows that."

"Where am I?"

"You're right here on the same line with me and Frances and Kathleen, God rest her soul."

"Where's Other Lily?"

"She doesn't appear here, dear."

"How come?"

"She was never baptized."

"But she was our sister."

"Yes, and we love her and pray for her, but that's not how it works on a family tree."

"Where's Ambrose?"

Mercedes looks at Lily. "Who's Ambrose?"

Lily looks back at Mercedes. "Will you read me a story?"

"Of course I will, dear, you go climb into your nightgown and pick one out, I'll be right there."

At three that morning, Mercedes slumbers beneath a finger of moonlight. As usual, her door is an inch or so ajar—she has nothing to hide and plenty to listen for. The door begins to open silently. Mercedes' eyes open. In time to see it swing to rest wide enough to admit a draft. Or a very small child.

"Who's there?"

No answer. The soft, barely discernible pad-padding of tiny feet. Approaching the bed.

"Trixie?"

Silence. Trixie never visits her room.

"Go 'way, Trixie."

At the corner of Mercedes' eye, a whitish glimmer. Her blood cools. Not Trixie. Mercedes raises her head. The thing moves into the slant of moonlight. And there—oh Mother of God—an unholy infant. Swathed in a mockery of the first holy sacrament. Mercedes tries but fails to say, "Out."

Dressed in the baptismal gown, stained with the Devil's swart embrace.

"Out"—a cracked whisper.

Two yellow eyes.

"Out out out out, *ou-ou-t!*" straight from her bowels.

James bolts through the door, flails, finds and yanks the electric light chain to see Mercedes shuddering, staring, teeth bared, rosary at her chest.

"What's happened?"

Mercedes speaks but her sobs snatch and tear the words; he grips her shoulders. "Look at me." He shakes her. "Look at me." She does. She pulls herself up and away from the void, then says, "I thought I saw something."

He nods and sits down on the edge of her bed. There is, and is not, any such thing as a ghost. This house, for example: James, honest with himself, admits that there are places and times which he avoids in his own home. Not out of belief—out of that spot on the back of his neck that stirs now and then for no reason. That's when he wishes he had the right to pray. Because that's what the unquiet need. "Pray for us" is what they're saying with their moans and midnight walks.

James runs his tongue over the dry bluish sheen of his lower lip and Mercedes notices how long his lashes are. He speaks to her—to her alone—oh it seems for the first time since she was a very little girl.

"Your grandmother. My mother. Saw something once. Or no. Heard."

Mercedes waits. Daddy has never mentioned his mother to anyone but me, now, at this moment . . . and perhaps once long ago to Kathleen. Mercedes holds her breath, not to startle the moment. So fragile. All the fine things, anything not smudged, all things that can never wither but break so easily, that's what he is.

"Music," he says. "It was a sunny day. She couldn't tell you what instrument or what tune, or even which way it came—whether in through the window, or right beside her. Just that she thought, 'That must be what heaven's like.' It was that beautiful. So she knelt down where she was in the kitchen and said a prayer of thanks because she'd had that little taste, see? And after that she was never afraid of anything."

Mercedes forms her small smile. She holds her tears in a reservoir. Tears could only dampen a moment such as this and set it to mildew, guaranteeing its decay.

A voice from the door. "What's the matter?"

"Hey, little buddy." James goes to Lily and scoops her up, Lily fastens her legs around his waist. She's too big to be picked up, thinks Mercedes, answering, "I thought I—" but she catches Daddy's warning look and revises her story; "Nothing, Lily, I rode the nightmare is all."

"Did you see the *bodechean?*"

James laughs at the old Gaelic expression. "There's no such thing, who told you about the *bodechean?*"

"Frances."

Shut up, Lily, for once can't you just shut up, but Mercedes says, "Frances was just teasing, there's no such thing."

"Mercedes, want to sleep with me and Frances?"

"No. Thank you, Lily."

"Give your sister a kiss goodnight, Lily."

They leave and Mercedes, thoroughly back to herself, rises and crosses to the center of the room, douses the light and returns to bed in the dark, scornfully recalling the days when she believed that long-necked creatures resided beneath her bed waiting to bite her ankles.

She kneels at the side of her bed and starts the rosary. Just in time, because she felt the first inkling of the long-necked things just now, when her mind's disdain wore off. Bedside kneeling in the dark is always the hardest, for imagine the things wrapping themselves around your upper legs. Pulling you under. Don't imagine anything past that, nothing like that is going to happen as long as you say your rosary. With a pure heart. Mercedes despises herself for these childish superstitions, knows them to be groundless, but can't stop the retractions in her thigh muscles all the same. These small flexings often lead to a dread feeling farther up that craves undoing, and it's this feeling more than all the others that serves to remind one that—while there are no long-necked creatures under the bed, and the *bodechean* is merely a pagan notion—there is certainly a Devil. *Holy Mary Mother of God, pray for us sinners, now and at the hour of our death, amen.*

Mercedes imagines her unknown grandmother bathed in sunlight, kneeling in thanks for the foretaste of heaven. Then she considers the visitation which she herself has just been vouchsafed. God gives us each something different.

Frances is in the cellar, holding a coal-oil lamp to the gap between the furnace and the blackened wall, where Trixie is wedged as far back as possible. Trixie's lace bonnet is askew, her white satin gown a sooty mess. Earlier this evening, just before supper, she scrowled out of Frances's hold in the attic and streaked down to the cellar for refuge. Cats don't enjoy dress-ups. She stayed behind the furnace until the house fell silent. Then she crept out and up the stairs. To Mercedes' room.

"Come on, Trixie."

Frances has to get Trixie undressed quickly, because if Daddy finds her like this again it will be into the creek with her.

"Trixie, please."

Trixie vigorously licks her front paw and washes her face.

"Trixie, *taa'i la hown, Habibti.*"

Trixie looks up, then suffers herself to be hauled from the corner. Frances unties the bonnet. "You looked so pretty, Trixie." And undoes the thousand buttons of the baptism gown. "Stay still, I'm almost—"

Trixie scratches the rest of the way out and bounds up the steps. Frances follows more quietly. When she reaches the top step, her lamp light splashes across Daddy's shoes. Trixie is long gone, thank goodness; she'll be back in two or three days.

James waits until Frances has washed and hung up the gown and bonnet.

Upstairs, Mercedes finishes the rosary. Even as she screamed, her mind had already identified what she had seen, but it had to wait for her body to catch up. The apparition explained, however, is not expunged. It was a demonic vision whatever the earthly agency. God works in mysterious ways, but the Devil's ways are even more arcane and often spiced with the absurd. Some would say funny. Mercedes would not. Funny is a fat lady playing the ukelele. Funny is a man dressed up as a woman in a Gilbert and Sullivan musical. Funny is not a crippled black cat got up like a devil baby in the family christening gear at midnight. Frances is a vessel. Like that morning before Mumma died and Mercedes and Frances both had coal smudges on their foreheads and Frances said she was visited by a "dark lady" in the night. Please, dear Mother of God, hear my prayer and accept the offering of thy holy rosary for the preservation of the soul of my sister Frances, amen.

No sooner is Mercedes back in bed than the light slices on again and she squints up to see Frances's head bobbing and lurching, he's got her by the back of the neck, Punch and Judy.

"Now apologize to your sister."

Mercedes looks away. She can't stand it when Frances grins with a bloody lip.

Later, when all is calm, Mercedes slips into the room overlooking the creek. She crawls into bed and spoons around Frances's chill back and encircles her thin waist. On the other side, Lily feigns sleep. All the sisters tucked up in one bed—this wonderful thing only ever happens these days on sad occasions. Frances has had another talking-to from Daddy, Lily knows that.

Mercedes feels ease. This is as close as she gets to a state of grace, curious as she knows this to be. It's a mystery. To experience the gift of peace with your bad sister in your arms. Nothing can get you now, Frances, *te'berini*.

Mercedes casts a net of thought prayers over Frances's sleeping form, lighter than air, than gossamer wings, finer than the finest silk to keep my little sister safe. Hush baby, sleep, thy mother tends the sheep. . . .

The Family Tree

THREE AND A HALF weeks later, Mercedes has unearthed another fossil. It was beached beneath a quarter-inch of dust on a forgotten page of a crumbling chapel registry. Another name. Perfectly preserved in its desert grave, waiting to be exhumed and grafted onto Mercedes' family tree; granted eternal still life in a meaningful context.

Late at night when all is blessedly quiet, when she's got a moment to herself alone, she sits at her desk, straightens her spine and begins to unscroll the family tree. She squints as though against a sudden light—it's . . . unscroll a little more . . . what is it? A riot of golds and greens and ruby-reds swirls and ululates across the page, what is it? . . . scroll it slowly open all the way and . . . where there was once a sober grid etched in ink with loving and dispassionate care, there is now a swaying, drunken growth, a what, a tree! A tree. Yes, she can see that now, it is in fact a tree.

Colored in with crayons. Every ancient name has been obliterated by a shiny red apple, each right angle beguiled into a serpent twist of bark; each vertical stroke has evolved into a leafy stem bearing fruit. The largest apples strain the lower boughs all in a line. These are the only apples with names, printed in an awkward childish hand: "Daddy," "Mumma," "Kathleen," "Mercedes," "Frances," "Other Lily," and "Lily." The Mumma and Kathleen apples have little golden wings and the Other Lily one has silver wings. Trixie's black face and yellow eyes peek out from a high branch amid emerald leaves. Meanwhile, at the base of the trunk, grass sprouts on the surface of the earth and a little blue creek flows by all innocent of the continued drama below, for a cross-section of the earth reveals tree roots thrusting down and branching out into the surrounding soil studded with glistening chunks of coal and worked by a sightless army of worms. And there, nestled among the pale subterranean branches, is a golden chest encrusted with diamonds. Buried treasure.

Mercedes' tears fall and bead on the shiny wax colors of the new revised edition of the family tree. She has never cried so bitterly or so quietly in all her life.

People have been known to go gray or snow-white overnight due to a fright or a sudden loss of all joy. But Mercedes' hair simply fades. Frances sees it happen. She was thinking of sneaking out of the house when she passed Mercedes' door and saw her light.

"Mercedes? . . . Are you awake?"

Mercedes is slumped over the desk, perfectly still. Has she died? Turned to stone? To salt? "Mercedes?" Frances approaches, leans down and looks. Golly Moses. How long has she been like this? Her gaped-back mouth all tight and wrinkled at the corners, her eyes crunched and seeping, perfectly still. Frances touches Mercedes' shoulder and Mercedes takes a big gulp of air, emerging from her silent picture to cry in a real-life way.

"What's wrong? Mercedes, what is it, what happened?"

Mercedes speaks from the back of her throat: "I hate her. I hate her so much. I wish I could kill her. I wish it weren't a sin, I wish she were dead, I wish she had died, I hate her, hate her."

Frances understands Mercedes and so does not embrace her but lightly strokes her newly pale braids. What on earth is Mercedes going on about?

"She wrecked everything," says Mercedes, "everyone was happy before she came along, everyone died, everything went wrong when she was born, she's spoiled rotten and I'm going to have to look after her for the rest of her life because she's a cripple, oh God I hate my life, I hate my life."

Mercedes sobs. Frances comforts her the way you would a dear and delicate moth, if moths could be comforted.

"Shshsh. Shshsh, it's okay now. It's all right now."

"What's wrong with Mercedes?" Reverent, worried, Lily asks from the door. How long has she been standing there? How much did she hear? Frances answers gently without missing a beat,

"She had a bad dream, Lily. Go back to bed."

Mercedes doesn't acknowledge Lily's presence. She just goes on crying. Lily retreats. Frances looks down at the brilliant scroll.

In bed, under the covers, there is a small unearthly glow. It emanates from a tiny grotto formed by sheets held up by Lily's knee. The source of the glow is the Virgin Mary. She is made of white phosphorescent Bakelite and towers four inches above a tin sedan in which Lily, Frances and Mercedes have lost their way in the middle of the night out the country. They saw a glow in the distance a little way off the road, in a farmer's field. And there she was. Our Lady. Everywhere there is the smell of lily of the valley. They must be right in the middle of a field of it but it's too dark to tell. Either that or the lovely smell is coming from her. The Blessed Virgin has a message for each of the sisters that they must never reveal. Not even to one another. Lily's message is this: Her leg will never heal. It will never be like the other one. She will always have one boot-leg and one good leg. There is a reason for this. Our Lady does not say what it is. "Now get back into your car and love one another."

"Yes, Our Lady."

"Lily."

It's Frances. Oh no. Lily has used her perfume without asking. But Frances doesn't even say anything about that.

"Lily."

Lily drives the car away from the grotto and out from beneath the sheets. She looks up at Frances. Frances has the scroll.

"What happened here, Lily?"

Tears form in Lily's eyes and roll down but she's not crying that she knows of. "I colored in the family tree."

"That was Mercedes' special thing."

"It was a surprise." Now she's crying.

"You know you shouldn't touch other people's things, Lily, especially when they've worked hard. You should have drawn your own."

"I couldn't help it."

Frances knows this to be true. She sits down on the edge of the bed.

"I'm sorry, Frances."

"Don't cry, Lily."

Lily tumbles into Frances's arms for a good snoggling cry and Frances hugs her.

"Frances?"

"Mm-hm?"

"Everyone didn't die."

"What do you mean?"

"Everyone didn't die when I was born."

"Of course they didn't."

"Daddy didn't die. Mercedes didn't die. You didn't die."

"Mercedes' feelings were hurt, that's all, Lily, she didn't mean it. She loves you. We all do."

Lily can't resist another look at her artwork. She peels open the scroll and reaches under the sheets for the phosphorescent statue. She and Frances look at the scroll together by the light of the Virgin Mary.

"You're a good artist, Lily. I like the worms."

"Thank you."

"What's inside the treasure chest?"

"Treasure."

"What kind of treasure?"

"Ambrose."

"Lily. Ambrose is just a story."

"I know."

The Virgin is losing her glow. The picture is no longer visible. It's time to go to sleep. Frances rolls up the scroll.

"What are you going to do with it, Frances?"

"We don't want Mercedes to see it anymore. I'll have to take it to the dump or burn it."

"No!"

"Shsh. We can't keep it."

"We could bury it."

Frances considers. . . . "In the garden."

Frances and Lily are crouched in the garden, working by the cautious light of a candle stub. The Virgin Mary is in Lily's pocket. Together they manage to dislodge the big rock—a catastrophe for a whole community of soft-shell creatures that go scrambling in all directions. Lily marvels at how they all managed to thrive under that rock without being crushed by it:

"For them the rock is the sky."

"Come on, Lily, we haven't got all night."

Even though Mercedes is the gardener of the family, she is unlikely to go digging under the rock, so the garden is actually quite a good hiding place. Daddy put the boulder in this spot, "the year he decided to make it a rock garden," says Frances. "Up to then there was a scarecrow, but one night it pulled itself out of the ground and walked away."

Lily pauses and looks at Frances, but Frances is calmly digging with a spoon, not using a spooky voice or anything.

"Nobody knows where it went. Maybe it'll come back and visit us someday if you're lucky, Lily. Anyhow, Daddy never made the rock garden because Mumma died around that time and he didn't have the heart to continue."

"Around the time that I was born, eh."

"That's right. You and Ambrose."

"Frances, you said Ambrose was just a story."

"I changed my mind."

"Frances, don't!"

"Don't be a baby, Lily, jeez, you're so easy to scare."

"He was just a story, Frances."

"All right, Lily, he was just a story."

"He was, Frances!"

"Lily, you think what you want to think and I'll think what I want to think. And if you're not mature enough to help me here then we'll just burn your stupid drawing in the furnace and Daddy will know about it, is that what you want?"

"No."

"Then quit whining about Ambrose, he was just a story."

Silence. Lily, satisfied, picks up a spoon and digs obediently.

Frances grins; "No he wasn't."

Lily controls herself and manages not to respond. Frances starts laughing. They keep digging. Frances calls softly, "A-a-ambro-o-ose . . . Ambro-o-ose, Lily wants you-ou-ou."

Giddy gales of laughter. Prickly lights in her eyes and the little white stripe. Frances rolls over in the dirt and shakes her hands and feet in the air like a dog and giggles demonically. The only thing to do when Frances gets like this is to ignore her until it wears off, otherwise you make it worse. Lily just keeps digging.

"That's deep enough." Frances is suddenly back in command. "We don't want to dig up the bones of the orange cat."

Lily draws back. She had forgotten about the cat, now only inches below. Frances lays the scroll in the shallow hole. "Rest in pieces."

Lily looks up sharply but it's okay; apart from a gleam in her eye, Frances is safely this side of the verge.

They each toss in a handful of dirt, then bury the scroll and roll the rock back into place. A perfect job. Just place these loose bits of dry corn husks around its base and no one could ever tell in a million years.

"Okay, Lily, go on inside now, I'll be right there."

"What are you going to do?"

"I'm going to say a little prayer."

Lily obeys. Out of the garden and onto the little footbridge over the creek in her steady uneven gait and *whap,* she catches a dirtball right in the back of the head. She turns. Frances is doubled over in the center of the garden. She's off again. Oh no.

"Frances, come on. Someone will see you."

Frances runs in a crazy limp out of the garden, down the bank and right straight splash through the creek, waving her arms, doing her impression of Lily—"Fwances come on, come on Fwances!" laughing, limping all the way back to the house. Lily follows slowly. Frances can't help it, Lily knows that. She just hopes Daddy hasn't heard them out at this hour. Because if he has, Frances will get a good talking-to. And there won't be anything Lily can do about it, except to bring her warm milk after and let her sleep with Raggedy-Lily-of-the-Valley.

But it's all right. Daddy is out. He isn't working, he just couldn't sleep. He went for a walk and wound up at the graveyard, longing for a drink. He drank salt air instead. Now at dawn he turns homeward, listening for the sound of pit boots along Plummer Avenue, expecting to hear the mine whistle. Then he remembers the strike. For no reason his throat tightens. His eyes sting but he isn't going to cry, there isn't time. He wants to be home when his girls wake up.

Porridge

"Here, Daddy."

Breakfast. It's a new day and the night is gone and I'm here with my girls. "Thank you, Mercedes. Eat up, Frances."

"I'm not hungry, Daddy."

"Eat."

Frances skims her porridge. It's still hot underneath but the surface has congealed to a thin skin and a few viscous strands cling to the end of her spoon.

"Don't play with your food."

"It's cold."

Daddy gestures to Mercedes, who adds another steaming spoonful to Frances's bowl. Frances grimaces.

"Men in the trenches would have given an arm for what you're turning your nose up at."

Frances pictures the severed arm. She sees an apple-cheeked young Tommy; he smilingly detaches one of his arms, sleeve and all, and says in a fetching cockney accent, "No 'arm done mate, can Oy 'ave yo' gruel now?" Don't laugh. Just stare down into the glistening gray muck. There are dead men under there.

"I said eat."

Frances places her spoon in her mouth. Snot.

"Swallow it."

Who will save Frances? Lily is eating every bite of her own porridge, little brat. Is there any way to sneak some into her bowl? Will Mercedes intervene discreetly? Frances racks her brains for a diversion. She knows her throat will not open again. It will gag and she'll spew and Daddy will—

"Answer your sister."

"What?"

Mercedes quietly repeats, "Are you all right, Frances?"

"Yes thanks, it's really good, Mercedes."

Who will save Frances?

"That godforsaken cat is in your garden again, Mercedes."

"That's okay, Daddy."

"It's digging." He sets down his spoon, "We shouldn't eat a thing from that garden with that animal around."

"Trixie never relieves herself there, Daddy."

Everyone turns and sees Trixie out the window, her tail bobbing around the rock. James tolerates Frances's cat because Lily is attached to the thing. But he is running out of patience, already composing a kind lie about how Trixie had a long and happy life but cats sometimes just run away. He gets up from the table.

Frances watches him head for the back door—oh thank God, thank Jesus, Mary, Joseph and all the saints, I will never sin again—she waits till he's halfway across the yard, then jumps up and empties her bowl into the garbage by the stove. Mercedes doesn't comment, but Lily looks suddenly worried.

"Relax, Lily, he'll never know," says Frances.

But Lily isn't worried about the porridge. She's been watching Daddy bending over the rock in the garden.

He comes back into the kitchen, but does not sit down. He stands at the head of the table with his arms folded and asks quietly, "Who moved the rock?"

Frances feels sick. She knows now that life was easy when there was just porridge. Lily turns bright red.

"I did, Daddy." Nice try, Lily.

Daddy strokes her hair. Mercedes is at a loss—if she knew what Frances's crime was, perhaps she could—"Perhaps I dislodged it while gardening, Daddy." That was pretty lame.

"I did." Frances speaks clearly.

"When?"

"Last night."

Silence. How is it possible to feel so cold and yet to be sweating at the same time? How long have we been sitting here? What's the big deal anyway?

Whack across the side of the head.

"I'll tell you what the 'big deal' is"—oh no, Frances, you said it out loud, you thought you just thought it but you said it—"the big deal is, you had your sister out in the middle of the night and she could have caught her death of pneumonia."

Frances: "So could I."

"You have the gift of health. Your sister is delicate."

"I'm fine, Daddy," says Lily, and sneezes.

Frances almost grins, but Mercedes looks down. She does not believe in accidents. James has not taken his eyes off Frances. "What in God's name were you doing?"

Frances considers. And answers, "We planted something."

"What?"

Lily saves Frances. "We planted a tree. For the family."

Mercedes looks at Frances as the penny drops.

James asks Frances, "Under the rock?"

"It's a really strong tree." Thank you Lily.

James looks at Frances. He should pave over the garden plot and park the car on it. But that wouldn't seem right. He should dig up what's there and put it elsewhere. But he can't. And perhaps, after last night, it is no longer there. He looks at Frances. Surely she was too young to remember. But if she does . . . What kind of person takes her baby sister out at night to exhume infant remains?

Frances meets James's eyes and says, "I told Lily that if we dug in the garden we might find treasure. But we didn't find anything."

James resumes his seat. He rests his eyes on the tea leaves at the bottom of his cup. Mercedes pours him some hot. He sips. Frances can't believe her luck. Mercedes says a prayer of thanks and apologizes to God for being ungrateful about her family. James says to Frances, "Eat."

"I've already finished, Daddy, look."

"So you have."

No. She could not possibly remember.

Water Babies

From breakfast on through all the day
at home among my friends I stay,
But every night I go abroad
Afar into the Land of Nod.

ROBERT LOUIS STEVENSON,
''THE LAND OF NOD''

A VERY YOUNG FRANCES IS standing in the creek in the middle of the night staring out. At us. Or at someone behind us. She is holding a bundle in her skinny arms. You can sort of almost see it from the corner of your eye but you can't see it at all when you look right at it. Like trying to look directly at a dim object in the dark. It's annoying. What is it? And just when you thought this was a still picture in black and white, the water around Frances's white nightgown lights up blue. The source of this light is a bright blue fish that's flicking and swimming about her ankles. It's beautiful. Lily wakes up screaming.

"Lily, Jesus Christ Almighty!" Frances is blanched and staring at Lily's shell-shocked form, silent now, and ramrod-straight beside her in the bed.

The overhead bulb goes on—it's James in a plaid panic. "What's happened?"

Mercedes appears behind him, a new line hovering at her brow.

"It's okay, she had a nightmare," says Frances, petting Lily's rigid back.

Lily turns and looks at James. He comes to her and picks her up. She wraps her arms and legs around him and lays her head upon his shoulder, eyes wide open. He rocks her gently from side to side, wondering a little at the recent rash of nightmares under his roof.

Lily says, "I dreamed I was a fish."

Frances shivers. Mercedes smooths her temples.

"In the creek," Lily continues. "And I couldn't breathe."

Mercedes heads down to the kitchen to make hot milk all around. Frances rolls over and rescues Lillian Gish from the ice floe. James leaves the room but returns a few minutes later, just ahead of Mercedes. He has Trixie. Trixie looks terrified but knows enough not to move a muscle when in this particular embrace. He puts Trixie down gently next to Lily, who buries her face in the astonished black fur. When Mercedes passes around the warm milk, James pours a little of his own into his hand and offers it to Trixie. Trixie gives him a look, then bends and laps it up.

"Do you feel better now, sweetie?" James asks.

"Yes," answers Lily.

Trixie curls up between Frances and Lily; James tucks them in and turns out the light.

Back in her room, Mercedes is finishing *Jane Eyre* again. She was thankful when Frances returned her favorite volume apparently unscathed. Now, with that mixture of satisfaction and regret with which one comes to the end of a beloved book, Mercedes turns the last page only to find Frances's unmistakable scrawl on the flyleaf. It is an epilogue, wherein Mr. Rochester's hand, severed and lost in the fire, comes back to life and strangles their infant child.

Mercedes closes the book and merely sighs. She is past weeping and gnashing of teeth. It is abundantly clear that her two sisters are working their way through everything that is of the slightest value to her and ruining it. Mercedes is resigned. For now. Someday she will marry someone wonderful. Perhaps not Valentino. But wonderful nonetheless. She will have her own family and they will be civilized. Frances will be allowed to live with them, but it will be Mercedes' castle. And her husband's too, of course. But not yet. Daddy needs her. Hail Mary full of grace, the Lord is with thee . . .

"If you were a fish, how come you couldn't breathe?"

Frances hasn't touched her milk. It's on the bedside table wearing a wrinkled skin.

"I was drownding."

"Fish don't drown."

"You were in it, Frances."

"In the creek?"

"You were little."

". . . I know."

"What were you holding?"

"Nothing . . . I don't remember. Go to sleep. It was just a dream."

Lily's hand glows red around the Bakelite Virgin—conductive scarlet threads beneath the line of life, of fate, heart and mind, her palm bleeding light.

Later that night Frances is awakened by a weight on her chest. She opens her eyes and looks into Trixie's intent face staring into her own at a range of about an inch. Trixie's black paw hovers white-tipped and frozen in midair. A wizened slimy strand of something like the throw-uppy bit of a raw egg dangles from the corner of Trixie's mouth. Frances blinks and Trixie turns back to the glass of tepid milk on the bedside table, ignoring Frances, wiping her milky face, dipping and drinking.

The first time Ambrose comes to Lily he is naked except for the decomposing bits of Frances's old white nightgown in which he was laid to rest. The shreds cling to him here and there, fluttering slightly because there's a bit of a breeze when Ambrose arrives. Safe and soundless in his garden womb, he has not been dreaming because he has not been asleep. He has been growing. His body is streaked with earth and coal but otherwise he is pale as a root. Although he is exactly the same age as Lily, he is full-grown like a man whereas she is still a little girl. This is because their environments have been so different. What color is his wispy angel hair beneath the dirt and soot? Reddish. He is standing at the foot of the bed. Frances is asleep. Lily is somewhere in between. She must be; to see such a thing, and not scream? To see such a thing and know it can't quite be a dream, because there is the foot of my bed; there is my sister sleeping; there is my rag doll; and here is Trixie curled between us with one eye open. And there is Ambrose. Although Lily does not yet recognize her twin.

"Who are you?"

Has she spoken this? She must have because the man who is looking at her from the foot of her bed opens his lips to reply. And as he does so, water gushes from his mouth and splashes to the floor. Now she screams. Now she is "awake"—back in a state which is a definite place on a map. Here is the place called Awake. On the other side of this line is the country of Asleep. And you see this shaded area in between? Don't linger there. It is No Man's Land.

Lily is safely back in Awake and expects to see Frances's exasperated face looming over hers. She expects the overhead light to snap on for the second time and for Daddy to pick her up again and wonder how she could possibly have two nightmares in one night. But there is no light, and Frances is still asleep. Lily did not scream after all. Although the sound of her cry was enough to wake her up, it was apparently no more than a whimper, because the house around her is still breathing regularly, expanding and contracting, dreaming. And see? There is no man at the foot of the bed. There's no water on the floor as there would be had he truly been here.

Lily doesn't tell anyone about this dream because it is too scary to tell. Even though the dream of Frances in the creek with the dark bundle and the bright blue fish caused Lily to cry out and wake the whole house, the dream of the Water-Man from which she awoke with a whimper was much more frightening.

A Child's Prayer for a Happy Death

> *O Lord, my God, even now I accept from Thy hand*
> *the kind of death it may please Thee to send me with*
> *all its sorrows, pains and anguish.*
> *O Jesus, I offer Thee from this moment my agony*
> *and all the pains of my death. . . .*
> *O Mary, conceived without stain, pray for us who fly*
> *to thee! Refuge of sinners, Mother of those who are in*
> *their agony, leave us not in the hour of our death, but*
> *obtain for us perfect sorrow, sincere contrition, remis-*
> *sion of our sins, a worthy reception of the most holy*
> *Viaticum and the strengthening of the Sacrament of*
> *Extreme Unction. Amen.*

BY SISTER MARY AMBROSE, O. P.

"PRAYER FOR A HAPPY DEATH" is from a children's paperback called *My Gift to Jesus*. The prayer is the last one in the book—which makes sense. The book was a gift from Mercedes to Lily for no reason. About twenty minutes ago Mercedes came in and said, "Here, Lily, here's a little gift for you for no reason in particular." Then Mercedes went to Helen Frye's house.

It's a hot sunny day and Frances and Lily should be down at the shore—Lily in the old English pram and Frances pushing it on the run, careering over rocks and pebbles, splashing through foam, both of them screaming with terror and joy. But instead they are dressed up in togas and turbans from the linen closet, confined to the house because Daddy says it's not safe to play outside. In fact he has driven Mercedes over to Helen Frye's house on Ninth Street and he plans to drive her home again too. The miners' strike has dragged into June and turned ugly.

Special company constables have been on the rampage: drunken goons on horseback wielding sticks and guns, knocking people down in the street—women, children, it makes no difference. The bosses are now a monopoly called the British Empire Coal and Steel Company, "Besco." This time, not only have they cut off credit at the company stores, they've cut off New Waterford's water and electricity. For the past week, sweating bucket brigades have stretched from the few wells to houses throughout town. At New Waterford General Hospital children lie parched amidst a new outbreak of all the old diseases with the pretty names.

People can't haul buckets indefinitely with so little to eat to keep up their strength. And the resumption of the almost daily sight of small white coffins has convinced many that their last drop of strength might be better spent hammering the guilty parties.

Once James dropped Mercedes off, he drove to Sydney to buy bottled water and kerosene with strict instructions to the girls to "keep inside." Apart from missing out on the sunny days, the girls haven't minded so much. It's been fun using only lamps and candles again, "like in the olden days." Frances would venture out on her own, but Lily is so worried by this prospect that she has already sworn to tattle if Frances risks it.

Having tired of playing "Arabian Nights," Lily and Frances are now poring over *My Gift to Jesus*. Like her sisters before her, Lily is already a good reader. But she hasn't had a chance to read the little book herself because Frances grabbed it, turned to the last page—as is her habit with all books—and read it aloud. Lily has understood everything in the happy-death prayer except for one word.

"What's a viaticum?"

"It's a holy word for clean underwear."

"Can I see the book now, Frances?"

Lily reaches, but Frances pulls the book away and explains, "When you're about to die and the priest comes and gives you extreme unction, he takes a set of clean underwear out of your drawer and blesses them. Then he puts them on you. Or if it's an emergency and there's no priest, anyone can bless the clean underwear. That's where Fruit of the Loom underwear comes from, it comes from the Hail Mary when you say, 'Blessed is the fruit of thy loom, Jesus.' "

"Did I get clean underwear that time when I almost died when I was a baby?"

"Yup."

"Blessed by Father Nicholson?"

"No, by me—Lily, look!" Frances has just noticed the name on the title page of *My Gift to Jesus*. "This book was written by a nun called Sister Mary Ambrose!"

Lily gasps obligingly, "Does she know our brother?"

"It could be a message to us from Ambrose himself."

Lily gazes in wonder at the title page while Frances deduces.

"Ambrose is working through that nun, and he also made Mercedes buy this book and give it to you so you'd know he's watching over you."

They look at one another, united by the discovery.

"Does he always see me?" asks Lily.

"Yes."

"When I'm bad?"

"Yup."

"Is he going to tell God?"

"God knows everything anyhow."

"Oh yes." This had momentarily slipped Lily's mind.

"Ambrose sees you when you're sleeping. He knows when you're awake."

"Like Santa Claus."

"That's blasphemous, Lily."

"Sorry."

"Don't tell me, tell God."

Lily folds her hands, squeezes her eyes shut and whispers, "Sorry dear God," following it up with a rapid sign of the cross. Making the sign of the cross after a prayer is as essential as putting a stamp on a letter. Otherwise your message isn't going anywhere but prayer limbo.

"Frances, you know what? God is really Santa Claus and Santa Claus is really God."

"No he isn't, Lily."

"But God gives us gifts and knows everything and so does Santa."

"Yeah, but Santa Claus doesn't give people leprosy and earthquakes, stupid, he doesn't give them the *Titanic* sinking or people getting their legs chopped off!"

Frances turns her attention back to the book and ignores Lily.

"Frances?"

No response.

"Frances?"

"What!" Slapping down the prayer-book.

"Is Ambrose going to bring me presents?"

"A lump of coal if you're bad."

"But what if I'm good?"

"Ambrose doesn't really care if you're bad or good, Lily."

"Oh."

"He just cares if you're okay. If you're happy."

"How come?"

"Because he loves you."

Frances looks straight at Lily. Lily puts on her most seriously attentive face.

"Don't you know who Ambrose is, Lily?"

"He's our wee baby brother who died."

"He's your guardian angel."

Lily's forehead puckers. "Everyone has a guardian angel, don't they, Frances?"

"Yes, but most people don't know who theirs is. You're lucky. You know who yours is. And that he's your very own brother, and he's watching over you. And he loves you. He really loves you, Lily."

"Don't cry, Frances."

"I'm not crying."

"Yes you are."

Frances wipes her eyes. Her throat constricts. Yes, she's crying. Why? She didn't feel sad until she started crying.

"Frances? . . . Frances, let's go up and look in the hope chest."

But Frances is crying.

"Frances, do you want to give Raggedy-Lily-of-the-Valley a bath? You can. I'll let you give her a bath if you want. . . . Do you want to wear my brace? You can, I'll let you."

Frances has dropped *My Gift to Jesus*. Lily picks it up and reads silently, poring over the bright pictures. When Frances feels better, Lily will ask her what INRI means. It's the thing written on the scroll that's always nailed at the top of Jesus's cross. INRI.

I'll ask Frances, thinks Lily. Frances will know.

★ ★ ★

Late that afternoon, Mercedes comes home crying too, but for a different reason. In the car she told Daddy it was because she and Helen had been talking about all the poor children in the hospital. James simply nodded. Mrs. Luvovitz has informed him that girls of this age are likely to become emotional. The last thing one ought to do is tell them not to cry. He watched Mercedes get safely into the house, then he turned the car around and headed back downtown, having forgotten to drop by the post office.

Mercedes tiptoes up to her room and closes the door quietly. She doesn't want to have to see anyone or explain anything. She lies face down and weeps into her pillow. Today a miner called Mr. Davis was shot dead. There was a riot at the power plant out on Waterford Lake. The miners went there to flush out the company police and turn the water and lights back on for the town. The miners had sticks and stones and cinders. The police had guns and horses, but the miners won. Except that some got shot and poor Mr. Davis who wasn't even in the fight was killed. He was on his way home with milk for his youngest, they found a baby bottle in his pocket. Now there are seven more fatherless children in New Waterford.

But that's not why Mercedes is crying. This afternoon, Helen Frye's daddy came home with a bullet in his wrist. While Mrs. Frye took the bullet out, Mr. Frye took a long drink from a medicine bottle and told Mercedes that he was "most regretful, because I know you're a nice girl, Mercedes. But I only have the one child, see, and I can't have her associating with the Pipers."

Mercedes' eyes filled up and her face felt scalded. She felt mortified, as though someone had caught her in a shameful private act, but she could not think of anything she had done wrong. Mrs. Frye just continued digging in Mr. Frye's wrist, while he turned white but didn't flinch and spoke in a kindly voice, words that cut Mercedes apart. He said Mercedes' father was a bad man. A bootlegger. A scab. An enemy of this town. Then Helen was told to go upstairs and Mercedes was asked to wait in the front room until her father came to pick her up in his automobile.

Now Mercedes curls onto her side and catches sight of Valentino perched in his frame on her dresser next to the china figurine of The Old-Fashioned Girl. Valentino invites fresh tears but they are tears of consolation. At least I still have you, my love. And The Old-Fashioned Girl reminds her how nice her daddy is. He is, he is a kind good man. And if— *if*—Daddy is forced to do certain things, it is only because he loves us so much and we don't have a mother to look after us. Fresh tears. Mercedes can hear Mumma singing, and this is too much. She covers her head with the pillow and forces the sound from her mind. She banishes the memory and focuses on what is important: my family. Helping my father, who is a good good man; who looks after his crippled daughter all day long. If Mr. Frye and everyone else could see Daddy with Lily, then they'd know.

Mercedes has grown calmer and her eyes drift now to the picture of Bernadette in the grotto with Our Lady of Lourdes. Bernadette has been beatified. Someday she will be a saint. They dug her up and she was sweet as a rose—that's the odor of sanctity. She was a little crippled girl too. Maybe people hated her father as well.

Mercedes has cried herself almost to sleep, but before she tumbles under, a plan forms in her mind. Tomorrow she will take Lily for a walk. They will go together to the hospital—not to the wards, she doesn't want Lily to catch anything, just to the reception area. And there Mercedes will have Lily give all their old storybooks and clothes, as well as several pies that Mercedes will bake, to the poor children suffering upstairs. Then people will see . . . What a good man . . .

It took James an unusually long time to drive to the post office because several streets were impassable. Rocks bounced off the hood of his automobile and a horde of young men descended and began to rock it to and fro. He gunned through them but found Plummer Avenue likewise swarming. A bunch of dismounted company police were being kicked, prodded and paraded toward the jailhouse. Women ran behind the prisoners, brandishing hatpins and using them, too. There would be trouble tonight.

James drove to the Shore Road, parked and made it on foot through side streets back to the post office. He could have put off the errand till tomorrow, but he considered that the post office and half the buildings on the main street might be burned to the ground by then, and he was expecting money.

He enters the post office, collects his cash and is about to leave when, "There's a letter here too, Mr. Piper."

James reaches to take the envelope from the clerk. Mail is fairly rare. Packages and pictures sometimes come for Frances—James vets them before handing them over, he has confiscated more than one bottle of

"Coca Wine: for brain fag and listlessness." At the moment, the post office is buzzing with the day's events and people are glued to the windows watching the mob go by, but it all fades to silent stillness around James as he catches sight of the name on the front of the envelope: Miss Kathleen Piper.

He loses consciousness for a split second. Like a blink inside the head, accompanied by the flash of a camera. Then the sound of excitement floods back in around him and for an instant he thinks the uproar is all about the fact that someone has sent a letter to Kathleen Piper. Someone has written to my daughter, not knowing—or perhaps knowing—she is dead.

Just the sight of her name. In letters scripted by a living hand, so unlike the letters carved in stone at the edge of town—this is why the light in his head flashed and faded on the fleeting notion that she was alive after all. That must be what insanity is like, thinks James. Except that the flash lasts for ever. Maybe that would be good.

He is back in the car before he can bring himself to open the letter. He remembers another letter so long ago. Anonymous. Horrible. It changed everything. He breaks the seal. He unfolds the page—a refined and ladylike hand. He reads:

Dear Kathleen,

I was so sorry to learn of your terrible accident. You are obviously a very brave girl. And you are also a lucky one to have such a nice father. Maybe one day you will be able to leave your wheelchair and run and play again. I hope so. Here is a signed photograph for your collection with my best wishes.

Yours truly,
Lillian Gish

James presses the electric starter on the Hupmobile and heads for home. He will take Frances out to the shed. And ask her to explain the joke.

That night, Mercedes, Lily and Daddy stand on the veranda and glimpse the torches processing through town. Frances is upstairs in bed with a damp cloth to her face. James has the car packed and gassed up in case they all have to leave in a hurry. The army won't be here for another couple of days and, until then, it's better to be prepared.

First the miners burn down Number 12 washhouse. Then they raid the company stores—they don't burn them for fear of setting the whole town on fire. Then they go to the jailhouse to lynch the company police. But the priest meets them and talks them out of it. There are enough fatherless children in New Waterford.

October 31, 1918

Dear Mr. Piper,

Your daughter is in grave danger. Knowing Kathleen to be of good family and blessed with prodigious musical gifts, I feel it my duty to you and to the world to sound the alarm. Sir, you are from another country and perhaps fortunate enough to be unfamiliar with the very term "miscegenation." It is a modern evil and it is weakening the fabric of our nation. It now threatens to claim your own daughter. Through cunning seduction and flattery, your daughter has been ensnared in a net of godless music and immorality.

I look on helpless to intervene because I am an invalid. I speak as one who knows to her own cost, when I say that by crossing nature's divide, your daughter courts her own ruin and can end only by yielding to the dark remnants of the beast in man. It is, perhaps, not too late. She is yet young. It is your prerogative to ignore, yea to condemn the report of a stranger. My conscience dictates this letter. Thus discharged of my Christian duty, I remain,

An Anonymous Well-Wisher

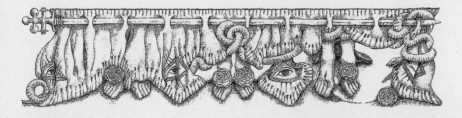

Book 4

THE OLD
FRENCH
MINE

Lest We Forget

LILY'S FOOT IS BLEEDING. She doesn't know it, because the bagpipes are drowning out the pain. This is what bagpipes are designed to do. But even if she felt the pain and saw the blood soaking the back of her stocking, Lily would not stop marching, because she is on top of the world. She is carrying the Nova Scotia flag up Plummer Avenue. Her heart and lungs are big and plaid like the tartan bags of air that feed the pipes. And for once Lily's type of walking is the ideal type. The sway and lilt of her unevenly matched legs go with the every-second-beat flex and swing of the music. Lily has a big open smile on her face and tears in her eyes—the pipes always make her feel tragic and elated all at the same time. With a poppy pinned to her tartan sash, she feels like a brave soldier. It's November 11, 1929, Armistice Day. Today we remember The War to End All Wars.

New Waterford is out in force. Plummer Avenue is lined. Even James is out—not in his capacity as veteran, but as proud father. Mercedes stands at his side in front of Cribb's Bookstore. Across the street, Luvovitz's Kosher Canadian is closed, the blinds drawn down. There is no danger of them forgetting this day, but Mrs. Luvovitz prefers them to do their remembering at home, far from the sights and sounds of Sacrifice and Honor. Frances is supposed to be here but she is at the Empire Theatre, watching Louise Brooks in *Pandora's Box* again before the authorities get wind and it gets banned.

The parade swings toward the Miners' Monument. Although it was erected in memory of the sixty-five who died in the explosion of '17, it has become a symbol of all the others who have been killed in battles both foreign and domestic: those like Mr. Davis, who were shot in the street, and all those who ever have been or will be blown up or gassed in a trench or mine. The pipes fall abruptly silent. Lily and the rest of the parade march onward to the stark beating of the drums, until they halt at the monument. Then it's two minutes of silence.

You can hear the ocean. You can hear birds and the wind. You can hear the poppies blow in Flanders fields between the crosses row on row, "we are the Dead. Short days ago we lived, felt dawn, saw sunset glow, loved and were loved." Men have stony expressions on their faces, their hands folded in front. Women look severe. Everyone remembers their dear ones who will always be young.

Then a wrenching groan, a high-pitched wail, the drones start up and the pipes are on the march again. This releases tears, although the bagpipes do people's keening for them. A primitive reed instrument awakens something very old, and puts sorrow in a consolingly long perspective. Perhaps because grass is the oldest musical instrument for all kinds of people.

Lily feels secure among all the hard hairy pale male knees keeping time between socks and swinging sporrans and swaying kilts. She feels a camaraderie with the men. As if they'd all fought the war together. She would like to be a soldier. She's ten. She would like to be a veteran when she grows up. She wouldn't be afraid of the pain or the bullets, she'd leap over the top and charge with bare knees into battle. Daddy got the DSO medal. She knows because Mr. MacIsaac told her.

It's only when the pipes and drums cease and the brass band at the rear strikes up "Rule Britannia" that Lily feels the first twinge in her left foot, the little one. Her brown boot, with the built-up sole that Daddy made specially, is firmly harnessed between the steel supports of her brace, but it has been rubbing the top of her heel because it's new. A red stain has spread around her ankle. Lily steals a look, but doesn't miss a beat. There are Daddy and Mercedes. There are Mr. and Mrs. MacIsaac. Lily gives them what she hopes is a manly smile. Many people, not just those she knows, smile back.

Lily is unaware of the stigma surrounding her father, and people— not only her family—conspire to keep her that way. There are plenty of children with braces on their legs, some with crooked backs too, but Lily is the only one out marching. She is also the prettiest child ever to have been stricken. And the sweetest. Lily has become well known in town thanks to Mercedes, but she has become well loved because of herself.

New Waterford hasn't changed much. The company stores have gone. Besco never reopened them after the looting of '25. Many miners went back to work with an eight-percent wage cut but many others were blacklisted as Bolsheviks and wound up moving south of the border to Boston, and to the mills and lumber camps of New England. It was the beginning of the exodus to points south and west which shows no sign of stopping. The crash of '29 rocked the world but registered as a ripple in Cape Breton, where it takes a while for the Depression to sink in because it had already been going on for so long. Besides, it is widely believed that Nova Scotia's catastrophe occurred in 1867 with Confederation. Anything since then has just been an aftershock. No one can imagine how the thirties could be worse than the twenties. And as R. B. Bennett is fond of saying, "Prosperity is just around the corner."

But nothing can dampen civic pride—the turnout today shows that. Cape Bretoners have reconciled loyalty to King and country with scorn and skepticism for all things "from away"—the foolish arses in Upper Canada and the useless bowler hats in Whitehall. They are fiercely proud of their veterans, yet bitter about the Canadian army that has so often invaded the coalfields. In spite of this, the armed forces are increasingly an option for the jobless and the working poor looking to get off this cursèd godforsaken rock that they love more than the breath in their own lungs. There is no such place as "down home" unless you are "away." By November 1929 the process is under way whereby, eventually, more people will have a "down home" than a "home." Remembrance Day tends to stir up a lot of mixed emotions.

On days like this, Prohibition seems doubly ludicrous. By evening, kitchens will overflow with music and family and conversation. Jugs and cups of tea will be passed around. Mounties will turn a blind eye to hotel bars and speakeasies and more than one brawl will add to the evening's entertainment.

James will not work tonight. And he certainly will not socialize, although this is the one night when bridges might be mended—he is a veteran, after all, and decorated. But this is also one of two nights in the year when he does not trust himself near a bottle, because he wishes to forget, not remember, the day the Armistice was signed. All over town, people are asking each other the ritual question "Do you remember where you were the day the war ended, b'y?" James remembers all too well. He was in New York City. He was in Giles's apartment in Greenwich Village.

He was walking through the front door because it was unlocked. He had called out but no one answered. He is walking down the hallway, the apartment smells like lavender, he is looking for Kathleen, he finds her— stop

Tonight James needs to be safe at home in the bosom of his family.

Frances is already home playing piano, imagining her future life as a white slave cabaret dancer in Cairo, playing Mumma's forbidden music from the hope chest—Daddy says it's colored music, put it away. She is bobbing on the bench to "Coal Black Rose" when James and Mercedes rush in with Lily. Daddy carries Lily upstairs and Mercedes follows. Frances leaves the piano and takes the steps two at a time to the bathroom, where Daddy unrolls the stocking that's stuck to Lily's tiny foot and Mercedes gets the carbolic acid. Lily doesn't cry out at the pain, she just looks over Mercedes' shoulder at Frances in the doorway. Frances says, "It's okay, little gingerbread boy," which is one of their special codes, adding, *"Hayola kellu bas Helm."* Lily's gaze does not waver as she replies, *"Inshallah."* James glances at Frances in the doorway but says nothing. Mercedes bandages Lily's foot, praying that there won't be a scene later.

Inshallah is Lily's magic word. It is from the language that she knows ought not to be used by day except in an emergency. Because the words are like wishes from a genie—don't waste them. Lily has not even a rudimentary understanding of Arabic; it is, rather, dreamlike. At night in bed, long after lights-out, she and Frances speak the strange language. Their bed language. Frances uses half-remembered phrases and tells fragments of old stories, weaving them with pieces of songs, filling in the many gaps with her own made-up words that approximate the sounds of Mumma's Old Country tongue. Lily converses fluently in the made-up language, unaware which words are authentic, which invented, which hybrid. The meaning resides in the music and the privacy of their magic carpet bed. Arabian Nights.

Later that evening, when Mercedes has gone into the kitchen to make cocoa for everyone, Lily slips off Daddy's lap in the wingback chair without waking him and quietly asks Frances to redo her bandage: Mercedes has wrapped it a little too tightly.

Sweet Sixteen

FRANCES HAS GROWN AN inch and a half. She is now five feet tall and old enough to quit school. And she would, except that Daddy will not hear of it. Frances wants to get out in the world and garner some practical experience so she can join the French Foreign Legion as a nurse. She wants to cross the desert disguised as a camel driver by day and a seductress by night, smuggling secret documents to the Allies. Mata Hari and her seven veils. Except that Frances would escape the firing squad at the last second. But Daddy only ever has one response regardless of the extravagance of Frances's ambitions: "Even spies—especially spies—need an education."

Frances has already shamed Mercedes by flunking two grades. Not that it makes much difference, seeing's how they were both put ahead a year when they started, owing to the fact that they could already read and do long division. So by Frances's calculations she has really only flunked one grade.

Frances always sat at the back of the class with the hulking boys until the teacher realized it was best to move her up front. She has become pretty tight with the Corneliuses. Cornelius the younger has turned out nice, his friends call him Puss-Eye. Everyone expects him to be a priest because no one can imagine him as a miner or a soldier. Cornelius the older is nasty, his nickname is Petal. Frances saw Petal's thing three years ago but she has never shown him hers. From Petal, Frances extorted forbidden information and cigarettes in exchange for false hope. Petal always thought Frances was going to let him demonstrate his lessons one of these days, but Frances would just tell him, "You're nothing but a brute. Piss off." Petal quit school last year and moved to Vermont to cut wood and terrorize Americans, so aside from Puss-Eye and Mercedes, who don't count, Frances is without a worthy ally at Mount Carmel. Unless you can call Sister Saint Eustace Martyr an ally.

She is the principal and therefore Frances's arch-enemy. Not because she has threatened to expel Frances, but because she refuses to. And how else is Frances going to get out of school? Frances has done many bad things to this end. None of them, however, seems to have been quite bad enough for Sister Saint Eustace, a woman whose faith—judging by her belief in Frances—could move mountains.

"You have God-given ability, Frances. When are you going to apply yourself?"

Silence. Smell of beeswax. Frances fidgets.

Sister persists. "There are scholarships available for bright students, but you'll have to buckle down and start achieving consistently."

"Yes, Sister Saint Useless, thank you."

Frances thinks Sister Saint Eustace does not notice.

Or: "Why do you do these things, Frances?" This could refer to anything from theft or defacement of other people's property, to reducing a fellow pupil to tears by telling her that her parents have just been killed in an automobile accident, "Your mother's head came right off."

"Why, Frances? When we know that deep down you're a good girl."

"I'm sorry, sister. I'll try to behave in a way that's worthy of all the special efforts you make on my behalf."

"What about what's worthy of you, Frances?"

Silence. Frances glances up at poor disappointed Jesus on the cross. She glances down at her nicotine fingers.

"What do you want to be when you grow up, Frances?"

"A cabaret parasite."

Sister's expression does not change. Frances grows beet-red under the beady blue gaze. Finally: "You know, Frances, sometimes it's the wildest girls who end up with the strongest vocations."

No way, no way I'm being a nun.

"But you don't have to become a nun to get a good education and pursue a satisfying career. Women can do anything nowadays. You're an intelligent girl, Frances. The world is your oyster."

Yeah, slimy and smelly.

Frances wonders, what will it take to get free? Because all Sister Saint

Eustace does is poke at an old and tender bruise that reminds Frances what a bad apple she really is.

Frances has been going stir-crazy waiting for her life to begin. She has cut the sleeves off most of her dresses and shortened them herself—uneven is all the rage. She has decided she has a perfect figure, which is none. She removes the ribbons from her braids and ties them around her forehead and she has experimented with the bejeweled-brow look, courtesy of Mercedes' opal rosary. In the toe of an odd stocking in her drawer she keeps a tube of Rose of Araby lipstick she swiped from MacIsaac's. She has scorched her hair in an effort to straighten it, and always before her mind's eye is Louise Brooks, with her jet-black shingle and fringe.

Louise Brooks has usurped Lillian Gish in Frances's heart and on her wall. Lillian survives now only in an honorary capacity, alone on her virginal ice floe. Louise smolders from beneath a black widow's veil, smirks in a tuxedo, flirts over the rim of a champagne glass, simpers on Jack the Ripper's knee, and sprawls in a wicked heap, naked but for a handful of feathers. She is the best and the worst girl in the world. She is also the most modern. Frances longs to be sold into a "life of sin," forced onto the stage and into "houses of ill fame" where life is tragic but so much fun.

In the meantime, she plays hooky down by the shore or at the picture house. Lately she has taken to walking and trotting the Shore Road all nine miles into Sydney, where she heads for the docks of the Esplanade and hangs around the ships. She's thinking about stowing away. She chats with merchant sailors from all over the world and entertains them with her own skinnamalink stepdance-Charleston for pennies. Lets the odd nasty one touch her chest for a quarter before taking to her heels.

The only thing that keeps Frances from running away is Lily. She has to make sure that Lily is okay before she can let her life begin. What "okay" means is not clear. Frances will know it when she sees it. For now, she contents herself with a fresh diversion: on November 12, she follows James to his secret place in the woods:

It was difficult because she didn't have a car to follow him in and, besides, he would notice that. So she went on the floor of the back seat of his Hupmobile, under a blanket.

When the car stops, she hears him get out. Then she hears another automobile drive up. Sounds like a truck. She hears James's voice and another man's, soft and deep. She waits until their footsteps scuff away, then she carefully rises and peeps out the window. There's a shack with smoke coming out the top of a tin chimney—I was right!

Her elation is such that she reflexively ducks back down, as though she had made a noise. She peeps out again in time to see James come out of the shack and stand with his back to her. Nearby is a truck, its trailer covered with a tarpaulin stretched up and over a frame of wooden ribs like a covered wagon. The other man comes out of the shack carrying a big barrel on his shoulder.

He is familiar to Frances but she cannot place him. He is a substantial man, though not unusually tall, with wide shoulders and chest; obviously strong, but there are no sharp edges to him. His body is a pile of cushions, his face is an open invitation to come in and relax. Honest round forehead, large eyes—there is an overall quality that Frances racks her brains to identify. Then it comes to her. He looks kind. Something about him reminds Frances of Lily. Maybe that's why he seems familiar. The man rolls the barrel off his shoulder and into the back of his truck, where Frances sees a name stenciled, "Leo Taylor Transport." This too is familiar, but just out of reach.

Frances watches as the man carries barrel after barrel and case after clinking case while James waits. When the man has finished, he ties the canvas flaps of the tarp together. James takes a roll of bills out of his pocket and peels off a few. The man says, "Thanks, Mr. Piper."

And James says, "All right, Leo. Drive safe."

Let Me Call You Sweetheart

"You know why you have a boot-leg, Lily?"

" 'Cause I got infantile paralysis when I was a wee tiny baby but God wanted me to live."

It's a rainy Saturday afternoon. Frances and Lily have been playing Covered Wagon on Mercedes' bed. Mercedes is off volunteering at the hospital and Daddy is out Frances-knows-where. The chenille spread is the wagon cover and behind them are their children: Diphtheria Rose, Raggedy-Lily-of-the-Valley, Spanish Influenza, Maurice and the rest. They are a pioneer family bound for the frontier, shortly to be scalped. Lily has finally got the reins.

"You caught it in the creek."

The horses stop. Lily waits.

"You caught it in the creek because Mumma tried to drown you as soon as you were born."

"Frances"—quivering lip, this is the worst thing Frances has ever said—"Mumma loved me, she wouldn't hurt me."

"You were a dark baby. You and Ambrose."

"Frances, Daddy says—"

"He's not your daddy."

"He is so!"

"Shut up, Lily, or I won't tell you anything."

Whispering, "He is so!"

Frances gets up and heads for the door. "Never mind, Lily, 'cause obviously you don't even want to know who your real father is."

"Yes I do."

Frances takes a long look at Lily, as though assessing her ability to withstand the truth. Then: "Your father is a black man from The Coke Ovens in Whitney Pier."

Lily takes it in.

"Mumma tried to drown you 'cause you were dark." Every time Frances tells the true story, the story gets a little truer.

"I saved you, Lily."

Lily bites her lip. Frances's lips have gone white-hard. Her throat is a white rope.

"From drownding?"

"Drowning, not drownding, stupid."

Frances tosses the dolls onto the floor and begins to make the bed. Lily's silky black eyebrows tremble. "Mumma killed Ambrose?"

"That's right." Suddenly offhand, an efficient plump of the pillow.

Lily starts to cry.

Frances points out reasonably, "She was afraid Daddy would kill her."

"But he wouldn't!" Lily sobs.

Frances watches for a moment. She always feels immensely relieved when Lily starts to cry. She sits beside Lily, puts an arm around her and strokes her sweet head. Dear Lily.

"It's okay, Lily . . . Daddy couldn't ever hurt anyone."

"Ever."

"I won't tell you any more, you're too little."

"I am not!" Lily pulls away, swatting the tears off her cheeks.

"Yes you are, Lily. You're a sweet little girl."

"Tell me, Frances! I'm big."

"Little."

"Big!"

"Tiny."

"NO!"

"Oui."

"TELL ME!" Lily bright red, fists pounding the bed.

Frances flops back on the pillow, hands folded behind her head, and casually sings, one foot resting on the other knee and bobbing time, "Mademoiselle from Armentières, *pa-a-arlez-vous?*" Lily starts tearing apart the freshly made bed. "Mademoiselle from Armentières, *pa-a-arlez-vous?*"—bedspread yanked out from under Frances—"Mademoiselle

from Armentières"—strewn sheets, rosary attached with a safety pin—
"hasn't been kissed in forty years"—Lily could pass out with rage—
"inky-dinky *parlez-vo-o-ous*"—she whirls around the room, grabs a big
book and tears off the spine. She rips up hunks of pages and throws them
out the window. She whips the gutted binding down after them like a
blown-off shingle, spins back on her sturdy leg, her steel brace propelling
out to the side, and spots The Old-Fashioned Girl that plays "Let Me Call
You Sweetheart." It holds a yellow parasol. It lives on Mercedes' dresser
on a doily all its own. Lily grabs it.

"Tell me, Frances, or I'll smash it."

"I'm not telling you anything, you're a maniac."

Lily's arm swings up, "Tell me."

"No."

Lily pauses—the enormity of the idea of throwing The Old-
Fashioned Girl to the floor threatens to sink in, so she simply lets the
figurine drop. It hits the floor. The parasol and the head. Clink. Roll, roll,
ruddle-ruddle. Lily looks in shock at what she's done. Frances delivers the
punch line.

"If you were doing all this to get back at me, you didn't, all you did
was wreck Mercedes' precious things."

Again. Oh no. Lily stands with parted lips and puckered forehead. Oh
no, oh no, oh no.

"Okay, Lily. I'll tell you"—Lily can't remember what Frances is
talking about—"but you have to swear."

Lily just stands there.

"Don't worry, Lily, we'll clean it all up."

"But some things are broken."

"We'll fix them, don't worry. Swear."

"I swear."

"You have to swear on something."

"Um . . . on Raggedy-Lily-of-the-Valley."

This makes Lily feel teary because she imagines how she'd feel if
someone came along and did to Raggedy-Lily-of-the-Valley what she has
just done to The Old-Fashioned Girl. Raggedy-Lily-of-the-Valley with
her head off. Little bits of gray material coming out. But Frances has other
stakes in mind.

"Swear on your boot-leg."

"On my little leg."

"May it be cut off if you speak of this again."

Lily looks down at her legs: the strong right one, and the wispy left one. In its sincere beige wool stocking, which sags like empty skin within the steel harness; its high narrow shoe with the mild horse's face, the iron bit clamped under the sole. Her heel is much better now, there's just a scab from Armistice Day.

"Okay," says Lily. Don't worry, little leg, I'll keep my vow.

"Okay. Well. Mumma went crazy from shame of what she did with the man from The Coke Ovens. Plus she was dying of a wound she got because Daddy had to cut you and Ambrose out of her stomach with his bayonet." Make yourself cozy, now. "It was the middle of the night. Daddy left her sleeping and went to get the doctor. But she got up even though she was cut open." Frances has slipped into the eerie voice of the stray-orange-cat story. It's the voice she uses when she is telling the truth. "I was at my bedroom window wearing my tartan housecoat. I saw Mumma down in the creek. Ambrose was lying on the bottom. She was just about to do the same thing to you. But she looked up and she saw me watching her so she stopped. There was a bright bright moon and I just looked her in the eye like that till Daddy came and dragged her back to the house with you. Then she died."

"Poor Mumma," Lily weeps.

Frances blinks, finally. "Poor Mumma? She tried to kill you, you idiot, I'm the one who saved you."

"Why didn't you save Mumma?"

"No one could save Mumma."

"You saved me."

"Yes, you dunce, I saved you."

"Thank you, Frances." Lily hugs Frances. "Does Daddy know?"

"That I saved you? Yes."

"Does he know he's not my real daddy?"

"Yes, but you can never mention it, Lily, it would really hurt him. 'Cause even though you're not his, he loves you more than the rest of us."

"He loves you too, Frances."

"Yes, but he loves you the most."

"I want him to love you the most too."

"It's all right, Lily, it's supposed to be this way."

"I love you the most, Frances."

"What about Daddy and Mercedes?"

"I love them the most too."

"There's no such thing as loving everyone the most."

Mercedes spent the morning at New Waterford General Hospital. She read aloud to a veteran who had been gassed in the war, emptied bedpans, changed the water in vases and generally made herself useful. She'd have brought Lily, but Daddy wants to make sure Lily's foot is completely healed before she ventures out. After the hospital, Mercedes went to Mount Carmel Church and helped the nuns polish the communion rail and dust the altar. She lit a candle, knelt at the base of the beautiful eight-foot Mary and said a few prayers for Mumma and Kathleen and Valentino and all the poor captive souls in purgatory.

Valentino died three years ago. The day she heard the impossible news it was all Mercedes could do to keep from running to Helen Frye's house. She found the strength to forbear. It's simple, really: just don't move, and you won't do anything you'll regret later. Mercedes spent that day sitting, enervated, on the edge of her bed, staring at Valentino's picture. When she got up, it was to replace his face in the frame with a poem she had come across in *Reader's Digest* called "Don't Whine."

Mercedes always crosses the street when she sees Helen Frye. Helen looks wistfully at Mercedes, although she has given up saying hello. The Fryes must know by now how wrong they were, no doubt Helen has shed her share of hot tears. Good enough for them. Mercedes hasn't wasted time on silly girlfriends since Frye. She has been too busy with school and family. Here is the order of priorities: God, family, school, piano, friends.

Mercedes will soon turn seventeen—November is the one month when she and Frances are the same age. Mercedes is in her final year of high school. She is a definite for a scholarship to Saint Francis Xavier University on the mainland. Surely Daddy will be able to spare her by then. She tries not to be selfish about it, but she wants so badly to go to university. It's too late for her other ambition: to be the best student ever to grace the halls of Holy Angels. She has settled for being the best Mount Carmel has ever seen, and among the best in the province. All this and cooking and cleaning and babysitting too. Mercedes tries not to be proud—only grateful. Think of how many girls never even get to finish high school. Think of the poor children who share a single pair of shoes among a whole family.

Mercedes leaves the church, raises her umbrella and walks down

Plummer Avenue through the steady drizzle, nodding polite greetings left and right. Despite her youth, many people call her "Miss Piper." It seems natural. Partly because of her bearing and good works. Partly because of her grooming. She is swathed in tweed, crisp in a white blouse and black necktie, gloved, with a straw boater angled on her pale bun. She never fails to wear a hat and gloves, not just out of seemliness but because, summer or winter, she darkens rather too readily. In Paris, Coco Chanel has just invented the suntan, but word hasn't reached New Waterford. Beneath it all, Mercedes is decently corseted and petticoated. Frances has told her she looks as though she just stepped out of the Time Machine. But good taste is always in style. Truly, civilization is a thin veneer. For what have we to distinguish us from the beasts of the field? Besides, of course, an immortal soul? Manners, and suitable attire.

One effect of cultivating the virtue of charity is the realization that the Mahmouds over in Sydney require her prayers. So along with the dead, Mercedes prays for her unknown relatives. She is praying for them now, inwardly, as she passes the new gasoline pumps and nods to Mr. MacIsaac. It slipped her mind in church, but there is no such thing as an inconvenient moment when it comes to prayer. That's the marvelous thing about it. "Please, dear God, don't judge too harshly Your servants in Sydney who cast out their own flesh and blood. Amen."

Although Mercedes was too young to respond mercifully to the first twenty-five years of disaster, she has been working hard to make up for it. And there's plenty of time; this is, after all, only 1929. In the grievously wounded but still young twentieth century, Mercedes finishes her prayer with a discreet sign of the cross etched with her index finger upon her thumb and turns into Luvovitz's Kosher Canadian to buy a roast for Sunday's supper.

Luvovitz's Delicatessen has expanded to include fruits, vegetables, tinned goods, dry goods, and bins of bulk comestibles, because few people can afford to buy meat on a regular basis.

The bell rings as Mercedes opens the door, and Ralph Luvovitz looks up from behind the counter. The tips of his adorable sticking-out ears turn as red as the stripes in his apron when he sees her. Mercedes looks as young as she is the moment she smiles at him. They exchange pleasantries, avoiding and catching one another's eyes, as he draws out the process of measuring and cutting brown paper, unwinding a length of string, selecting just the right roast, wrapping it and tying it up. At the end of the process it seems to slip his mind that Mercedes is waiting for him to hand the package to her. Neither does Mercedes remind him.

"How is the clarinet going, Ralph?" she inquires.

"I've been practicing"—

"Good, are you—?"

"Are you—? Sorry—"

"Sorry."

Smile.

"Are you still able to come over Sunday evening?" asks Ralph.

"Oh yes. May I bring the girls?"

"Of course, that'd be grand."

Smile.

Mercedes reflects, not for the first time, that Ralph's shiny brown eyes and sandy curls are somehow more pleasing than Valentino's turban and charcoal glowers. Perhaps it's because, if she reached out right now, she could touch Ralph. She blushes afresh and fumbles for the roast. Ralph drops it.

They've known one another all their lives, but suddenly over the past few months they've become terribly polite. It is a change that is not lost on Mrs. Luvovitz, who is taking inventory across the aisle.

Mercedes is a good girl. A wonderful girl. I helped bring her into this world. I loved her mother like a daughter. But.

The problem is, if Mr. and Mrs. Luvovitz are to have grandchildren—Jewish grandchildren—well, it can't be a *shayna* Catholic *maidela,* now can it?

"Relax," Benny has told her.

"How can I relax? You want a Catholic grandchild?"

"A grandchild would be nice."

Mrs. Luvovitz gets choked up and can't continue the argument. Benny says, "Come here, come here."

She does. He says, "You want he should go away to school, and you want he should stay home." She nods. He says, "You want he should be a doctor, and you want he should be a grocer." She nods again, smiling now through tears. "And," says Benny, "he should marry a nice Jewish girl and move into a house down the street." She nods, stuffing a hanky in between his shoulder and her nose.

"You know, *liebkeit,* we're the ones who came here. If we'd stayed in the Old Country there'd be plenty of nice Jewish girls. It's not Ralph's fault we made him be born here." He pauses. "And it's not his fault that . . ."

But he doesn't have to continue. They both know. If Abe and Rudy had not been killed in the war, Mrs. Luvovitz would not have such a problem letting Ralph marry Mercedes.

Over the tins of Dutch Cleanser, Mrs. Luvovitz watches Mercedes count out the money for Ralph and she watches him meticulously place it in the cash register. She sees him slip a chocolate rosebud into Mercedes' hand before she leaves.

Mercedes exits Luvovitz's Kosher Canadian feeling light-headed. Maintaining the pink glow on her cheeks for several blocks is the thought of what her and Ralph's children would look like. Mercedes Luvovitz. Mrs. Ralph Luvovitz. Their children would be Catholic, of course.

Mercedes indulges herself until King Street, then reins in her thoughts and remembers to open her umbrella. I wonder if Frances and Lily went on their picnic. I hope not, in this weather.

She turns onto Water Street and sees that Daddy is not yet home. Just as well. I feel like a little lie-down before starting supper.

Mercedes mounts the stairs to her room. The house is quiet. Lily and Frances must have gone on their picnic after all. It's sweet of Frances to play with Lily so much—it means Lily's not constantly on my hands—but I could wish Frances had a friend her own age. A nice one.

Mercedes lies down on her perfectly made bed, and allows her eyes to travel contentedly about her room. She has only fine things. Books. On her bedside table she has framed the old photograph of Mumma and Daddy in the archway. And safely hidden is the one surviving photograph of Kathleen—hmm, what's it doing on the floor, it's always tucked inside *Jane Eyre* where Daddy won't have to come across it. Mercedes reaches down, picks up the photo and puts it on her bedside table. She'll tuck it back into the book after she has a little zizz.

Mercedes' eyes come drowsily to rest on the wall above her dresser where she has hung the portrait of Our Lady appearing to Bernadette in the grotto at Lourdes. Yellow roses sprout between the toes of Our Lady, and arranged in a halo about her head are the words she said to Bernadette, "I am the Immaculate Conception." A stream runs between them. The stream that became the healing waters of Lourdes and now provides three-times-nine thousand gallons every day. Our Lady appeared to Bernadette three-times-six times. She told Bernadette three times to drink from the stream, which Bernadette did after throwing away the first three handfuls of water. Our Lady told her three secrets that Bernadette carried to the grave. Bernadette escaped all the publicity by becoming a nun. In the convent she helped out in the hospital and the chapel and struggled to control her lifelong bad temper. When asked what she was doing, Bernadette replied, "Getting on with my work: being ill." Three days after the Feast of the Immaculate Conception she became bedridden. At three-times-twelve years old she died of asthma, tuberculosis and a tumor on the knee. She received extreme unction three times. Three nuns knelt by her at her death and now three million faithful a year flock to three basilicas at Lourdes, where the waters occasionally effect a miraculous cure.

Mercedes has become very sleepy thinking about Bernadette.

As her eyes drift down from the picture they naturally fall upon the figurine of the dear Old-Fashioned Girl. Mercedes' eyes lurch open. Diabolical.

The Old-Fashioned Girl has a parasol for a head and a head for a parasol. She is daintily holding up her own head of ringlets to the sun while the insensate yellow parasol is implanted in the empty neck like a flag. *Frances*.

Mercedes blinks back tears. It's always like this—the minute I have something good, something clean. She goes to the dresser, tidying her tears with a thin trembling wrist.

She examines the body. The pieces have been glued like that, there's no fixing this. At least not now. What to do with it, where to put it in the meantime where it won't be like an obscene smell, invisible yet oppressive. The hope chest. It's been kept locked ever since Frances dressed Trixie in the baptismal gown. Mercedes has the key.

She picks up the disfigurine without looking at it. It tinkles briefly. On the way, she picks up the photo of Kathleen, intending to replace it between the leaves of *Jane Eyre,* but Jane has flown. She is not on the shelf near the window. She is nowhere to be seen. Frances must have borrowed her. Again.

First things first. Mercedes will hunt for the book later. She puts Kathleen in her pocket and walks to the foot of the attic stairs. Listens. Silence. She mounts the stairs.

The attic is so empty. Nothing but the hope chest. Even the attic's one other distinguishing feature is an absence: a crisscross halfway up the wall where a crucifix used to be. Mercedes remembers when this was Kathleen's bedroom. Before she died here, peacefully in her sleep.

The hope chest is a good place to store things like the ruined Old-Fashioned Girl because the attic is so separate from the rest of the house. In a state of perpetual quarantine. It's really an abandoned room. That's why the sad feeling here, Mercedes supposes. Sad like a deconsecrated church. Maybe I'll put a crucifix back up here if I think of it next time. Or no, because then you couldn't store anything up here like the ruined Old-Fashioned Girl. Mercedes sees the practical benefit of having a nonroom in the house.

She opens the hope chest. The cedar smell clouds up soft and alive, resurrecting an old grief. Mercedes has no wish to linger here or to rummage in the past. She takes what is to hand—the baptismal gown is at the top of the pile from the Trixie incident—and wraps the Old-Fashioned Girl in it. After what the garment has been through this can hardly be considered a desecration. She closes the lid and locks it. She stands for a moment in the emptiest of rooms. Then leaves, quietly closing the door behind her.

Mercedes feels calmer by the time she arrives in the living room. Daddy will be home soon and she mustn't show that anything's wrong. She sits down at the piano. No doubt Lily knocked over the figurine by accident, she is a child after all—*jab jab jab* at that sticky C sharp, Daddy keeps saying he's going to fix it but never does—Mercedes is under the impression that she has forgiven Lily for the family-tree incident and now she is preparing herself to forgive Frances for mutilating the Old-Fashioned Girl. She turns to page thirty-two in *Everybody's Favorite Songs*. Oddly, Mercedes has always found it much easier to forgive Frances than to forgive Lily, even though Frances is satanically inspired and Lily is unarguably innocent. Mercedes needs to forgive Frances the same way Frances needs to comfort Lily.

Mercedes goes to touch down lightly on the keys but stops and reaches into her pocket, where she has forgotten Kathleen. She takes the photo out and props it on the music ledge next to the song book. Kathleen in her Holy Angels uniform, hands on her knees, laughing. She was beautiful. A slight blur around her hair because she wouldn't keep still long enough for the camera. There, says Mercedes to Kathleen with her mind, you can listen and watch and I'll play you a song.

Mercedes starts to play. And to sing sincerely:

" 'Darling I am growing old. Silver threads among the gold, shine upon my brow today, life is fading fast away. But, my darling you will be, will be, always young and fair to me. Yes! My darling you will be, always young and fair to me.' "

Trixie, Frances, then Lily quietly file in. Lily's face is black with coal except for a wide oval around her mouth. Mercedes sees them but keeps singing. Frances looks at Mercedes and figures, I guess she hasn't been up to her room yet.

Frances, Lily and Trixie sit on the sofa and listen.

" 'With the roses of the May, I will kiss your lips and say, Oh! My darling mine alone, You have never older grown.' "

Daddy is in the doorway. The song ends.

"That was lovely, Mercedes."

"Thank you, Daddy."

"Play something else, my dear," he says, crossing the room to sit in the wingback chair.

"Play 'Oh My Darlin' Clementine,' " Lily requests.

"What in the name of time have you done to your face?"

"We did a minstrel show in the cellar, Daddy," says Lily.

James looks at Frances. Frances just looks back. Daddy smiles at Lily,

"Come here, ya wee scallywag."

Lily jumps into Daddy's lap.

"Go on and play, Mercedes."

Mercedes plays and Daddy and Lily sing, cuddled together in the wingback chair. Frances watches them as though transfixed. Lily belts out her favorite part, " 'herring boxes without topses, shoes they were for Clementine.' " Lily always wonders what happened to Clementine, the miner forty-niner's daughter, "lost and gone for ever," where?

The song comes to an end; Daddy gently shifts Lily off his knee and rises.

"Tell you what, Mercedes, I'm going to fix that C sharp right this minute."

"Oh, thank goodness, Daddy, it's so annoying." Mercedes is a lady. She is able to chat with Daddy like that. Frances marvels. James opens the piano lid and looks in. "Give it a tap, Mercedes."

She does.

"Nothin' to it," says James, "I'll get my tools." Then he sees the photograph. The laughing leaning-forward girl with the halo of hurry, "Daddy!" The house is behind her and you can just see Materia in the kitchen window waving. Something bright in her hand. Flashed against the lens. James can hear Kathleen laughing at him, totally unafraid, nothing to be afraid of. Not like now in this room. Now is the dim past. Then was the shining present. He hears her laugh. He hears the water trickling in the creek and flash goes Materia's waving hand, although her face is barely visible. Kathleen is fourteen. You think you're safe. Until you see a picture like that. And then you know you'll always be a slave to the present because the present is more powerful than the past, no matter how long ago the present happened.

If only he hadn't let her go so far from home. If only he had gone with her to New York. None of it would have happened. She never would have got pregnant. Not that I regret Lily, Lily is my consolation, but my first girl . . . She'd be with me now. Oh my darlin'. The breath assaults James's lungs and he comes out of the black and white picture back into the room of living color.

And looks around. My good daughter. My bad daughter. And my dear daughter's daughter—in blackface. That isn't even worth getting riled about, although riled is what Frances tries to get me with something like that.

"What's this doing here?" he asks Mercedes, softly. There are no pictures of Kathleen anywhere. Not a spinning wheel in the kingdom, so to speak, and then you prick your finger.

Mercedes answers, "I'm sorry, Daddy."

Frances stares at James. "I did it."

Mercedes swivels on the piano stool. She wants to say to Frances, no, it will go much harder with you, you don't have to atone for the ruin of my silly possessions by taking the blame for this. But Frances deliberately digs her own grave. "Kathleen was my sister and I'd like to see her now and then."

James is getting whiter. The blue part of his eyes is heating up.

Frances stokes him. "Why can't we, anyhow? Was there something wrong with her? Was she a lunatic or something?" Casual insolent tone.

Mercedes can't find her voice. It's autumn in her mouth and all her tongue can do is rustle. Lily doesn't like it when Daddy looks at Frances like that. It's not Daddy anymore. Not her daddy.

"Was she a slut?" Frances, in a helpful tone of voice. Ahhh, that's just right. Look at him, all lit up like an Easter candle.

James says quietly to Frances, "Come with me."

Frances shrugs and gets up, nonchalant, grinning at Mercedes. Mercedes covers her face with her hands. James says to Mercedes, "Take your sister out for a while."

"Come on, Lily."

Lily's forehead has the bump in it but she obeys.

Frances saunters across the room toward James, who finally snaps at the sight of her slouching toward him, grabs the back of her neck and flings her through the doorway. Mercedes hustles Lily out the front door.

"Where are we going, Mercedes?"

"Out."

"I broke your beautiful thing."

"I don't care, Lily, just walk please"—down the porch steps.

"Frances glued it but I broke it and I tore up your book too, I didn't mean to."

"They're just things, Lily, they don't matter."

Lily is having a hard time keeping up but she has no choice, Mercedes has her by the wrist.

"I'm sorry, Mercedes."

No answer.

"Mercedes—"

"That's enough, Lily."

They walk-drag through town until they come to the cliff above the shore. Mercedes stands staring out at the gray sea. Lily sits with her legs dangling over the edge.

"How come I never saw that picture?"

"You know perfectly well, because Daddy doesn't like to dwell on Kathleen. It grieves him."

"Did you hide it?"

"Yes. In the book you destroyed. That's how it came to be out in the open."

"That's the book Frances likes to read. That's how come I accidentally wrecked it. Because Frances accidentally made me."

"Well, then. She has you to thank for whatever Daddy gives her."

"How come you put the picture on the piano, Mercedes?"

Mercedes freezes. How come indeed? Surely not on purpose. Mercedes turns her head slowly and looks at Lily. She sees her falling over the cliff to the rocks below. The only thing that would not break would be her withered leg in its steel brace.

Without looking at Mercedes, Lily rises and wanders back toward the Shore Road. She turns to see if Mercedes is coming, but Mercedes is kneeling at the precipice, facing the ocean.

"Mercedes," she calls. "Don't fall, Mercedes."

Mercedes makes the sign of the cross and gets up. God will forgive her. She has made Him a promise.

On Water Street, the outside walls of the shed thump now and then like a bass drum with a foot pedal at work inside it keeping the beat. In the shed the performance has begun. The upbeat grabs her neck till she's on point, the downbeat thrusts her back against the wall, two eighth-notes of head on wood, knuckles clatter incidentally. In the half-note rest he lights up her pale face with the blue wicks of his eyes, and the lyrics kick in *con spirito,* "What right have you, you have no right, no right to even speak her name, who's the slut, tell me who's the slut!" The next two bars are like the first, then we're into the second movement, swing your partner from the wall into the workbench, which catches her in the small of the back, grace note into stumble because she bounces, being young. *Staccato* across the face, then she expands her percussive range and becomes a silent tambourine. Frances gets through this part by pretending to herself that she's actually Raggedy-Lily-of-the-Valley, which makes her laugh and provokes his second verse, "I don't want to hear you speak her name," accidental note to the nose resolves into big major chord, "Do—You—Under—Stand—Me?" We've gone all stately; it's whole notes from here on in. She flies against another wall and he follows her trajectory, taking his time now because we're working up to the finale. One more clash of timbers and tissues and it's finally opera, "I'll cut the tongue right out of your head." She sticks her tongue out at him and tastes blood. Cue finale to the gut. Frances folds over till she's on the floor. Modern dancer.

The first thing Mercedes did was bring Frances Spanish Influenza and the rest of her dear children, arranging them lovingly on her bed. Even though Frances didn't register their arrival, Mercedes knew their presence would comfort her. Then she got a basin and a cloth and cleaned Frances's face.

The swelling makes Frances look even younger than sixteen, especially with all her dolls around her. She speaks finally, her words a little thick. "Where's Trixie?"

"It's okay, Trixie's fine."

Frances hurts all over, which makes her feel restful. It's a lovely feeling that she hardly ever gets.

Mercedes squeezes out the cloth, "You shouldn't make him angry like that."

"He deserves it."

"You're the one who gets hurt."

Frances swallows carefully. "I'm sorry about your things."

"It's all right, Frances. You didn't have to take the blame for the photograph."

"Yes I did."

"Why?"

"It's the way it is, Mercedes. You can't change the way it is."

"I don't agree, that doesn't make any sense, he shouldn't beat you for something I did."

"Well, he wouldn't beat you."

"Well good, then, no one need have got beaten."

"Yes, someone did need to. Besides, it lets me get back at him."

"For what?"

Frances looks at Mercedes and smiles slightly, which makes the fresh seam in her lower lip gleam.

"For the thing you don't know. And what you don't know won't hurt you."

Mercedes says nothing. Frances reaches for Diphtheria Rose, hugs her and closes her eyes.

Mercedes has told Daddy that the picture has been burned to nothing on the stove. But it's a lie. She can't part with it. She leaves Frances sleeping, but before going to the coal cellar to keep her promise to God, she climbs the attic stairs for the second time today. Mercedes knows that Daddy never looks in the hope chest. The photo will be perfectly safe there.

When the house is quiet, Trixie lopes up the stairs into Frances and Lily's room and silently leaps onto the bed. She snuggles down amongst the dolls in the crook of Frances's arm. She watches Frances sleep for a while. Then she lays her head upon the pillow, extends her paw and rests it against Frances's forehead. Neither of them moves till morning.

We Are the Dead

. . . All by myself I have to go
With none to tell me what to do
All alone beside the streams
And up the mountainsides of dreams . . .

ROBERT LOUIS STEVENSON,
''THE LAND OF NOD''

AN OPENING IN THE earth a third of the way up a steep slope of lime-stone, thin grass and scant soil. Crazy pine trees grow parallel to the slant here and there. An archway in the earth. No inscription. An abandoned bootleg mine. A drift mine, the type that cuts into a hillface and burrows horizontally.

Every time people find an old mine around here, they think they've found the old French mine. There's no treasure associated with the old French mine, it just happened to be the first hole excavated for the purpose of extracting "buried sunshine." This is the sort of thing that becomes important when you don't have cathedrals.

"It's the old French mine," says Frances. "No one else knows it's here."

Frances and Lily stand at the base of the hill looking up. Behind them are the woods, where Frances has just blazed a trail in the pine trees with the kitchen scissors. She brings a hand up to shade her eyes in the manner of a French Foreign Legion commander, the overcast Cape Breton sky notwithstanding. Her left eye socket has healed to pale yellow, but her right one is still a pouchy mauve—wounds sustained in my last hand-to-hand bout with the Algerians, *mon Dieu!*

Frances cuts what she intends to be a plucky figure in her blue Girl Guide uniform. Her neckerchief is neatly knotted, her beret tweaked at regulation angle, her leather pouch buckled to her belt. The only things missing are badges. She has yet to earn one. She has yet to attend a second Guide meeting. Lily is in her Brownie uniform. Daddy has finally let her join because she hasn't had so much as a cold for a long long time. Frances was supposed to take her to her first Brownie pack meeting this afternoon, but brought her here instead. They walked all the way, and it's miles. Frances told Lily she would earn her hiking badge.

"There are dead men in there, Lily. And diamonds."

"Like in Aladdin."

"That's right."

"Let's go home now, Frances."

"We're going in."

Frances reaches for Lily's hand, but Lily backs away. "Come on, Lily, just for a little visit."

"No, Frances, there's dead people in there."

"Dead people are completely harmless."

"What about ghosts?"

"There's no such thing."

"Then who're we visiting if they're all dead?"

"Ambrose."

Lily searches Frances's face. "Ambrose is dead."

"No he isn't."

"He is so, he drownded, you *said.*"

"Yes, he drowned, but he isn't dead, Lily, he's an angel, remember? He became an angel, it happens. And he's in there. That's where he lives. I think it's time you met him."

"No."

"Come on, I'll be with you."

"No."

Frances seizes Lily's arm and pulls her along, like trying to get a dog up stairs.

"You'll earn a badge for this, Lily."

"I don't want to go in there, Frances." Lily's voice is shaking with fear.

"You can't get your wings and fly up to Guides if you don't earn your guardian angel badge."

Frances starts laughing and Lily knows it's going to get bad. They've started up the slope, Lily twisting in Frances's grasp. Frances grapples her into a sack of potatoes over her shoulder. Lily ceases to struggle. They climb up to the mouth of the mine. They enter.

There's nothing much to see—a few rotting ribs of wood and pit props, a rusted shovel. Frances carries Lily forward. It gets darker. The air is musty. They follow a bend in the tunnel and lose sight of the light at the entrance. Frances walks on slowly into the dank and shapeless dark.

Lily asks quietly, "What if we get lost?"

"We won't. Ambrose will find us."

Lily whimpers.

"He loves you, Lily, don't be afraid."

"I want to go home."

"We are home. We're in his home."

Frances stops and puts Lily down. Her fingers feel for the snap on her Girl Guide pouch. She withdraws a cigarette, and strikes a match against her belt buckle. The tongue of fire illuminates: *a pool of still water inches from their feet, dear God, how deep is it? And over there, against the wall*—Lily screams. Frances lights her cigarette and blows out the match.

"There's someone here, Frances." Lily's voice is shaking.

"I know."

"He's standing over there. On the other side of the water."

Frances takes a big puff. "What's he look like?"

"He's got overalls on. And a pick. And a peaked cap."

"Is there a lamp on his cap?"

"Yes. The teapot kind."

"He must have been dead quite a while."

Frances blows invisible smoke rings.

"Frances"—Lily's fear is spilling over.

"It's not Ambrose, Lily. It's a dead miner."

Frances lights another match: *the pool, the seeping wall*—Lily cries out again as the flame disappears.

"It's not a miner, Frances."

"What is it?"

"He's got a mask on."

"A Halloween mask?"

"A gas mask. He's got a rifle with a bayonet on the end."

"A dead soldier."

Frances lights another match: *the black water, stones and earthen walls—*

"He's gone," says Lily.

"Ambrose took him away 'cause he knew you were scared. Baby. Brownie baby."

"Ambrose isn't here."

"Yes he is."

"Where?"

Frances drops her cigarette and it sizzles against the unseen pool. "In there."

Lily looks down, dizzy from the dark. "Angels live in heaven."

"They live wherever the hell they want."

"I'm telling. You smoked and swore."

"Go ahead and tattle. Ambrose and I will still look after you no matter what."

"There's no such thing as Ambrose."

"At night he dives down in this pool and swims in an underground river till it comes out at the surface and turns into our creek. He takes a breath and swims in the shallow water, long and white, all the way till he gets to our place. Then he climbs out over the top of the bank and slowly walks, dripping, across our yard and opens the kitchen door. He walks past the oven. He walks into the hall past the front room. He walks up the stairs without a sound, and past the attic door. He comes into the room where you're asleep. He stands at the foot of the bed and looks down at you. He has red hair.

"And then he leaves. But he can't swim back. He has to move the rock in the garden and go down a tunnel that's too small for him now, until he gets to the sad and lonely mine. He walks for miles in his bare feet past all the quiet soldiers and miners resting against the walls. And every time he makes the journey back to the pool, his heart breaks. So you see how much he loves you, Lily, to make such a trip night after night."

Silence. Lily pees her pants.

Frances's footsteps trot away and around the bend until Lily can't hear them anymore. Her Brownie stockings are soaked. She passes out.

When Frances doesn't hear Lily cry or holler, she runs back through the darkness and lights another match. Oh my God, "Lily!" But Lily lies motionless, dead of a heart attack at ten, it could happen, "Lily!" Frances shakes her, splashes water on her face, and she wakes up. Frances piggy-backs her out of the mine and slides half the way down the hill in stones and dirt. When they get to the bottom, she props Lily against a mossy tree and catches her breath, hands on her knees.

Lily opens her eyes. "Frances, I peed."

"That's okay, we'll go straight home and change, come on."

Lily stays sitting. "Frances. What if Ambrose is the Devil?"

"He's not the Devil. I know who the Devil is and it isn't Ambrose."

"Who's the Devil?"

Frances crouches down as if she were talking to Trixie. "That's something I'll never tell you, Lily, no matter how old you get to be, because the Devil is shy. It makes him angry when someone recognizes him, so once they do the Devil gets after them. And I don't want the Devil to get after you."

"Is the Devil after you?"

"Yes."

"Jesus can beat the Devil."

"If God wants."

"God is against the Devil."

"God made the Devil."

"Why?"

"For fun."

"No, to test us."

"If you know, why are you asking me?"

"Daddy says there's no such thing as the Devil, it's just an idea."

"The Devil lives with us."

"No he doesn't."

"You see the Devil every day. The Devil hugs you and eats right next to you."

"Daddy's not the Devil."

"I never said he was. . . ."

Frances has got a dry look, tinder in the eye; her voice is a stack of hay heating up at the center, her mouth a stitched line. "I'm the Devil."

This is the moment Lily stops being afraid of anything Frances could ever say or do again. Stops being afraid of anything at all. She reaches out and takes Frances's hand. The white hand that always smells of small wildflowers, lily of the valley. The hand that has always done up Lily's buttons and laces, and produced wondrous objects. She holds Frances's hand and tells her, "It's okay, Frances."

Frances's bruised face crumples and her forehead drops to her knees knocking her Girl Guide beret askew. Her stick arms encircle her legs and she cries. Lily strokes the sinewy back while Frances mumbles something over and over.

Years later, Frances remembers that she was saying, "I'm sorry, I'm sorry, Lily, I'm sorry."

But memory plays tricks. Memory is another word for story, and nothing is more unreliable.

The First Miracle

*My own soul cries out in anguish, it thirsts so much for
purification and cleansing. Even while I sleep my soul groans
for complete surrender to Jesus. Ah my Saviour, my heart bleeds
with pain and love. Oh, Jesus—You know it—My Jesus!*

"THE SECRETS OF PURGATORY,"
AUTHOR UNKNOWN

WHILE FRANCES AND LILY were at the old French mine, Mercedes was
home in the coal cellar keeping her promise to God.

"Through my fault, through my fault, through my most grievous
fault." Penance has not only eased her soul, it has been the occasion for
Our Lady to put the idea into Mercedes' mind of a Lourdes fund for Lily.
Why didn't I think of it before? But Mercedes knows the answer. She
wasn't worthy to receive the inspiration until she acknowledged her sins
and humbly begged God's forgiveness.

Naturally Mercedes has made a full confession: "Father forgive me,
for I have sinned. . . . I wished my lame sister dead of a fall, I grieved my
poor father, I allowed my favorite sister to suffer for my sin. I have a
favorite sister." She has been assigned a standard penance of prayers, but
she has devised an additional private penance here in the cellar.

Although she has told no one of her penance, she has told Daddy and
Frances about the Lourdes fund so that they may contribute, and she has
told Lily so that Lily may have hope. There is nearly two dollars in the
cocoa tin already and it's only been a week. At this rate, Lily will be able to
go to Lourdes when she's fourteen. That's a good age for a cure. The brink

of womanhood. Think how perfectly lovely Lily would be without her affliction.

Mercedes rises, takes off the white shift and hides it behind the furnace. She stands naked for a moment in the darkness and says a prayer of thanks to the Immaculate Heart of Mary. Most Blessed Virgin, Merciful Mother, Virgin Most Powerful, Seat of Wisdom, Tower of Ivory, Mystical Rose, Queen of the Apostles, Martyrs and all the Saints, Mother Undefiled, pray for us. White Rose of Purity, Winsome One, the Daintiest Jewel that God hath ever made, Great Casket of Mysteries, Princess Fair, that death may be but a prelude to thy kiss, amen.

Then she gets dressed and goes upstairs to wash her tongue before everyone gets home.

She has set the table for supper by the time Lily and Frances arrive rather late from Brownies and Guides. Lily goes straight up to the bathroom to launder her uniform and woolen stockings "for a cleanliness badge." Frances goes straight to bed to avoid the meal. No one has invented a badge for that yet. Mercedes tells Daddy that Frances is "indisposed" knowing he will not inquire further. Lies like that are not a sin, they are a sacrifice. Mercedes goes upstairs to get Lily.

Lily is kneeling barefoot at the tub which is how Mercedes notices that the wound on her left heel has reopened. That's not good. It's two weeks now since Armistice Day. Mercedes wrings out Lily's Brownie uniform and soaks the bad foot in warm salt water.

"We'll have the doctor look at it tomorrow."

Lily has noticed something different about Mercedes lately. For example, now—her movements. They've gone . . . glidy. Mercedes gets a clean dressing from the cabinet. She binds the wound gently and efficiently, not too tight this time, so why does Lily feel frightened as she watches the white cloth go round and round and round her little foot?

"There."

"Thank you, Mercedes."

Mercedes smiles at Lily with the peace that penance brings. Lily makes her mouth stretch east and west simultaneously. And again she feels a little scared because Mercedes' smile is the kind of smile you figure must be meant for the person standing behind you, but behind you is the wall.

They have sardines on toast for supper since no one is very hungry tonight.

★   ★   ★

When Lily crawls into bed, Frances is already asleep. And soon, so is Lily.

It's Ambrose. Standing at the foot of her bed, looking down at her the way he does. Lily is in that place again between the lines. This time she looks at him carefully. His wide green eyes, wincing even in this dim light. High smooth forehead with the hint of a bump. His pale body, green shadows drowned beneath his skin. Ivory belly, strange soft segments nestled between his thighs. Hairless but for his head of fine-spun angel orange.

Lily asks him, "Who are you?"

She is prepared for the flood but he does not open his mouth. Instead, he turns his palms to her. They are blank.

She asks him again, "Who are you?"

He opens his mouth and the water pours out but Lily stays in the in-between place and does not make a sound until she and the bed and Frances sleeping next to her are soaked. It's not so bad. The water is warm, having been inside him. When all the water is out of him, he is still looking, looking, his empty palms facing her.

She asks for the third time, "Who are you?"

Ambrose speaks his first words. He has a dark voice because he lives in a dark place. "I am No Man."

"Don't be afraid, Ambrose. Don't be afraid. We love you."

Ambrose says, "Hello."

"Hello," says Lily. "Hello, little boy. Hello."

Lily wakes up because Mercedes is sponging her head. "She's waking up."

"Ambrose," says Lily.

"She's delirious." Mercedes' voice feels like surgery on Lily's skin.

"Who took my skin?"

"Soaked with fever."

Lily buries her face in her drenched pillow because the light is an eye operation.

"The light is off, Lily, see? There's no light on."

Daddy has arrived with the doctor. It's a good sign that Lily's fever has broken, unless her temperature goes back up. Gangrene. Somewhere in the scalpel light Lily hears him talking to Daddy and her sisters, "You did the right thing, Mercedes." They'll have to keep an eye on her for the rest of the night, if her temp goes up, if it goes up . . . They go out into the hall, Lily can't hear them anymore except that Mercedes cries out something, then Frances comes back in and sings songs to Lily. Nice ones. Beautiful sad ones in minor keys, long story songs that our ancestors sang on the boats coming over in other languages.

That was midnight. At 3:30 A.M. Lily wakes up. There's a bright moon glazing the window. On either side, Frances and Mercedes are slumped in chairs under bedsheets lit like snowdrifts shadowed blue. It's Christmas Eve. The shepherds have fallen asleep beneath their flocks of snow. Lily sits up in bed. Her skin is no longer sore. She feels cool and calm, a midnight clear. She walks between the snowdrifts and their deep sleepers to the window because she has been invited. Oh, it's not the moon at all, there is no moon tonight, the light is coming from the creek.

Ambrose is in the creek. He is leaning out to wave, his left arm above his head, his right arm stretched along the lip of earth. His lower body is concealed by the embankment, he looks like a merman waving to Lily in the slow wide lullaby of the ocean, *hello* . . . His skin has changed from white to amber and the glow has wakened Lily from her bed of fire into soothing rose milk. She puts a hand to the window, *hello* . . . Ambrose is the drowned sun, he is the buried sunshine, he's saying, *come Lily, come. My sister. And I will heal you. A garden locked, a fountain sealed, many waters cannot quench me.* He says, *the spring in my garden pours down from Lebanon, come to me and I will give you rest.* And Lily says, *yes.* She is asleep but her heart is wakeful, *yes I'm coming, Ambrose. Wait for me, dear brother, I am coming.*

Lily leaves the snow sleepers by the window and walks down the stairs, through the kitchen, out the back door and over the coal clinks in the backyard in her bare feet, she shouldn't be able to walk at all with her wounded heel but there's no pain. Just the glow of Ambrose waiting for her in the creek, her big baby brother. He opens his arms. She goes to him. He picks her up in her white nightgown and cradles her, her head resting in the crook of his left shoulder, his right arm encircling her body. She has never felt so warm and peaceful, *are my eyes open or closed,* it doesn't matter. There is almost no sensory change between the air and the water, it takes her a moment to realize why she feels lighter now and even more tenderly embraced—it takes the sight of her own hair fanning out from her head and the thickening of the soft orange light to let her know that now she is under water, her cheek resting against his breast, her body curved around its first companion, *I would take you to my mother's house, to the room of she who conceived me*—Lily has never got used to being alone. They turn in the water and turn again, then Ambrose lifts her above the surface once more and the creek rains down from her. He lays her gently on the bank and her heart breaks. Her tears begin to flow because he is leaving—*don't go!* He sinks into the water on his back—*take me with you!* His body turns white again and shimmers into segments until all the pieces disappear. Lily lies face down at right angles to the creek, her head hanging over the edge, arms outstretched toward the spot where she last saw her brother.

That's how Mercedes finds her at 5:00 A.M., in the first snowfall of the season.

Mercedes blamed herself for the fever that was consuming Lily and might result in the loss of her leg or worse. That was why she went straight to the coal cellar after the doctor's visit. While Frances sang to Lily in the dark, Mercedes was naked under burlap, kneeling by the furnace, offering up her sacrifice to God.

She cups the lump of coal in both hands, elevates it and bows her head; "Through my fault." When she did this last week she was serene, a foolish smile on her lips. This time, however, she weeps hot tears. This time she is truly penitent. That was the problem the first time. Pride. She was proud of herself for staging her penance in the cellar, for establishing the Lourdes cocoa tin. She was pleased with herself as she bathed and bandaged Lily's foot with an expertise she thought surpassed that of the nurses at New Waterford General. Her piety was pride in the Devil's guise, her penitence nothing but a fresh occasion of sin, oh how often must we learn the same lesson? God reacted swiftly and smote Lily. "Through my fault," Mercedes can barely get out the words, and as she takes the first bite of coal, chews and swallows, sorrow overwhelms her. She is so bitterly aware of how she hurt God, and of how God in His infinite mercy has given her this second chance of which she is not worthy. "Through my most grievous fault." She takes another bite of coal. . . .

When Mercedes finished in the cellar, she rose shakily, changed back into her nightgown and went upstairs, where she washed the soot, snot and tears off her face, scrubbed her tongue as best she could, got her opal rosary and went in to keep watch on Lily. She fell asleep in a chair opposite

Frances. When she awoke for no reason at 4:55 A.M., Lily was gone. Mercedes obeyed an ancient reflex to look out the window and down at the creek.

The following evening, when Lily opens her eyes and looks into Mercedes' praying mouth, it occurs to her for the first time that she must be dreaming, because why has Mercedes got a black tongue?

Lily slept through extreme unction and she slept through the doctor saying no point even amputating the leg now, and was she in the habit of sleepwalking? She slept through Daddy laying his head on her chest and sobbing. She slept through Frances bribing and threatening God, "You bastard, I'll be good, okay? Just don't murder her and I won't smoke anymore, okay? I won't swear, I won't make my fuckin maniac father mad anymore, and I'll say the rosary ten times a day and be a goddamn nun, okay? Amen."

But what woke Lily were Mercedes' whispered prayers.

Lily asks, "How come you've got a black tongue, Mercedes?"

Mercedes cries, "Oh thank God—Daddy! Daddy!"

He swerves into the room—"Oh thank God"—and kneels next to Mercedes at Lily's bedside.

Lily says, "I'm hungry."

Daddy and Mercedes laugh and hug each other and thank God again. Frances loiters in the doorway and tells God, "There's no way I'm being a nun out of this."

Mercedes is careful to avoid the slightest idea of Lily's miraculous cure being at all connected with her own acts of contrition in the cellar. That would be inviting more of God's infinite mercy. So she is relieved when Lily offers an explanation of her own.

"Ambrose cured me. He washed me in the creek."

"Who's Ambrose?"

"He's my guardian angel."

Mercedes tells the priest. He nods but tells her that it is of the greatest importance not to be premature about these things. Rome requires more than an isolated event, while the laity require almost nothing to make a shrine out of a creek and a saint out of a ten-year-old girl. Best to keep quiet and watch for signs.

So Mercedes does. She tries not to dwell on the signs that are suddenly evident in retrospect: Lily's shriveled leg—saints are often stricken in childhood. Her pretty face—the mirror of her soul. The tragic circumstances of her birth—poor motherless child. Just imagine if Lily were revealed to have a healing power. Or if she were the instrument of a posthumous miracle by Bernadette at Lourdes. Mercedes does her best to chasten these thoughts, knowing from bitter experience how the Devil masquerades. He is a mocker and a mimic, a dealer in reflections and parallel lines. Just look at all the supposed saints the Church had to burn a few centuries ago. Saints and satanic vessels tend to start out the same way. You have to watch closely to see which force will rush in to claim the highly conductive soul of the candidate—for it is bound to be one or the other. Mercedes knows that if the Devil catches the slightest whiff of ambition on her part, he will come and get Lily.

But since Mercedes can't help but want Lily to be revealed as a saint, she tries to want it only for Daddy's sake. The ultimate vindication.

Frances doesn't need to tell Lily any more Ambrose stories after this because he has become Lily's story. Frances has finally succeeded in giving him to her. Lily is okay. For now. Frances can get on with other things. Her life.

She raids the Lourdes tin. She puts on her Girl Guide uniform and stows away in the Hupmobile. Once at James's still, she slides out and hides in the bushes till Leo Taylor's truck pulls up. She waits till he's finished loading and has returned to James to get his pay, then she makes a break from the trees to the truck, leaps into the back and disappears behind the crates and barrels.

"Thank you, Mr. Piper."

"All right, Leo. Drive safe."

Frances pokes her head out between the tarpaulin flaps and watches the Shore Road speed away beneath her. She turns and grins like a dog into the sunny sea wind, and lets her braids fly out behind her.

The truck slows when they reach Sydney and stops in the Coke Ovens section of Whitney Pier. She ducks as Taylor gets out, comes round, and undoes the tarps for his first delivery. When his broad back is turned, she hops out, lightening his load by an additional forty ounces. She waits behind a tar-smelling timber of the C.N. rail bridge until he drives away. Then she walks over to the run-down clapboard house and knocks at a big steel door.

> If I should take a notion,
> to jump in to the ocean,
> 't ain't nobody's business if I do, do, do, do . . .
>
> I swear I won't call no copper,
> if I'm beat up by my Poppa,
> 't ain't nobody's business if I do. . . .

Saturday, August 31, 1918
Dear Diary,

  I don't know where to begin. I have to get it all down now while it's fresh. I'm here under my tree in Central Park and we have all afternoon till supper-time. I'll have to go back a few days because despite all that whining about nothing ever happening,

  I realize now that tons was happening and it was all leading up to what I have to tell you which is EVERYTHING.

  . . . I have no shame in front of you, Diary, for you are me. You won't squirm, you can't be shocked, you know that nothing in love is nasty so I will try to be as free with you as I am in my own thoughts. Lest I forget, let me offer up a sincere orison of thanks for Giles. She is the least curious person on the face of the earth. Without her total lack of vigilance my life could never have got started. If Daddy knew what a lackadaisical gatekeeper she is he would be down here in a second to board me with the nuns. Which reminds me, I'd better write him. Oh but I'm teasing you, aren't I, Diary. You're in an agony of anticipation. Be still, open your heart, and I will begin at the beginning and unfold it for you as it unfolded for me. . . .

Book 5

DIARY OF A
LOST GIRL

Baby Burlesque

A SIX-INCH PANEL THWACKS OPEN and two brown eyes take aim at her beneath a single eyebrow. Frances holds up a bottle of James's finest. The panel slides closed and after a moment the steel door opens. Standing there is a big man. Wavy black hair, nose like a fist, arms like cannon, would-be olive skin but he obviously doesn't see much sunlight. Young and, Frances has to figure, dopey. He stares down at her blankly, blocking the inner gloom she is so longing to glimpse.

"Close the friggin door, Boutros, it's broad fuckin daylight, b'y."

A small man elbows the younger one aside and, with a glance not at Frances but over her shoulder, grabs her arm. "Get in, get in."

She's in.

The interior of the speakeasy lives down to its exterior. It's the only drab house in The Coke Ovens. Peeling gray paint, boarded windows, you'd have to know what you were looking for to find it because it appears deserted—with the exception of the upper story, where a few tired petunias and chewed marigolds cling to life in a window box overlooking the slag dump of Dominion Iron and Steel. Above is the train bridge. This is Railway Street.

Frances blinks into the dusty shadows and the room takes shape. Benches line the walls. Wallpaper strips with traces of lords and ladies flap from ceiling corners dingy with nicotine and neglect. On the floor, a genuine brass spittoon awash in brown slime, and several rusty tin cans that serve the same purpose. A pile of cigarette butts has been swept to the center of the floorboards. A makeshift bar—sheet of scrap metal on two oil drums—bottles and barrels, not a mirror, not a shot glass, no engravings of ships or trains, no regimental photo, no boxing heroes grace the walls. In the far corner stands a scarred player piano.

Frances looks into the taut sallow face of the small man. His black stubble matches his eyes.

"Who sent you, you're not selling cookies." He snickers. Frances feels suddenly ridiculous in her Girl Guide uniform, which she thought was the perfect disguise.

"It's a costume," she falters. "I'm a . . ."

"You're a what?"

She can't answer. Her eyebrows quiver. She's mad at herself—baby. Sooky baby, Frances. She bites her cheek and looks down.

"I asked you a question."

She looks up at him. He is something new. Not a nun, not a bad boy, not her father.

"Get outta here. Go on, beat it."

He shoves her toward the door, Frances stumbles and blurts out, "I'm an entertainer."

He stops and laughs, hands in his pockets—a mean mirthless laugh, his sharp tongue protruding past his lower lip as he jingles change with one hand. Beside him, big Boutros hasn't changed his expression—still just looking at her. Maybe going to jump me and won't give me no quarter neither, won't take no. Frances looks around, but there's nowhere to run. The dumb giant is planted between her and the door, why didn't she leave when the greasy little man told her to? Frances wants suddenly to high-tail it home to Lily and Mercedes.

"What's your name, kid?"

Frances says, "I have to go now. Sorry to bother you."

The little man gestures to her to "come here." Frances walks slowly back to him. He snatches the bottle from her hand. Everything about him is a coiled spring ready to pop you in the eye. Frances doesn't see him move, she's just suddenly sitting hard on her tailbone on one of the benches.

"Please, mister, I just want to go home."

"Come on, sweetheart, what's your name?"

Frances doesn't reply. He grips her chin between thumb and forefinger—she realizes he's stronger than he looks—he shakes her head till her neck burns. She starts to relax.

"You gonna be nice, now? Hey? You gonna answer me?"

This isn't so hard after all. "Fuck off," she says.

He seizes a fistful of her hair and yanks her back to her feet. Frances is elated at the power of the word, unleashed here for the first time on a grown-up. She laughs at him and spits, "Who do you think I am, look at the bottle, stupid."

He smacks her efficiently, one eye already on the label. He examines it, lips still parted and curled. He looks back at her and shakes his head slowly. Frances straightens her beret. The man tosses the bottle to Boutros without looking and asks her, "He know you're here?"

"No. But he will."

"Bullshit."

Frances just shrugs.

He repeats, "Bullshit, you tell him, he'll kill you—"

"He'll kill you second. You touched me." She puts her chin up and looks down her nose. "Daddy wouldn't like that."

The man considers this. Then he says, "Which one are you?"

"Frances."

He narrows his eyes. "What do you want, Frances?"

"A job."

He starts to laugh again but Frances just looks him steady in the eye. He shuts up and asks, "What can you do?"

"I can dance. I can sing and play piano."

He looks her up and down. "What else?"

She twists her mouth into a sneer she hopes is hard as nails. "I can do anything."

He gives a short chuckle. Then another, and nods. "You're all right, Frances." Without taking his eyes off her, he says to Boutros, "Say hello to your cousin, b'y." Frances looks up at Boutros. Concrete with eyeballs. She turns back to the small man. "What are you talking about?"

"I'm Jameel. I'm your uncle, doll."

That's when Frances sees, between yellow-gray curtains in the dusk of a rear doorway, a puffy woman staring at her in a way that shocks her. Only people who know me really well hate me like that. Who can she be? Then, with a sickening half-turn of her stomach, Frances identifies the other side of a coin she knew and loved so well.

"Camille, come here and meet your niece, dear," says Jameel.

But Camille just turns and disappears into the back room. Frances hears her slow heavy foot up the stairs. It's too horrible. Not these men, not the brown sputum in the cans, the butts on the floor, the stench of liquor and puke—but the fact that that hateful woman is Mumma's sister.

The following Saturday, without waiting for James to leave on his midnight rounds, Frances gets out of bed, puts on her Guide uniform, ties two sheets together, knots them and fastens one end to the radiator. She climbs out the window and rappels down the side of the house. Lily reels the ladder back in once Frances has landed safely. Lily will sleep fitfully till just before dawn in the expectation of hearing a cinder against the windowpane. In helping Frances, she has chosen the lesser of two evils: even though it's terrible not to know where Frances will spend the long night, it is more terrible still to picture what Frances's face will look like if Daddy catches her. "Please dear God, please let Ambrose look after Frances."

> Ain't she sweet? She's a' walkin down the street.
> Now I ask you very confidentially, ain't she sweet?

Well-off people purchase liquor discreetly and consume it in a civilized manner at home. Ordinary people pass the jar in a convivial kitchen. Loose pegs and young trouble-seekers come to Jameel's blind pig in the Pier to fight, play cards and pass out. Miners, merchant seamen and steelworkers, some as sweet and others as sour as soldiers. A few genuine formaldehyde drunks, the odd alienated contemplative just passing through, a vet with no visible injuries. No music—no one even cranks the old player piano. This place is not sufficiently jovial to inspire more than a caterwauling chorus at closing time. The clientele are white with the exception of one or two of the American sailors. Certainly no one is here from The Coke Ovens itself. There are no women. There are no tourists—this isn't Harlem. No slumming scions. Frances is the only fallen princess to have crossed the threshold. Her aunt Camille doesn't count because she is not here voluntarily. She stays upstairs until it's time to come down and empty the spittoons and swab the piss from the doorstep.

Frances arrives outside the steel door, takes a last breath of coke-oven air and enters the dim roar of the speak, passing under Boutros's arm as if it were a bridge. The air is palpable, not just with smoke but with the dark mass of male voices and limbs, work-soiled clothes, the smell of axle grease, sulphur and sweat. A shifting, pitching anchorage of hard dirty hulls in the night, and Frances swims among them without so much as a paddle or a spar. What would be more frightening? To be noticed and netted? Or accidentally crushed? She finds Jameel and gets up the nerve to order a drink in what she hopes is the voice of experience, impatient for her first real taste of sin. Jameel tells her to forget it and get to work.

She looks about. Work . . . No stage. No footlights. Certainly no hushed turning of heads at her approach to the piano. Where to begin? Frances wishes for a fairy godmother to swathe her in ostrich feathers; in breasts, hips, lips and lipstick—a husky contralto which she imagines to be Louise Brooks's voice. No such luck. Five foot nothing, flat as two bumps on an ironing board, hips like chopsticks—at sixteen Frances is as grown as she'll ever be. She stands before the piano since there's no stool. It's missing a few teeth, the rest are edged in decay, still others are intact but silent. Its pocked and yellowed music rolls date from a long-dead turn-of-the-century parlor.

Frances turns to the indifferent bass throng and feels her knees turning to water. To stop herself running away, she kicks up her heels in the fake tap dance that earned her so many pennies on the docks. No response. Not even a "boo"—she is invisible. A tobacco-streaked wad of mucus lands next to her shoe by chance. She gags briefly, closes her eyes, clenches her fists and wills herself into song, belting at the top of her narrow lungs, " 'Mademoiselle from Armentières, *parlez-vous?* Mademoiselle from Armentières, *parlez-vous?* Mademoiselle from Armentières, she hasn't been fucked in forty years, inky dinky *pa-arlez vou-ous.*' " To no avail. What is shocking in the schoolyard passes unnoticed at the speak.

She goes through her repertoire but it's no use. Who wants to look at a skinny Girl Guide doing a solo second-hand foxtrot picked up from the movie screen, never mind listen to her spindly kewpie-doll voice? Jameel doesn't. He wants her out on her ear. He grabs her neckerchief, she writhes free and, in a desperate last-ditch sally, lands on someone's knee and steals his drink—"Hey!"—she downs the shot, gasps in shock, then quips in moving-picture parlance, " 'Oh gee baby, how did the angels ever let you leave heaven?' " She weaves out of reach between slim hips and broad shoulders, steals another from a man with three jacks—"What do you think you're doin?"—and knocks it back, promising, " 'I've got what ain't in books,' " coughing, sputtering, blowing a kiss. Jameel follows with a bottle, calming the waters, signaling to Boutros "Get rid of her." When Frances has downed her third drink in quick succession from a " 'great big good-lookin some-account man,' " and is convinced that her esophagus and chest have been burned away, her feet suddenly sprout wings, they become hap-hap-happy, she cranks the player-piano. The mechanical thumping of a hobnail army renders "Coming thru' the Rye" and Frances wriggles out of her uniform and down to her skivvies via the highland fling cum cancan. They start watching.

On Monday, Frances skips school and heads for Satchel-Ass Chism's barber shop. She shows him a picture of Louise Brooks. He shakes his head.

"I don't know how to cut ladies' hair—"

"I'm not a lady."

"Listen, dear—"

She grabs his scissors, lops off one of her braids and says, "Now fix it."

"Lord love ya, girl!"

The other men glanced up from Chinese checkers at her entrance; they raised an eyebrow when she plopped down in the barber's chair, and now they grin at her. "That's the stuff."

Satchel-Ass shakes his head and does his best. "I don't know why you don't go into Sydney to a proper beauty parlor."

The checker players chuckle and lisp and call him "Pierre."

"I don't got time to be gallivanting off to Sydney," says Frances, savoring her new gun-moll grammar, "I got things to do."

Twenty minutes later she emerges onto Plummer Avenue, her head a bobbing mess of rusty bedsprings. Canada just got another sweetheart.

She swings into MacIsaac's Drugs and Confectionery. "Hello, Mr. MacIsaac, may I please have a packet of pins?"

"I like your haircut, Frances, it's right jazzy."

When he turns, she swipes a pack of Turkish tailor-made smokes. He hands her the pins along with a lemon drop and asks her, "What are your plans when you graduate next year, lass?"

"Why, I think I'll go in for teaching, Mr. MacIsaac. I believe it is most important that children get a good start in life, and that's what a good teacher can give them."

"You're smart, you girls. You've a gift, each and every one of you."

She pops the lemon drop into her mouth and leaves the pins on the counter.

She enters the schoolyard throng at morning recess. Frances has decided that today is her last day of school. If she isn't expelled after what she plans to do, then there's no justice. She lights a cigarette and looks around for the means to her end. Inside, Mercedes is washing a blackboard. She looks out the window to see her sister smoking right out in the open. And what on earth has Frances got on her head? A strange little cap . . . of hair. Good Lord. By the time Mercedes gets outside, Frances has taken off somewhere with Puss-Eye Murphy. What can she possibly want with poor sweet Puss-Eye?

Actually, "Puss-Eye" mutated into "Pious-Eye" some time ago, until now most people call him "Pius" or "Father Pie," so certain is everyone, including himself, of his priestly vocation. So Mercedes stands on the school porch, beating shammies against the stone steps, unable to shake an uneasy feeling, even though she knows that any girl would be perfectly safe with Cornelius "Father Pie" Murphy.

When the bell rings to signal the end of recess, Puss-Eye staggers from one of the derelict outhouses on the edge of the playground and runs sobbing through games of shinny, skipping ropes and hopscotch, across the street into the ballpark, all the way home. Why is he holding his crotch? Mercedes scans the sea of pupils for Frances and spots her strolling away from the outhouses. What in heaven's name has happened? Students pour up the steps and past Mercedes, speculating as to the nature of Frances Piper's latest crime—"Kicked him in the nuts." "Put a snake down his combinations." Mercedes watches till Frances is out of sight, then she takes a deep breath, collects her brushes and shammies and returns to class, hoping for the best.

That afternoon James receives a note from Sister Saint Eustace. Frances has been expelled.

Midway through supper, Frances arrives home and joins her family at the kitchen table. "Mmmm, boiled mush with mush."

Lily is amazed at the sight of Frances's shorn head but, before she can comment, James excuses her and Mercedes from the table. They set down their knives and forks and leave without a word. James stands and raises his hand. Frances doesn't wince. She doesn't even look up, none of her involuntary muscles contract in expectation. She just reaches for Lily's fork and starts eating. James lets his hand drop to his side. He says, suddenly tired, "Don't bring it home." She just chews. He carefully moves the plate out of her reach. "Do you hear me, Frances?"

She looks up, affecting good-natured distraction. "What's that?"

"If you're going to live here . . . whatever you get up to . . . keep it away from Lily."

Frances reaches for the plate and says, "Don't worry, Daddy."

He feels more than tired as he looks at her. The insolent face, the freshly hacked curls. Lost. And gone forever. What happened to her? My little Frances. James sighs. He can't think about all that right now. There's too much of it. It's too dark in there, and he doesn't have the energy. He watches her, elbows on the table, humming as she chews. Then he leaves without having laid a hand on her. She's as beat as she'll ever be.

Frances told Puss-Eye she needed his advice about a terrible sin someone had confessed to her. Once inside the darkness of the boonie with its antique reek, Frances knocked him down and, with a fistful of his hair and her knee gouging his breastbone, she jammed her other hand down his pants. She grabbed and jerked while he cried. The harder he got the harder he cried, he couldn't help either one and it didn't take long, he was only fifteen.

Frances wiped her hand on the floor and left. Mission accomplished. It's not like I hurt him or anything.

Puss-Eye's mother knew at the sight of him when he arrived home, he didn't have to say much except to name his attacker. His father was dead, lucky for Frances, and Petal was far away. Widow Murphy went to the school and told Sister Saint Eustace, in as few words as possible.

If there was any lingering faith on anyone's part that deep down Frances was good, it has been obliterated.

The next morning, Mercedes arrives at school early as usual and has just enough time before the bell to fill a bucket with soapy water and wash away the cinder scrawl on the side wall, "FRANCES PIPER BURN IN HELL."

Cheap Women 'n Cheatin' Men

Put another nickel in, in the nickelodeon,
all I want is having you and music, music, music.
I'd do anything for you, anything you'd want me to . . . ,
all I want is loving you and music, music, music.

NOW THAT THERE'S ENTERTAINMENT, men start bringing the occasional date to the speak. Jameel sets up a couple of tables. Puts on an apron. The women watch the show with varying degrees of disbelief, scorn or fascination while their men affect indifference. Frances has gutted the player piano of its music rolls and she hammers away at the keys, at first playing Mumma's old vaudeville music from the hope chest, and then by ear from the records that sailors bring her up from New York City.

Frances is a bizarre delta diva one night, warbling in her thin soprano, "Moonshine Blues" and "Shave 'em Dry." Declaring, an octave above the norm, " 'I can strut my pudding, spread my grease with ease, 'cause I know my onions, that's why I always please.' " The following Saturday will see her stripped from the waist up, wearing James's old horsehair war sporran as a wig, singing, "I'm Just Wild about Harry" in pidgin Arabic. She turns the freckle on her nose to an exclamation mark with a stroke of eyeliner, rouges her cheeks, paints on a cupid's-bow mouth and dances naked behind a homemade fan of seagull feathers, " 'I wish I could shimmy like my sister, Kate.' "

She invests her early profits in face paint and costumery. She'll start out as Valentino in a striped robe and turban. While one hand teases the

piano keys, she removes the robe to reveal Mata Hari in a haze of purple
and red. The seven veils come off one by one to "Scotland the Brave" and,
just in case anyone's in danger of getting more horny than amused, there's
always a surprise to wilt the wicked and stimulate the unsuspecting. For
example, she may strip down to a diaper, then stick her thumb in her
mouth. " 'Yes my heart belongs to Daddy, so I simply couldn't be
ba-ad. . . .' "

Her act is fueled by "jazzoline," for at first Frances takes most of her
pay in liquid form, till she gets wise. Drink is just a means to an end: it
inspires her one-woman follies, and it makes her untouchable when she
takes the men outside one by one. Because the real money is not in the
speak. It's out back.

Frances is a sealed letter. It doesn't matter where she's been or who's
pawed her, no one gets to handle the contents no matter how grimy the
envelope. And it's for sure no one's going to be able to steam her open.
Frances will bounce in your lap with your fly buttoned for as long as it
takes for two bucks. Expensive, but consider the overhead in wardrobe
alone. A hand job costs two-fifty—she has a special glove she wears, left
over from her first communion. Another fifty cents buys you patter, a
song, any name you want to hear. Touch her little chest and cough up an
extra buck; nothing below her belt. That's the menu, no substitutions. If
she laughs at you don't whack her or she'll holler for Boutros.

Frances starts to make money. Once she has acquired enough trinkets
and trash to keep her gussied, she starts saving her money in a secret place.
It's for Lily. Not for a "cure"—Frances does not subscribe to Mercedes'
devout yearnings. In fact, Frances is unsure why she is sure the money is for
Lily. She is putting it away "just in case." In case what? In case.

Frances remains a technical virgin throughout. What is she saving
herself for? She can't say. It's a feeling. There is something left for her to
do. "For Lily." What, Frances? Something.

Every night, when the last drunks are being peeled off the floor and
deposited outside, Frances passes through the tired curtains to the back
room and changes. One night, early in her career, she tiptoed up the back
stairs and discovered her Aunt Camille sitting in a kitchen, playing solitaire
under a dim yellow bulb. Again Frances was struck sad by the sullen heap
so like and unlike Mumma. Camille was too absorbed in her cards to
notice Frances peering around the doorjamb. Frances watched Camille sip
her tea and cheat.

Frances can't help but wonder how Camille wound up here, married to Jameel. But then, look where Mumma ended up. Maybe Camille eloped too. Frances's reflections on the subject of romance are summed up by the last scene of *Pandora's Box:* when Louise Brooks finally gives it away to a fella for free, he ups and kills her.

Frances has no desire to penetrate any further the shabby mystery of Aunt Camille, so she hasn't repeated her foray into the upper domestic reaches of the speak. Come closing time she removes her costume among the crates and kegs of the chilly back room and washes her face and hands at the pump. She never washes the costumes. She climbs into her beige woolen stockings, her black button boots, Girl Guide uniform and beret, and heads back to New Waterford.

Lily is always faithfully at the window, ready with the sheet, even though Daddy never gets home before Frances on weekends anymore. James doesn't want to be there when Frances "sneaks" in or out. He doesn't want to know where she goes. In the mornings he glances into her room, half expecting to find her gone. Run off with a man, perhaps. Perhaps dead in a ditch.

"Rapunzel, Rapunzel, let down your hair!" rasps Frances, and Lily lowers the knotted bedsheet. Frances is usually fairly sober by the time she climbs in the window, unless she has nicked a jar for the road.

"Want a sip, Lily?"

"No thank you."

"C'm'ere, dollface." Lily steps onto Frances's feet and they spin about while Frances sings, " 'Let's dance, though you've only a small room, make it your ballroom, let's dance'—"

Mercedes stands in the darkened doorway, spectral in her white nightgown.

"Join me in a nightcap, toots?"

"Frances, you're drunk."

Frances rattles, "The-sheet-is-slit-who-slit-the-sheet-whoever-slit-the-sheet-is-a-good-sheet-slitter. Say it fast, Lily."

"Frances, it's time to go to bed." Mercedes tries to sound calm and bossy at the same time.

"Piss on you, sister." Frances laughs.

Occasionally, if she's feeling up to it and Frances is sufficiently intoxicated, Mercedes will seize her round the waist, carry her to the waiting tub and bathe her forcibly, uniform and all. Otherwise Frances would not be fit to live with, for she only ever washes her face and hands. And she never washes her uniform. Mercedes rifles the Guide pouch in search of soiled hankies but finds only a dirty white glove.

"Where's your other glove, Frances?"

"I only use one."

"Oh. Well, it may as well be clean."

Mercedes wrings it under the hot water, asking, "Isn't it rather small for you now?"

"It does the trick."

Mercedes does not inquire further.

On relatively sober evenings, Frances curls up next to Lily and whispers whiskey in her ear: "Lily. We are the dead"—Lily pretends to be asleep—"except we don't know it. We think we're alive, but we're not. We all died the same time as Kathleen and we've been haunting the house ever since." Lily prays for everyone, in case Frances is right.

On quite sober evenings, Lily confides her fears.

"Frances, do I have to go to Lourdes?"

"No. You don't have to do anything you don't want to do."

Lily tucks her little foot between Frances's ankles.

"Frances. Al akbar inshallah?"

"In fallah inti itsy-bitsy spider."

"Ya koosa gingerbread boy kibbeh?"

"Shalom bi' salami."

"Aladdin bi' sesame."

"Bezella ya aini Beirut."

"Te'berini."

"Te'berini."

"Tipperary."

Every night, pissed or stone sober, Frances puts her money in the secret place for Lily.

Lady Bountiful

MERCEDES GRADUATES TOP OF the class of 1930. Ralph Luvovitz is second. Mercedes gives the valedictory address, in which she urges her fellow young citizens to learn from the mistakes of the past, to seize the numerous challenges of the present and to put their trust in God and His only begotten Son, Our Lord Jesus Christ, amen.

James sits near the back of the auditorium with Lily and the Luvovitzes. It's inadvisable for Frances to be seen near the school premises, so she is absent this evening, although earlier in the day Mercedes entered her bedroom to find a new boxed set of Morocco-bound *The Complete Charlotte Brontë* on her dresser. Oh, Frances! The expense. The dubious source of the requisite funds. The generosity. Mercedes cried and hugged Frances and told her she loved her. Frances told Mercedes not to leak all over her uniform.

After the commencement ceremonies, Mercedes, Lily and James repair to the Luvovitz house for tea. Lily wonders again, but does not ask, why all the mirrors are always covered in Mrs. Luv's house. Mercedes and Ralph play happy-sad klezmer music on piano and clarinet while Mr. Luvovitz sings and dances to the delighted embarrassment of Mrs. Luvovitz.

As Mercedes' and Ralph's heads incline closer over the old Yiddish songbook, Mr. and Mrs. L exchange complicated looks across the parlor. James doesn't notice—he simply enjoys the music, unaccustomedly re-laxed. A civilized evening with old friends. We should do this more often. He savors a feeling of normalcy for the first time in years. In the increasing absence of Frances, it has become possible for James, now and then, to feel like a good man.

"Have another *ruggalech,* James."

"Thank you, Ben, don't mind if I do. They're delicious, missus."

Ralph escorts them home and lingers on the veranda with Mercedes. He tells her he is going away. Not for good. They can write.

"Promise me you'll write, Mercedes."

"Of course I will, Ralph."

His parents have scrimped and saved to send him to McGill University in Montreal.

"I thought you were going to Saint F.X." Mercedes keeps her voice steady. Saint Francis Xavier University is only a day away by train. It's where she plans to go. When her family can spare her. But Montreal . . .

"It's a great opportunity."

"Of course it is, Ralph."

He's leaving next week, it's all very sudden. He's going to live with the Weintraubs, friends of his mother's relatives who recently emigrated from Munich. They've lined up a job for him in a bakery. Ralph is going to be a doctor. He is a scrupulous boy and so does not make any rash proposals of which he is as yet unworthy. He will wait until he has finished his undergraduate degree, then he will ask Mercedes to be his wife.

"Mercedes . . ."

"Yes, Ralph?"

Mercedes' heart beats so rapidly that she fears it has set the ruffles of her yellow silk blouse aflutter. Ralph leans abruptly down and brushes her lips with his own. Then he is away, leaving Mercedes breathless.

Upstairs, she cools her cheek against the scarlet leather of her brand-new edition of *Jane Eyre.*

Mercedes and Ralph exchange fervid newsy letters all that summer and through the fall. Their correspondence gives Mercedes strength to endure; to postpone the beginning of her life. She has turned down her scholarship to Saint Francis Xavier University, for how can she think of leaving home when Lily is still a child? Mercedes is so accustomed to doing everything for Daddy's sake that it seems natural to assign this sacrifice to him as well. But deep down another purpose has been emerging: Frances needs looking after. More than Daddy. More than Lily. What if I were far away at school in Antigonish and Frances didn't come home one night?

In the meantime, Mercedes is not at a loss for worthwhile work. She has her project: Lily. There have not been any more overt "signs" since the night of Lily's illness last November. Mercedes does not include—indeed tries not to notice—the reddish highlights that have since appeared in Lily's hair. And she reminds herself that miracles alone are not sufficient to indicate that special closeness to God which is sainthood; the Life too will be taken into account. To this end, she redoubles her charitable efforts with Lily in tow.

The abundance of free time on Mercedes' hands now that she is no longer at school dwindles to a pittance once she has scheduled the needs of her community. She learns a valuable lesson: if you think you are good, just try doing good. You'll soon find out how inadequate your little drop of goodness is. Especially in a mining town. Especially in the Depression.

Mercedes bends with grim determination to her mission—if it were enjoyable to immerse oneself in the malodorous misery of the less fortunate, it could not be counted a sacrifice. Offer it up for the poor souls in purgatory. And remember, time is of the essence: saints who are revealed in childhood rarely live to adulthood. Lily's life has already been painful and Mercedes expects it to be short. She prays. Lily need only survive to celebrate her fourteenth birthday. In the Lourdes tin there is almost thirty dollars.

Mercedes has observed Lily's particular gift with the veterans. On the top floor of the pleasant west wing of New Waterford General Hospital, there live a handful of men whose injuries and lack of family have rendered them permanent residents. Some have no arms or legs. Three were gassed—they are perfectly fine and whole other than their lungs. They sit quietly near the window wearing their oxygen masks till the sun goes down and it's time to lie perfectly still in their oxygen tents. Their eyes have enlarged and the lines have dropped away from around their mouths behind the masks. They look like big children—maybe that's why they like to see Lily coming. They are child grown-ups and she is a grown-up child.

Lily doesn't flinch when she meets the man with no face, just a blank stretch of baby skin with nose holes and a lipless mouth that doesn't quite close. He doesn't mask his missing face because he never goes out and everyone on the ward is used to him; what's more, he can't frighten himself, he has no eyes. His great pleasure is a cigarette and, now, touching Lily's face. He has found the bump in her forehead and it amuses him. He swears he was uglier before and shows Lily a picture to prove it. Lily agrees that he was putrid-looking and he laughs. Mercedes notes this as worthy of inclusion in The Life of Saint Lily, for Mercedes has never known this man to do more than grunt an obscenity, much less laugh.

Lily is not repelled by the veterans. She feels badly for them, they've been terribly hurt, but pity is a poison unction. Lily has experienced pity but she didn't know what to call it, she only knew it made her terribly afraid. As if she had disappeared and become a ghost. Having experienced her own disappearance, she is conscious of how important it is for people to be seen, so when she looks at them—even the blind one—she also looks *for* them, just in case they too have got lost and need finding.

They play gin rummy until she learns poker. The gas men are the only ones who never laugh, though they enjoy themselves.

On the way home, when Mercedes quizzes her, Lily always feels she has somehow let her sister down when she answers truthfully, "I had fun."

Every evening, when the day's ministrations are done, Mercedes indulges herself with a gloriously blank sheet of paper: "Dear Ralph . . ."

There are things Lily could tell Mercedes that would have quite another effect, but it never occurs to her to do so. For example, Mr. MacIsaac has stopped drinking. He tells Lily she has healed him. He tells her she has "the gift." It happened one day when Lily asked to see where he grew the medicine. Mr. MacIsaac took her back to his greenhouse.

Mr. MacIsaac is also a veteran, though of the Boer War. It too was a bad war. He has said there's no such thing as a good one. He and Lily both limp on the same side and he likes to tell her they'd run one heck of a three-legged race together. He tells her how like she is to her beautiful sister Kathleen, "God rest her soul." Especially now that the red is coming out in her hair. "Fairy hair" Mr. MacIsaac calls it, a twinkle in his kind bleary eye. "Don't worry, lass, that's a good thing."

They went through a canvas door into the greenhouse. The air was mysterious to breathe, damp like an underground lake. There were plants in boxes everywhere, each with a special power but none, it seemed, that could cure him.

But the miraculous thing was overhead. Lily looked up at the glass roof. The sun came out from behind a cloud and filtered through the tiny panes. Before her eyes a host took shape. Shadows of green and gray, a ghostly army in uniform, smiling down at her. Forever young.

Glass photographic plates. Mr. MacIsaac collected them—so many were discarded after the war, there being no demand for additional prints of such photos once their subjects had been killed.

"They're my children," he said. "We were never blessed with our own, so I think about all the people who lost theirs and how maybe I'd have lost mine too anyhow, things being what they were."

Mrs. MacIsaac had died early that year and people expected Mister to follow soon at the rate he was going, constantly quietly soused.

Lily said, "I'll be your child."

He laughed his wheezy laugh, then covered up his face. He reached for her hand and placed it on his bald head. After a while he gave her back her hand and looked up again. He asked her to do something for him.

"Whenever you pass by my door, say a Hail Mary for me. Will you do that?"

Lily promised she would, and she did. Still does. She didn't tell anyone because it seemed private. Soon people were saying it was a miracle that Mr. MacIsaac had quit the bottle. Even though there was barely a soul in town who didn't owe him money, there was no one who wouldn't rather see him spry behind his counter.

MacIsaac would live long enough to extend credit right through the Great Depression, and die a rich man on paper.

Lily did not feel disloyal to Daddy when she told Mr. MacIsaac she would be his child. Frances would say, "That's because Daddy's not your real father." But Lily knows he is. Just as she knows that it is possible to love everyone the most. Even if she can't help loving Frances most of all.

The Ginger Man

Jameel has been charging admission on show nights. He makes Boutros wear a fez. He has replaced the faded curtain with a beaded one. There are ashtrays. There are glasses. He ups the price of poison. He's still paying Frances a nickel a night. In September he has the nerve to demand a cut of her earnings from her private customers. What he gets is a new deal.

"Look, buddy, I've turned this dump into a cultural Mecca, so don't you be talking to me about cutting you in, you're cutting me in, pal, I'm in for fifty percent of the door or I walk and talk."

"Fuck you."

"Sixty."

"Forty."

"Auryvoir."

He grabs her arm. "Forty-five."

"Kiss my arse."

"Fifty."

"Gimme a light."

He lights her cigarette. "All right. You're in now, so if you foul up I'll cut your throat just like I would a man's."

"Get me a decent piano in here."

Boutros neither confirms nor denies Jameel's threat, he just counts out half the evening's admissions and hands it over to Frances.

"Hey Boutros," she says. "I didn't know you could count, b'y." She winks at him and heads for the back room to change out of her diaper and merry widow.

In a place like this it's best to get a man's status—the threat of throat-cutting and only throat-cutting simplifies a woman's survival. Frances trades in her coins and two-dollar bills for larger notes at the bank in order to fit it all into her hiding place.

When the sweetheart of Whitney Pier turns seventeen there's a cake and presents and everything. The clientele, which has grown more checkered along with Frances's reputation, sings "Happy Birthday." A woman whom Frances calls "The Countess" because she looks like the lesbian in *Pandora's Box* gives her a one-way ticket to Boston. The Countess has got a big education and some kind of setup down there—she's described it to Frances a thousand times but Frances, though she keeps her eyeballs pointing in the same direction no matter how much she's had to drink, still can't get it straight whether this woman runs a nightclub or a home for wayward girls. "My intentions are entirely honorable, Fanny," says The Countess, at which Frances yawns in her face and winks. A stoker named Henry gives Frances the latest Bessie Smith, "Black Mountain Blues." She gives him a big sloppy kiss, then holds her hand out for a quarter, and everyone laughs. Archie "White-Socks" MacGillicuddy, who everybody knows is a sissyboy, comes wearing his thing outside his pants gaily gift-wrapped with a bow and a tag, "For Frances." Frances tells Boutros to open it for her, "Go on, Buttress, good things come in small packages." Boutros declines. Leo Taylor shows up at the front door in time to see Jameel parading through the crowd bearing a pint-size painted whore with a parasol on his shoulders. Taylor yells over the din, "Mr. Jameel, I got what you ordered."

Jameel sets Frances down and numerous hands cover her eyes before she can turn around, "Who toined out the lights?!" Boutros leaves with Taylor. After a few moments they return, veins bulging in their necks, inching a good-as-new upright piano through the door.

Taylor delivers the booze on weekday afternoons so he has never seen the place in action, which has been just fine by him. He dislikes drunks, and prostitutes dismay him—they are all someone's daughter. This one is small enough to be a child but surely that's impossible—he is just as glad that her face is obscured by someone's hands. There's no missing the oversize red ringlets of her wig, however, or her hands spinning the parasol—lily white to the wrists, where two sleeves of grime begin. Grime that has accumulated through contact with nothing but time. And he can't avoid her scent as he sets down his end of the piano before her. She smells like a neglected baby, that sad sour-milk pee-stain smell. Taylor leaves and comes back with a piano stool, but she's already seated with her back to him, demurely rendering "Let Me Call You Sweetheart." It disturbs him: such a little-girl voice.

Frances doesn't miss a sweet beat as Boutros gets up off his hands and knees and is replaced by the stool.

Leo Taylor leaves feeling a bit sick. The steel door closes behind him and he hears the piano become a pie-anny as schmaltz transmogrifies to boogie. He steps up into his truck and starts the engine. He would like to go home and kiss his wife and kids again for the road but there's no time. Along with liquor, he's hauling live lobsters to New York City for all the fine old families and newly minted gangsters who can afford them.

He points his truck south on Highway 4 and conjures his wife's voice and image to keep him company. He calls up every precious detail: rusty wire hair, dark brown freckles across her light brown face, sharpshooter eyes. Lean and mean, it makes him chuckle. They commune all the way to the Strait of Canso, till he's off the island and he figures he ought to let her get some sleep. "Good night, Addy," he says, smiling at how she'd raz him for his sappiness if she could see him chatting to her out loud in his truck as it rolls onto the ferryboat. He sees her wry smile as she reaches up to kiss him, "Good night, Ginger," she says. "Drive safe, baby."

Leo Taylor is not called Ginger because he is a light black man. He is dark like his sister, Teresa. He is called Ginger because he brews real ginger beer from a West Indian recipe passed to him by his mother, Clarisse. Clarisse used to sell it but Ginger can afford to give it away as a treat. He has the strong arms and soft belly of a happy man. He often counts his blessings, wondering how he got so lucky in life. A good job, healthy beautiful children and a tough wife.

That night, Frances crawls into bed next to Lily as usual but before long awakens from another nightmare. There are dreams Frances is used to by now, like the one where she gives her own amputated leg to Lily but it's the wrong size. There are dreams she'll never get used to, where she puts Lily in the oven by mistake and cooks her but Mumma doesn't seem to notice that the roast is Lily and neither does anyone else at the table. But tonight Frances awakens with her throat constricted in a silent scream— Mumma in the garden on the scarecrow stick, wearing the old fedora and one of her baggy flowered dresses all crusty down the front, and she's holding the steak-and-kidney-pie scissors with a bit of pink gristle hanging off. But the worst part is she has no face. Mumma!—

Frances is determined not to watch to the end of this silent picture, in case it becomes a talkie. She needs to sleep in a place of no dreams. A place both empty and utterly silent. The attic, being in a state of permanent shock, is both.

Trixie follows as Frances drags a blanket and a pile of cushions across the hall to the door of the attic stairs. She opens the door, but both she and Trixie hesitate. The problem is that, although the attic is not haunted, the stairs leading up to it are.

Frances stands barefoot at the bottom looking up into the narrow passage. She feels a tightness at her scalp as though she still had braids. In the darkness, her body distends and contracts wildly as though she were an elastic band—suddenly ten feet long and curved, then very small like a young child. "I forgot to put my housecoat on"—Frances sees her green tartan housecoat in her mind, "but that's silly because I haven't had that housecoat since Mercedes and I were little and everything matched." Frances is on the first step. A wet chill down her spine restores her body to its normal size and she is seized with fear because she can hear voices. Just below the water, they are still fish voices but they are bubbling to the surface, in a moment she will understand what they are saying. Frances starts babbling quietly with her hands over her ears and forces herself onto the second step. Damp shadows slipper by, Kathleen is up there. No she isn't, that's just the kittens, *stop*—they have to be baptized—*don't*— "who's the killer?!"—*don't*—"you're the Devil!"—*don't, don't, don't, don't,* all the way up the stairs till she gets to the top and opens the door.

Arriving in the attic is like arriving in the desert after almost drowning. She closes the door behind her. Trixie leaps silently onto the window ledge. Frances lies on the floor. She closes her eyes and sleeps deeply and blankly, no longer any need to fear death by dreaming.

Frances awakens the next day more sober than she's been in almost a year. She finds a train ticket to Boston in her Guide pouch but doesn't remember how it got there. She goes to the station in Sydney and scalps it for cash. She has no intention of leaving the island until she has made enough money for Lily. And accomplished something else too. What, Frances? Something. She will know it when she sees it. She is a commando in training for a mission so secret that even she does not know what it is. But she is ready. Every night the obstacle course. Maneuvering behind the lines. Camouflaged to blend with the terrain.

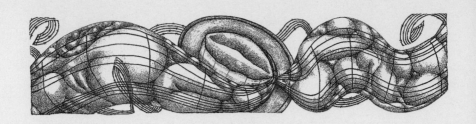

Your voice is sad whene'er you speak . . .

The night before the war ends, Kathleen unties an emerald sash from around the waist of her scandalous new dress of pale green silk chiffon, and winds it round and round the brim of her lover's charcoal fedora. She runs her hands up the diamond-studded shirt front and slips her thigh between the stripes of the wide black-and-tan pant legs.

There are mixed clubs they can go to uptown. And there is a private place in Central Park. They have to be careful, but it's hard. They are so young, they forget that the world is not as in love with them as they are.

And tears bedim your loving eyes. . . .

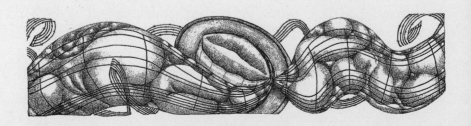

Book 6

THE GIRL GUIDE

Don't Whine

BY MAY 1931, MERCEDES is downright worried. She hasn't heard from Ralph in eight weeks. She won't ask Mrs. Luvovitz about him because it is unladylike for a girl to seem to be pursuing a boy, and Mercedes doesn't want to appear "fast"—especially in the eyes of her future mother-in-law. And besides, if Ralph were in trouble his parents would know, and they appear to be quite unperturbed. Nonetheless, Mercedes drops into Luvovitz's Kosher Canadian several times a week, the darnedest items having slipped her mind—"Oh, Mrs. Luvovitz, would you believe I forgot to pick up a pound of blood pudding for Daddy."

One Thursday afternoon, Mercedes returns to Luvovitz's to buy a box of salt she forgot that morning. As Mrs. Luvovitz rings up the purchase she smiles a little oddly at Mercedes and inquires, "Well now. And how's your father, dear?"

"Oh he's well, Mrs. Luvovitz, thank you."

The two of them nod and smile at each other yet neither makes a move to leave. Mercedes asks, "And how's Mr. Luvovitz?"

"Oh you know Mister, he's grand, dear, just grand."

Mercedes chuckles and nods.

Mrs. Luvovitz asks, "How are your sisters?"

"Lily is grand, thank you, and Frances seems—well, I worry a little about Frances, she's . . . still finding herself, you know . . ."

"We all worry, dear, but she's a—deep down, you know, she's fine."

"Thank you, yes."

Mrs. Luvovitz reaches for a tin of Ovaltine and hands it to Mercedes. "Have you ever tried this? This we get from England."

"Oh, really? No, I never have."

"Here, try it, you'll like it."

"Oh"—Mercedes reddens and reaches for her purse, unsure as to— but Mrs. Luvovitz places a hand on hers and, in the familiar scolding voice that puts Mercedes back at ease, "Ay-yay-yay, what do you think you're doing, put your money away now."

Mercedes says, "Thank you very much, Mrs. Luvovitz, that's awfully nice of you," and feels foolish, aware she must be thanking Mrs. Luvovitz rather too profusely because Mrs. Luv's smile has turned a bit pink. In fact Mercedes has never before seen such a sustained smile on the dear lady's face. Mercedes smiles back, longing to ask, "Have you heard from Ralph?" Instead she thanks Mrs. Luvovitz once again and turns to leave, but Mrs. Luvovitz pipes up, "Have you heard from Ralph?"

Mercedes turns back. Now she is truly worried. "No I haven't, oh dear—"

"He's fine, he's fine, our friends write he's fine, he's perfect, it's just—"

"Oh, well, that is good news—"

"We haven't had a letter from him and I wondered—"

"Oh dear." They look at one another a moment, then Mercedes shakes her head. "I'm afraid I haven't had one in quite some time either."

Mercedes is both bewildered and embarrassed by what follows. Mrs. Luvovitz squeezes Mercedes' hands between her own and says, with her chin wrinkled in a smile against tears, "You're a good girl, Mercedes, a wonderful girl."

"Thank you, Mrs. Luvovitz." Mercedes drops the Ovaltine into her net bag and almost forgets the salt, adding, "I'll let you know as soon as I've heard from Ralph."

But Mrs. Luvovitz has turned back to the shelves and is carefully straightening a box of steel wool.

Three weeks later, the longed-for letter arrives. Mercedes carries it up to her room, taking the stairs an unaccustomed two at a time. She flings herself onto her bed, kissing the envelope before her head hits the pillow, and spends a moment lying on her side just caressing the seal. Dear Ralph. His features have smoothed and his voice has deepened in her mind over these past many months. She sighs, catches sight of her red cheeks in her dresser mirror and commands, "Don't be such a silly chit, Mrs. Ralph

Luvovitz"—which makes her giggle and she hugs her pillow and buries her face in it at the same time. Finally she composes herself enough to open the letter. "Dear Mercedes"—dear Ralph—"I feel conceited even writing this to you because you are such a swell girl and could have any fellow in the world instead of settling for me anyhow, but I feel I had better say it because maybe you'll think I'm a coward if I don't. Here goes. I am terribly sorry if I ever led you to expect . . ."

When Mercedes can get up, she crosses to her dresser and removes Ralph's picture from the frame to reveal the poem with which she replaced Valentino's picture almost five years ago. She returns to her bed and sits perfectly still, willing all her leaping blood back to low tide until, even if she tried, she could not so much as make a fist. Little by little her temperature drops as she stares at the words of wisdom in the frame, erasing Ralph.

By evening she is perfectly calm. Lucid, in fact, for the first time since she conceived her little crush on the grocer's son. A Hebrew. Heavens. Meanwhile there are those who need me whom I have neglected.

Mercedes walks downstairs with her head perfectly balanced on her neck, one hand lightly gracing the balustrade. Tonight Frances will get a bath, no two ways about it. Mercedes enters the kitchen, goes directly to the Lourdes tin and counts the money. Hmm. We'll have to do better than that, now won't we? She lights a burner on the stove and dispatches the crumpled photograph of the boy with sticking-out ears. She cooks a large supper for Daddy. It pains her to realize how she has neglected her culinary duties of late. And Daddy is so kind about it, saying only, "I'll pick up some cold cuts on the way home, Mercedes, don't you go to any trouble." Mercedes plans to keep the table groaning from now on. Poor Daddy.

Mercedes has told no one of the letter, so when Mr. and Mrs. Luvovitz drive into Sydney for the joyous reunion with their son early in June they are unprepared to meet his wife. Marie-Josée is petite and plump in just the right way. Dark and pretty. Catholic and pregnant. This dire accident in no way obscures the fact that she and Ralph are very much in love.

DON'T WHINE

Today I saw a lovely girl with golden hair,
envied her and wished I were so fair.
When she rose to go, she hobbled down the aisle.
She had one leg, wore a crutch and a smile.
Oh God forgive me when I whine
I have two legs, the world is mine.

Then I stopped to buy some sweets.
The lad who sold them had such charm.
I talked with him—my being late was no harm.
As I left he said to me, "You've been so kind.
You see," he said, "I am blind."
Oh God forgive me when I whine
I have two eyes, the world is mine.

Later, I saw a child with eyes of blue.
Watching others play, not knowing what to do.
"Why don't you join the others, dear."
He stared ahead, he could not hear.
Oh God forgive me when I whine. . . .

AUTHOR UNKNOWN

Dark Ladies

FRANCES IS CHANGING INTO her Guide uniform in the freezing back room of the speak one March night in 1932. Although she feels the cold more than many people, she welcomes it because it makes her outfits seem so fresh. Tonight she gets a bit of a start: a flaccid female voice plops against her like a jellyfish, "You're no good."

Frances looks up. The darker patch of gloom is unmistakably Camille.

"Oh hi, Aunt Camille."

"You're trash."

Frances pulls on her ripe woolen stockings. "We're all sisters under the mink, honey."

"Why don't you kill yourself."

Frances bursts out laughing and leaves.

At first glance, in her Guide uniform, it's hard to believe Frances is eighteen and not a child of twelve. At second glance, it's hard to believe Frances was ever a child. Camille watches her go and wonders, what did my sister ever do to deserve that? But then, what did I ever do to deserve my life?

When Mahmoud's eldest daughter Materia ran off with the *enklese* bastard, Mahmoud gave his second eldest daughter to Tommy Jameel, thinking that his being Lebanese was enough. It was not enough. Mahmoud knows that now; Jameel is no son-in-law of his.

Luckily there were three daughters left so he was able to make up for the first two. They're all happy. Two married nice Lebanese Canadian boys from Sydney and the youngest married a doctor—*enklese,* but a good one. And his sons all married well: three got wives from the Old Country, which is ideal. Three married Canadian girls: one Lebanese, two Acadian. One son is a priest, God is great. That makes forty grandchildren so far, twenty-four of whom are Mahmouds, and fifteen of those are male. *Mneshkor allah.*

Camille could have had her pick of husbands. She really was the most beautiful in that many-sons sort of way. She could have been Camille MacNeil, Camille Shebib or Camille Stubinski. Instead she is Camille Jameel. She doesn't blame Pa—Pa she reveres. And how could she blame Materia, whom she idolized? So she hates Frances, the slut who lives only to dishonor the memory of poor Materia.

Camille is a simple woman who wanted a simple life. Instead she got a complicated one. She giggled and batted her eyelashes and where did it get her? Jameel's gin joint. Pa gave Jameel a big dowry, God only knows where that money went. Camille is not talented. She would have been good at the things she was raised to be good at. The world should not be organized to require heroines, and when one is required but fails to appear we should not judge. We should just say, poor Camille, she turned into a bitch the way most people would have—and stay out of her way.

In her heart, though, there is still expectation. A clearing in the woods. Not when she looks at her five sons, who were absorbed by their father as soon as they were big enough to carry a crate or run with a message. Not when she looks at her husband, who never even bothered to shave on their wedding night—he examined himself and the bedsheet right after to make sure he hadn't been cheated. No. The clearing in her heart is where Camille pauses like a deer, and waits for Pa to see her.

The following night, the inky specter waits once again in the back room. Frances actually gets a bit nervous—Camille is the type of woman who sits like a lump, then picks up an ax one day.

"Hi, Aunt Camille, what can I do for ya?"

"You're shit."

"My, that's a lovely ensemble you're wearing."

"You're a disgrace to my father."

"How's he doing, I keep meaning to drop by."

"You're not fit to set foot in my father's house."

Frances snaps shut her bulging Guide pouch and leaves. Camille has just given her an idea.

★   ★   ★

The address is in the phone book. Frances finds her way to a house on the hill. She flits from hedge to tree. From shrub to side wall—the coal chute is just big enough for a child. Once she is inside her grandfather's house, there are quite a number of secret vantage points. And plenty to steal, one hardly knows where to begin.

There's a grate on the inside wall of the opulent front room. Frances's face can often be seen there through wrought-iron vines, but no one ever thinks to look. The closet beneath the stairs is full of soft dark things. When its door stands open a crack it is possible to discern a thin white stripe interrupting the sliver of gloom. That's Frances peeking out. Hands seeking furs and shawls have brushed right past her curls, hardly pausing to register them as just so much more mouton. And if, one night, the occupant of the master bedroom upstairs awoke and looked under the bed for no reason, he might see her lying there with her arms folded across her chest, staring up at the spot where his heart sleeps. That is, if she is not peering at him through the brass bars at the foot of the bed.

Frances drinks in her grandfather's long lean frame, his skin the tone and supple texture of aged deer-hide. She can't see Mumma anywhere but in the color of him, in the liquid ebony of the eyes—though his are sharp—and the waviness of the steel-gray hair. She is pierced with a sudden longing for her grandmother and wonders how it is possible to miss what you never had. She is surprised to locate one family resemblance, however: there is something of Mercedes in the angles of Mahmoud's body, his carriage and immutable spine. Frances concludes, not for the first time, that she herself is a changeling.

She always brings back a present for Lily. A sterling silver tail comb with tortoiseshell teeth. A moonstone ring. A braid.

Lily strokes the dry black braid as though it were a creature prone to sudden death by fright.

"It was Mumma's," says Frances.

"Can I keep it?"

"It's yours."

"Where did you get it?"

"I found a trapdoor like in *Arabian Nights*. It leads to an underground garden. There's everything you can think of down there just growing on the trees. Jewels, hair . . . And babies that haven't been born yet."

Lily assumes this is Frances's way of talking about the old French mine. She doesn't like to think of Frances there alone, looking for treasure. Robbing the dead. Lily begs to accompany her but Frances says the Arabian garden is a "solo mission." When Frances brings Lily back a single pearl, however, Lily starts to worry because it means that Frances has been diving. She is afraid Frances might decide to drown in the pool at the old French mine. Lily knows how tempting it can be to breathe water so she asks Ambrose to watch over Frances. Please, dear brother, deliver our dearest Frances from drowning as you delivered me.

The first time Frances stayed out all night, Mercedes was frantic. She changed in and out of her nightgown, wrung her hands and several times was halfway out the front door—but with no idea where to search she soon returned to her vigil at the kitchen table. Besides, what if Frances should telephone while she was out?

Mercedes did her fretting silently so as not to worry Daddy, who was in a much-needed and uncharacteristically deep sleep in the wingback chair. In the morning, Lily came down to find Mercedes peeling onions at the kitchen table.

"What are you cooking, Mercedes?"

"Nothing, Lily, go back to bed."

"It's morning. . . . Is Frances home yet?"

Mercedes wiped her eyes with her onion hand by mistake and found herself unable to do anything but gulp.

"Mercedes—"

"I'm just slicing onions, Lily, don't be foolish."

"Don't worry about Frances, Mercedes, I asked Ambrose to look after her."

Mercedes seized Lily and hugged her. Lily felt something hard pressing across her spine—Mercedes had forgotten to put down the paring knife—but Lily was too polite to say anything. James came into the kitchen rubbing his hands together, refreshed despite a night in a chair in his clothes, "Who feels like bacon and eggs? I'll cook."

"Oh Daddy," said Mercedes, "don't worry about Frances, she's sure to turn up."

And she did, that afternoon, with a tiny carved ballerina for Lily.

Now Mercedes has ceased to worry when Frances disappears like a cat for days, confident that she is being watched over through the special intercessions of Lily. Mercedes puts it down as another sign and adds it to the lengthening report she will one day soon make to the bishop.

Mahmoud never misses the braid because he has no idea it survived the Materia purge. Frances found it under the red velvet lining at the bottom of Giselle's jewelry box. It was a close call.

Mahmoud was in bed and out like a light at the other end of the room. Frances stood at her late grandmother's vanity and surveyed the loot laid out before her. Silver brushes, combs and hand mirrors. A rosewood jewelry box. She lifted the lid and up struck a hurdy-gurdy orchestra along with a pink ballerina. Frances shut the box instantly and turned back toward Mahmoud, who groaned, rolled over and looked straight at her. They just stayed like that, staring at each other, until she realized he was still asleep. She waved at him. She gave him the finger. She returned to the jewelry box and opened it a hairbreadth—yes, now she could see the little dancer lying flat on its face. Frances slipped a finger through the crack and pinned the thing in dead-swan position while she opened and plundered the box. She checked for a false bottom in case of cash, lifting the red velvet lining, and that was how she stumbled upon the black braid lying coiled in its jewelled nest. It must have been Mumma's because why else would it be hidden? Artifacts of lost girls are always forbidden. Frances stuffed the braid and the jewels into her Guide pouch leaving only a strand of genuine pearls. She extracted the ballerina by its roots, little red bits of velvet trailing from its pointed feet. She considered laying it on Mahmoud's pillow like an eldritch gift from the tooth fairy, but decided Lily might like to have it. Finally, she picked up the strand of pearls and carefully severed its string with her teeth. She removed one pearl, then coiled the rest back into the otherwise empty rosewood box and tiptoed from the room with her booty.

What Frances really wishes she could steal or be stolen by, however, is Teresa, who still works for Mahmoud. Teresa of the black and white candy. Queen Teresa, disguised as a maid. Frances is not fooled by her big purse and simple dress. It almost seems vain for someone with a face like Teresa's to dress in clothes so humble that they serve only to highlight the beauty of the wearer. When Frances first spied Teresa letting herself in through the kitchen door with her own key she had the wild certainty that Teresa was now Mrs. Mahmoud—my step-grandmother! But Teresa left at six that evening, having set out Mahmoud's supper, and Frances realized she had her own home to go to—with lucky children in it, no doubt.

There's a kitchen door to the cellar and Frances loves to sit behind its splinter of light and watch Teresa work. She does this for hours, until she turns into the dough that Teresa is kneading, or the glass that Teresa pours milk into, or the apron that she wipes her hands on. It's so peaceful that one time Frances fell asleep and tumbled all the way down the cellar steps. She hid when Teresa came down to see what the commotion was, and even though Frances was longing to say, "It's me, I hurt myself," all she said was, "Meow."

One day, a man comes and eats lunch at the kitchen table while Teresa works. His name is Ginger—"Come on in, Ginger, darlin." He is her darling but not her husband—Teresa calls to Mahmoud in the living room, "My brother's here, sir." Ginger wears overalls but he's not a miner, he's too healthy-looking. Frances recognizes him right away—he is the one who used to drive Kathleen back and forth to school in a black Model T Ford. He dropped off Kathleen the day Teresa gave Frances the black and white striped candy. He called to Teresa and they drove away together and Kathleen took Frances's candy and threw it into the creek. Frances even remembers what they had for supper that night—steak-and-kidney pie. Frances wonders why stupid details like supper stick in her mind when there are other things that she'd give anything to remember, like the last time she felt her mother's touch.

Mr. Mahmoud comes in while Ginger is there and says, "Hello, Leo"—and Frances nearly loses her balance on the steps again, jolted by the collision of two men in her mind. Frances sees the name stenciled on the back of the booze truck, parked out front of James's still, then the truck dissolves into the Model T Ford but the stenciled name remains: "Leo Taylor Transport."

He says, "Hello, Mr. Mahmoud."

Mahmoud asks in his dusky accent, "Have you got my special order?"

"I sure do, Mr. Mahmoud, and strong like you like it."

The surprise of recognizing Leo Taylor outweighs the surprise of seeing her grandfather guzzle a brown bottle of "special order." Frances would never have pegged him for a drinker. He isn't, of course, it's only ginger beer. And when Teresa pours out glasses for herself and her brother, Frances realizes that, along with the fact that she too is thirsty. When she watches the fizzy gold slide past Teresa's lips and ripple down her throat, Frances feels a craving. Leo Taylor sips his slowly.

Frances watches and remembers when she told Lily that her real daddy was a black man from The Coke Ovens. It was Leo Taylor she was thinking of, having seen him at James's still. She told Lily this story in order to find out if it was true. Like the old orange-cat story—how it smothered Ambrose, and Daddy buried it in the garden. Like the story of how Mumma drowned Ambrose in the creek, and the one about the old French mine. Frances needs to say a story out loud to divine how much truth runs beneath its surface.

On her narrow journeys up the attic stairs by night Frances has seen a picture she did not know she owned: Kathleen with a black-red stomach, sweaty hair, two tiny babies alive between her knees. There is no one else in the picture except the person who is looking at it—*that must be me.* There is a voice way at the back of Frances's mind, hollering into a wind. She can't make it out yet, it's just a sighing sound, it's sighing a question. The question is, *how did the babies get in the creek, Frances?* The voice is getting closer. It's on the first step. Partly to drown the voice and partly to enlist help in traveling to meet it, Frances tells herself another story.

There at the top of her grandfather's cellar steps, behind the crack of the door, watching Teresa and her brother drink ginger beer, Frances murmurs aloud, quickly and under her breath like Mercedes saying the rosary: *Kathleen is Lily's mother, Ambrose drowned because we don't know why, Kathleen was not married, she had a tumor in her belly but she didn't really, there was a secret father, it was Ginger—he drove her and they fell in love on the way to school, that's why Daddy says don't play that colored music from the hope chest— he sent Kathleen to New York Town but Ginger followed in his truck, Daddy took her home again but it was too late, she died of twins—do you know the Ginger Man, the Ginger Man, the Ginger Man, do you know the Ginger Man he lives in Ginger Lane. Amen Lily and Ambrose.*

"Goodbye, Ginger honey," says Teresa at the kitchen door, "drive safe."

Teresa washes the glasses and Frances pads away down the cellar steps. Part of her story is true. And part of it is true enough. Frances will find out where he lives and buy herself a case of ginger beer.

She shimmies up the coal chute and out into a stab of sunlight.

Ginger has seen a little girl on the Shore Road between New Waterford and Sydney. She strays along the edge of the ditch looking every place but where she's going. Why is she allowed to wander the highway alone like that and why is she not in school? Who's her father? Where's her mother? She always wears a Girl Guide uniform, which is strange because she doesn't look old enough to be a Girl Guide, more like a Brownie.

The third time Ginger passes, they're both traveling in the same direction and he slows down a little, thinking maybe to offer her a ride, but he decides against it, not wanting to frighten her. She looks up, though, at the slowing truck ahead, and he sees her face in the side mirror. It hurts him. Who would let their little girl walk the Shore Road alone day after day? He never would. He has three daughters: two Brownies and one Guide.

He shivers and drives on. He glances at the St. Christopher medal hanging from his rearview mirror. Ginger has never had an accident, he is a good driver, but lately he has felt funny about the road. He used to see it all at once and drive as naturally as blinking and breathing, but now it's as though he sees each piece of road individually the moment his wheels roll over it. To either side, each stone and tree stands separately, and he has lost the knack of expecting the road to unfurl around the bend. Driving is his living—he can't afford to be spooked.

Ever since his last trip to New York Ginger hasn't felt right. Never quite rested, or quite awake. It's as though a window has been left open inside his head, admitting a draft. He can't get to it to close it. But he can look out it, even though all he sees is fog. It rolls into his mind, obscuring his ease, setting him to shiver. Still, he looks and looks. Because out there in the fog he can feel something looking back at him.

His wife, Adelaide, knows there is something not right but how can Ginger explain to her what he cannot explain to himself? He heard some music in New York. That sounds crazy, he knows it, so the least he can do is keep it to himself. Can music cast a spell? Yes. Everyone knows that. And everyone would laugh at him if he said it out loud.

It was in a club up in Harlem. Ginger had time on his hands waiting for a shipment of dresses to haul back to Mahmoud's Department Store on

Pitt Street. Whenever Ginger is in a place that's filled with other black people it's as though he is relieved of a weight that he was unaware of until it came off him. He walked up Lenox Avenue feeling light. In Harlem Ginger felt happy but lonely too. Home and not home. He entered a small club on 135th Street that welcomed Negroes in the audience, not just on stage. A trio was playing quiet music for a quiet crowd. The whole scene was highly unusual. No floor show, no horns or hi-de-ho. Piano, bass and flute. Ginger stood and listened.

The piano player was at the core of the trio. A slim man with long fine fingers, hand-tooled wrists. So good that he had come to prefer playing between the music. This was not for everyone and the pianist hadn't had a new suit in a very long time. Threadbare trousers, white shirt open at the long handsome throat. A charcoal fedora angled low, and around its base a shimmering green silk band.

Three minutes or three hours later, Ginger recognized the number as "Honeysuckle Rose," but this did not prevent him from confusing his left arm with his right when he went to lift his glass of beer. The odd thing was, Ginger had homey taste in music. If it could be sung by the whole family, it was great by him. He certainly didn't claim to be any kind of connoisseur. And yet when the pianist allowed his fingers to settle like mist onto the keys for the next interstellar tune, Ginger had to stay and listen.

It was on the night drive back up to Cape Breton that he became aware of the fault line opening inside his head, and twice he had to remind himself to stop when the land ended: once because it was time to coast onto the ferry, and once again because he was home. He hugged Adelaide as though she were the first solid food he'd had in weeks.

Still, he hasn't been able to shake the unease, and sights like the lost little Girl Guide are bothering him perhaps even more than they normally would. The third time he sees her, Ginger means to tell Adelaide, but it slips his mind only to return that night in a dream. He sees the thin white face in the side mirror up close—the serious brown green eyes, one freckle on the nose. It still looks like a child, but an unspeakably old one. It is the saddest face he has ever seen. Ginger wakes up even though it's not a nightmare. For the first time it occurs to him that the little Girl Guide may be a ghost. What is she saying to him with her eyes? "Here is how I died. . . . Pray for me." Ginger wipes his face—it's wet but none of the rest of him is so it couldn't have been a night sweat. How strange. He goes and checks on all his children in their beds. When he returns he looks down at his rusty-haired wife, who appears ready for a fight even in her sleep. Thank God for Adelaide.

Ginger means to tell his sister Teresa about the little Girl Guide and about his dream the next day at lunch when he brings Mr. Mahmoud his ginger-beer treat, but again it slips his mind.

Jameel squints down at Frances. "What for?"

"Just tell me."

Frances has awakened him in the middle of the day, he's jaundiced as the sun.

"Why?"

"Because I'll burn your fuckin house down if you don't."

Jameel horks out last night's nicotine. "You just watch yourself, that's all I'm sayin, Leo Taylor's got a mean wife."

"It's not his wife I'm interested in."

"He lives in the purple house on Tupper Street."

Frances turns to leave; Jameel shakes his head and warns, "Just don't come cryin to me."

But she ignores him.

Ginger Taylor gets a jolt when he looks up from the shell in his youngest child's hand to see the little Girl Guide standing in his backyard staring at him. She is a ghost. What does she want?

"May I have some of your ginger beer?"

Adelaide comes to the back door. "What do you want?"

Frances looks up at her. The woman's reddish hair indicates to Frances the ability to see through people. Best not to answer.

Adelaide doesn't take her eyes off Frances. "Who is she, Ginger?"

"I don't know, honey." Then he turns back to Frances, "What's your name, little girl?"

Frances walks away. The child moves to follow her but Ginger picks him up.

Adelaide and Ginger watch Frances trail off down the alley, then Adelaide says, "That's not a little girl." And walks back into the house.

Salt

THE FIRST THING MAHMOUD notices is that one of the sterling combs is missing. That leads him to the rosewood jewelry box. He opens it. An empty metal post pops up and rotates to the strains of "The Anniversary Waltz." The box is bare but for the pearls. Shaking with disbelief, he snatches them up—they slide down their severed string and spray across the floor.

"Teresa!" he roars.

She's up in an instant, wiping her hands, white grains of *burghul* clinging to them—she's making *kibbeh*—and the next instant she's lucky he hasn't called the police; "Get your things and go."

Mahmoud contacts his youngest daughter and she organizes a bucket brigade of female relatives. The family is hugely attentive anyway, but full-time housekeeping for an old man is another matter. They'll have to find a paid replacement because Mahmoud's family is so successful that there are no spare females lying around.

A line of Irish girls and colored girls and country girls is paraded before him but Mahmoud can't seem to decide on a new Teresa, so it falls to Camille to take up most of the slack. She is the closest thing to a widow there is.

What enrages Mahmoud is that he let himself be lulled into trusting Teresa—into thinking she was different. That's when the viper strikes. He should never have forgotten her color. They can be the nicest people in the world but, like children, they mustn't be overburdened with responsibility. They're like the worser sort of woman in that way, even the men—which reminds me, I wonder if the brother was in cahoots.

It's enormously aggravating at Mahmoud's age to have to explain every little thing to each of the female relatives looking after him. They all do their best but the evil truth is, none of them knows him like Teresa did. And—this is the most evil truth—none of them makes Lebanese food as beautifully as she did. Better than his own wife, God rest her soul and God forgive me. Teresa seemed to read his mind. She made everything so easy. And Mahmoud knew that, when the time came, he could have accepted her most intimate ministrations without yielding a particle of his dignity. Now that is a good woman. And what is her price? Above rubies. Damn it. What were a few trinkets in exchange for that? He'd have willingly given her the whole kit 'n' caboodle, every bauble and—what am I thinking? I'm a foolish old man. And what is my price? An ass if I'm not careful. I need my daughters at a time like this, my own flesh and blood, this just goes to show it.

It wounds Mahmoud to observe that the thefts do not end with the departure of Teresa. They resume under the increasingly continuous care of his daughter Camille.

Mahmoud blames himself. In the Old Country he never would have given a daughter to Jameel, because there the crucial distinction between their two families would have been clear. The Jameels are Arabs. We Mahmouds are more Mediterranean. Closer to being European, really. Such distinctions are apt to get blurred in the new country, where you open wide your arms to a brother from home who speaks the same beautiful language as you. The same shapely humorous language with earth and water in it. What a relief it is to sit down to a meal or a game of cards with someone, a Jameel for example, who shares this language. What a relief from the chill of English, which is exactly like immersing your tongue in ice water. And after all, to the *enklese* you are all "black Syrians." Mahmoud didn't recognize until too late that his Old Country standards had eroded to the point where he had given his most beautiful daughter to a dirty half-civilized Arab. Poor Camille, a good girl who has borne sons only, and five of them—what a waste. And he's lost Teresa to boot.

Tears are shed by Mahmoud sitting next to his bed. He has come up here to get away from a bungling granddaughter. He sits in the skirted chair that matches the bedclothes—Giselle's taste, French provincial, God rest her soul—and his eyes fall upon the carved mahogany reproduction of Dürer's *Praying Hands* hanging on the wall. My wife bought that. A distant tremor for Giselle gives way to hot tears because they are Teresa's hands.

Go ahead, cry it out and be done with it. Then get down on your knees and thank God that your daughter Camille has been polluted by her no-good Arab husband into a petty thief, and that you fired Teresa for Camille's crime. Thank God, because you know that otherwise, and not too long from now, you would have asked Teresa to marry you.

Mahmoud slides from the chair and clunks to the floor on his knees. It must have been God who intervened when the pearls went flying, because if Mahmoud had been thinking for himself he never would have believed the thief could be a woman to whom he had entrusted the housekeeping money every week for the past fifteen years. It was God speaking straight out of his mouth. Thank you. Infinite wisdom, infinite mercy, I am not worthy.

Mahmoud kneels and weeps into his own praying hands. Beneath the bed, Frances listens, fascinated.

Teresa is crying too, but with anger. She sits on the loveseat in her home under the hand-tinted photograph of Bridgetown and wonders what she's going to do now. Worse than the loss of her job is the loss of her reputation. And what is its price? To have been unjustly accused. And of something so far beneath her and everything she comes from. How dare he? Hateful old man. Like all the rest only worse. Nasty, low-down, filthy Syrian—oh sweet Lord, I am trying but You make it hard. How is it possible to forgive and to live at the same time?

It always ends this way: not-colored people can't stand it when a colored person gets too good at something. Teresa blames herself for believing that she was indispensable to Mahmoud. Pride goeth before a fall. She did everything for him. She remembered all the names and all the birthdays of all his grandchildren, and shopped for the endless stream of presents that bore his name. She remembered which son liked what dish and cooked accordingly when they came for supper. She knew when to mend a sock and when to throw it out, where he had left his diamond tiepin and his reading glasses, she banked his money, paid his bills and soothed his corns. If she hadn't done her job so well Mahmoud would not have resented her and fired her on a vicious lie. Yes he would. He'd have fired her for being lazy "like the rest of your people." It ends the same way no matter what, leaving you to suck salt and pray Jesus to take away the hate.

Hector reaches over and brushes away a tear, which causes her to weep afresh. They have been married thirteen years. All day long Hector sits faithfully under his blanket waiting for her to come home. Thank the Lord for Ginger, Adelaide and their kids, thank God for good neighbors, otherwise Hector would have died of loneliness by now.

Hector wasn't fired, he was never unjustly accused of anything and, unlike dear Ginger, he never resorted to making a living through illegal means. Hector had a good job at the steel plant. He and Teresa were married fourteen months when a half-cooked beam fell and caught him on the side of the head. Now he can go for little walks if you hold his hand, but mostly he gets pushed along in his wheelchair.

Hector and Teresa had put off having children because he was going to be a minister and they were going to move to New York City and have American children and a better life. Teresa pats Hector's hand, then goes to fetch a fresh diaper for him from the linen closet. She long ago gave up imagining what their children would have looked like.

Jameel barges into Boutros's bedroom on the second floor and says, "Tell Leo Taylor to come here tonight and bring a case of ginger beer."

Boutros turns from his open window and says, "I'll pick it up myself, Pa."

"Shut up and do what I say."

"How come?"

Jameel reaches up and clips Boutros a sharp one on the back of the head, "That's how come."

"Ow."

Jameel laughs and explains, "Your cousin wants him, b'y."

Boutros doesn't say anything. Jameel shakes his head, Jesus, I have to spell everything out for this kid, takes after his mother—"Queen a' Sheba, friggin Frances, b'y, she's after his black arse."

Boutros is trembling. With someone as big as Boutros, it's hard to tell. He is nineteen. Soon he won't be able to stop himself from belting his father. Jameel laughs at Boutros, grabs his big face in both hands, squashes the cheeks together and slaps him affectionately. "Do what I say, go on."

Jameel leaves and Boutros turns back to his open window. He picks up a battered oilcan from the ledge and finishes watering his marigolds and petunias.

The name Boutros means Peter. And Peter means rock. And upon this rock, Jameel has built his booze can. It is Boutros's curse to be the eldest. He has four younger brothers. Most of them are just like Jameel and therefore well suited to being the eldest, except for the middle brother, who is obviously headed for the priesthood. Boutros dreams of saving enough money to buy a farm; of marrying his cousin Frances and taking her and his mother, Camille, away to the country, where they would all be happy. They'd have a lot of children and he would love them all, but especially he would love his wife, and make his mother's last years the happiest of her life. Frances is a painted drunken whore on the outside but Boutros sees through that because he loves her and, one day soon, intends to save her.

"Pa wants you to come tonight and bring a case of ginger beer."

Ginger looks up at Boutros filling the doorway. Adelaide calls from the kitchen, "Take it yourself, buddy."

"Puppa says for mister to come."

"It's okay, Addy, I won't be long." Ginger goes for his jacket.

"Not now," says Boutros, "tonight after midnight."

"What for?" Adelaide wants to know.

"I don't know, Mrs. Taylor, Pa says."

"It'll cost him," says Adelaide, pouring some hot into Teresa's cup— Adelaide's been making mincemeat pies and offering to beat the can off old Mahmoud.

Ginger says to Boutros, "Tell him I'll be there." But Boutros doesn't leave right away. He remains for a moment, looking down at Ginger. Finally he turns and goes without a word.

"Did you see that?" Ginger asks the women, returning to the kitchen table. "Gawking at me like I was a ghost?"

"That whole family's right nuts," says Adelaide, thinking not only of the old vulture who fired Teresa, but of mean Camille—twenty years in The Coke Ovens and she's never said hello to a soul. Then there's the New Waterford branch. Too bad Ginger has to be mixed up with any of them.

"Lord have mercy on them," says Teresa, folding her hands around her cup.

"Mercy my foot," says Adelaide, "here, baby." Adelaide sets a plate of Nellie's Muffins in front of Ginger. He gives her a kiss, sits down and hands the jammiest one to Hector, who grins with delight.

Adelaide cooks all that good plain Nova Scotia stuff. She comes from a community in Halifax called Africville. She is proud of her African Irish United Empire Loyalist blood, proud to have been baptized in Bedford Basin, and never tires of telling tales of the 1917 explosion—I was spared for a reason: to punch you in the nose, buddy—to dance with you tonight, honey—to see my babies grow.

Later, when Teresa and Hector have gone and they've put the kids to bed, Adelaide says, not looking at him, "Don't go to that place, Leo."

"I have to, baby."

"Then come right back, don't linger."

"No desire to."

"Come here," she says, looking at him.

He smiles and obeys her.

Ginger carries the crate up to the front door of Jameel's speak. He hates this place. He can hear the usual party going on inside. He can smell the booze from out here and it smells like the raw material used to make vomit. He feels sorry for Jameel's wife.

On second thought, he'll go round the back. Ginger dislikes using a back door, but in this case he'd rather enter unnoticed by the crowd that turns like one queasy beast every time someone walks in—never mind the floozie on piano, who smells like a sick baby. I should quit this job—see if I can get on at the steel plant. But Ginger knows there's no work to be had there or anywhere else. Not even for white men.

It's like a blow to his stomach when Ginger walks into the cold storage room and sees the Girl Guide uniform filthy and strewn across the empty kegs, stockings, beret, the little pouch. He looks about instinctively for the nude body—this is what happens to little girls who aren't looked after, I should have found out who she was, I should have given her a drive . . . He calms down a little when he doesn't see her. But that's not to say she hasn't been dragged outside by one of Jameel's drunks and raped. Ginger is suddenly enraged—to be working for a man like Jameel, to be helping keep a place like this going in the very neighborhood where his own daughters are growing up. Ginger pounds on the door. Boutros opens it and says, "Pa's over there."

Ginger shoves his way through the crowd with his crate, past the tart on piano—" 'Jeepers creepers, where'd ya get those peepers' "—and finds Jameel. "Jameel, what happened to that little girl with the Guide uniform?"

"That's Mr. Jameel to you, boy."

Ginger drops the crate and grabs Jameel by the collar.

"Where is she, you devil?"

A cold pain on the back of Ginger's neck and he's looking at Boutros's shoes. Jameel is laughing down at him. "He wants it *ba-ad!*"

A cold drop splashes onto Ginger's forehead. He looks up. The prostitute in the orange wig is chug-a-lugging a bottle of ginger beer. He can see the white underside of her chin and her grime collar.

"She's right here, Leo b'y," smirks Jameel, "Help yourself. Cash only."

She looks down at Ginger with serious green-brown eyes. Golden froth trickles out the corner of her smeary red mouth. He covers his eyes with his hands.

"I'm quitting, I'm not driving anymore," is all Adelaide can get out of him twenty minutes later.

He needs a good cry so let him. "You've been working too hard, let's throttle back a bit, eh b'y?"

All he can do is nod and sob against her until he falls asleep.

Adelaide hugs him and counts five weeks since that last New York run. Something's not right.

In the morning it all seems like a bad dream. He tells Adelaide, "Jameel's got a little girl hustling there." Adelaide listens. "And it made me think of our own girls and what would happen if—"

"I know, honey." He's too sensitive. "Why don't you take it easy today?"

"I'm all right, Addy, I feel fine."

And he climbs into his truck.

He drives away and realizes he forgot to tell Adelaide the whole point of the story—that the child prostitute is the little Girl Guide who came into their yard that day, and that he's seen her on the road and in the side mirror of his dream. But he forgot. And what was it Adelaide said about the Girl Guide that day? "That's not a Girl Guide." Well obviously not a real one, he knows that now.

I'll tell Adelaide tonight, he thinks, and turns onto the Shore Road.

Harem Scarem

AT FIRST, FRANCES WONDERED when Teresa was going to get back from her holiday or her illness or whatever it was. But this afternoon, as she walks the Shore Road to New Waterford, a horrible thought occurs to her. What if Teresa has been fired? What if Mahmoud pinned the thefts on her? He'd be crazy to—why, just yesterday Frances helped herself to a Royal Doulton shepherdess and a Chinese fisherman from the piano, and Teresa had been gone three days by then.

In his truck, Ginger realizes that he's been searching the Shore Road for the Girl Guide. He wants to talk to her, that's all, but not at the speak. He wants to find out who her father is, where her people are, if she has any. And if she doesn't, maybe he and Adelaide can help.

Frances doesn't look or stop walking when she hears the truck braking on the soft shoulder behind her.

"Hey there."

She stops but does not turn.

"Excuse me, little miss."

She turns and looks up at him leaning out the window of his cab. I was right, thinks Ginger, twelve at the most. She walks to the truck, steps up on the running board and gets in beside him. She has already pegged him for a nice man . . . this may take some time.

"What's your name, dear, who's your father?" as he pulls back onto the road.

"My name is Frances Euphrasia Piper. My father is James Hiram Piper, my grandfather is Ibrahim Mahmoud. I don't know his middle name."

Ginger doesn't take his eyes off the road. He is shocked, can't think what to say.

"Is that right?" he says. "I knew your sister Kathleen."

"I know."

He glances at her. She's looking at him.

"I used to drive her, you know, I'm Leo Taylor."

"I know."

Ginger sees a tree go by on his left. Then a rock. Another rock. He says the normal thing and feels as if he's lying even though he isn't. "It was a real shame her passing away like that so young, she was a really pretty gal."

"I know. I saw her."

"I guess you seen photographs, eh?"

"I remember her perfectly well."

"But you wouldn't've even been born yet." He chuckles, which really is a lie.

"I was going on six," she says. "I remember everything."

Ginger brakes and pulls over, pebble by pebble.

"What's the matter?"

"I thought you were a child."

"You're Teresa's brother, eh?"

"Yeah." He feels a bit dizzy. It's the driving, I can't drive anymore.

"How come she's not at my grandfather's anymore?"

"She got fired. He said she stole but she didn't."

"He'll be sorry."

He sits up. "Look you, does your daddy know what you're doing, and why are you doing it anyway when you got a good home and a family?"

"Because I'm bad."

He looks at her. "No you're not."

"How do you know?"

Ginger takes a breath. His eyes water and he says, "I can tell by looking. In your eyes. You're not bad . . . you're just lost."

"I know exactly where I am."

"That doesn't mean you're not lost."

He reaches out and cradles the side of her face in his hand. She's got wise eyes. They make him feel so deep dry sad that something must be done. "I want you to come home with me and talk to my wife, she's a good woman."

"Do you want to be my friend?"

"I'd like to help you, honey."

"Then take me with you where you're driving."

"I can't do that."

"You did it for my sister."

"I never took your sister halfway 'cross the continent."

"Where did you take her?"

"School and back, what do you think?"

"Little Ginger Man . . . I need someone to look after me. I'm full-grown, but I'm just a little girl inside. I want you to find me 'cause I'm lost, I'm lost in a deep dark place, please, please, please, oh you smell nice."

He takes her hand away and pushes her, not roughly, to the far end of the seat. "Where do you want me to drop you?"

"The Empire."

He guns into New Waterford and Frances hops down in front of the picture house. It's a talkie today, but Frances buys a ticket anyhow. She has some thinking to do. She knows now what it is she must accomplish for Lily. There remains, however, one piece of unfinished business.

Camille has often imagined herself a widow. She would return home and look after Pa and he'd realize she was the only daughter who really loved him. It has weighed on her that he has been all alone in that big house since Mumma died with only a colored woman to wait on him. Camille has cried over that. It's the only thing she has cried over since the early days of her marriage, when she still had the energy to cry over herself. So now that Teresa is gone, Camille is in her element. Her one regret is that she is obliged to return home nights.

Camille knows that Teresa is not a thief. The jewels that went missing from Ma's rosewood box have reappeared at the speak, encrusting Frances's fingers, dangling from her ears and glittering round her scrawny neck. The silver tail of a comb pokes out her Guide pouch. If Camille could incinerate Frances with her eyes, Frances would have been blown away by now, but Camille has a good reason for keeping mum about the jewels.

She frisks her father's house top to bottom to find the breach where the pest has got in. Down in the cellar she glimpses the guilty crack of light framing the swing-trap at the top of the coal chute. She nails a board across it for now and goes upstairs to the front hall, where she telephones the hardware store.

Frances waits patiently inside the closet until Camille gets off the phone and returns to the kitchen, then she bounds soundlessly upstairs two at a time into the master bedroom, where she prepares for tonight's performance. Her last on this stage.

Camille has sealed up the rat hole but she doesn't breathe a word about the rat. If Pa found out that it wasn't Teresa who stole, then he would hire her back and send Camille home to her husband.

Mahmoud has spent the day at his store as usual, sitting out front, carving soapstone and playing checkers with the other old fellas while his sons run things. They have expanded the business and now they are a major Maritime import/export company with a big warehouse in Sydney and headquarters in Halifax. Shipping is next. Mahmoud never played the stock market, never bought on credit, and it has paid off. The world economy lies in ruins, but the family business is expanding. The Mahmoud boys honor their father by allowing him to feel that he is still the boss, hence "Sure, Pa, whatever you say," before going ahead and doing what they know is best.

Mahmoud has passed an agreeable day growling at his grandsons and watching the street go by. Everybody knows him, everybody respects him. He wears a plaid shirt and a dove-gray jacket and tie just as he did every day of his working life. Today is Wednesday, so on his way home he looks forward to stuffed *koosa* the way Teresa makes it. He's been forgetting like this lately. It's not so bad if he remembers before he opens the front door. Then he can prepare himself for her absence. But if he makes it all the way to the kitchen, and over to the stove to taste what's in the covered dish—"Teresa!" he calls in disbelief at how she has murdered her specialty with salt—only to turn and see Camille at the top of the cellar steps.

"What is it, Pa?"

"Nothing."

He does not blame Camille. The best cook of the family is not quite as good as Teresa, and Camille is the only bad cook. Another effect of her wrong marriage—an unhappily married woman is necessarily a bad cook—and therefore his own fault, as well he knows. Just as it's his fault she's a thief. Well, why shouldn't she have her mother's pretty things? She has little else, not even a talent for food. He forgives her.

"Are you starved, Pa?"

He grunts and shuffles away. He doesn't want to see her sallow smile, she makes him feel tired. He'll just have a snooze before attempting supper, which will taste, as usual, like the Dead Sea. He forgives her because he does not love her.

He comforts himself with the thought of his other daughters whom he does love—please God the one with grown children will be widowed soon and deliver me from Camille, God forgive me I didn't mean that.

After supper, Mahmoud drinks a big glass of water and falls asleep in his mauve satin chair in the front room. Nothing quenches his thirst or his fatigue these days. He thinks a lot about Giselle. Not in the ordinary way, as of the dear departed, but as though she had just stepped from the room. And for the first time in thirty-two years he admits the memory of Materia. She appears with her black braids and mischievous smile. He is unaware of the smile on his own lips—*la hown, ya Helwi*. She looked like her mother and she ran off at about the same age Giselle was when Mahmoud married her, but that was different, oh very. That was in the Old Country where they had everything in common.

The Old Country was part of Syria then and a lot of people were emigrating to America. He and Giselle ended up in Cape Breton because of the lying mongrel of a sea captain who took their money, then dumped them on this barren rock. Days of peering at the horizon waiting for land and finally—land! Waiting to see the Statue of Liberty loom up, to dock at Ellis Island before ferrying to the blessed isle of Manhattan. They dropped anchor in Sydney and the captain turfed them out—"What's the difference, it's an island, ain't it?"

Jameel's father was on that boat too. Mahmoud had no way of knowing that Jameel senior was fleeing creditors in Syria, because he said he was fleeing the Turks and the Druses like everyone else. And when asked for his own story, Mahmoud replied, "the godforsaken Muslim devils." In fact, he and Giselle left because her family was set to arrest him and stick her in a convent. But it was different from what happened with Materia and the *enklese* bastard—for one thing, he and Giselle were both from the same race, culture, language and faith. Although Giselle's family did not see it that way. They were doctors and lawyers, spoke more French than Arabic, considered themselves more Mediterranean, even European. They were from Beirut. He was an Arab from the south. He had returned to Lebanon, land of his birth, having spent his boyhood picking cotton in Egypt. Don't tell me what it is to work.

He took Giselle to a better place across the ocean and gave her everything her own family would have and more. As soon as he could, he forbade her to work, even though, being the good woman she was, she resisted at first. He honored her, never laid a hand on her in anger—never had to. He gave her a beautiful house, servants, jewels each anniversary. A silk negligee from Beirut to make up for the fact she'd never had a wedding gown; three shades of Mediterranean blue and a veil with a fringe of real pearls. The veil was purely for fun, of course, a romantic joke. The sight of her in this outfit was unimaginably exciting.

If only her arrogant family could have seen what Mahmoud achieved in the New World.

"Pa? . . . Pa."

He wakes with half a moan to see Camille. She's got her coat on and the room is dark.

"I'm going home now, Pa."

"Where's your mother?"

He's speaking Arabic but she replies in English to help him back to his senses, "Wake up, Pa, do you want something before I go, a nice cuppa tea?"

Oh. What? It's time for bed, where's Ter—? Oh. "No, no, no, I'm going to bed."

Camille goes to help him but he casually swats her away as he rises.

"I'll turn the light on for you, Pa."

"No, no, go home, Camille." Oh, his life—what has become of his life?

There is nothing more for Camille to do: she has laid out his pajamas, he doesn't want the light. Mahmoud reaches the foot of the stairs and with a slight wave of his hand he says without turning, "Thank you, Camille."

If his other daughters could hear Pa saying thank you—"He never says thank you to me." "Me neither, dear." "He's never said anything to me except 'Close your legs.' " Mahmoud thanks Camille because he does not love her.

Camille watches him slowly mount the stairs until he disappears into the darkness of the landing. Then she leaves, although she knows it's a sin to leave an old man alone in that big house all night even if he does insist. "Am I the only one who cares?" she wonders.

But he is not alone. There is someone else who cares enough to keep him company through the long lonely night.

★ ★ ★

Mahmoud awakens smiling a few hours later to the sound of an Arabic comedy routine. A husband and wife chiding each other about faithfulness. Then they break into a love song. He had this record and many others brought over from Beirut. He and Giselle used to sit side by side on the sofa and never tire of laughing at the same jokes. Then she would dance for him and he for her. But only when the children were out. And only sometimes. But what precious times . . .

His smile dies upon his lips when the impossibility of what he is hearing hits him. What, is he dead? Is there a thief in the house? Playing his scratchy old records? Why?

He puts on his velvet robe, ties the cord around his waist and creeps down the stairs. He is dead. He must be. There is Giselle.

Beyond the archway, the front room is aglow with candlelight and three shades of Mediterranean blue. Swirling and swaying and quarter-turning, hips beckoning, fingers twining in air, wrists caressing one another above her head, the pearls of her veil swinging to the rhythm of the reeds, the drums and the wailing voices of the love song.

Mahmoud is filled with desire and his heart hurts, stirring again after such a long period of inactivity, never having been particularly athletic. She has seen him and now she is luring him into the dance. Ohhh. He travels through the archway, he does not know how. She bends forward in her circle of firelight, the blue silk wafts open at her breasts in shadow—come closer, the better to see me, *Habibi*. Her eyes are full of fun above the veil and her fingers tickle the emptiness between her and her beloved, closer, closer. "Giselle," he whispers, reaching out to her. She giggles and he laughs too, not knowing what's funny, "Giselle," he whispers, *"Habibti."*

But she slips out of the ring of light and vanishes. He calls her but she does not answer. He picks up a candelabrum, knowing better than to turn on electric lights when seeking a vision, and searches the ground floor; the cellar. He goes back up to the front room. He blows out the candles and turns on the electric chandelier because he can feel she is gone. The record has ended, there's just the repetitive sigh at its center—he removes the needle and returns to his bedroom. He opens his wife's oak wardrobe where all her fine clothes still hang among mothballs. There at the back is the shimmering blue with its whispering veil. He must have been dreaming. But what about the candles? The record? Losing my mind. Or else it was an impostor. I don't care. He reaches out to touch the silk, which is impossible to feel if there is a lifetime of work on your hands. He touches it but does not feel it—just as he saw what he could not have seen. *I don't care what you were, come back to me Please Please Please Ohhh.*

It's his last thrill and his last sting of love, as fresh and painful as youth transplanted over time and an ocean. There is nothing left for him now except to die, but that will take a while because he is a creature of habit, and he has got into the habit of being alive.

Thief in the Night

IT WOULDN'T MATTER TO Frances if Ginger were a cruel man. She would do the same thing. Kindness or cruelty, it's all by chance and what's worse anyway? It's easier to endure cruelty so maybe kindness is worse. The only question is, how do you get a nice man to do a bad thing?

She stops drinking. She wants all her wits about her for what lies ahead. Frances without liquor is a bit scary to her customers. No more cutie-pie patter or kisses for gin, she takes cash up front and services them cold-bloodedly with the communion glove. Dripping with her grandmother's jewels, she no longer bothers to change out of her coal-smeared Guide uniform, and at the piano she plays Chopin while speaking blues lyrics in a loud monotone despite a chorus of boos. When she strips, she doesn't sing or shimmy, she undresses like an automaton and bellows in a leaden voice, " 'IRENE GOOD-NIGHT. IRENE GOOD-NIGHT. GOOD-NIGHT IRENE GOOD-NIGHT IRENE I'LL REAM YOU IN MY DREAMS.' " She's no fun anymore, soon they'll look elsewhere. It's almost as though Frances despises her customers when she's sober, and what could be more insulting, because what right has she?

Frances wants three thousand bucks for Lily before retiring as a dive diva so she ups her price. This does not go down well either—some men try to dine and dash while others take the insult out on her face. Boutros has broken one man's wrist and crushed another's cheekbone, but Frances doesn't care if her clients hit her, she just cares if she's raped—she doesn't want anything interfering with her plans.

Ginger Taylor has been gone in his truck a week and a half now. Frances has kept his purple house under surveillance. She knows he'll be back tomorrow because she gets close enough to listen. She has motive. She has means. She watches the moon and awaits her opportunity.

Tonight Boutros follows Frances home as usual. He has given up trying to walk with her because she tells him where to go every time. So he escorts her secretly all the way to New Waterford and watches her slip around the back of the house on Water Street. He waits out front for the glow of her candle to appear in the gabled window at the very top of the house. Tonight as he waits, the headlights of a passing car catch two yellow gleams at the attic window—there's a demon up there, crouched and lying in wait for Frances! Boutros is halfway to the veranda when he sees her light appear and cast a halo of black fur around two yellow eyes. He watches her come to the window, sit on the ledge and cradle the cat. His face softens. He is glad to see that he is not her only friend.

As yet, Boutros has not caught anyone attempting to ambush Frances on her way home. But if he ever does, the fella will die. Snap. Simple as that.

When Ginger Taylor returns the next day, he lays Christmas in August on the kitchen table. Rolls of white lace trim and colored ribbon, yards and yards of fabric. A swatch of sun, moon and stars against a smoky midnight blue, a bolt of emerald polka dots on iridescent black, spring flowers for the girls, gray flannel for the boys. Candy, pineapples and a whole deer dressed on ice in the back of the truck.

Adelaide's eyes water at the sight of the fabric. The ladies she sews for buy some fine cloth but nothing so jazzy. She has made gowns for most of the white weddings in Sydney. She uses silk, satin and organdy for her ladies, and her imagination for her family. Often there's a nice piece left over from a job, but if the lady doesn't ask for it back Adelaide gives it away to a neighbor because it is contrary to her own professional code to dress her children in leftover piecework. She'd sooner turn flour sacks into perfect pinafores, and she does. The Mahmouds were Adelaide's biggest customers till the Teresa fiasco, and when you add that times are worse than ever, Leo has no business throwing money away on all this nonsense.

Madeleine, Sarah, Josephine, Cleo, Evan, Frederick and Carvery swarm at the sweets, shrieking, sharing, fighting, and Adelaide wants to know, "What in the name of time is all this, mister?"

Ginger beams at her. "It's a whole lot of nothing for no reason."

She fingers the fabric. "What did you do, rob a bank? You better've." They've been saving for the kids for school, how could he?

He heads her off. "I got so happy, Addy, I had to go out and waste some money or else bust, because I love you. Because you are the best woman, you are the toughest, the meanest, the prettiest and I can't believe that I got you!" He jumps her in a spinning bear hug.

"You're crazy, you know that? You're right nuts, and put me down, b'y!" She packs a bony wallop to his soft shoulder. "Put me down till I beat the can offa ya!"

And he does. "Come on," he says, feinting with a right jab, and she comes at him with a left hook, wiry she is—jab, jab at his upraised forearms and dancing fists, socks him a good one right in the breadbasket, till she has to double over because she's laughing so hard she might pee, and she can't see to box him anymore for the tears streaming down her face.

"Invite the neighbors," he tells her. "I'm going to get Trese and Hector. Evan, honey, I want a big fire out back."

Evan hops to it. He is the oldest at twelve.

Barbecued deer and boiled corn, enough for the neighborhood, and the neighborhood is there in the backyard. The sun is down, the fire is high and so is the moon. Hector sits under his blanket wide-eyed and smiling, tapping his foot in reel time to the fiddle of the very old Mr. Prince Crawley. Teresa feels well for the first time since she was fired. She had forgotten the sweet joys of society, of just yakking with people, surrounded by kids and food and music. She has made a fish curry fit to cure the dead—renewing her claim to the local West Indian cooking crown—and a tub of ice cream to cool the flames. She goes so far as to let Adelaide persuade her to sing—"Only for you, Addy, and only this once." Teresa starts up one her mother, Clarisse, always sang for her and Ginger:

" 'Sly mongoose, Sly enough but the dog knows your ways. Sly mongoose, Sly enough but the cat is on your track—' "

And what good's a song if you don't dance it? Teresa is an excellent dancer when wild horses have got her up and moving. Once moving, she is nothing but happy—

" 'The mongoose went in the missus' kitchen, Took up two of her fattest chickens, Passed them into his vestcoat pocket, Sly mongoose—' "

The crowd joins in, the going gets wild, Hector is laughing and clapping and the little girls have all got up to join Teresa. Her smile is a mile wide, her hips have gone saucy, fingers snapping, palms percussing, "Go, girl!"

" 'You look to me like a mile and a quarter, You look to me like you require some water, You look to me like your blood's out of order, Drink bush tea, Drinky bush tea—' "

She begins to improvise verses, and it gets hilarious because she makes up all kinds of rhyming gossip about everyone there, and people throw made-up verses back at her. At last Teresa takes the song back to the chorus and everyone sings, then shakes the firelight with appreciation. Teresa hasn't caught her breath before she notices Adelaide alert as a cat staring at the backyard fence. Before she can say, "What's the matter, dear?" Adelaide has pounced—over the fence and down the alley.

Adelaide pelts after the small fleeing figure and catches it easily by the collar.

"What's going on, eh? Why're you hanging around my family?"

"Fuck off—ow."

Adelaide has got the fine art of arm-twisting.

"What's your name, girl?"

"Harriet Beecher Stowe, ha ha—ow!"

Teresa has caught up. Frances sees her. And can't help but speak to her.

"Hi, Teresa."

Adelaide looks at Teresa. "Who is she, Trese?"

"I don't know, Addy."

"Teresa." Frances looks up at her. "Don't you remember me?"

Frances forgets to lie. She forgets about Adelaide pinning her wrist behind her back, she is tempted to tell Teresa everything. Because Teresa would understand. Teresa would touch her forehead and everything would fall away, all the weight of everything Frances knows and doesn't know. The terrible weight of her heavy heavy mind.

"Dear God," says Teresa. She has just seen the double row of precious stones on Frances's fingers. "Where did you get those rings, child?"

"I found them." It's sweet like milk—she called me "child."

Ginger arrives but stops a little way off. Adelaide turns to him, "It's her again, I don't know who she is or what the hell she's after."

No sooner said than Adelaide has an answer to the latter question: glancing down at her prisoner, she sees Frances staring at Ginger with a cool cool look on her face.

"Who is she, Leo?" Adelaide says sharply, watching his face.

He looks back at the phony Girl Guide and Adelaide knows the next thing she hears will be a lie.

"I don't know, Addy."

Leo has never lied to her before. Adelaide's talent for seeing through a lie could be called a sixth sense, but she doesn't figure there's anything spooky about it. To tell truth from a lie is easy as salt and sweet.

"Never mind," she says to her husband and his sister. "Go back and enjoy yourselves, I'll be right there." But they hang. "Move, will ya Jesus-Christ-on-the-Cross move!" And they do.

Adelaide shifts Frances's wrist an eighth of an inch and so gets her undivided attention. Then she leans her face close in till they are eyeball to eyeball. Quietly, and with intent, "You come around my house; you touch my babies or my husband, and I will kill you."

"Yes ma'am."

Adelaide lets go of Frances's wrist and returns to her own backyard.

Teresa and Leo have told everyone that Adelaide caught a peeping Tom, a white fella, and put the fear of God into him. Everyone laughs because they pity anyone who crosses Adelaide, and when she comes through the gate looking so grim, they laugh some more. Adelaide marches straight into the house and straight back out with her mouth organ. She plays "The Old Rugged Cross." It's bluesy this way, which is how it sounds best. This one always makes Teresa cry, the way "Ave Maria" does a tired Catholic. Laughing and crying all in the one night, it's been a wonderful party.

Except for the dirty Girl Guide with Mrs. Mahmoud's rings. How on earth did she come by them? On the black market? In the gutter? The actual thief must be long gone by now. Teresa was too shocked at the sight to think what to do but now she knows there is nothing to be done. No point seizing the rings or telling Mahmoud, he would never believe her, he's proven that much. And he doesn't deserve the truth—forgive me, Lord, only You know what we each deserve—anyhow, why get Adelaide all het up about what can't be fixed? "The Old Rugged Cross" reminds Teresa to turn the other cheek and not to dwell, what's done is done.

Prince Crawley joins in on fiddle, several sing and Hector hums. It ends the evening in just the right way.

Teresa wheels Hector home down the street and shakes off an unsettling question. How did the little waif know my name?

Ginger makes sure he's in bed ahead of Adelaide. He feels ashamed to be mimicking the sound of sleep as she undresses and crawls in next to him. He's done nothing wrong, but how could he possibly explain? A little white lie and for no reason. It doesn't matter.

She watches him for a while, then softly calls him by his secret name—not "Ginger," another name. It's private. He stirs a little but doesn't open his eyes. She kisses his shoulder and lies down next to him. She'd do anything for her family.

The next day.

Adelaide arrives home from Beel's Grocery with an envelope of bright new buttons.

"Josephine, Evan, come here till I annihilate the both of you, what's this?"

"I'm sorry, Mumma—Sorry, Mumma."

Two soft earlobes pierced between stiletto thumbs and forefingers,

"I'll tell you what's this, this is your baby brother Carvery playing with the stove!"

"Yes ma'am—Yes ma'am."

Release earlobes, ah.

"He is your brother. You are responsible for him and you are responsible for each other."

"Yes, ma'am—Yes, ma'am."

"You never, ever let your family come in harm's way."

"No, ma'am—No, ma'am."

Then she threatens them with retribution by their father when he gets home and the two children breathe a sigh of relief, because what they'll get from their father is "Well now, how did that happen?" and a seat in his cushiony lap.

At the kitchen table.

Adelaide sits down to her buttons and bolts of precious fabric. Princely knickerbockers for Frederick, gentleman trousers for Evan, white shirts and collars for them both, Sunday dresses decked with ribbons for the girls, a swashbuckling shirt of sun, moon and stars for Leo and a matching one for baby Carvery. And finally, although she is mortified to spend the time on it—"I'm only doing this to please you, mister"— sleeveless, slinky, low-slung, black satin and tropical green polka dots. When you see Adelaide in this dress, you'll have to ask her to dance just to feel her slip through your arms like a flashy fish.

At the matinee.

"Has the picture started?"

"Nearly over with."

"One, please."

Ginger hands over his nickel and enters the Empire. It's a silent, *Diary of a Lost Girl* starring Louise Brooks. Not many people. It should be easy to spot Frances if she's here. He stands at the top of the raked aisle and waits until his eyes resolve the shadows into shapes. The outline of her beret. Front row center, but she's not alone.

The picture ends, "IF THERE WERE MORE LOVE IN THIS WORLD, NO ONE WOULD EVER HAVE TO BE LOST." The lights come up and he watches Frances rise from her seat. Her companion looks to be a child, though Ginger is wary of jumping to that conclusion anymore. But no, it's definitely a real little girl, he sees that when she stands and turns to collect her sweater from the back of her seat. A really pretty child, with long red-gold hair past her waist, familiar in some way. Now that he sees Frances next to a real child he can't imagine how he ever mistook her for one. Actually, her face looks quite old. He watches. The two of them start along their row to the aisle and the long-haired child seems to stumble to one side. Then again, and with each step. She must have hurt herself somehow, he thinks, but he understands when she rounds the last seat in the row and walks towards him up the aisle. Pretty little gal, what a shame. The youngest Piper child, of course, and that's who she reminds me of, her older sister Kathleen. The closer she gets, the more uncanny the resemblance.

Ginger waits for Frances to see him. But if she does, she doesn't give any sign. She's chatting to her little sister, "Next Saturday is *The Wind* starring Lillian Gish, it's about a beautiful girl who goes out West but when she gets there the wind buggers her mind."

"How does it bugger it?"

"Don't say 'bugger,' Lily, say 'derange.' "

"Derange."

Frances puts an arm around Lily and walks right past Ginger.

"Hello, Frances."

The long-haired child turns and gives him her green eyes—so like the girl Kathleen, but so unlike too because Kathleen never once looked at him. Frances doesn't turn, just yanks the little sister after her, nearly knocking her off balance. Ginger is confused. Is this a slap in the face? If so, what for? He feels like someone's dirty secret. But I'm not. I haven't done anything wrong and don't intend to. Don't want to!

But he has to talk to her. Tell her she can't be skulking around his house like that, and not to be coming on like a whore with him, he's not that kind of man. Yes, he has to talk to her as soon as possible. That means the speak. Tonight, Saturday.

Ginger has no intention of ever entering that Pandora's box again, so he doesn't even bother to leave his house until 3 A.M., when he knows she'll be leaving.

"Sorry, Addy, I forgot to tell you, Jameel said for me to come at closing."

The second lie. How is Adelaide to protect her family when she doesn't know what from? She had seen with a chill that the fake Girl Guide bore no good will toward her husband. Like a fiend she looked at him: starved but patient.

Adelaide hears the front door shut behind Ginger. She rolls over in bed wondering, what does she want with him? And what could Leo possibly see in that dirty little white thing? Crazy girl, bad pixie, nobody's child . . . Adelaide sits up with a jolt as it hits her: he feels sorry for her. Oh no. Oh no, no, no, no, no.

Ginger waits behind a wooden support under the rail bridge as the clientele spills out of Jameel's. The piano is going a mile a minute—"The Funeral March." With the last of the revelers gone, Ginger goes around back. He figures he'll catch her before she gets into whatever car takes her home. He watches from the corner of the building as she comes out. In the cast of light he sees she's back in uniform but still in makeup and costume jewelry. A lot of those men in there, and the women too who laugh along, they see her as their clown. The whore part is bad enough, but who ever heard of a whore clown? Ginger wonders what it must be like to see through the eyes of those who could find her funny or sexy. She locks the storage-room door and Ginger is about to reveal his presence when she takes off into the dark—what? Where'd she go?

He doesn't want to holler, doesn't want Jameel in on this. He goes around the front. No waiting car, and he's heard no engine. Overhead, the rat-a-tat of a stick along the railway ties. He looks up through the trestle-work at the shadow feet flying between the slats and follows at a trot below. The ground rises to meet the rail line and he runs up the bank, getting winded, but she's still sprinting ahead, taking the ties three at a time with her arms flying out from her sides. By now they're on the edge of town, she tosses away her stick. He bends over to get his breath—he's not the sporty type. When he straightens up he can see her way ahead in the moonlight, seeming to jump up and down on one spot in a wild step-dance but getting smaller, smaller. He trots on.

To his left the water gleams dark silver beyond the cliff, the sound of his breath and pounding chest drown out his own footfalls along with the crickets and frogs singing now in the high weeds that line the tracks. They're traveling parallel to the Shore Road. She's running the whole way, this is how she gets home. Lord. They're way past town, it should be safe to call, "Fra—" and he's flat on his face on the piss-reeking tracks, his gut shocked airless, his back only now registering the impact that sent him flying forward—something grabs a fist of his hair and slams him into the gravel again and again and again, and darkness.

Tonight, Frances extinguishes her candle before she steps into the attic. It's the moon. Four rectangles of light have swooned through the latticed window onto the floor. The moon may drive men mad but it can calm a savage girl, for it is cool, precise, it is lucid. Especially in such an empty room. Frances pauses and allows herself to be soothed. Then she goes to the window. It's a good night for gazing.

One floor below, at the rear of the house, Lily is at her bedroom window watching the creek. Her lips are moving slightly as though whispering to someone down there, but there's not a soul to be seen, just shimmering segments of the moon in the water. Across the hall, and directly beneath the attic window where Frances has just seated herself, James is sound asleep, dreaming plentifully, the way he has since Frances receded from his life. He is a little boy again, and it's just he and his mother in a field of wildflowers. Mercedes is sleeping too, in her spare room, the whites of her brown eyes just showing in slits through nearly closed lids. She dreams of steel, of the color gray, of skeins of gray hair on a loom.

Frances strokes Trixie in her lap and realizes she's been followed home. She can see Boutros down there, though he can't see her. He's peering up, waiting for her candle to appear and warm the room. He's staring at the windowpane, but all he can see there is the moon.

Frances hasn't kept herself a technical virgin just to be raped by something the size of that—and why else did he follow me home? In her head is *The Catholic Wife*. Years ago she rifled Ralph Luvovitz's room when they were all supposed to be playing klezmer music downstairs, and robbed him of *What Every Boy Should Know*. *The Catholic Wife* was easier to come by but is much more complicated. A Catholic wife must keep a graph in her head at all times, plotting the ponderous journey of the ovum, stolid as an icebreaker, to its point of intersection with a zillion speedboats. On average, there are six or seven days a month when this is fairly likely to happen, whereas the rest of the time it's fairly likely not to happen. That's the rhythm method. Like comedy, it's about timing. Rhythm is a sin, of course, but only a venial one and sanctioned by the Holy Father in Rome, provided you are without lust when performing the generative act and not hoping not to get pregnant. (Unless you are performing the generative act in order to ward off your husband's lust for another woman, in which case it is a sin for you to give in to his lust, but one mitigated by your intention of preventing him from committing a worse sin with a woman not his wife. Go to confession, you're fine.) Every other type of birth control is a mortal sin for which you go directly to hell if unshriven at the hour of death.

Frances gets her period almost not at all but its scantiness is completely regular. Tonight is the first of the five or six probably fertile days. And this makes her shudder at the thought of Boutros loitering down there in the yard, because it's bad enough thinking about him going up her, much less a chip off that massive block coming out her nine months from now. She'll have to speed things up. She is irritated. Why did Ginger Taylor have to turn out to be a nice man?

Via Dolorosa

"Coupla drunks jumped me outside Jameel's."

The third lie.

"Ow, Addy, easy!"

Adelaide picks out another wood splinter and jabs carbolic at Ginger's chewed forehead. Luckily, that's the strongest part of the skull. Lucky too that his nose and teeth only grazed gravel while his forehead took the railway tie. Luckiest of all was being lulled awake by the warm buzz of the steel rails beneath him in time to roll over and let the noon coal train pass. Who's his guardian angel?

"I want to know who she is and no bullshit."

"What?" But it's useless to pretend. Why did he for one second think she'd buy it? "She's one of the Piper girls from New Waterford."

Adelaide gets a chill, but she just nods and says, "Frances." She knows the bad one is called Frances.

"I don't know what she wants. I went after her last night but I got jumped before I could ask her, I don't know by who or how many."

Adelaide looks at him. Waiting for the rest.

"I'm sorry, Addy. I gave her a drive once, that's all, I don't know why I lied before." He's feeling suddenly tired. "She's the little girl at the speak and I wanted to help her. I thought we could help her."

Adelaide folds a soft white dressing for his brow. "There's a lot of trouble in that family, Leo. That girl is not right in the head. She'll see you in jail for rape."

Ginger is shocked. "I would never, never—"

"The Pipers have money. You're a colored man, and that girl is after you."

★ ★ ★

With the dressing round his head and his face scabbing over nicely, he knocks at the steel door.

"You want a fuckin raise, b'y, is that it?"

"No, Mr. Jameel, I just quit, tell Piper I quit him too."

"Tell him yourself."

Ginger turns to leave, saying, "Then I guess he'll find out when I don't come for your order." Ginger wants a wide berth between him and all things Piper.

"Fuckin nigger, get the fuck off my property—Boutros!"

Ginger is already leaving but he won't run. He glances behind him to see the big son in the doorway. Ginger's not scared of Boutros, despite the crack on the neck he got when he grabbed Jameel that time—the boy was just protecting his father. Ginger knows fellas like that are sooner pussycats than fighters.

"Fuckin nigger," mutters Jameel. "Get the car, b'y," to Boutros without looking at him.

"Daddy, I'm going to get married."

Jameel wheels and swats Boutros across the face, "Get the fuckin car!"

That was around five o'clock.

"What kind of trouble?" Ginger asks.

Ginger knows the basic facts about the Pipers—what everyone knows and what he picked up driving to and from their house for years. Nowadays he hauls Piper's booze, but that only ever takes him to the still in the woods and all Piper ever says is "Thank you, Leo, drive safe."

But Adelaide knows what Teresa has told her. Teresa would never dream of telling such things to her little brother. Ginger was a sweet child, and keeping him from everything unpleasant is second nature to her. Besides, there are some things that are right to tell a woman friend, but otherwise indecent to repeat. Some things, when discussed with a dear husband or brother, are only poison. Good women discuss these things the way epidemiologists identify and track disease without alarming the public. This is woman's work. Men are unfitted for it by nature and should be protected from it the same way women shouldn't have to go down the mines. Men are so innocent.

"Tell me, Addy."

The time has come for inoculation. Adelaide takes a deep breath.

"The mother committed suicide. That was Mahmoud's daughter, Materia, who ran off with Piper. Mahmoud disowned her. Their daughter, the one with the voice who you drove—"

"Kathleen—"

"She had a baby out of wedlock, the little crippled gal. Piper killed his daughter by not calling the doctor when she was dying in childbed. Pearleen Campbell works at Ferguson's Funeral Parlor, she washed the body, there was a homemade cut in the belly, Pearleen and Teresa were girls together that's how Teresa knows. Years ago, Teresa took a big check to Piper from old man Mahmoud. Next thing you know, the singer girl goes to New York City, meantime her mother's in rags. The singer girl was a bitch. The mother died the day after her daughter was put in the ground, not a mark on her but her hair reeking of gas when they brought her to Ferguson's. Teresa went to the mother's funeral and saw the girl Frances laughing. That's what I know, so God knows what else there is, or what that Frances girl was b'ought up with. She's got a reason to be crazy, b'y, but that don't make her innocent."

That was after supper. Ginger had changed into his sun moon and stars shirt for the meal to mark his release from everything bad. Johnnycake and molasses, beans and Cape Breton steak—take a pound and a half of baloney; slice it; now scorch it. A celebration, even though quitting the rum-running business means less money again. Ginger never realized how important the Mahmouds were to his family until Teresa lost her job, and Adelaide lost customers, and he lost most of the legitimate side of his trucking business. And now here goes the illegitimate side of her. . . . Things have been worse than usual for everyone lately; the Taylors have had it good by comparison. At least they have a future saved up for their kids. They can start living on that.

The children are in bed. Teresa has just arrived with Hector, who holds out a date loaf for Adelaide with his big drooly smile.

"Thank you, baby!"

"Where's your man, Addy?" Teresa asks.

"Out New Waterford telling Piper he's quit."

"What's he quit for?"

"Sit'll I pour us some tea."

Thank God for tea, thank God for Teresa who I can talk to. Hector nods in his wheelchair while Adelaide tells Teresa the whole Frances story and finishes up with "I said to'm don't go out there, but he told me it's 'unmanly' not to look a feller in the eye when you're quitting him after all these years." She takes a sip of tea. "At least it's all over and done with."

Teresa hasn't said a word.

"Trese?"

"Yes dear, she's crazy, they're all right nuts." But Teresa is distracted and she gets up. "I just want to look at Carvery before I go."

Teresa loves to look at Carvery asleep. He looks like Ginger did when he was a baby and Teresa used to look after him. When she married Hector, she wanted to have a baby as sweet as Ginger. Carvery has inherited his father's nature too. Sound asleep in his tiny sun moon and stars shirt. Sweet, sweet baby boy.

"Aunt Teresa?" It's Evan whispering.

"Yes, darlin?"

"Sticky Leary snuck in the cloakroom and stole my lunch today, he called it nigger food."

"What did he do with it?"

"He said he threw it away but I saw him eat it."

"He was hungry."

"Mumma said I should beat the can off him. Do you think I should?"

"I think he doesn't have enough to eat."

"Why doesn't he just ask for some without calling me dirty names?"

"He's ashamed so he tries to make you ashamed."

"I'm not ashamed of anything. I should just beat the holy crap out of him, eh, Auntie?"

"If you want to do the real Christian thing, you put half your lunch in his pocket every day without letting anyone see. And the rest of the time you forget about him and concentrate on getting where you're going. You're big and strong. You can beat any boy your age, but you start with that and the game in the schoolyard's going to be 'who can beat Evan?' Then the older boys will get after you and when the teachers come out you'll be the one gets blamed. You want to be a boxer when you grow up?"

"No, I want to be a veterinarian."

"Then forget fighting and concentrate on schooling and you'll beat the lot of them, 'cause, sweetheart, most of them are going nowhere but underground."

"Or the steel plant."

"That's right."

Teresa comes back downstairs. "I told Evan not to fight, he asked me."

"Good, I told him to ask you." Adelaide believes that all children should have enough grown-ups around who love them so that one can tell them to fight, one can tell them not to and one can tell them not to worry so much.

Teresa leaves with Hector. It's early, they didn't even play cards. Adelaide stands in the open doorway and watches them go. Talk of anything to do with even an offshoot of Mahmoud must still upset Teresa. I'll have to think of something nice to do for Trese. I'll make her a shawl. It's hard, though, because Teresa wants always to give. It embarrasses her to get.

Teresa pushes Hector home down the alley so as to be totally alone. She is in shock about it being Frances Piper. Mahmoud's disowned granddaughter. The thin-faced goblin with the unkempt curls and Mrs. Mahmoud's rings. She somehow slithered into the house—she's small enough—and stole out of revenge in broad daylight. She stole my job. My good name. My brother's good name. She stole food from his table. And now she's after stealing him.

Teresa couldn't tell Adelaide about the jewels just now. To add it up with the Ginger story, out loud with her best friend? No. That would be to have all the bitterness poured into one cup so you could see just how much you had to drink. It makes Teresa dizzy to contemplate it, she will lose her mind with anger—Oh Jesus, sweet Lord, please don't let me hate. Look after the cruel and the crazy people, and let me look after my family, amen.

Even as she prays, Teresa makes a sickening realization. Frances recognized her that night in the alley with Adelaide. *That means she's been watching me. During the day in Mahmoud's house when I thought I was alone. The girl who laughed at her mother's funeral.* Teresa shivers. *And she was watching while I danced and sang my mother's song.*

The thief you must fear the most is not the one who steals mere things.

Ginger's not home yet. Eleven o'clock. Adelaide is uncharacteristically lying to herself. "He stopped at Beel's for a game of cards, he got a flat, he decided to do one more run for Piper at twice the price, I'll hear in a minute." She must be really scared to be doing this when what she knows is "She's got him." After the lying phase is the pissed-off phase, "Foolish, head-up-his-arse eejit, he can pack and shack up with the honky slut from hell," when what she knows is "She's sick, she's dangerous, she's with him now."

At six o'clock that evening, Jameel and Boutros arrived at the place in the woods where Piper makes the moonshine and cuts the liquor.

"Fuckin nigger up and quit," says Jameel, getting out on the passenger side.

James despises people who say "nigger." A civilized man need not resort to barroom slang for emphasis.

"Plenty where he came from," is all James has to say as he hands barrel after case to Jameel and Jameel hands them to Boutros and Boutros slings them into the back of the brand-new black 8-cylinder Kissel Brougham where the seats have been removed and curtains put up.

James looks at Jameel as little as possible. He regrets that his line of work necessitates contact with someone like this. Short black whiskers against a yellowish complexion, oily jet hair and the fusty smell of fried bread. James despises Jameel with his "nigger this" and "nigger that" because it's obvious to him that Jameel is shit-scared of being seen as colored. A man who wears his fear on his sleeve is a fool. Besides, thinks James, while Jameel is not black, he sure as hell is colored, 'cause he sure as hell's not white. James is grateful that all his girls turned out so fair. But there's obviously a morbid tendency in the blood they inherited from Materia that made Kathleen lean toward color. James has taken delivery of another crate of books. He has dipped into Dr. Freud in an effort to discover where to lay the blame for Kathleen's perversity. Freud calls women "the dark continent." James couldn't agree more. He doesn't hate blacks, he just doesn't want them near his bloodline.

"You're going to have to do it in three or four runs," says James, counting the money.

"Look, Jimmy, we should buy our own truck and get one of my boys driving." James lets Jameel call him "Jimmy" because it is better than having Jameel's greasy mouth on "James." Also, when you let someone call you by not-your-real-name, you are reminded every time he says it of what a foolish arse he is.

"I don't take partners, Jameel, you buy it, I'll hire it."

The back of the car is full and now Boutros closes the brimming trunk. James can see Materia in that boy. The same vacancy—standing there staring at me like he's going to say something, then doesn't. Nothing to say, that's why, not a thought in his head. Creeping idiocy in that family, that's another thing.

Boutros starts the car. Jameel slides in next to him. "See ya in a coupla weeks, Jimmy."

"I better see you in an hour."

"What for?"

James bends into the open passenger window. "I hired Leo Taylor because I knew I could trust him with merchandise, and until I'm convinced about a replacement I want you personally responsible."

"What are you talkin about, b'y? Boutros'll do the runs."

"You'll accompany him."

"You trust a nigger over my boy, is that it?"

"This is business, Jameel. I expect to see you back here in an hour or not at all." James straightens away from the window.

Jameel sticks his head out, "Fuck you Piper, you fuckin uppity sonofabitch, did you know you're supplying my place with Piper pussy, eh boy? And that she's fuckin your precious spade, Leo Taylor?"

James glances through the windshield at Boutros, who's still staring at him. Jameel smirks. James can't lay a hand on him with the big fella sitting there.

"Who are you talking about, Jameel?" he asks evenly.

"Your daughter Frances, b'y," with a good buddy grin.

"I don't have a daughter by that name."

Man, he's cool.

"If I don't see you here in an hour, Jameel, I'll assume our deal is terminated."

He turns and walks calmly towards the shack.

Jameel is enraged, head and shoulders out the window, "Everyone's had her, b'y! Everyone but you, I guess, or have you had her too?"

Boutros floors it and Jameel's head cracks against the outer chrome. "Shit!" Boutros gets a row of knuckles to the ear but he doesn't seem to notice, he's concentrating on James in the rearview mirror disappearing into the shack.

Inside, James has his first drink in thirteen years. He'll get this Jameel transaction over with in a few hours. Then he'll get hold of a rifle and go over to Leo Taylor's place for a talk.

"Slow down, you'll have the Mounties on us."

Boutros doesn't register the order.

"I said slow down."

But Boutros takes Low Point at a steady seventy. Boutros doesn't say a word throughout the next three runs, which makes it no fun for Jameel, who can usually count on "Yeah Pa, that's right Pa" whenever he leaves space for a breath. Jameel sulks in the car while Boutros takes the booze from Piper, who is drunker every time and likewise dead silent. That's how an *enklese* gets you, thinks Jameel, with silence. Ice, they use, they're smart but they're not quite human. No feelings. When it comes to his son Boutros, however, Jameel doesn't think "silent," he thinks "dumb."

Boutros is calm because he has decided that tonight is the night. He'll take money, what he's rightfully earned, from his father's safe, then he'll go get Frances and they'll drive. Wherever she wants to go. Forget the farm, forget his mother, that was the dream of a child, the grown-up knows that he has to get Frances off this island right away. There are too many men here who need to be killed, first among them her own father. What kind of a man disowns his daughter? Frances is a diamond, passed from filthy paw to paw but never diminished. The men who handle her can leave no mark because her worth is far above them. Hard, helpless, buried. You can hear it in her voice and see it in her eyes, she is waiting for a strong and fearless miner to go way down and rescue her up to the surface where she can shine for all she's worth.

Boutros has to get her away tonight, before something happens, he doesn't know what. He had a terrible feeling when his father taunted Piper about having had his own daughter. Boutros knew it must be true. For Frances to do what she does right under her father's nose, Piper must know she's already ruined, and he knows because he ruined her. But Boutros knows that no one is that powerful to be able to ruin something God created good. That was proven by Job. The Devil can try, but he can't triumph.

Why did Adelaide believe Ginger when he said he was going to square things like a man with Piper? Because she was tired of not believing him. When people get tired they sometimes do things they wouldn't normally do. Materia went for a nap with her head in the oven. That's not in Adelaide's line. When she gets tired, she stops tasting for truth. In a moment of fatigue she wanted everything to be all right, but wishing never made anything right. This is what happens when Adelaide stops being tough for a second.

If Adelaide weren't in such a hurry she would run out and lose her supper into the toilet, but there isn't time, so she walks shaky to Beel's Grocery on the corner. "Have you seen my man tonight, missus?" is a rhetorical question. Mrs. Beel goes straight to Adelaide's house to mind the children while Adelaide takes care of her trouble. Wilfrid Beel is there with his philosophical white hair. He offers her a drive wherever she might need to go.

"I'll let you know, Wilf."

She leaves and walks to Teresa's house.

Earlier that evening, Ginger had just laid Carvery in the crib when he saw a light down in the garage. He went out and opened the double doors onto the blazing headlights of his truck. He stood for a moment, temporarily blinded, and heard a soft crying.

"Hello?" he said.

Again the soft whimper.

It's coming from the cab. Ginger opens the driver's side and sees a dark shape huddled against the opposite door. A small voice says, "Don't tell on me."

His gullet leaps in fear. It's her. Instinctively he hits the lights and they go out in slow motion.

"I'm scared," she says, her voice muffled behind her hands.

"I'm not going to hurt you."

She says something he can't understand, barely audible and obscured by sorrow.

"You can't stay here, Frances."

The crying starts again—quiet, rhythmically regular, drained of passion. Like a child who's already cried itself to sleep, then reawakened and is now no longer crying to be heard, having given up on that.

"What's wrong?"

Soft hiccup, the voice is drenched and exhausted, ". . . hurt me."

"What?" he says, stepping up on the running board. She rustles away from him in frightened reflex.

"Shshsh, shsh, I'm not going to hurt you, what's wrong?"

"I already got hurt."

"What happened?"

"I can't tell you."

"Yes you can. But, Frances, you can't stay here, come into the house."

"No-o-o." Fresh terror, fresh tears.

"How can I help you if you won't come inside?"

"Take me to a safe place."

"Where?"

"A place I know where he can't get me."

"Who?"

"My father."

"Frances. Did your father hurt you?"

No answer. Sound of a hand wiping a wet nose.

"What did he do?"

She sounds more grown-up now. Brave. "I made him mad."

"Tell me what he did to you."

Her voice goes cold. "It's my own fault"—sniff—"I'm no good, he's right. Why should anyone care about me, why should you, I'm bad for everyone."

Ginger has found a match in his pocket. As he lights it, she recoils and covers her face with her hands, "No!"

He looks at her, curled up in the corner, so fragile. He reaches out, gently pries a hand away from her face and, just before the flame dies, "Oh my Lord." He's shocked. Who could do such a thing?

"Don't look at me, I'm ugly."

"You're not ugly."

"Yes I am, go away."

"You're hurt. I'm going to help you, I'm going to get my wife."

"No!" she hisses.

Her life depends on this. "No one can know. I came here tonight 'cause you're the only one I can trust. If anyone knows, if he finds out where I am, he'll come and kill me." She takes a deep breath. "I can understand if you're not willing to help me, you have enough troubles, thank you anyway." The passenger door clunks open in the dark.

"Wait, wait—"

She pauses, her feet dangling.

"—where do you need to go?"

"It's about five miles out of New Waterford. No one knows about it, it's an old mine. I've got food and money. If I can stay there a couple of days, he'll think I'm already off the island. Then it'll be safe to hitch a ride to the ferry and go."

"Go where?"

"Just go."

He hesitates.

"Forget it," she says. "Sorry to bother you, Mr. Taylor."

"I'll take you."

Silence.

"I said I'll take you there, Frances."

". . . God bless you."

"Just wait here a minute."

Boutros is serene behind the wheel. They're heading back to Sydney, it's the last run of the night, the sun's long gone, it was a too-hot day. If Frances agrees, they'll drive to British Columbia. He wants to grow things. Cherries. And grapes, for wine. The thought of his own orchard, and Frances free and flourishing among rows of gnarly trees in bloom, full fruit, heavy vines—he pictures stuffing their own grape leaves with rice and lamb, he loves to cook, anything that consists of something wrapped around something else. Driving is a wonderful place for dreaming.

Boutros doesn't enjoy violence. It's just the job he's always done for his father. Mostly it consists of walking into other men's violence and turning it off for them, like groping for a switch in a dark cluttered basement. To do this he often has to hurt them. He rarely gets angry. Though he got angry last night with Taylor on the rail tracks. Boutros spared him for Mrs. Taylor's sake. She's a hardworking woman and doesn't deserve to be a widow. And Taylor seems to have learned his lesson and backed off.

"Slow the Jesus down, ya moron!" Jameel's nerves are shot.

Up ahead comes Leo Taylor's truck. It whizzes past them on the land side of the Shore Road. The one-second aperture of his headlights has taken a picture for Boutros which is just now coming up in black and white through the film on his eyes: Frances in the cab, looking straight at him, her face a battered mess. Taylor at the wheel, laughing at her.

"What the fuck are you doing!" Jameel grabs the dashboard and goes slamming into the passenger door as glass collides in the back—"Shit!"—and the Kissel fishtails out of the U-turn, speeding after the truck in a wake of rye whiskey.

"Leo Taylor's got Frances."

Jameel screams, "So what the fuck what?" and begins slapping Boutros.

Boutros puts up a hand to keep his line of vision clear, they're gaining on the truck.

"She's my cousin."

"She's a whore!"

"Don't talk about her like that."

Jameel starts laughing. Boutros trembles.

"You sweet on her, b'y? Eh? You sweet on the whore? You smelled her? Ha ha."

Boutros blinks hard.

"You gonna cry now, crybaby?" Boutros does have tears in his eyes. "Eh, little sissy-boy, sooky-baby, eh, little mama's boy gonna cry now, eh? Go ahead, go on—"

The windshield explodes with Jameel's head, shattering Boutros's view of the road. He sticks his face out the window just in time to swerve out of the way of an oncoming carload of nuns. His hand is still around the back of his father's neck as the Kissel hurtles off the road, over the ruts and along the cliff at eighty till the terrain changes abruptly to silent air. Jameel is dead before they hit the rocks below.

The nuns turn around and drive back, dropping off three of their number to investigate while the other three drive back to New Waterford to get an ambulance. By the time the rugger-playing one picks her way down to the water's edge, there is only one man, his neck all but severed. The other man is found the next day. The engineer didn't quite manage to stop the coal train in time, but the big man lying on the tracks was already dead.

"I'll just talk to Piper and turn right around and come home," Ginger had told Adelaide just after nine.

"I love you. . . ."

It gave him a twinge when she said his private name, but he wasn't lying for his own sake, and this time there was a reason—to protect that poor beat-up girl waiting for him in the truck. In a couple of days she'd be gone right off this rock, and that gave him a light feeling even as he told the lie.

It's a cloudy night but Ginger gets a good look at Frances as they pass the fires of the steel plant. There's blood crusting her nose and filling the gully that meets her upper lip. The lip is split and fat on the left side. Her left eye is likewise puffy and blacked. That Piper is more than just a negligent father. This explains everything.

"What happened to you?" she asks, and for a second he isn't sure what she means because he's been concentrating on her injuries.

"Last night," he says, "fella got me." He feels himself blushing. "I was following you home, along the tracks. I wanted to ask you something."

"What?"

"Well I know the answer now, I was just going to ask you why you kept coming around me."

"Because you're the only good man I know."

Ginger feels ashamed. Sydney is behind them now. He picks up speed on the Shore Road.

"I'm sorry I ignored you at the picture house," she says. "It's better for Lily's sake if she doesn't know anything."

"That's your little sister?"

He turns. There's just enough dark to swallow her wounds and light her eyes. She gives him a calm, knowing look. It's like an invitation to rest—it says, don't try any more, stop fighting, I know. I understand something that's so deep you think it's behind you. But it isn't. It's inside you. Let me touch it.

"Lily," he says. "That's a pretty name." He sounds foolish to himself. Something has hit his stomach like a fiery drink and it's spreading out through his limbs. He shakes it off. "You and me make a fine team, eh?" he chuckles.

"What do you mean?"

Her voice is so grown-up he feels callow but he presses on. "I mean the two of us with our wracked-up faces, what a sight." He turns to her and laughs, and she smiles slightly, as he's glad to see by the light of an oncoming car. Frances keeps one eye on the road as the headlights of the Kissel slice by the truck.

"Can this thing go any faster?" she wants to know.

★   ★   ★

At Teresa's house, Hector rocks quietly by the kitchen stove and follows the conversation with his eyes. Adelaide is sick with worry.

"I have to go out there, Teresa, she's got him, oh my God," she leans over and holds her stomach.

"Settle down now, I'll tell you what we're going to do, Addy. First we're going to find out if she's home, 'cause if she is there's nothing to be worried about—we'll get Wilf Beel to drive us out and, okay, here's what we're going to do, listen now: I'll go up to the door and say old Mahmoud is dying and wants to see his granddaughters at the last minute, and if Piper says forget it, I let him know there could be money in the will, you know? And then I say Mahmoud also says for them all to come or none, so we'll know if Frances isn't there—what're you doing, girl, sit down."

"Where's Hector's gun?"

"What do you want with it?"

"Don't ask foolish questions and shut up with your foolish ideas."

Hector stares wide-eyed at Adelaide and points a finger at the top cupboard. Adelaide climbs onto the kitchen counter and Teresa seizes her around the knees.

"I'm warning you, Trese."

"Addy, come on now—"

Woomph, a back foot to the stomach. "I'm sorry, dear." Adelaide fishes the rifle from on top of the cabinet. "Thank you, Hector."

"That thing doesn't even work anymore," says Teresa, still on the floor.

Adelaide fires it into the ceiling, Teresa screams.

"It works." Adelaide hops down from the counter, calm the way people are when they've gone over the edge.

Teresa talks fast. "All right, Addy, we'll get Wilf and we'll drive till we find them, no point going out to their house, you're right, she's not there, she's with him, so let's calm down and go get a ride."

By the time the Jameels left with their last load, James was stone-cold drunk. He climbed into his immaculate 1932 close-coupled Buick sedan and started it up. It's a tan color. Gangsters have black cars. He drove at a moderate speed back to New Waterford. He had decided not to bother finding a rifle. The best close-up killing is done with a bayonet. A rifle is

really just an appendage, useful if the blade gets stuck in the ribs and you
have to shoot free. But once you've been around for a while you know
how to avoid making noise. Under and up.

"Stop."

Pine branches bend and squeak against Ginger's truck. This isn't even
a road. He cuts the engine.

"We have to walk from here," Frances says. "Take my hand."

He does. It's necessary, after all she knows the way, he doesn't and it's
such a dark night. Such a slim soft hand.

Mercedes is dusting the piano. She has taken all the figurines and doilies off
it and she is about to apply the lemon oil when Daddy comes in, "Give me
the keys to the hope chest, Mercedes."

He reeks of liquor. Mercedes is scared.

"What's wrong, Daddy?" But she knows enough to have the keys in
her outstretched hand while asking.

"Don't worry, my dear, I won't be long."

He takes the stairs two at a time without hurrying. Mercedes screws
the lid back on the lemon oil, wipes her hands and follows him up two
flights to the attic. He's on his knees with the contents of the hope chest
scattered over the floor.

"What happened to The Old-Fashioned Girl?" he asks gently, holding it in his hand.

"I knocked her over while dusting, Daddy, I didn't want to hurt you
by saying so."

"I'll get you a new doll, Mercedes." He goes back to rummaging.
"I'm sorry about this mess."

Trixie hops down from the window ledge and hugs the wall on her
way out. Mercedes feels icy cold. He sounds so strange, just two inches off
to the side of his normal self, how does it add up with how drunk he must
be? The smell reminds her of how sick she always feels even when she's
feeling fine.

He finds what he's looking for at the very bottom, "Ouch." He was
prepared to find it in need of a quick grinding, but it's razor sharp, though
he remembers laying it in the chest dull with the war. Just as well, he
thinks, as he sucks a bead or two from his fingertip.

"Where are you going, Daddy?"

He pats her heavily on the head, this man who never touches her. "You stay and look after your sister."

"What are you fellas doing up there?" Lily from the bottom of the attic stairs.

"Go back to bed," Mercedes orders.

James trots down the attic stairs, calling back to Mercedes, "I have to find Frances."

"No!" Mercedes has shrieked it.

Lily is shocked—the sound is stranger than Daddy kissing the top of her head with a long knife in his hand. Mercedes leaps into the dark shaft of the attic stairway, catching and propelling herself by the palms of her hands against the walls. James seizes her by the wrists as she lands in the hallway, and nearly drops the bayonet, now at an angle. Lily doesn't take her eyes off it.

"I'm not going to hurt Frances. I'm after the man who's been at her, that's all." He's starting to feel the liquor now. "My little girl . . ."

He wheels to face the top of the stairs leading down to the front hall and he puts his bayonet hand on the railing, "I'll be right back."

Mercedes puts a hand over Lily's eyes. Then she pushes her father down the stairs.

The ground slopes sharply upward. They've reached the hill with the drift mine cut into it.

"There's a bit of a climb," says Frances.

"I'll go in front." He bends to the hill and they start up.

She gasps and her hand slips from his, he flings out an arm catching the sleeve of her uniform, "You okay?"

"Yes." She gets up. ". . . Ow."

"Wait now." He lifts her into his arms. Light as a feather. She slips an arm around his neck of necessity and, with quiet dignity, "Thank you." He carries her up the hill.

"There." He places her gently on the ground before an arch of complete darkness.

"You can go now, Mr. Taylor."

He is nonplussed. He can't just leave her here, in the dark, can he?

"Wait, Frances, don't you have a flashlight, have you got a blanket or something in there?"

"Don't worry about me, I'll be fine. Goodbye."

She turns, becomes pure shadow, then is swallowed by the mouth of the mine.

"Frances?"

But she doesn't answer. He shifts his weight. He leans into the darkness, "Frances."

He hesitates. He enters the pit.

Feeling his way with one hand along the damp wall, the other hand outstretched, walking slowly, slowly, listening for her steps, "Frances?" Why is he whispering, and why does she not answer? Step, step, step over the uneven floor. He lets go of the wall and lights a match—nothing but the dank shine to one side of him and below, his dusty boots looking up at him so trusting. The light goes out. Step. Step. Both hands outstretched now, he walks for two long minutes. He stubs his toe on a stone sending it scudding for an instant, then three counts of silence before a wet plonk. That sound is called cutting the Devil's throat—no splash, deep water. His heart kicks, he claws for the wall but it's farther away than he thought, which pitches him to the void in the opposite direction—he throws himself toward his feet, hurting his shoulder. The floor was closer than he thought. He lies curled on his side for a moment almost sick with relief. To fall into God knows how deep a flooded shaft in the dark—the first heavy sinking, then panicking, losing up from down, that's how you drown even when you're quite a good swimmer.

He takes a big breath and no sooner returns to his feet than "What if she's fallen in?" He didn't hear a splash, but then she slipped away so quickly, it could have happened before he stepped into the mine, either that or—he lights his last match, yes a wide pool, black water—she may have slid beneath the surface, intending all along to drown herself tonight. The match goes out. He lowers himself carefully to the floor, stretches out on his stomach and dips an arm down into the water, a prayer in his head, his heart full of dread, feeling around. Cold. Nothing. Something silky. *Oh Jesus!* He travels screaming over cinders, yanked along by a sudden vise grip round his wrist, down into the water, plunging head and shoulders, waist, his knees grab the lip as he clutches an unseen arm in both his hands, hauling her up along with himself, breaking the surface with a torrent the sound of a hefty rag mop.

She's naked. He finds her armpits and lays her on the rough ground, she doesn't answer, her eyes are closed, he can feel that, he fumbles for her mouth, opens it, gasps for his own breath—drowning people try to drown their saviors—slips a hand beneath her head and presses his mouth onto hers, opening the cut in her lip, he tastes blood and it reminds him of life, still warm, he breathes into her, she coughs and starts to cry.

"Are you all right, Frances, I didn't mean to hurt you, honey, here." He wants to tear off his jacket, shirt, wrap her up, but his clothes are soaking wet so he folds her in his arms instead.

"I'm sorry," she cries, "I'm sorry," and clings to him.

"It's okay, it's okay," he pats her shoulder blade.

After a moment her shivering subsides and she strokes the back of his neck, kisses his cheek, grazing his ear, "Thank you," she rests her thigh between his legs and brushes his mouth accidentally with her lips, "sorry."

"That's okay."

"Don't leave me, please, I'm so frightened of the dark," closer.

"I won't leave you, but—" he's embarrassed to find he's hard, he didn't know till now he wanted her, still doesn't know, "excuse me," and he moves to release her.

"That's okay," she whispers, kissing his mouth, moving next to him, "ohhh," she says and her fingers sink into his shoulders. He pulls her a little closer without meaning to, she sighs again and reaches down, "that's okay little Ginger Man," her voice is so gentle, she undoes his pants and slides against him, "that's okay . . ." and she says his secret name. He moans. Misery and desire, because with that she's onto him and all around him and he can only move inside her.

Ginger's private name must not be written down. It's bad enough that Frances knows it.

When Mercedes' hand uncovers Lily's eyes, Lily sees her father lying bunched up at the foot of the stairs. The bayonet has landed a safe six steps above him. In retrospect, Mercedes calculates that he was highly unlikely to land anywhere near the blade, considering the position of his hand on the railing and its loose grip on the weapon at the time of the fall. Furthermore, he was sufficiently drunk to render the fall likely nonlethal. But Mercedes faces the fact that she merely pushed. And calculated later. She has not read Dr. Freud. She takes no solace in the subconscious. She takes responsibility. She decides in that moment to stop her penance in the coal cellar. It appears to her suddenly as so much whining. Yes, she will confess this sin of pushing her father. But she knows now that no good act is ever unaccompanied by evil. That is what original sin has done to us.

That is what makes us human. The necessity of sin itself is the cross we must bear.

God did not put me on this earth to stand by while my sister Frances is killed. Beaten is one thing. Wrongly touched is one thing. Stabbed with a bayonet is another. Push. Be strong enough to carry the burden of sin that goes with doing the right thing. There is only one saint in this family and I'm not it.

God has made Mercedes a judge. No one loves you for that. Not like a crippled child who's prone to visions. Whom Mercedes prizes. Not like a fallen woman who makes people laugh. Whom Mercedes loves.

Mercedes is standing straight as steel, staring down at James. Brown-eyed people are popularly believed to be soft somewhere. And warm. Look again.

Lily walks carefully down the stairs in her bare feet, holding onto both railings. She bends over James. A line of spit runs from the corner of his mouth. She strokes his hair and gives him a kiss on the cheek. His eyelashes flutter. She looks up at Mercedes, and says, "He's not dead."

"Good. Now go to bed."

Curled deep in the hope chest left open by James, Trixie hears Frances call her name and leaps out, padding down the stairs, across the hall and into the room Frances used to share with Lily. But Frances is not here. There's just Lily kneeling at the window, her hands folded on the ledge, looking out. Trixie brushes the soles of Lily's feet as Mercedes swishes past the bedroom door, the bayonet flashing in her hand. Up in the darkness of the attic, Mercedes dumps everything back into the hope chest as quickly as possible, pressing its lid down snug against air and moths.

Frances's eyes burst open. She had a dream about Trixie just now. Frances was calling and calling her but Trixie was locked in a box and smothered. It was just a dream. Don't move. Don't wake this man who's crushing me now.

Frances doesn't want to have to stand up and lose any of his goodness down her legs. And she'll have to stand up if he awakens because he'll be clamoring to get out of here, wondering what in the name of God he's done, and if he leaves she'll have to go with him because she sure as shooting doesn't intend to walk the five miles home. Not in what she hopes is her delicate condition. She'll lie still for another couple of hours.

★ ★ ★

"Wiggle your toes."

James groans and lolls his head. Mercedes pours more ice water on his face and he uncrumples with a jerk.

"Good," she says. She gets behind him, hooking her hands under his arms, and yanks him into a sitting position.

"Help me now," she orders. He slumps onto his knees. She gets him standing, then hauls him like timber into the front room, where he collapses onto the couch and passes out again. She looks at him with her arms folded for a moment, then leaves and returns with a blanket. She tosses it over him.

Advancing steadily toward the front of her mind is the memory of what she and Frances can't know together out loud. She has kept this memory on top of a pile of things at the back of her mind. Not buried. Right there where she can see it every time she passes the open door. But as long as she keeps it in the back room, she can believe that it belongs with the rest of the old junk. As long as she doesn't talk about it, it can remain overlooked by amateurs and experts alike: the gilt frame covered with dust, the painting gummed over with neglect—who would guess what a piece of work lies dormant there.

But it has stirred. Torn itself from its frame, and now it's coming closer and closer—stop. That's far enough.

Mercedes takes the cap off the lemon oil and picks up her dust rag. If she's going to look at what just arrived behind her eyes, she has to have something to occupy her hands.

It was here in the living room. The painting from the junk pile is called *Daddy and Frances in the Rocking Chair*. But there never was a rocking chair, in this room or any other. Just the pale green wingback. Mercedes' white rag goes round and round, bringing up the mahogany sheen on the piano.

It was the night of Kathleen's funeral. I got up because Frances was gone from our bed. You could see her imprint in the snow sheets and pillow. I looked out at the creek but she's not there. Good. Maybe she's gone downstairs for something to eat. She must be hungry by now, she hasn't had anything but imaginary food for two days. I will go downstairs too, and make cinnamon toast. I pictured myself and Frances eating cinnamon toast and drinking cocoa at the kitchen table, but I didn't put on my tartan housecoat or my slippers, which is how I know now I didn't really believe in the cinnamon toast. Bad things happen when Frances gets out of bed. I'm not afraid of the dark. I had two long french braids. On my way down the stairs I heard a sound like a puppy. I walked down the stairs towards the light spilling through the front-room archway on the right. To the left is the dark kitchen and a smell like the inside of someone's body. In the front room the reading lamp will be on, the yellow one with the pleated shade that stands over the wingback chair. I get to the archway. I was right, it is the reading lamp. Frances is there looking at me already. I wonder how long she's been waiting for me. She had blond ringlets then and no laugh lines. She's sitting on Daddy's lap, sideways, facing me. Rocking. He's rocking her. But it's not working, she's wide awake. He doesn't see me because he's looking into her hair. His mouth is open a little, an upside-down new moon. He's making the sound. The skin on his face looks pulled back by an undertow, his head is straining forward not to drown. His right hand hovers, barely touching the halo of yellow fuzz Frances gets from turning on her pillow, and his left hand is under and up her nightgown like a puppeteer's. He says something I can't hear, then breathes up hard through his nose, then "my little girl," and the chewed-up word "beautiful," then he shoves her down between his legs and pins one hand across her chest, the other one still operating underneath, they're both facing in the same direction now but Frances turns her face to keep our eyes together. His head snaps back and he jams her up between his legs once, again, three times and a half, until he trembles at the ceiling. That's when the fear goes out of him and he crumples around her and cries into her hair. Frances and I keep looking at each other until he falls asleep like that, then she crawls out from behind his arms and walks over to me. "It doesn't hurt," she says. Now I see a piece of him behind the narrow opening in his pants. I go get the crocheted comforter from the sofa and I put it over him without looking again, it's rude to stare. Sizzling comes from the kitchen across the hall. I don't like that smell of kidneys cooking. "Me neither," says Frances. We go back upstairs to bed and I sing songs to her until I fall asleep. The next day, Frances sucked on dough and Mumma died in the kitchen.

The piano is a mirror but Mercedes is not staring at herself, she's staring at her father passed out beneath the crocheted blanket.

"Mercedes?"

"What are you doing up, Lily?"

"Is Frances home yet?"

"No."

"Are you worried this time?"

"Yes."

"I know where she is. Ambrose told me."

Lily can't tell Mercedes how she knows where Frances goes when she doesn't come home. That would mean tattling on Frances for scaring the pee out of her that day at the old French mine when they were supposed to be at Brownies and Guides. It would also mean revealing that it was Frances who told Lily about Ambrose in the first place, and where he lives now and what he does at night. If Mercedes finds that out, she might start treating Frances as though she too were special to God. Frances wouldn't like that. She might run away. Or worse, if Mercedes finds out that Ambrose is a gift from Frances, she might think Ambrose is evil.

Mercedes knows Frances is bad but loves her anyway, because however hard it is to be the good one in the family, it is harder still to be the bad one. Lily understands that. Who in the world does Lily love more than Frances? Not even Daddy. Who in the world does she fear more than Mercedes, whose cocoa tin has filled twenty times over against Lily's fourteenth birthday, when they will journey to Lourdes along with throngs of other special people who come to bathe in Our Lady's own creek and leave their specialness behind for ever? Lily has promised herself, her little leg, that—number one—she will never let it be cut off. And—number two—she will never let it be obliterated by a miracle. The idea of betraying so valiant a limb, which has carried and marched beyond the call of duty. To say, here is your reward: to cease to be—to become, instead, a false twin for the good leg. Her bad leg is special because it is so strong. Lily has learned, however, that to others it is special because it is weak. No one, not even Our Lady, will get their holy waters on her little leg.

I can't tell Mercedes the true history of Ambrose, thinks Lily. Mercedes loves me because I'm special to God. If she thinks I'm special to the Devil, I might have to run away. I saw through the cracks in Mercedes' fingers how Daddy wound up at the bottom of the stairs.

"Where?" Mercedes has no expression on her face.

Lily looks up at Mercedes and the bump appears faintly in her forehead. "Ambrose says not to worry. It's not a bad man she's with."

Lily is fairly sure that at least the latter part is true. Daddy was away at work today, Mercedes was off cleaning the sacristy at Our Lady of Mount Carmel Church and Lily was in her room starting a diary—"Dear Diary,

Allow me to introduce myself"—when Frances ran down from the attic and past the bedroom door, where Lily caught a glimpse of her and cried, "Frances!"

But Frances clattered down the front hall stairs, catapulting over the last five steps, hitting the floor with a thump and a spring to the door. Lily took the stairs as fast as she dared, "Frances, what happened to you?" stumbling and clinging to the railing halfway down. "Frances!" cried Lily.

"Fwances!" she mocked back, yanking open the door and turning to grin up at Lily, the left side of her face all bloody, her Guide neckerchief soaked. Tears sprang to Lily's eyes but Frances said as though stating the obvious, "Don't worry, Lily, it's not real blood."

And she was gone.

Lily went up to the attic but all she found there was the empty coal scuttle. She touched the lip of it and her finger came away red. She tasted it. Salt and iron. She washed the scuttle in the bathroom and took it back down to the cellar.

Lily can't tell Mercedes that Frances beat herself up. Mercedes might think Frances is crazy. That too can be grounds for specialness to God.

"Go get dressed, Lily."

Mercedes has never driven the car before. James always parks it in second gear so it has stayed in second the whole way, Mercedes gripping the wheel and peering forward into the lit-up darkness.

"She has a beat-up face, but the man didn't do it."

"I know, Lily."

Lily looks sharply across at Mercedes and tests her cautiously; "I saw how it happened."

Mercedes returns the look. "Did he see you watching?"

"I don't think so."

"Don't worry, Lily, he'll never touch her again"—It's on the tip of Lily's tongue to say, "It wasn't Daddy," but she doesn't. The fog has settled and they are in the midst of a soft void—it's as though they've ceased to travel forward at all, the car just rocking gently side to side. Mercedes returns her eyes to the blind windshield—"I won't let him."

They crawl along in silence for a while. You can tell where the edge of the road is by reaching out through the passenger window till you feel the pine needles going by. Lily loses herself in this task but gives a start when something chilly alights on her other hand.

"Say a little prayer with me for Daddy, Lily." And Mercedes closes her hand around Lily's. "Let us ask God to forgive him."

"Because he knows not what he does . . ." says Lily.

"Let's say a decade of the beads."

"Did you bring a rosary?"

"We don't need a rosary, Lily. We have faith."

But Mercedes needs to count something, so she counts the nubs of the wooden steering wheel, a nub for each whispered prayer, allowing them to slip beneath her fingers. One. By one. By one.

By the time Mercedes' left hand has gone three times around the steering wheel, her other hand has drained the warmth from Lily's and they both of them are cold. An increase in the pressure of their backs against the seat tells them that the road has started to ascend. The last strands of fog caress the car, releasing it back into time and space and night.

"Glory be to the Father, and to the Son, and to the Holy Ghost, as it was in the beginning, is now, and ever shall be—"

"Turn here."

"That's not a road, Lily."

"I know."

They lurch and rumble through squealing branches till the back of a truck appears in their lights. Mercedes feels her eyes and stomach go watery. She reads the name stenciled there, "Leo Taylor Transport."

"He's not a bad man, Mercedes."

Their lights fade from the rear of the truck. They get out of the car. Mercedes has brought Daddy's old pit lantern. She lights it.

It's a sin for Lily to let Mercedes think it was Daddy who beat up Frances. But he has done it in the past. Surely truth can be borrowed across time without perishing. Shelf life, so to speak. Though Lily knows the man in the mine with Frances did not hit her, she is nevertheless worried. In the movies, when a girl is interested in a man she gets dressed up, powders her nose and puts on a little lipstick. But what kind of man is it for whom a girl would see fit to render herself more attractive by bashing in her own face?

Lily and Mercedes walk slowly, scraping their way through the woods, pinning back boughs for each other. Lily strains to spot the trail that Frances blazed in the trees that November day almost three years ago. She hasn't mentioned the trail to Mercedes. After all this time, you'd never notice the marks unless you knew they were there. Frances carved each one with the kitchen scissors. Scissors have not changed since ancient history. The Egyptians had scissors and eyeshadow and jewelry and pet cats just as we do, it's in a beautiful golden book that Lily got for Christmas from Daddy, *Secrets of King Tut*. But they didn't have the wheel.

"Do you think the Egyptians had the wheel, Mercedes?"

"I'm sure I neither know nor greatly care."

"I think they did but it was too holy to them to draw it. Or else they wanted to keep it a secret."

Mercedes stops. "How much farther?"

"We're halfway there." They've just passed the tree marked with an "R"—the fourth of seven letters, each spaced seven trees apart.

"After all," Lily continues, "they worshiped the sun and the sun is round." Lily counts seven trees and stops again.

Mercedes holds the lantern up to a gouge in the bark where Lily is peering.

"What are you looking at?"

" 'O' " Lily reads. Then turns to Mercedes. "We're almost there."

Mercedes knows only that her sister is being guided. She looks down into Lily's eyes, and Lily feels her back open up like a book on either side of her spine, onto a dark and endless corridor full of something Mercedes craves. This is the look of Reverence. Like the look of Pity, it is frightening. But Lily has learned how to remain Lily while receiving such a look. She holds her eyes the way you might hold your arms when looking up at someone who is in danger of falling from a high place: still, steady, outstretched. This discourages the person from jumping and killing you both, for perhaps they just wanted to know there was someone waiting below to catch them. The way Lily looks when she calmly holds out her eyes in this manner is what the lookers of Pity and Reverence call "beatific."

"Are you tired, Lily?" Mercedes asks gently, allowing Lily's back to close up again.

"No. We're almost there."

And they walk on. "S." And finally, "E."

"Up there." Lily points.

Mercedes raises the lantern to the sudden incline of the hill. "You'd better wait here, Lily."

"No. I better come."

They hold hands and traverse the hill. Unlike Frances, Mercedes paid attention at Guides and learned how to climb a steep hill without falling, how to swim safely across a current.

Mercedes knows that Frances is no stranger to men, she only wonders how Frances has avoided pregnancy for so long. But tonight is different. For Daddy to be upset, it has to be. "Different how?" Mercedes wondered, as soon as James was prone at the foot of the stairs. She has been going over that question and she has come up with an answer. It was Lily saying that Frances was not with "a bad man" that tipped Mercedes off. It must be that Frances is in love. Planning to elope with this man, whoever he is. But why elope? There must be some obstacle. The man must be married.

What would become of Frances, on the run with a man not bound by law to look after her? How long could anyone, man or woman, put up with Frances? Who else but Mercedes knows how to love Frances? And where would Frances and her lover be by the time he'd had enough? Hundreds, perhaps thousands of miles away, maybe in another country. Frances stranded, without money or love, would die far from home. Mercedes can't bear the thought. It burns her throat and salts her eyes. Dear Frances. My little Frances, alone, dying and no one there to love her because no one there remembers.

Mercedes bends to the hill, they're almost there, "Hurry, Lily." Thank you God, thank you Jesus, Mary and Joseph and all the saints, for Lily, who is divinely inspired. If Lily's premonition proves correct and prevents Frances from running away, then that will be a miracle indeed. Time enough to contact the archdiocese once Frances is safely home.

The old pit lantern lights up the rim of the arch—torn earth, a fringe of tangled grass, a limestone gash and, within, the gleaming textures of the walls. Cave paintings would never last in here, too damp.

Mercedes calls softly, "Frances."

Lily whispers, "The tunnel goes around a bend, then there's a pool of deep water."

Please God, let it be a good man.

They walk in.

"Frances."

Frances will hide, Mercedes thinks, so she proceeds slowly, casting the lantern from side to side, examining every nook and cranny. Lily keeps her eyes on her feet, waiting for the yelp of fear when Mercedes sees the dead miner, the dead soldier. But it doesn't come. As with so much else of what she remembers, Lily wonders, was it just a dream? Did that happen? Was that really me?

The corridor begins to curve to the left.

Frances has heard her name and shoves Ginger off her. He wakes, cold with misery, full of apology.

"Shut up," she says. "Someone's coming."

She feels around for the rock under which she hid her uniform.

"Stay here, Frances, I'll go and see who it is."

"It's my sister and Christ only knows who else," scuffling into her clothes.

He's bewildered. The water of the pool was not as cold as this.

"Frances, I didn't mean to take advantage of you."

She laughs, hauling on her shoes.

This time they both hear her name.

"Sweet Jesus." He feels for his fly and buttons up. Her footsteps start away. Ginger flails out and catches her bicep, so fragile.

"Ow." She writhes but he won't let her go.

"Where are you going?"

"Home."

"What's the matter with you, girl?"

"Get your hands off me."

"I'm sorry I touched you, if I got you in trouble, if I hurt you—"

She laughs. He lets her go.

"Look"—she's all business—"just forget about it. We both got what we wanted."

"You wanted me to help you."

"You did, thank you. If this doesn't work then I'm probably infertile, since you obviously aren't."

At this he seizes her again, pinning her elbows against her ribs. "What do you mean?" He's shocked by his own anger.

"Relax, buddy, I don't want anything else from you. And I won't tell anyone if you don't."

But he doesn't let her go. His hot breath is on her face. He feels he could break her in two right this instant, just like that, and it scares him. Frances knows better. If a man is going to hurt you badly, the first blow will come within three seconds. It's been over ten now, and he's still just hanging on and heaving air.

"Come on, Leo. You liked it, I could tell."

"I saved your life."

"My fuzzy arse, you did."

He falters, not wanting to take it in just yet.

"What about your daddy, you can't go back, he'll kill you."

She goes all haughty and upper crust. "My father has never laid a hand on me." He lets her go. A light appears around the bend. Frances walks toward it.

He never does see who or how many have come for her. Of everything, perhaps he's most ashamed of staying behind, cowering in reliance on her promise not to tell. But what would happen to his family if he were killed here tonight? Disgrace and destitution.

At the thought of his family, Ginger emerges from what seems to him now to have been a narcotic haze. There in the dripping mine, his head feels clear and whole for the first time in he doesn't know how long. Since New York. His heart is heavy, leaking and frayed, but it is his own. He feels acutely present in every particle of his body and his body is more worn than it was last time he looked—like the body of a loved one, long thought dead, who returns looking older but so much more like himself than anything recorded in memory or photographs. He is filled with the joy and sorrow of the reunion with himself. Forgiveness.

The sun is about to show. The rifle jiggles on Adelaide's knees and she can't help a yawn. Teresa exchanges a look with Wilfrid Beel. Wilf says, "There's a hunting cabin down this road I used to use, if it's still there it's a likely spot—"

"Never mind, Wilf," says Adelaide. "Let's go home, he's probably there waiting on me by now."

Teresa is relieved. They've been driving Addy around all night wearing her out with dirt roads, they drove halfway to Meat Cove, and it's finally worked. Teresa wasn't worried that their search would turn up anything. She just wanted to keep Adelaide away from the Piper house with that rifle. She's got a short wick, her sister-in-law, God love her. No good telling her that Ginger wouldn't touch that ghost of a girl with a ten-foot pole.

Adelaide is right. When they pull up in front of her house it's light enough to see through the windows of the locked double doors that Ginger's truck is safely inside the garage.

★   ★   ★

When Frances greeted Lily and Mercedes in the mine she just said, "Did you bring the car?"

Mercedes was so relieved she didn't at first notice Lily straying round the bend whence Frances had appeared. "Lily, we're going home now."

"What about the man?"

"He has his own vehicle," answered Mercedes. She did not wish to see what lay around the bend. It was enough for her that Frances was content to leave it behind.

Once home, Frances refuses to take a bath, "I had one last night." When Mercedes tries her strong-arm matron thing, Frances resists like a cat, clinging hands and feet to the sides of the tub till Mercedes gives up. Then Frances washes her hands, her face and feet while Mercedes stands waiting with a fresh towel.

"Are you in love with him?"

Frances just snorts.

"Do you plan to see him again?"

"What, are you jealous, Mercedes?"

"I don't want you to get hurt."

"Maybe you're a lezzy, Mercedes, did you ever think of that? Have you tried it? Want to? We could." Frances laughs without finding it funny, nothing seems that funny anymore, she has a delicious tired feeling creeping up.

"Are you hungry?" asks Mercedes.

"Yes."

"I'll make us some cinnamon toast." And she turns to leave.

"Mercedes?"

Mercedes pauses in the bathroom door but does not turn. Frances continues, "I'm going to be good from now on. I'm going to have a healthy baby."

Mercedes takes a breath and lowers her head.

"Mercedes?"

"Yes?"

"Can we have cocoa too?"

"Of course."

"Come in for a cuppa?"

Wilf and Teresa politely decline. Adelaide enters her house, dog tired.

Ginger has made tea and tea biscuits, and he is freshly bathed and changed. He says to his wife, "Addy, I'm going to tell you everything, and then you can tell me if you want me to leave."

"Gimme a cuppa tea first, Leo." She sinks onto a kitchen chair with a physical relief that would make sense if she had spent the night walking instead of driving.

By the end of his story Adelaide's freckles are more prominent than before, but that could be because she's tired. He breaks the silence that follows with "You want me to go?"

"No."

"I can only stay if you can forgive me, otherwise there's no point."

She looks at him across the tea. It's as though a mist had cleared from his face. He's back. She gets a retroactive shiver at the thought of how he's been lost and wandering in a wilderness not his own.

"Can you forgive yourself?" she asks.

"I think I have. Because, you see, she's gone right out of me."

"I believe you."

"But do you forgive me?"

"That's what I said."

"You said—"

"I forgive you." She never cries. So when she does, the tears are hot pepper.

"I'm sorry," he says.

She wraps him up with her long muscles, graceful bone blades, reddish halo. "Don't ever leave me."

"I never, never will."

"I love you."

"I love you."

She runs a hand over his half-inch of soft rough hair, squeezes his shoulders, loses her narrowness in the fold of his belly and feels her back supported by his arms, which are as strong as they look. They hold each other and think about all their children and feel in themselves no limit to what they can make together, what they can give to each other. She slips her hands onto his hips. Upstairs the baby awakens. Morning.

A New and Glorious Morn

Across town, Camille makes her first pot of tea as a widow. The word isn't in yet about her son but she knows about the loss of her husband. A very young Mountie banged on the door just before midnight. She hadn't been going to open up for him, thinking it was a raid; then she figured, what's the difference? It's not as though her husband has kept her in the style to which a successful gin-slinger's wife might reasonably expect to become accustomed. So she opened up and the Mountie said with a long face, "I'm sorry, missus, but I have some bad news for you." Then he came out with the anticlimax of a lifetime.

The first of Camille's sons to arrive home had difficulty opening the front door against the weight of her steamer trunk.

"Ma, what's going on?"

She lumbered down the stairs with a hatbox in one hand and a suitcase containing her wedding gown in the other. "Your father's dead, I'm going home."

Now Camille fixes a cup of tea the way Pa likes it and carries it up the stairs to his bedroom. It's dawn. He doesn't know she's here. She's going to surprise him.

Mercedes sits on the piano bench and watches James until his eyes snap open at dawn. It's a habit he got in the war. She takes a reading on his position.

"What do you remember from last night?"

James blinks, crystal-blue and innocent.

"Wake up," she says. The last thing Mercedes wants right now is to see him as a tousled little boy. He jerks to a sitting position, where he finds his headache waiting for him. It tightens over his scalp and he ages the forty years back to reality.

"What happened?" he asks.

"You got drunk and fell."

He winces and looks at the floor. Then he remembers, "Where's Frances?"

"Frances is sleeping, sit down."

He's fully awake now and has registered Mercedes' unaccustomed tone. He looks at her, and sits back down slowly. "What did I do?"

"You tried to touch Lily."

His hands fly up to keep his shattered face from spilling onto the carpet, a moan oozes out between his fingers. Mercedes feels a twinge of compunction, then thrusts the point of her lie under and up, "I had to drag you off her."

He doubles over, caught in the ribs, his moan turns to a squeak. Mercedes gives quarter. "She didn't wake up."

His head starts shaking no behind his hands, he leaves the sofa without straightening up, to do so might be to lose his guts, and he staggers out of the room, out of the house like that. Mercedes hears the car engine start. If her father chooses to drive himself over a cliff, so be it. And if Mercedes burns an extra millennium in purgatory as a result, that's simply the cost of doing business with God. The bottom line is that she has rescued Frances. Finally. Mercedes is neither a saint nor a sinner. She is somewhere in between. She is why purgatory was invented.

Over a late and unusually hearty breakfast, Frances reads about the accident in the *Cape Breton Post*. Jameel, well, that doesn't much matter either way, her days as a booze queen being over, but Boutros—that is a relief. The way he looked at her. Not like the other fellas. Brooding, as if he wanted something she didn't have for sale. What that could be, she could only imagine as rape.

"Are you sure you want more porridge, Frances?"

"Look, Lily, that's our cousin and our uncle by marriage."

Lily refills Frances's bowl and reads the headline, " 'Hero's Death For Whitney Pier Man.' " The story reports that the brand-new 1932 8-cylinder Kissel swerved to avoid a carload of Congregation of Notre

Dame nuns on their way back to Holy Angels from an evening spent at a massed choir practice.

"Mercedes was there!"

"So what, Lily?"

"Well she said Sister Saint Monica offered her a drive home but she said she wanted to walk, but if she'd taken the drive then the sisters wouldn't have passed the car with our cousin and uncle in it and they wouldn't've crashed."

"Yeah, Lily, and if a zillion invertebrates hadn't died around here a trillion stupid years ago, we wouldn't have a gravel driveway."

Lily reads on. "It says the Mounties got to the car and knew someone else was driving because 'Mr. Jameel was lodged in the passenger side of the vehicle. Boutros Jameel was found on the rail tracks. After having crashed to avoid the nuns, he walked two miles toward New Waterford in the throes of death, presumably in order to fetch a doctor for his father.' "

Frances is thoroughly creeped. Imagine that enormous living dead man slouching toward New Waterford, set to heave himself on her with his dying breath. Just how hard it was for him to be killed is a measure of what she would have been in for if he had ever got his massive mitts on her.

The young Mountie guides his cruiser over a well-worn dirt track through the woods, following a crudely drawn map. Jameel was a half-decent businessman. He kept a strict account of all his transactions in a small leather-bound notebook that the Mountie found tucked in his breast pocket at the crash site. Jameel had been careful not to use any real names, however. His code name for James: The Enklese Bastard. The penciled map leading to the distillery of The Enklese Bastard was an incautious but temporary measure—he drew it according to James's instructions over the phone when Taylor quit.

X marks the spot, but when the young Mountie pulls up this morning expecting either to nab his man or to lie in wait, all that's left of X is a charred patch of earth and some smoking planks. So much for *corpus delicti*. The Mountie turns round and heads back to Sydney. He doesn't see the tan Buick sedan parked in a gully nearby.

"Is she going to holler rape?"

"No."

The *Cape Breton Post* is on Teresa's kitchen table. She and Adelaide have agreed that Ginger picked as good a time as any to quit Jameel's. Hector is in his usual place, rocking. Teresa pours Adelaide more tea.

"What makes you so sure?" Teresa asks.

" 'Cause she got what she wanted, so she said."

"What's that?"

"A baby."

Teresa is struck dizzy but doesn't let on. She sits down carefully and commences to stir and stir her tea, asking, "Do you believe that?"

"If she timed it right, sure. You can tell if it takes, you know, I always could right from the first one."

Adelaide feels bad suddenly because here she is talking to Teresa about how a woman knows when she's pregnant, while Teresa herself is bound never to be so, though it's what she wanted most.

Adelaide has always wondered how a head injury could injure a man's sexual power. That steel bar never fell on Hector's privates, his seed must be good as ever, and he's not downright paralyzed, just all over reduced. If it had been Adelaide, she'd have seen if he still worked, then she would have got a baby from him. Hector loves children. They could have managed. She and Ginger would've helped look after it. But Adelaide knows Teresa is different, altogether finer. She's like royalty, the real kind, not snobbish, just innately fine. You can't picture Teresa straddling a broken-down man for his seed. So if Hector still does work in that way, Adelaide's certain Teresa hasn't tested him out. Teresa's in her forties. Soon she'll be too old, if she isn't already.

"Addy, what if it's true?"

"Don't worry, Trese, I've got something in mind."

"Addy—"

"Trese, don't ask, 'cause I'm not telling anyone beforehand, I don't want anyone changing my mind this time or driving me all over hell's half acre." Adelaide gives Hector a pat on the head and goes home to get supper. "Thanks for the tea, girl."

Teresa sees her to the door and returns to the kitchen, where Hector is staring up at the top cupboard with a worried look in his eye.

"Don't worry, honey," she tells Hector, "it's still there."

But she goes to the back room to fetch the stepladder, intending to take a look just to be sure. Teresa is not one to clamber on kitchen counters.

★   ★   ★

Adelaide has told no one of what she intends to do. She has forgiven Ginger. She has forgiven Teresa for taking her off the scent last night. But it has been demonstrated that, in this matter, she can trust only herself. She has planned it carefully and this time no one is going to stop her.

Just after supper, she gets on her bicycle with the long wicker baskets attached to the sides. When her business was thriving she could carry whole bolts of fabric in them. Today she carries something else in one of them. She rides the Shore Road to New Waterford. The beginnings of a beautiful sunset.

Adelaide could wait three months and find out if Frances really is pregnant before doing what she means to do. But what's the point? If she's not pregnant she's likely to start harassing him again. Coming around. The most disturbing part of Leo's disturbing story was that Frances knew Adelaide's secret name for him. She'd practically have to have been in bed with them to know that. And a girl who would inflict an injury on herself, risk drowning to get what she wants—wouldn't such a girl also use blackmail? Accuse Leo of rape if he doesn't give her what she wants? Adelaide pumps the pedals harder, ignoring the blazing sky to her right and the sparkling water to her left.

Mercedes is walking home from her talk with the priest. He has agreed to inform the bishop. His Grace will then decide whether it is appropriate to interview Lily with regard to the growing list of remarkable events— without, of course, letting Lily know the reason for his inquiry. Mercedes lifts her face to the slanting sun. Everything has turned a ruddy gold, God's blessing at its most gentle, "all's right with the world." The calamities of Frances have peaked just as Lily's sanctity is at its most evident and Mercedes is grateful to find herself up to handling both. Tomorrow she will go to confession and obtain absolution for wronging her father.

When she gets home she is disturbed to see that the car is still gone, and she withstands a wave of dread at the sight of Sister Saint Monica waiting for her in the front room. Mercedes knows Sister Saint Monica via the massed choir, where they struck up an immediate, if formal, rapport. But "bad news" is all Mercedes can think at the sight of wimple and robes at this particular moment. Lily has shown the sister in and given her a cup of tea and a date square. Mercedes seats herself in the wingback chair and gently dismisses Lily, steeling herself to receive the news of her father's death.

But no. It's something else altogether. Sister Saint Monica was at the wheel when Boutros went careering across their path to his death, and she had seen, moments earlier, Frances in a truck with a colored man.

"I meant to tell you immediately, Mercedes, but the accident temporarily removed it from my thoughts."

Mercedes confides in Sister Saint Monica as to Frances's likely predicament.

"God forgive me."

"Sister, you are blameless in this situation."

But both women know that no one is blameless.

"Had I reacted swiftly, it is likely Frances would not have succeeded in putting herself in the way of temptation."

"Sister, I would not have burdened you with this knowledge, except for the fact that I must make plans for Frances and I don't know where else to turn for sound advice."

"Of course."

It's the least Sister Saint Monica can do. There is much to discuss. At what point Frances ought to leave New Waterford, the place of her lying-in . . . "I'll arrange for the convent at Mabou. They have an excellent infirmary."

The knowledge that it is to be a colored child is most useful in determining its future. First of all, there is now no question of keeping it. Illegitimacy is a terrible but invisible blot, whereas miscegenation cannot be concealed. Neither mother nor child deserves to live thus doubly stained. Such is the charitable view. Therefore, the second issue becomes the selection of an appropriate orphanage, bearing in mind that adoption is unlikely under the circumstances, for how many good Catholic white families would be willing to take a colored child? Particularly if it turns out to be a male child. As to good Catholic colored families, there are few, that community being predominantly Anglican on the island and Baptist on the mainland. And perhaps it's as well, thinks Mercedes, for doesn't that branch of the human family commonly have difficulty raising its own children, never mind those of other people?

"Thank you, sister."

Sister Saint Monica glides down the street in black and white, past

Adelaide on her bike. Adelaide can't for the life of her imagine how anyone could take a vow of chastity, then she flashes on Teresa and has no trouble picturing her as a nun. She lifts the lid on her wicker basket to check her cargo as she dismounts in front of the Piper house.

Back at Teresa and Hector's, the rifle is gone from on top of the kitchen cupboard. Hector is beside himself, making squeaks that generate a little drool down his chin, all his language in his eyes. Somewhere inside his head he's still all there, but moved into a cramped rear apartment overlooking the old brain. Teresa tries to reassure him. "Hector honey, now settle down, everything's going to be all right."

"Mercedes," calls Lily from the front-room window, "there's a lady coming up the walk."

"Don't holler, Lily, who is it?"

"I don't know."

Mercedes opens the door and is about to explain that deliveries are taken at the back when one look indicates that the woman is not here selling anything.

"May I please see Miss Frances Piper?"

Mercedes knows now precisely who this is.

"My sister is indisposed. Won't you step in?"

Adelaide casts a glance back at her bike and Mercedes adds, "I can assure you it will be safe there, but you're welcome to bring it onto the porch if you'd rather."

"Yes, I'd rather do that."

In the front room, Adelaide takes up the spot on the sofa lately vacated by Sister Saint Monica.

Frances spotted Adelaide from the attic window. Her stomach is still squirting fear as she creeps down to the upstairs hall. She would climb from a second-floor window but she dares not do anything to dislodge the new growth within her. Frances is no longer dressed as a Girl Guide. She has put on an old shift of Mumma's from the hope chest. Shapeless and roomy. Although only one day pregnant, Frances considers it none too soon to dress the part. Faded floral print in tropical reds and greens. It still smells like Mumma—dough, rose water, moist skin and cedar. In order to escape the house it will be necessary for Frances to descend the stairs and pass the front-room archway. But how? She hovers at the top of the stairs.

Mercedes doesn't take her eyes off the visitor.

"Lily, go and make a fresh pot of tea, please."

Lily leaves reluctantly. She has rarely seen a black person up close. She is fascinated by Adelaide's freckles. Adelaide takes a good look at Lily too, the baby that came out of the gash in Kathleen Piper's belly.

When Lily leaves the front room she is hit on the side of the head with Raggedy-Lily-of-the-Valley. She looks up to see Frances at the top of the stairs miming a zipper across her mouth. Lily picks up Raggedy-Lily-of-the-Valley and goes quietly up the stairs.

In the front room, tea has failed to materialize but Mercedes has forgotten it, mesmerized by what Mrs. Taylor is saying. "We would welcome the child into the family as our own. It would never know, and neither would anyone else." Adelaide's eyes sharpen ever so slightly when she adds, "But you'd have to take responsibility for your sister, miss."

With this last remark, Mercedes is stung out of the feeling of awe that stole up on her at the woman's astonishing offer—out of the question, of course, but Christian in its intent, however misguided. A little moisture deserts Mercedes for all time and evaporates to fall as rain elsewhere.

"Mrs. Taylor. Insofar as it is possible for anyone to be my sister's keeper, I am that. As to the possibility of a child—and it is yet to be confirmed—I should likewise assume responsibility for its welfare."

"Could you love it?"

Mercedes is, again, astonished. Her anger travels in like a thunder-head on a clear day. Adelaide isn't afraid. She's waiting for an answer.

"You may go now, Mrs. Taylor."

Mercedes gets up but Adelaide remains seated and says, "You see, I could love it. And I have less reason to than you do, dear."

There is nothing endearing in the "dear."

"I don't need you to show me where my duty lies, Mrs. Taylor."

"Girl, duty is your problem." Now Adelaide gets up and leaves, adding, "Keep your sister away from my man or I'll shoot her, pregnant or not."

And she goes. Mercedes starts shaking. Luckily there's sherry in the medicine cabinet.

On her way through New Waterford, Adelaide reflects on the strangeness of the Piper family. As if there weren't enough indications, on her way out of the front room she encountered the girl Lily pushing a big old baby carriage, jam-packed with dolls and a live cat, out the door. She must be thirteen or fourteen and still playing house. Adelaide watched as the lame girl clunked the carriage down the porch steps, the rusty wheel-springs straining under what seemed to be an enormous weight. What the hell else has she got in there, wondered Adelaide—jugs of moonshine?

Teresa has a bicycle too. It's Hector's old one. It's got a crossbar, of course, and Teresa is none too pleased to have her dress draped astride it but that can't be helped. At least she's tall enough not to look completely ridiculous. She used to ride this bike in the old days, but as a passenger on the handlebars in front of Hector, who pedaled and swerved to make her squeal and giggle. As she wobbles along now she marvels, was I ever that girly? She was a real girly girl. A princess. Everything had to be ladylike, the table set just so when he came to her mother's house for supper. It was perfect because Hector was a gentleman too, or at least was growing up into one, because at that time he was still a waggy boy. They were not too young, though, to plan for the future. His education and ordination as an Anglican minister. Moving south of the border. They wanted lots of children. People like us are the ones who should have children, they agreed. Teresa had a dream of founding a dynasty of people who would be a high example not only to their own race, but to all who knew them.

　　Way down beneath this noble aim, at the bottom of the well, was a voice stranded without a rope or a ladder, howling up, "I'll show them! I'll show them all!" Exultant, exuberant; its ferocity was the strength behind her ladylike dignity and determination, though she could barely hear it. She had no awareness of the power of the hopeful rage within, which could move mountains, climb out of wells in triumph. She did not know her own strength. With Hector's accident the voice got louder but it was still muffled by her determination to bear all patiently with the help of the Lord. At the unjust loss of her job there ceased to be any competition for the voice at all, and she could hear it plainly. It no longer said, "I'll show them," it was saying, "I'll get them." It had changed to hate. The hate that she prayed for Jesus to take away. But it was also part of what had kept her going so how could she do without it now? That kind of hate is a species of animated scrap metal. Rusting, corroding inside, leaching into the vital organs. Teresa is sick with it. It can kill.

Adelaide pulls up in front of MacIsaac's Drugs and Confectionery. Mr. MacIsaac is closing up for the evening, she catches him on the way out.

"Mr. MacIsaac, I'm Addy Taylor from the Pier."

"Hello, Mrs. Taylor."

He extends his old red hand and she shakes it. His eyes are clear these days but still kind.

Adelaide reaches deep into her wicker basket. "Have a swig of this, Mister Mac."

She uncorks a brown bottle. MacIsaac shakes his head, being two years on the wagon.

"It's the best ginger beer you ever tasted," says Adelaide.

He smiles. Takes it and drinks. It is. Sweet up front, then sears the back of your throat till your earwax tinkles.

"What do you call it?"

" 'Clarisse's Island Brew.' "

"Are you from the islands, Mrs. Taylor?"

Adelaide laughs, "I'm from Halifax for a hundred and fifty-six years, mister, where're you from?"

"From here for eighty or ninety years, and as far as I know before that it was the Isle of Skye, the Isle of Man and, let's see now, the Isle of Wight."

"Your people had a taste for islands."

"You'd think we'd've learned by now, eh?"

He wheezes and she laughs. He orders three cases for the store to see how it goes.

Frances is risen from the baby carriage now that Adelaide has ridden off on her bike. "Like a witch on her broom," thinks Frances with a shudder. She has sent Lily home, claiming the need to "commune with nature."

Part of Frances's new health regime is moderate exercise. It's hard to know what to believe about pregnancy when, in movies, miscarriages are a narrative convenience as close as the nearest flight of stairs, while in books like *Great Pioneer Women* the broads all fight bears and harvest corn right up to their accouchement. Frances has decided upon the happy medium of regular oceanside walks. Romantic heroines are always being ordered to take the sea air. Unless they are tubercular, in which case they are banished to the land where the blood oranges grow. Frances hasn't noticed any tubercular tendencies in herself. In fact, with the conviction of her pregnancy her self-image has evolved into that of a much larger woman. Slow and curvaceous, with a bosom instead of a chest.

Trixie has come along for the walk. Something about her attentive behavior, as well as the trotting gait necessitated by her missing paw, makes Trixie seem more canine than feline. And she is in the habit of casting quick glances up at Frances, checking in the way a dog does. They arrive at the edge of the cliff. Trixie follows as Frances traverses the stony slope, eschewing her former habit of skidding headlong on her hands and heels. At the bottom, Frances pauses and takes a deep salty breath.

She turns north and begins to stroll as though through warm water, or as though rhythmically across the endless wet sand of a beach she has never visited but would know instinctively how to tread. This kind of walking goes with her new hips, which have become what is commonly described as "child-bearing."

They walk on. This is the best of the summer. Not yet eight in the evening, the sun has brought out the green of the ocean and bathed the sky in a soothing balm of fire. Days like this are so precious. Frances stops and looks out at the sea, which trembles at the caress of the sun. Mumma feels near . . . as though she had never gone away. Frances is feeling a familiar yet unnameably old feeling. One she hadn't known was ever hers to forget. Happiness. Unlike her imaginary new body, this feeling is genuine.

Trixie looks up and sees Teresa standing on the ridge above. Backlit, Teresa is magnificently darker and brighter than ever. Seen from far below like this, her great height is higher still. In this light, at that height, everything becomes a precise charcoal line. Teresa's body is a bold vertical stroke. Bisecting her middle is a horizontal line half as long as she is tall. Against the red-gold blaze of evening. Frances looks up and experiences an arrow through her heart at the crucivision. The arrow is love, its pain spreads outward and the pain is faith, the source that launched the arrow was sorrow. "Teresa," thinks Frances, and her lips move around the name as she stretches her arms up and holds them out to the woman standing far above.

The horizontal line across Teresa revolves like the needle of a compass till it disappears into the vertical stroke of her body, and the next instant a shot rings out. Frances jolts through the air and onto her back against the gravel shore.

Precious Blood

No one knows just how much Hector understands, not even Teresa. She long ago ceased to look for signs of dear Hector, it being the only way she could come to terms with his loss. And besides, the doctor said Hector was brain-damaged into a cheerful vegetable. Although his only memories from before the accident are smell feelings, Hector has learned to understand English again the way a child learns, in nouns and verbs and concepts. He could learn to read again too if someone thought of teaching him. Unlike a child, however, he will never be able to speak the words himself. What's left to him is the speech of dogs.

"Hey, hey, Hector, what's the matter b'y?"

Old Wilf Beel has caught up to Hector's wheelchair and pulled him to the side of the road. Hector makes his sounds and paws at Wilf's jacket, his mouth foaming with panic, and Wilf asks, "Are you lost, Hector?"

Hector groans in frustration, then erupts into rage when Wilf actually points the wheelchair back homeward and starts pushing.

"Whoa, whoa, whoa, b'y—" says Wilf. But Hector flails at the armrests and wrenches his head around in an effort to see Wilf.

"Did you want to go visit Leo and Adelaide, is that it, Heck?"

And Hector can only bob his head and beam joylessly to get the message across loud and clear, YES! JESUS CHRIST ALMIGHTY, YES!

"Oh, well, I don't mind taking you there."

And Wilf turns the chair around again and pushes Hector along, if more slowly than Hector was traveling under his own steam, at least in a much straighter line.

"Where's Teresa at, eh Hector?"

Hector ignores the question but Wilf doesn't notice.

Teresa is in a state of disbelief. Minutes ago she was gliding along the Shore Road on the bike, having got the hang of it in the course of eight or so miles. She caught sight of the figure on the beach below because of the bright colors it wore, kindled by the full light of the setting sun. The dress looked familiar. Teresa laid down the bike and walked to the edge of the cliff for a better look. The sight of the dress awoke an emotion detached from context. Sympathy—and . . . pity. Yes. She felt sorry for her. The woman who answered the door in that dress, oh, long ago, a blond child at her feet, she was married to—it's Materia Piper's dress. A strip of goose-flesh streaked down Teresa's left arm at the recognition of the dress and of the wearer, whose aimless rhythm and bearing also said Materia. There was a small black dog down there too, trotting at the woman's heels. Did the Pipers have a dog back then, Teresa tried to recall as she slowly paralleled them along the cliff, the rifle threaded through her folded arms.

That poor woman . . . Teresa always wished she had done some nice little thing for Materia, since she was the only person Teresa had ever met who truly seemed worse off than herself.

Teresa doesn't believe in ghosts, nevertheless she expected any moment the figure to shimmer and disappear into ocean light.

"Perhaps it is a sign," she thought, "asking me not to harm her daughter."

And Teresa took pity on the woman who was not strong enough to live, but was strong enough to pierce through death to protect her child.

Teresa had resolved to go in peace when the figure ceased walking, turned and looked up at her. The Devil's face housed in a shape of pity. Teresa watched Frances raise her arms in triumph, a mocking smile twisting her lips, and hiss the name "Teresa." Teresa swung the rifle through a hundred and eighty degrees, caught it with her shoulder, aimed and fired. The demon jerked back and flopped like a rag doll.

Now Teresa is suspended with the smoking rifle floating out in front of her, trying to get ahold of what she's done.

Hector is exhausted by the time he's in Adelaide and Ginger's kitchen.

"Hector, honey, just settle down now, we're going to go find Teresa, okay?"

Ginger has already headed over to check Teresa's house. It's alarming. Hector does not go places unattended. But he won't settle down.

"Hector, did something happen to Teresa?"

He shakes his head "no" in a way that's understood only to those who know him. Then he nods his head "yes" twice as urgently till finally it dawns on him. He points. Up to the top of Adelaide's kitchen cupboard.

"What is it, Hector? You want something? There's nothin up there, b'y, what d'you want?"

He gives a series of frustrated groans but does not lower his pointing arm, though it begins to waver. Adelaide shrugs, moves to the counter and is halfway climbed onto it when she freezes in recognition.

"Oh Jesus, Hector."

She turns and he nods solemnly, "Yes. Yes. Yes. Yes. Yes."

"Good boy, Hector," she says as she grabs her sweater, "stay here with the kids," and she's out the door.

Teresa starts breathing again and the rifle regains its weight against her shoulder and in her hands. It's done. Her heart starts making a racket in an effort to wake up her mind. She reaches out, grasps the barrel in both hands and hurls the rifle end over end onto the beach below, where it discharges again in a hail of pebbles. This second shot is the one she hears, and it sets her running like a starting pistol in the ears of a sprinter. She pounds along the cliff, running and running, she doesn't think where until she swings with the rail tracks toward New Waterford, and still all she knows is what she sees flashing by, not what she intends. Number 12 Colliery, colossally idle to her right, the little company houses, whipping by like telephone poles past a steamed-up train. She's not running like a lady, she's running like a champion. The next thing she notices is that she's bounding up the steps of New Waterford General Hospital, and from this she surmises that she has come to get help for the girl she has killed.

Thundering toward New Waterford beside Ginger in his truck, Adelaide shouts, "Stop!"

It's Hector's bike lying near the tracks on the ocean side of the road. Adelaide hops down from the truck before it has rolled to a stop and dashes across. Ginger follows and joins her where she's standing at the edge of the cliff staring down.

"Oh my Lord."

Trixie is curled around Frances's head. She has spent the ten minutes since the shooting painfully kneading Frances's scalp with her never-trimmed claws. Two people have come sliding down the hill and now they're crunching toward her and Frances.

At their approach, Frances repeats the words she has been mumbling, "Ow. Trixie, stop it."

Frances's eyes have gone to slits, the only color on her face is her tiny nose mole, she has become scrawny once more, a little woman in a big dress.

In each hand there is a stone of equal weight. It is time for sleep.

"Should we move her?"

"We ain't got much of a choice," Adelaide replies.

It's hard to know where the wound is and therefore where to take hold and lift her up because there's so much blood. Trixie keeps kneading and for once she can't stop talking. Ginger slips his arms under Frances and lifts her carefully. She's so clearly not faking this time that he wonders again how he could possibly have bought her earlier performances. He decides to give himself a break and admit that she is a great actress. Adelaide picks up the rifle and they start back up the slope. Trixie follows, her eyes full of mendicant pleading. She watches the truck pull away, then streaks across the field for home.

Frances bleeds into Adelaide's dress with her feet resting across Ginger's knees. He tries for a compromise between speed and smoothness.

Teresa has been given a cup of tea in the front hall of New Waterford General Hospital. The head nursing sister was the first to come across her. If it had been that nice young intern from away, the hysterical woman would have been given a shot in the vein instead of a cup of tea. The head nurse, however, has noticed that, whether they drink the tea or not, the mere act of reaching out to receive something that must not be spilled seems to have a profoundly calming effect on all but the downright insane.

"Now dear, if the girl is dead, why does she need an ambulance?"

Teresa balances the teacup in both hands and puts her first real sentence together since the shooting, "There's a chance she may still be alive. She's down by the shore. She's been shot."

This is an example of how tea can work better than narcotic oblivion.

The head nurse rises immediately and swishes away to get the ball rolling. Teresa adds, "I shot her."

Nurse hears her, thinks, "First things first," and keeps walking toward Emergency.

The wasted ambulance is dispatched in time to narrowly avoid a collision with Ginger's truck, Ginger having abandoned smoothness in favor of speed. Frances's eyes have started to go fishy, and though Adelaide and Ginger have been shouting to her throughout the brief drive, Adelaide had no way of knowing that pricking Frances's scalp might keep her from slipping away.

Teresa has raised the teacup to her lips for a first sip when Adelaide breaks through the front doors and hollers, "Can we get some service around here?" Two young nurses run to support Adelaide, who is soaked in blood, and she snaps, "Not for me!" She swivels to indicate Ginger coming through the doors carrying Frances, and catches sight of Teresa hunched in a chair against the wall, drinking tea. The head nurse returns on silent shoes. She has a trained eye so she walks past Adelaide without turning a hair, takes Frances from Ginger's dripping arms and carries her to meet the gurney now hurtling toward them powered by the two younger sisters. Nurse lays Frances down on the move, they ram through a set of swinging doors and disappear into the operating theater.

Luckily the head nurse was in the war. She has a way with bullet wounds.

This time, Lily hasn't a clue where Frances might be. Ambrose has not come through. Mercedes shoos Trixie from the wingback chair to find a smear of blood in her place. Still wet.

"Trixie, come back here."

But everyone knows cats don't come. Mercedes searches the house till she finds Trixie in the cellar between the furnace and the wall. If anything has happened to the cat, Frances will be devastated.

"Come here, Trixie."

No.

Mercedes reaches but Trixie scurries farther back. Mercedes goes up to the kitchen and returns with a saucer of salted kippers, but that's the bait Frances always used to get Trixie in trouble.

Lily joins in the effort. "She might come if you speak Arabic."

Mercedes has a kink in her neck. "Oh for heaven's sake, Lily—"

"Trixie. *Inshallah.*"

Trixie puts forth a paw.

"Trixie," says Mercedes, *"taa'i la hown, Habibti . . . ya Helwi."*
Trixie slinks forward.

Mercedes examines Trixie on the kitchen counter— *"Te'berini"*—
daubing the blood with a damp cloth until it becomes clear "there's no
wound."

Lily picks up the bloody cloth and touches it to her tongue. Mercedes
shoots her a sharp look. Lily tastes and says, "I think Frances is in trouble."

"Oh God," thinks Mercedes as the dry sobs fight for air, "I will do
my best, O Lord, but when will you let me rest?"

Mercedes calls the hospital, then grabs her hat, "Stay here, Lily."

"When's Daddy coming home?"

But Mercedes is already out the door.

Mercedes falters at the sight of the Taylor truck parked out front of the
hospital. She enters and comes face to face with Mrs. Taylor and a man
who must be her husband, as well as an unknown woman with her hands
folded around a teacup.

"What happened?" Mercedes asks, standing at attention with her
back to the grief-green wall. Teresa is lost in a prayer world of her own.
Mercedes pegs her as a good woman. The only one unstreaked with
blood. My sister's blood.

"She's been hurt," Adelaide answers. "We found her and brought
her here. I'd have called you but there's been no time to think."

Mercedes turns to Adelaide, whose cotton dress is spattered scarlet
with guilt. "You can tell your story to the police," she says, forcing the
tremor from her voice, "once you've thought it through."

Teresa starts praying audibly. Mercedes closes her eyes and joins in
the prayer. She does not allow herself the luxury of tears. Tears won't keep
Frances here. Mercedes' stomach is spuming, her throat is in spasm. She
recedes from the turmoil of her body, to that uncontaminated place just
above her brow where prayer is forged. Prayer will keep Frances here.

A young nursing sister from reception appears.

"Your sister is still in surgery, Miss Piper. Would you like a cup of
tea?"

When the young nurse returns with three more steaming cups,
Mercedes is seated next to Teresa. They are holding hands, praying silently
together, eyes closed, heads bowed. Adelaide takes the tray from the
nursing sister and thinks to herself, "I could write a book. I really could."

Lily arrives carrying a carpetbag. Ginger notices the black tail trailing out from between its wooden handles. He gets up and gives her his chair.

"Thank you, sir."

Lily places the carpetbag on the floor beneath her chair. It stirs slightly. Adelaide and Ginger exchange a look. Lily doesn't ask about their bloodstains. She will know soon enough if she has two sisters, or one. Mercedes has heard Lily's unmistakable clanking entrance but she doesn't open her eyes. She does not wish to leave hold of her unknown partner in prayer. This good strong woman. You can feel the power of her faith.

The thing about an abdominal wound is the blood loss. The head nurse has performed some lovely field surgery on Frances but timing is everything and now it's touch and go. Nurse comes out to the motley crew waiting in reception and asks Mercedes, "What's your blood type, dear?"

At the far end of the recovery room, Lily has got an IV tube growing out of her right elbow, feeding a bloated bag that hangs from a metal stand and sprouts a second tube that runs into Frances's hand. Mercedes is standing straight as a virgin soldier at the foot of the bed staring at her sisters. The white curtains are pulled back from the bed since the room is empty of neighbors.

Frances hasn't moved, her eyelids haven't fluttered during her silent meal of blood. Mercedes is trying to think what else to promise God in exchange for Frances's life when it occurs to her that Lily's third miracle may be under way. But no, don't think of it, don't admit pride, ambition, into the sickroom, pray only. Mercedes treads softly the fifty feet to the door and leaves so as not to disrupt Lily's work.

In reception, Mercedes' and Teresa's hands are praying together once more. A young nurse places a hand on Mercedes' shoulder because she has twice failed to hear her own name. Teresa looks up at the touch.

The nurse says, "Your sister is awake, Miss Piper."

Mercedes jumps up but the nurse continues, "She's asking for a woman called Teresa."

Teresa rises, lets go of Mercedes' hand and follows the nurse up the stairs. Mercedes watches Teresa ascend the stairs and wonders how it is that Frances knows her.

"Who is she?" Mercedes asks the nurse at the desk.

"She's my sister," Ginger answers.

There is a blessing in all this, thinks Mercedes, looking at him. If Frances is pregnant, she is sure to miscarry as a result of the wound. He doesn't look like a bad man. But the wife looks like a woman who could kill. Came to insult me on the pretext of Christian charity, left my home, hunted my sister down and shot her like a dog. She'll pay. She'll hang.

Adelaide looks away.

Mercedes rises. "Sister?"

The young nurse looks up from the desk; "Would you like more tea, Miss Piper?"

"May I use your telephone please?"

"Of course."

Adelaide and Ginger wait and watch as Mercedes calls the police.

The head nurse tweaks the blood bag, tells Teresa, "Be brief," and closes the curtains in accordance with Frances's request. She withdraws to sit within earshot and arm's length, poring over her racing form.

Teresa is surprised to see a cat curled at the foot of the bed.

"Frances. Teresa is here."

The crippled girl with the sea-green eyes turns from whispering in Frances's left ear to stare up at Teresa. Frances opens her eyes but doesn't turn her head.

"You should go around where she can see you, ma'am," says Lily.

Teresa crosses to the right side of the bed thinking how much Lily looks like her singer-girl mother.

"Teresa." Frances's voice is mostly air.

"Yes?"

Teresa reluctantly crouches down until she's squatting at the side of the bed—she is not going to kneel, no matter what she has done. She looks into Frances's close-up eyes. Hazel. Rather, brown with broken bits of green lodged or floating.

"Teresa. Tell me about my mother."

". . . I didn't know your mother."

"You came to her funeral."

"Yes."

"You must have known her a bit."

"A little bit."

"What did you know?"

Teresa takes a breath. "I felt sorry for her, that's all," and she is surprised to find sorrow in her throat. For whom? Someone she never even knew.

"You gave me a candy."

"I did?"

"Peppermint licorice."

"I don't remember you."

"I had blond hair then."

Teresa thought the blonde had been the other one, the one she's just been praying with. "You were too small to remember that."

"I remember everything."

Frances closes her eyes for a moment, retaining the picture of Teresa's magnificent face on the insides of her lids. Teresa waits. She looks for the little girl to whom she gave the candy. Frances opens her eyes again.

"And I remember you came and stood over my bed and touched my head so I wouldn't be afraid."

"I didn't do that."

"Who did, then?"

And Teresa does a nice little thing of the type she always meant to do but never did. "It was your mother, child."

Frances closes her eyes till it seems she has fallen back asleep, then she smiles and says, "Thank you, Teresa."

And falls asleep.

Downstairs, Mercedes paces with a gait slightly less formal than a military slow march. The reassuring footfall of the Royal Canadian Mounted Police interrupts the bagpipe lament in her head.

"Miss Piper?" He's awfully young, isn't he? "What seems to be the trouble?"

Mercedes arches one eyebrow slightly, foreshadowing the type of schoolteacher she is destined to become.

"My sister is in critical condition with a bullet wound inflicted by the woman you see sitting there." She gestures without looking.

The Mountie looks at Adelaide and asks, taking out his notebook, "Is that correct, ma'am?"

Mercedes snaps, "Of course it's correct, look at their clothes!"

And as she turns she finally reads their bloodstains and cross-references them with the spotlessness of the woman upstairs. "Oh my

God." Her scaffolding of pride collapses and her face falls so far that even Adelaide might begin to forgive her, but there's no time for that because Mercedes is traveling up the stairs, leaving the Mountie at a bit of a loss. He turns to Adelaide, "Ma'am, I'll have to ask you to come with me down to the—"

"In a minute, b'y," she says, brushing by him and up the stairs.

Ginger follows, then so does the Mountie. It's been a rough couple of days for the rookie. Last night he broke the news to a woman of her husband's death in a car wreck and she took it like a weather report. Today he failed to obtain evidence of illegal alcohol production and just now he nearly fainted—he can handle the sight of blood so long as he isn't ambushed by it. He follows the procession up the stairs, determined to redeem himself with an arrest.

Mercedes is running now, slipping on beeswax, she reaches out and catches the doorjamb of the recovery room, propels herself through, sees the curtained bed at the far end standing like a draped chalice. She hurries toward it praying. There's a sound coming from within. The head nurse sees the look in Mercedes' eyes at twenty feet, rises, sets aside her racing form and catches Mercedes' wrists before she can tear at the curtains. Mercedes starts breathing again under the nurse's iron gaze, and listens. Someone is singing. The head nurse releases Mercedes and gently parts the curtains.

Teresa towers over Frances, singing softly, a West Indian lullaby. One hand rests lightly on Frances's forehead. Frances and Lily and Trixie are all asleep. Nurse and Mercedes look on and are joined by Adelaide, then Ginger, then the Mountie. "Now, what seems—" Mercedes silences him with a look.

Teresa finishes the song. She turns to the constable. "I'm ready to go."

Lily and Trixie open their eyes. Teresa goes to move from the bed but is prevented by Frances's grip on her hand. Frances, her face still marked from the self-administered beating of the day before, turns to her audience filling the parted curtains and speaks, "Mercedes?"

Why does Frances suddenly have an English accent, wonders Lily.

"I am truly sorry to have brought shame and anguish upon my family. Officer, arrest me, do your worst, for finding myself with child and without a husband, I betook me to the brink of the roiling deep where I did shoot myself. O, that I had died."

Frances turns her face upstage and allows a sob to escape her. Then the nurse clears the sickroom. "Show's over, folks."

And that's how Frances took Teresa's hate away.

Nine and a half months later, Teresa gives birth to a perfect baby girl she calls Adele Claire. Adelaide was right. Hector still works.

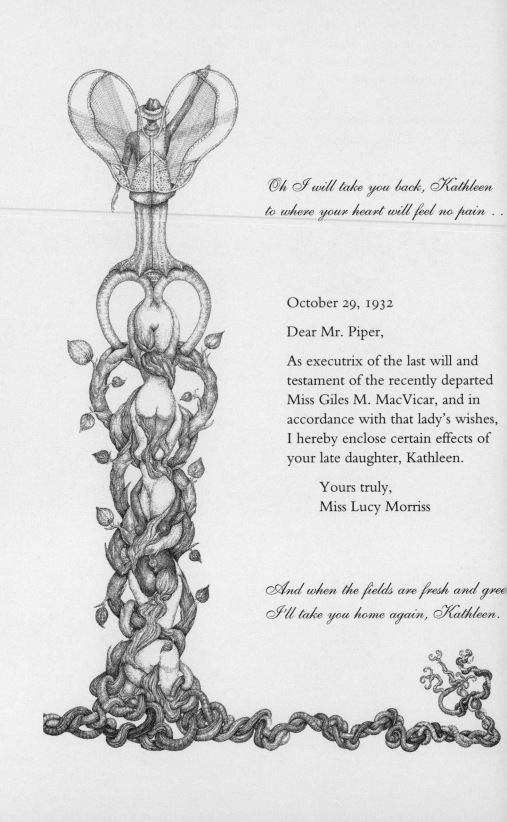

Oh I will take you back, Kathleen
to where your heart will feel no pain . . .

October 29, 1932

Dear Mr. Piper,

As executrix of the last will and
testament of the recently departed
Miss Giles M. MacVicar, and in
accordance with that lady's wishes,
I hereby enclose certain effects of
your late daughter, Kathleen.

    Yours truly,
    Miss Lucy Morriss

And when the fields are fresh and gree
I'll take you home again, Kathleen.

Book 7

THE BULLET

Blessed Art Thou amongst Women

THE HEAD NURSE'S STITCHES were a thing of beauty. They've been out for a month or so now, leaving only a shy smile below Frances's ribcage on her right side. It is the sly widening of this smile that indicates forces at work within Frances. She strokes her belly and returns the smile, *Hello*.

Mercedes notes with approval, "You're putting on weight." Frances has just risen from the steaming bathtub and Mercedes has wrapped her in a big towel warm from the radiator. It's the first of November but Mercedes has been burning coal since "the accident" in July, knowing Frances to be prone to chills. And Frances has permitted herself to be immersed, bathed and dried, docile as a drugged child.

It's been so peaceful, Frances's convalescence. She sits at the table without jittering and eats large meals. She smiles instead of grinning. She has ceased her roaming and spends the days under a light blanket on the veranda and, when well enough, strolling of an evening to the sea cliff with Lily and Trixie. Frances has become clean and soft, sweet to smell. And her face. It is fuller. Her eyes are calm, no longer furtive. The white stripe across her nose, emblem of glee, has not appeared, not once. She has breasts. Ripe. At their centers, mauve haloes resolve into walnut erections, the only part of her body not in lush repose. And her hair-of-all-directions has begun to shine. A bonnet of crackling copper lights and pure blond threads. Frances is pretty. Yes, that's what it is.

"It's been four months, high time I had something to show," replies Frances, tranquil beneath the comb Mercedes is drawing through her wet curls. Mercedes stops, looks down and plucks a golden strand from the comb.

"Frances, that's not possible."

The nurse told Mercedes that, what with the shooting, nature would take care of Frances's predicament. It would be like a particularly bad period. Mercedes has been waiting for Frances's cramps to start, but Frances must have suffered in silence, because how could she possibly still be—

"Look at me." Frances stands naked, serene on the bathroom tiles.

Mercedes looks. And blushes with a prickly flush. No good pretending she has been looking after a child. She has been washing, stroking, feeding, drying a woman who is blooming like a hothouse rose. The nipples look ready to burst and scatter seed, the russet pubic hair hangs proud like a bunch of grapes. A fig leaf would not do in this case—ripe and uncooked, pink and grainy as that fruit, Frances's whole boatful of genital cargo, from lip-wrapping-lips to clitoris in the prow, is in constant rock-abye motion in response to the new deeper tides of her body. She is almost always somewhat aroused, can feel her soft-sided barque opening, closing, taking on water from within. Her body is making love to itself. Until now, Frances had no idea what all the fuss was about.

For once, Frances is stripped of irony. She is in the presence of something bigger—namely Herself. Or at least the self implied by her new body. This is how the Blessed Virgin visits us. She inhabits our own flesh and makes love out of it. Nothing is ironic in the moment of first love. And Frances is in love. With her body, and what it is bringing forth.

"Frances. You couldn't still be pregnant. Not after what happened."

Frances replies, "Especially after what happened." She takes her white nightgown from the radiator and slips it on over her head, saying, "Thank you, Mercedes."

Mercedes aches after Frances leaves the bathroom. Suddenly bereft, she sinks to the floor and leans her cheek against the enamel tub. The last of the water sucks down the drain and, before she knows why, her tears are flowing. It's the same grief that's been waiting, bottled, against the day of Frances's death. Why has it been uncorked and sampled now? "Frances . . . my little Frances." Mercedes manages to get the bottle stoppered, hurriedly fumbling as though unaware that it is a magic bottle, capable of refilling itself eternally.

She splashes cold water on her face and realizes she cried because Frances really has gone away—her Frances, that is. This new Frances says thank you; is careful of her health, looks forward to being a mother. My

Frances is not a mother. My Frances is a child. Naughty but so dear. My child.

James has had his first stroke. But no one knows it, not even James. He just looks, and feels, older. One side of his face has slid a bit on its foundations. His left eye now always slightly sleepy, the left side of his mouth permanently triste. And he can't make a good fist with his left hand. A state of "just woke up" along that whole side of him.

The stroke itself was actually a pleasant, if strange, experience. It happened after he torched the still in the woods that day of the disasters four months ago.

James soaked the still in gasoline, lit it and ran. The thing blew sky-high, which is why the young Mountie found little more than smoldering earth. Perhaps it was the boom that triggered James's stroke—set a delicate patch of artery wall to trembling till it caved in and flooded a small surrounding area of his brain. Neurons drowned.

When he awoke, he was disoriented as to time. He noted the sun was in the same place as it had been when he ran and dived from the explosion. He got up and walked a few steps before the new imbalance of his body caught up with him and he fell to the left.

James had plenty of reasons to feel dizzy at that particular moment, considering all he'd recently been through. The idea that he might have had a small stroke would have seemed absurd to him. Overkill. He picked himself up and walked carefully from tree to tree until he reached the exploded fringe of the clearing, then he got down and crawled to the blackened spot on the ground where his industry had been. It was cold. That was how he knew at least twenty-four hours had passed.

He fell asleep. Or passed out. He opened his eyes next on a sky full of stars and a high new moon. For a moment he had no past. He was no one, no man. He was the clear night air. The next instant, however, he was a pit full of memory. Corroded shapes of used-to-be things, now twisted beyond recognition. He got onto his hands and knees, his head a wrecking ball, blind with pain. Molten glue sludging through the veins of his left side where his blood should flow. The right side of him had its first taste of dragging the left side like a wounded comrade as he struggled to his feet and, with his right hand, gripped a tattered sapling for support. He stayed there long enough for the sap to fuse his hand to the slender trunk and he left a layer of skin behind when he freed himself and staggered on.

He dropped carefully to his knees every so often when gravity got the better of his new inner-ear alignment. He'd hang his head to let a fresh wave of blood assault his brain. It hurt like hell but it was the only way to avoid fainting. Sometimes he'd fall farther with the weight of his head, from his knees onto his hands, his left hand failing to open on impact, taking the stony earth on bare knuckles. After this moment's rest, the healthy soldier would lift the wounded one back up and continue the next few yards, the right palm seeping blood, the left hand torn at the knuckles.

His car was a hundred yards from the site of the still. He had covered twenty-five when dawn broke. Then he slept. Or passed out.

But the stroke itself was blissful. He had a dream, only more so. He saw his mother. He was a grown man just as he is now:

As in other dreams of her, she is accompanied by distant but everywhere music. An old-fashioned tune on the piano, ineffably sweet and full of meaning, unnameable and yet as familiar as the beating of his own heart. He knows his mother is in the music. His tears well up and fall, refreshing him. He is in a clearing of bright green woods. Not pine, not dark like around here, but old deciduous growth, tall and embracing. There is a birch tree among the oaks and elms. He knows this is his mother. He looks at the white bark of the tree and recognizes her dress.

He lies down, curled beneath the birch, and he hears her voice, *Hello*. He knows that if he turns to look into her face she will go away, so he concentrates on a blade of grass before his eyes, and she speaks to him, calling him by his Gaelic name, *Hello, Seamus. Mo ghraidh. M'eudail.* His tears soothe his face, parched to kindling.

He speaks to her. He tells her he is sorry. He feels her hand, cool on the side of his face. He knows she is healing him, but he also realizes that with this she is preparing to send him away from her, "No!" He feels she is condemning him back to a hell he can't quite recall, "No!" He opens his eyes.

Then shut them against the sun. And resumed his journey to the car.

> Try as I like to find the way
> I never can get back by day
> Nor can remember plain and clear
> The curious music that I hear.

"If Daddy is dead, it will be up to me to look after this family."
It was dusk of the day after the shooting. Frances was in the clear

thanks to the nurse who'd seen worse, but James was still missing. Mercedes was allowing the possibility of her father's death to surface in her mind. She was sitting on the veranda, watching the street and peeling a pomegranate—an extravagant impulse, purchased from an old West Indian woman at the corner of Seventh Street.

"If Daddy is dead, I'll have to start teaching. I'll sell his tools."

Mercedes was reassured by her logical train of thought, though a little startled by the caboose: "If Daddy is dead, we'll be better off."

She bit into the sweet wine cluster. "If he isn't dead"—for Mercedes had to face this possibility too—"my job will simply be more demanding."

By the time she discerned the outline of the Buick behind the headlights, Mercedes' plans were firm enough to withstand the recognition. She observed the car creep along in second gear, genuflecting at every pothole in the street, and her first thought was "I'll have to learn to drive."

She folded her arms and watched as the car pulled into the driveway and jerked to a halt. As its lights died, she saw James's head loll back and his mouth fall open. A moment later she heard him fumbling for many seconds with the door handle. It opened and he got out. In the falling dark, she saw him descend slowly to his knees. He walked like that up the stone path to the veranda.

The one thing Mercedes hadn't counted on was that her father might return a penitent. Such a thing might interfere with her plans. She had no energy left to be the daughter of a good man. She had only energy enough to be the head of this family.

By the time he reached the steps and began to drag himself up them on all fours, she was near enough to hear the effort in his breath and realize that he was not penitential but merely sick. She had assumed he didn't see her so she jolted in her skin when he spoke, "Hello, my dear."

He was by now in a heap against the front door. Her reflexive mortification was replaced by the cool sense that it was just as well to have everything in the open between them. Yes, I watched you fall and did not stir to help.

James raised his eyes and looked at her. His eyes had turned younger, bluer. Or maybe that was only an illusion created by his face having got older. Mercedes couldn't see that yet, all she saw was that his eyes looked young and half his face was in shadow. It wasn't until she saw him under electric light later that night that she realized it wasn't a shadow at all, at least not in the usual sense.

She rose from her spare wooden chair and got her father into the dark house.

"Daddy!" Lily swung wildly down the stairs, barefoot in her nightgown, and wrapped herself around him, "Daddy, my daddy."

Such a baby still—Mercedes tried to think it fondly.

James patted Lily's head more awkwardly than usual.

"You hurt your hands," Lily cried, holding them in hers and feeling: his left one curled defenseless with its serrated knuckles, his right one strong but scabbed over at the palm.

"I'll make some tea," said Mercedes, gaining an inch in height en route from the front hall to the kitchen stove, shivering slightly at the unaccustomed breeze passing through the new spaces in her spine.

James swayed a little with just Lily to hold him, it was time for him to fall again but she didn't let him.

"Watch out now!" Afraid he'd injure her.

"It's all right, Daddy, put your hand on my shoulder."

He resisted, preferring to teeter toward the wall, but she caught him round the middle and held him fast, guiding him to the living room, trusting her strong right leg.

He found himself laid out for the second time in two days. Lily lifted his legs onto the couch and turned on the reading lamp. She saw at once the blow to him and her tears welled. She sat by his side and placed her cool hand on his injured face. He closed his eyes, too exhausted not to allow himself the relief of tears. They formed between his long blond lashes and rolled through the new hollows of his face.

"I love you, Daddy."

Mercedes arrived in the archway of the front room with the tea tray and stopped in the pool of light cast by the reading lamp. She fell through a crack in time without spilling a drop. When she returned, the tea was still piping hot and Lily was exhaling the same warm breath across James's chest where her head lay sleeping. James was stretched out on his back, asleep or comatose, and Lily had laid herself like a cool leaf alongside him, her right hand closed beneath his chin like a nighttime flower.

James slept for most of the following week. When awake, he would eat a little of whatever Lily brought him, then listen while she read aloud. Fairy tales and Freud, until he was well enough to realize that he had lost interest in his old favorites and preferred to have her read the *Halifax Chronicle* cover to cover. Things were getting interesting in Europe again.

By the time Frances got home from the hospital, James was sitting up and whittling himself a cane.

Lily and Mercedes had their hands full with two convalescents but they thrived on it. And the patients themselves were angels—uncomplaining, appreciative, recovering. Mercedes could not remember a happier time, for even when Mumma was alive there had been a cloud, a constant threat of turbulence. But now all is calm. All is bright.

The only distressing thing about these halcyon days was James's tendency to talk about Materia. It's normal to speak affectionately of the dead. But because it had been delayed for fourteen years, Mercedes experienced it as something of a painful intrusion. She was grateful that he hadn't yet mentioned Kathleen.

James carved the top of his cane into a dog's head and went for a slow walk with Lily. He started a new project out in his workshed. He picked up his shoemaker's tools again for the first time in many years. The work goes slowly, he's having to retrain himself around his bad left hand. And he won't say what he's making. The shed is off limits to everyone but Trixie. It's to be a surprise.

All this and heaven too—until the day that Frances rises in the tub and Mercedes can no longer deny that her sister is still pregnant.

Sisters of Mercy

"THE SISTERS WILL BE ready when the time comes, Mercedes."

"Thank you, Sister Saint Monica."

Mercedes has conferred with Sister Saint Monica in the geography classroom at Holy Angels, beneath the color print that still has pride of place over the blackboard. Saint Monica: patron of mothers. Scourge of African concubines.

"Have you discussed it with Frances?"

"Not yet, sister. I'm concerned she may refuse to part with the child."

"In that case, it's probably best not to discuss it with her."

"That's what I thought."

"There are other ways."

"Kinder ways."

"Quite right."

Wheels have been set in motion. Five months from now, Frances will lie in at the convent infirmary at Mabou. Then the infant will be relayed to an appropriate orphanage.

"That's a lovely print, sister."

"Thank you, Mercedes."

It's time Mercedes had a talk with Lily. Lily is thirteen. Mercedes had been going to delay the talk until the onset of menstruation but it looks as though Lily is going to be late starting—perhaps it's another sign. Perhaps she'll never bleed at all. That certainly would be an indication of God's favor. In any case, what with Frances's condition soon to be all too apparent, it's high time.

"Lily. Do you know where babies come from?"

"They come from God."

They're in the kitchen making tea biscuits, arms powdered white to the elbows like ladies' opera gloves.

Mercedes reddens. "That's right. But God works through our flesh to create new life." That's rather good. Mercedes relaxes. This may not be so bad after all.

"I know that, Mercedes," says Lily, looking decently down at the dough beneath her fists.

"How do you know?" snaps Mercedes.

"Frances told me."

This is going to be difficult after all.

"What did she tell you, Lily?"

Lily blushes a little, very prettily too, and continues to knead the dough.

"Well?" Mercedes is waiting.

"It's a private thing, isn't it?" says Lily, and she glances sideways, biting her lip.

"Yes. It's very private. It's between two people and God."

Lily says nothing.

"Lily, I'm not—I don't—I'm not trying to make you feel ashamed or embarrassed, I just want to prepare you for certain . . . wonderful— things that will occur as you mature." Lily's hands have kept working but Mercedes has stopped and gone to the pump to hide her embarrassment.

Lily answers with natural delicacy, "It's all right, Mercedes. I got my period for the first time last March and Frances told me what to do."

So. What else is it not given me to know around here, wonders Mercedes, pumping vigorously. Lily steals a look at her older sister. Suddenly she is aware of having hurt Mercedes' feelings. It hadn't occurred to her that Mercedes might feel left out of such a thing. It had only occurred to her that Mercedes might prefer to be left out. Lily would apologize but feels that would only intensify her sister's humiliation.

"Mercedes, is Frances really going to have a baby?"

"So she's told you."

"Yes, but I wasn't certain it was true."

"It's true." Mercedes rinses away all traces of flour and dough, then reaches for a cake of lye and asks, "Did Frances tell you how she came to be with child?"

"Yes."

Lily is quite flushed by now, not with guilty knowledge but with the delicate mortification of one whom it pains to trespass on the privacy of another.

Mercedes scrapes a bristle brush over the moistened lye and scrubs her way from fingernails to elbows.

"Well? What did she tell you, Lily?"

Lily works the dough reverently, shaping it with care.

"She told me that she became pregnant after the night she passed with Mr. Taylor in the mine—"

Mercedes' hands are sterile.

Lily continues with dignity, "But that she miscarried as a result of the shooting."

Mercedes turns off the pump with her wrist and holds her hands up, allowing them to drip-dry towards the elbows. She asks, "Then how does Frances explain her present condition?"

Lily answers, "The bullet." And goes on molding the dough.

Mercedes contaminates her hands with a clean tea towel, drying, drying, drying them. "She told you that in order to avoid telling you the truth, Lily."

"No. She believes it."

Mercedes pauses. Folds the towel. "Well that's not how women get pregnant."

"I know, Mercedes."

Mercedes has lost patience. "Well will you tell me then what in the name of Our Lord Jesus Christ on the Cross it is you altogether do know of the factual acts of life!"

Facts, Lily thinks but doesn't say. Instead, she removes her apron and leaves the kitchen saying, "Excuse me."

Mercedes is flummoxed. That girl is a cipher. Saint or no saint, why can't anyone in this house ever just have a straightforward conversation?

Then she sees the sculpture:

Modest penis and vagina in coital embrace, already beginning to sag owing to the dough being overworked.

"Frances, why did you tell Lily that story about the bullet?"

"Because it's true."

This is the last thing Mercedes expected to hear. She was ready for an obscene joke or another lie, not this. What Frances is this? The same strange one who rose from the tub the other day.

"Do you really believe that, Frances?"

Frances is bundled supine on a camp cot on the front porch watching the afternoon street go by. Trixie is chasing moths in the yard. Frances does another un-Frances thing. She reaches out and takes Mercedes' hand. Frances's hand is warm. She smiles.

"I'm happy, Mercedes. I'm happy."

Frances's smile is true. It contains the memory of all her other smiles, the false grins of a lifetime, nothing has been banished from her face—but something immeasurable has been added.

"Everything's going to be all right, Mercedes."

Mercedes squeezes Frances's hand and tucks the blanket up around her.

"Don't worry, Mercedes, I'm not crazy."

"I'm not worried." Frances will always need me.

"Don't be sad, Mercedes."

"I'm happy, dear." And Mercedes smiles through tears as she smooths back the curls from her sister's brow.

"Mercedes."

"Yes, dear?"

"Don't be upset about Lily. She was too shy to say the words so she made a sculpture."

"You're right," says Mercedes, serene, rising to leave, "Lily's a complete innocent."

"Either that or she's possessed by the Devil."

Mercedes turns sharply.

"Just kidding, Mercedes."

And the white stripe appears across Frances's nose, momentarily ruffling Mercedes' best-laid plans.

"When can you start, Mercedes?"

"I can start today, Sister Saint Eustace."

Mercedes savors the wood-polish smell of the principal's office at Mount Carmel High School. The well-worn books ranged upon the shelves, Jesus on His varnished cross, broad oak desk with immaculate inkwell and pen, crisp memos scrolled into pigeonholes. This is the type of office Mercedes would like some day. Someday I will cut off all my hair and enter the convent. I will teach. Or perhaps I will join a contemplative order.

Mercedes nips this fantasy in the bud, for it strikes her that her whole family would have to be dead or married before she herself could become the bride of Christ. And since marriage is extremely unlikely for any of them, her dream is tantamount to wishing them all dead. Or no. Frances could come with me as an invalid. Couldn't she?

"How is Frances?"

"Oh she's grand, Sister Saint Eustace, hale and—"

"Is she going to keep the child?"

Mercedes is flustered at the frankness of the question, even though she does not delude herself that the whole of Cape Breton Island is not fully apprised of the latest Piper scandal.

"Well I think—I should say quite possibly Frances may decide to put it up for adoption."

"Really."

Mercedes feels suddenly hot beneath the glare of Sister Saint Eustace's spectacles. Why? I haven't done anything wrong.

Sister continues, "God works in mysterious ways. Frances might finally come into her own. Raising a child."

"Oh quite possibly, sister, without a doubt."

Mercedes smiles and knows she is lying but is uncertain how to frame it as a confession of sin this Sunday, for is it one? Yes. And no. My head hurts.

"Shall I proceed to the grade ones, sister?"

"Yes."

Mercedes rises. "Thank you, Sister Saint Eustace."

But Sister Saint Eustace has returned to her paperwork.

James is enjoying his retirement. The wingback chair is surrounded by a growing turret of books. This is his other project, along with the secret one in the shed. He has opened the last of the crates and emptied the shelves of all the books he never had time to read. First he counted them all: a hundred and three. Then he began stacking them in the order in which he intends to read them, the last ones forming the foundation. It is a slow ruminative process. He knows what he intends to read first, however, and has set it aside accordingly for the pinnacle of his wall: Dante's *Paradiso.* Having gone through *Inferno* years ago, he has decided to cheat and skip over *Purgatorio,* eager for the beatific vision and the reunion with Beatrice.

He rests now from his labors, in his chair behind his partially constructed parapet of words, and allows his mind to drift in place. His capable eldest daughter making things go. His wild middle daughter settling down to raise her colored child—oh yes, he hasn't forgotten that. He has simply forgotten how such a thing was ever able to call murder into his heart; the birth of an innocent child. And Lily. My consolation.

He is startled from his reverie by the distant boom of a cannon. Lily is standing beside his chair combing his hair, "It's okay, Daddy—"

"Wha—?"

"It's eleven o'clock." But James is still bewildered. "In the morning." Lily gathers up a lock of his hair and begins to braid it, explaining gently, "It's Remembrance Day."

"Oh."

They observe two minutes' silence together, then James calls in his voice that has faded to straw, "Frances."

Frances and Trixie enter slowly. "Yes, Daddy?"

"Play something, my dear."

"What would you like me to play?"

"Any old thing."

She starts, " 'Swing low, sweet chariot, comin for to carry me home—' "

"That's lovely."

" 'Swi-ing low, sweet cha-ario-ot, com-in for to carry me home. . . .' "

At four-thirty, Mercedes arrives home from her first day as a schoolteacher to witness the latest phenomenon: Frances playing "The Maple Leaf Rag" while Daddy dozes in his chair, his head sprouting a mass of tiny braids. Frances breaks off from playing and leaves; "I'll get supper, Mercedes."

Mercedes has no objection. Frances has recently revealed a natural talent in the kitchen. She cooks and cooks. Roasts and curries, stews and casseroles. It's mystifying. Frances is like one of those strange persons who awake one morning and play the complete works of Bach with never a lesson.

"Daddy," says Mercedes. He uncrinkles his eyes and blinks in several directions before focusing on her. She's standing over him with a brown paper package. "This came for you." She deposits it in his lap and leaves.

James looks at the postmark. New York City. The address is written in a spidery hand—old-ladyish. He notes with relief that it is not the same hand that formed the infamous letter of years ago. Who could it be, then? It takes him a while to undo the strings.

Inside is a lavender note folded on top of a bundle wrapped in white tissue paper.

Supper.

Mercedes takes her seat at the head of the table. Lily places a platter of *kibbeh nayeh* in the center, followed by a bowl of *tabooleh,* a brimming casserole of stuffed *koosa* and a pot of *bezzella* and *roz.* Mercedes unfolds her napkin and wonders where Frances learned to cook—or not cook, as the case may be—their mother's food. The *kibbeh* looks just like Mumma's except that in the center there is the impression not of a cross, but of a jack-o'-lantern grin—

"Frances."

"Yes, Mercedes?"

"Oh, never mind."

James's slow foot is heard in the hall together with the syncopated clunk of his cane. He makes his way into the kitchen and over to his chair at the end of the table opposite Mercedes. Mercedes catches Frances's eye but Frances doesn't register anything unusual, oh for Pete's sake— "Daddy," says Mercedes.

"What's that?"

". . . Nothing."

Fine. Let him eat with his hair in braids. Whom does it injure? Better than provoking a scene at table. As in the bad old days.

They say grace. James does not express surprise at the Lebanese feast spread out before him. He presses his portion of *kibbeh* flat with his fork, drizzles it with olive oil, tears off a bite-size piece of flat bread, wraps a bite of *kibbeh* in it and eats. Modestly, the way he always has, even when he worked in the pit, aware of how intimate an act eating is.

"You've outdone yourself, Frances," he says. "It's every bit as good as your mother's."

Mercedes knows she ought to be glad but this strange new peace between Daddy and Frances unnerves her.

"Thank you, Daddy," Frances replies, pulling up her chair, "I learned by watching."

"Then you've got a photographic memory. That's a sign of genius."

Mercedes' eyebrows approach the ceiling—let's just say it's been a day full of surprises. She picks up her fork and gingerly tastes the *kibbeh*. It is more than delicious. It's as though Mumma were here. Mercedes closes her eyes for a moment in reminiscence of a precious time she knows could not have been: when Mumma was alive and we were all so happy. When was that time, where was that country? Rain begins to drizzle against the kitchen window, Frances lifts the lid from the steaming pot of *bezzella* and *roz* and Mercedes remembers: it was during the War. In the kitchen with Mumma and the Old Country. So happy. Mercedes opens her eyes again.

"What's wrong, Mercedes?"

"Nothing at all, Lily."

Mercedes permits herself to relax a little. She leans back in her chair and observes with satisfaction the flawless table manners of her family. She basks in their warm but civilized conversation. Everyone, it seems, has had an interesting day. Frances apportions second helpings. Lily reaches with her napkin and removes a spot of food from the left corner of James's mouth, a small service for which neither thanks nor embarrassment is required. All quiet at the kitchen table.

Frances pours boiling water into the teapot and Mercedes is alarmed to notice James catch sight of himself in the kettle. Bristling with braids. The right side of his mouth breaks into a smile big enough to make up for the left side having lost the knack, and he laughs so hard that he falls dangerously silent between wheezy exhalations. Frances and Lily laugh too, until their throats ache and the tears stream, elbows thunking onto the table rattling the cutlery. Even Mercedes joins in and, once started, is unable to stop even after the others have recovered, then caught it again from her.

Exhausted, they fortify themselves with a pan of succulent Nellie's Muffins straight from the oven. They sip tea. Listen to the rain. Outside, the whole world is hungry and forlorn. But in here is a little island of contentment.

At last, Mercedes thinks, we are a family. Daddy is senile, Frances is crazy, Lily is lame and I'm unmarried. But we are a family. Soon to be one more. And for the first time it crosses Mercedes' mind to keep Frances's child.

Certain Effects

"FRANCES," SAID JAMES AFTER the glorious Lebanese supper, "come here. I have something for you."

Frances joined him in the front room. She sat on the piano bench and he handed her the white tissue-paper bundle.

"What's this?" she asked.

"One or two things that belonged to your sister Kathleen." Then he left the room.

Frances fishes a new candle from a kitchen drawer. She walks up the attic stairs, where the voices are louder than ever. She pauses, wishing they would speak one at a time and stop yelling. "I'm listening," she says. But the hollow din rages on, so she continues up.

Now she and Trixie sit on the floor of the attic with the lighted candle. Frances looks down at the bundle in her lap. She parts the tissue folds. Lying on top of a soft pile is an old exercise notebook. The cover is imprinted with the Union Jack, the flag of Nova Scotia and the crest of Holy Angels Convent School. In a space marked *"Name:"* a grandiose signature spells "Kathleen Piper." And in the space marked *"Subject:"* in equally florid strokes, "La vie en rose!"

Frances picks up the notebook. Turns to the last page first, and reads:

O Diary. My loyal friend. There is love, there is music, there is no limit, there is work, there is the precious sense that this is the hour of grace when all things gather and distill to create the rest of my life. I don't believe in God, I believe in everything. And I am amazed at how blessed I am.

★ ★ ★

Then Frances turns back to the first page and begins:

> *8 pm, February 29, 1918, New York City*
> Dear Diary,
>
> No, I will not use that form of address. That is a relic of childhood. This book will serve as a record of my progress as a singer. I will record only relevant facts which will prove useful as my training progresses. No gush . . .

Wax drips from the guttering candle stub by the time Frances arrives once more at the last page. She closes the diary. "Goodnight, Kathleen."

She turns her attention to what remains in the tissue-paper package. Then she opens the hope chest.

The next day, James joins Frances on the veranda.

"Are you warm enough?"

"Yes thanks, Daddy."

But he has brought an old tartan blanket and spreads it over her and Trixie anyway. "There." He sits to the right of her on a kitchen chair next to her camp cot. He looks off at nothing in particular and starts talking, "I went down to New York because I got a letter."

Frances doesn't interject. She doesn't look at him. She knows he will fly away if she does that, so she relaxes and listens to his story.

"It was the day of the Armistice. I got off at Grand Central Station and I walked all the way to where she was staying because I couldn't get a cab. There were crowds. I didn't know the war had ended. . . ."

He trails off. They sit still and silent for a long comfortable time until he says to the middle distance, "Well it's time I did a tap of work." He picks up his cane and shuffles off to the shed. Trixie follows.

It takes six days. Mercedes leaves them each morning on the veranda and every afternoon she sees them when she returns up the street. It's as though they hadn't moved—although Lily assures her that they have been duly fed and watered. They look so peaceful sitting side by side, with their eyes settled on separate pieces of sky. Like old friends. Daddy and Frances.

Mercedes would like to sit and chat with an old friend, but she doesn't have one. She had Helen Frye. And most of all, she had Frances. Where is Frances now?

Mercedes can see James's lips moving as she approaches. What is he telling Frances? Day after day? He has always fallen silent by the time Mercedes is within earshot.

Walking home from school up Water Street on the chill seventeenth of November, Mercedes can see his breath. He is talking and talking, but by the time she reaches the veranda his words have given up their steamy ghosts. She greets them as usual on her way into the house, and finally hears something.

"How did the babies get in the creek, Daddy?"

Mercedes freezes on the threshold. Then walks briskly into the hall and, without removing her coat, runs up the stairs to her room. She leans against her door, slips a hand inside her blouse and feels for her opal rosary.

James reaches out his curled left hand without looking. He finds Frances's head and bonks it, saying kindly by way of answer, "That's all over and done with."

"I was there," says Frances. "Wasn't I?"

James rises. "Think I'll do a tap of work." And makes his slow way to the shed. His story is done.

Frances stays looking at the sky in fifteen shades of gray.

Benny Luvovitz takes James and Lily out in a sleigh and helps James cut down just the right tree.

On her way home from school, Mercedes opens MacIsaac's jingle-bell door to find Frances sucking on a cinnamon stick chatting and chortling with the old man, who's nursing a ginger beer. He looks up, "Merry Christmas, Mercedes." His shelves are not as full as they were in better days, but he reaches down a dusty box of peanut brittle.

"Thank you, Mr. MacIsaac."

"It won't be long now, eh?"

"What's that?" asks Mercedes.

"The great event." Mr. MacIsaac looks at Frances and beams. Mercedes stuffs the candy into her schoolbag, saying, "Come, Frances, time to go home." She forgets to buy the headache powders that she went in for.

Mercedes takes Frances's arm and sets a rapid pace down Plummer Avenue past shop windows with nothing for sale but empty space, "for lease, for lease, for lease"—at least there are no prying eyes behind those counters.

Frances wants to pop into Luvovitz's to buy raisins for mincemeat.

"I'll get the raisins, Frances, you go on home. It's cold."

"No, I'd like to say hi."

Mercedes has the exact change ready in her hand, but Mrs. Luvovitz sets out a stool for Frances, saying, "When it's your time, *taier,* you call me," and offers her expert opinion as to the sex of the infant, "You're carrying high so probably it's a girl, or else maybe just an extra-smart boy." Mrs. Luvovitz winks. Frances smiles and asks, "How's Ralph?"

Mercedes picks up a tin of Magic Baking Powder to avoid Mrs. Luvovitz's mortifyingly considerate glance in her direction. Mrs. Luvovitz hesitates, then produces a photograph of the world's most perfect grandson. Jean-Marie Luvovitz.

Frances hoots, "He's got the sticking-out ears!"

"What're you saying, 'sticking-out ears,' I'll 'sticking-out ears' you!"

But Frances laughs and so does Mrs. Luvovitz. Mercedes holds her head up and comes to the counter. She glances at the photo, then looks straight at Mrs. Luvovitz and says politely, "Congratulations."

Finally outside, Mercedes says, "It's probably best that you not leave the house these days, Frances. It's too cold for you to be out traipsing, you'll catch your death."

Frances doesn't answer. She turns up Ninth Street.

"Frances." Where on earth—? Oh good Lord.

Frances knocks on Helen Frye's door. Mercedes watches from the darkness of the street as the door opens and Helen appears in the square of light. Frances turns sideways, setting off her shameless silhouette, and looks back toward Mercedes as though waiting for her. Mercedes sees Helen slowly raise her hand in greeting. But Mercedes makes no move in reply. After a moment, Helen's hand drops once more to her side. Mercedes hears Frances say, "Merry Christmas, Helen."

Frances rejoins Mercedes in the street and they turn homeward again. Frances slips an arm through Mercedes'. Mercedes shivers.

At home, Daddy and Lily have begun decorating the tree. "This time next year, there'll be a wee holy terror crawling under the tree," says James, painstakingly threading a kernel of popcorn. Frances starts baking. In the front room, Mercedes catches sight of a check on the piano; made out by James in his wavery handwriting, to Our Lady of Mount Carmel Relief Fund—three zeroes. She crumples it up and tosses it into the fire. Bootleg money or no, this family cannot survive on a female junior teacher's salary. Daddy may wish to ease his conscience by giving away his

ill-gotten gains, but Mercedes puts the welfare of her family first. Someone's got to.

Immediately after supper that evening, Mercedes pleads homework
and a headache, and retires upstairs. A small lie. It's not her head that hurts.
Once in her room, she switches off the light and lies fully clothed on her
bed. She can hear Christmas carols from downstairs—Frances at the piano,
singing along with Daddy and Lily, " 'God rest you merry gentlemen, let
nothing you dismay. . . .' " Tears fill Mercedes' eyes. It is not fair that
Frances should bask in Daddy's affection and the approval of sundry
shopkeepers for something that ought to have her hiding her face in
shame. It is not fair that Sister Saint Eustace managed to make Mercedes
feel like the bad one—when everyone knows that she's the good one. It is
not fair that Frances will have a baby, while Mercedes was denied a
husband. None of it is fair, but that is not why Mercedes is weeping freely
against her pillow. She does not begrudge Frances the new affection she
has inspired on all sides—Mercedes was the first to love Frances, after all.
She knows she could even find the strength to bear the mortification of
raising the child. But she cannot bear to lose Frances. And that's what hurt
this evening on their walk home. The new Frances is no longer a wayward
child. Or even a scarlet woman. The new Frances is at home
everywhere—especially in her own growing body—and does not lack for
friends. Everyone seems to think that motherhood is the best thing that
could possibly happen to her. Everyone but Mercedes. For she knows that
once Frances has a child, Frances will no longer need a mother.

Mercedes covers her face with her arm and allows her heart to open
up along its oldest wound. Where will my baby Frances go? She will
disappear. She will die and I'll have no one to love and look after. Little
Frances will become a forlorn ghost child, crying on the stairs at night, cold
and transparent, with her fuzzy golden braids and her brave stare, *"It
doesn't hurt."* And I won't be able to comfort her.

Mercedes cries until she is dry and empty once more. Then she rises
and sits on the edge of her bed. Downstairs they're singing "O Holy
Night." She reaches into the drawer of her night table, finds a fresh hanky
and blows her nose. She rebraids her hair in the dark. There. Don't whine.
Fix it.

January gales freeze the ocean waves midcrest, pine trees tinkle in their
glass dresses, and it's warm inside.

" 'Hitler Appointed Chancellor.' "

Lily is scanning the headlines for James.

"There's going to be another war," he says. And adds another book to his wall.

Frances bellies up to the piano and plays "My Wild Irish Rose."

"Sing, Lily," says James, dropping into the wingback chair.

Upstairs, Mercedes studies by correspondence with Saint Francis Xavier University. Upgrading her earning power.

February will never end, but never mind.

Lily holds the newspaper at the proper distance from James's new glasses so he can make out the photograph: Chancellor Hitler and His Holiness Pope Pius XI. Shaking hands.

"Yup," says James. "You watch."

And he drops off suddenly to sleep the way he does now.

March comes in like a lion.

" 'Franklin D. Roosevelt Inaugurated President.' Do you want to see the picture, Daddy?" Together they look at the photograph of the tall bespectacled man standing on a hustings swagged in the Stars and Stripes, waving. " 'Pledges to Put America Back on Its Feet.' "

April Fool's Day. The morning sun floods through the attic window.

"Diphtheria Rose," says Frances.

Lily hands her the tattered, still pretty doll. Frances holds Dippy Rose over the open hope chest, and recites: " 'Golden lads and girls all must, / As chimney sweepers, come to dust.' "

Frances lays her next to Spanish Influenza, Typhoid and TB Ahoy, Small Pox, Scarlet Fever and Maurice. Trixie and Lily look on reverently. On the floor next to the open hope chest, the baptismal gown is laid out.

"Music please, Lily."

Lily winds up The Old-Fashioned Girl and sets her down to turn on the floor, her head balanced prettily on her hand. She tinkles, " 'Let me call you sweetheart, I'm in lo-o-ve wi-ith you-ou. . . .' " Trixie follows the figurine with her eyes, ready to pounce should it stray from its circumference.

Frances picks up the baptismal gown and lays it gently over her dolls. "Next time I open this box, it will be to dress my baby in this gown."

"And to get your dolls again."

"No."

Frances moves to lower the lid but Lily stops her halfway.

"You forgot this, Frances."

"That's yours, Lily."

The photograph of Kathleen. The one that Mercedes kept in *Jane Eyre* until Lily tore the book apart, it seems so long ago. Lily contemplates it for a moment. Mumma is in the background, in the window.

"What's that in Mumma's hand?" Lily asks.

"Scissors."

"She's waving."

"Yes."

Her eyes still on the photograph, Lily sucks in her upper and lower lips by slow turns, releasing them gently through her teeth.

"This picture belongs to Mercedes," she says, finally.

"No it doesn't."

"I don't want it." Lily looks away.

"She's pretty, isn't she?"

Lily doesn't say anything. Doesn't look up.

"She's your mother, Lily."

The Old-Fashioned Girl has stopped turning but Trixie keeps watch just in case. Frances continues gently, "She died. It wasn't your fault."

Lily sits very still and listens, veiled by her hair which she has been wearing loose of late, it sweeps to the floor around her like a curtain of fire.

"She went to New York," says Frances. "She was an opera singer. Something happened there. Daddy brought her home. She lay in this room and never said a word. Ambrose drowned in the creek. It was an accident. You didn't drown, you got polio instead. I was there."

The more Frances tells, the more she remembers. As though it were all parked, waiting behind the flimsiest of stage scenery—a scrim perhaps—and suddenly exposed by a trick of light; the countryside dissolving to reveal the battlefield, present all along.

"The night you were born. I don't know why I brought you to the creek. I loved you. It wasn't because I didn't love you. I carried you into the water. I held you and I prayed." Frances strokes her belly, feeling for a kick inside, but it's all quiet.

"Did you baptize Ambrose too?"

"Yes."

They sit for a long moment together, not talking, breathing in the soft cedar cloud.

Frances puts The Old-Fashioned Girl back in the hope chest, then turns and looks at Lily, who is growing up.

"Lily. If you want to ask me something, I'll tell you the truth."

Lily has dropped the photograph of the laughing girl. She looks up. "Ambrose loves you, Frances."

Frances takes Lily's hand and places it against her belly. "Here. You can feel him. He's awake now."

Lily feels the ripple. She presses her ear against the site.

"What do you hear, Lily?"

"The ocean."

The car horn blasts outside; Mercedes has learned to drive. Frances and Lily go to the window and wave down. Daddy is standing by the car, leaning on his cane, he smiles up. Lily turns away from the window, intending to close the hope chest before going downstairs, but she sees that Frances has already done so. She pauses at the top of the stairs and says, "Are you coming, Frances?" Frances turns and goes directly to join her sister at the top of the stairs. No need to close the hope chest, for she sees that Lily has done so already.

It's a lovely day for the drive to Mabou. Frances would rather have had her baby here at home with Mrs. Luvovitz, but she relented because it seemed to mean so much to Mercedes—"They're equipped for emergencies, Frances, it's safer even than going into hospital, please dear, if only for my sake."

James stands holding the passenger door open. Mercedes pulls on a pair of kid gloves as Frances climbs in beside her.

"Frances, I have to tell you a secret."

"What?"

"I'm pregnant too."

Mercedes' smile trembles for a moment, then she bursts out in a high-pitched giggle, "April Fool!"

The car lunges in reverse down the driveway. Frances watches her sister's laughing profile and reflects that Mercedes has been under a strain.

Blue Dress

DADDY AND LILY ARE very happy together at home alone. It's so peaceful. Three and a half weeks pass. Lily doesn't realize the extent of James's latest limitations until he starts to smell a bit rank. She helps him into the bath once a week. She lays out fresh underwear daily and bleaches the rest. Fresh and clean. She checks on him if he's too long in the toilet. He sometimes falls asleep there. She tidies him, then wakes him up. He still spends an hour a day working in the shed but he misses Trixie's company. They haven't seen her since Frances left. Lily expects Trixie to show up at the foot of Frances's bed in Mabou. Meantime, Lily has had to put mousetraps in the cellar and kitchen.

On April 25 the telegram arrives: *it's a boy stop coming home wed stop.* Lily and Daddy toast the new arrival with milk. They consider a battery of names—Isador, Ignatius, Malcolm, Rupert, Bingo, George, Sebastian, Christopher, Pius, Lief, Horace, Romulus, Patrick, Pierre, Cornelius, Michael, Alec, Eustochium, Felix, Augustus, David—and decide on all of them. Until Lily comes up with Aloysius, which seems to say it all.

"Aloysius," says James. ". . . Aloysius. Yes."

"Aloysius," replies Lily.

The first of May, month of Immaculate Mary. Lily is still in her white dress and headgear from the noon procession up Plummer Avenue to the church. It seems an appropriate outfit in which to greet her sisters and her new nephew. She has strewn the stone path to the house with Queen Anne's lace and daisies. "Welcome Home" in Gothic script hangs from the veranda eaves. In the kitchen, bread sculptures cool on the table—

Madonna and the Infant of Prague, and a *pietà*. She has prepared a feast: a roast cooked to the size of a wallet with raw turnip slices, cranberry sauce, baked potatoes—the two that failed to detonate in the oven—tea biscuits and molasses. Date squares, pits in. Upstairs, lily of the valley exhale on Frances's pillow. All is in readiness. Last but not least, a big blue cake with white writing, "Happy Birthday Allowishes."

The morning rain has turned to evaporating diamonds in the afternoon heat. Lily has had her eyes peeled on the street for the past three hours.

"Here they come!"

James joins her on the veranda. As soon as the car gets within range, Lily waves and runs back into the house to get the new camera. She gets a shot of the car as it turns into the driveway. Mercedes is waving now too but in the background Frances is, of course, more concerned with the bright blue bundle at her breast. Click. The car pulls to a stop. Mercedes' hand goes up to her window. Click. The driver's side opens. Click. Mercedes steps out, still waving, click. She runs up the path to Lily, click, click, click. And grabs the camera, jerking Lily's head forward at the same time because the new camera comes with a strap. She hisses at Lily, "Not a word, do you hear me? Not a word."

Mercedes glances up to include James in this proviso but he's on his way down the steps with his cane, walking to meet Frances, who has stopped halfway up the flowered path. Mercedes moves to overtake him but "No, Mercedes," says Lily.

Mercedes is surprised. But she obeys, understanding that Lily is up to something saintly.

James reaches Frances, puts out his arm for her, and she takes it. Together they walk to the house. Frances is wearing a sky-blue dress to go with the darker blue bundle she cradles with her free arm. When they reach the foot of the veranda, Lily sees that it is not a bundle at all, but Frances's breasts. Huge and leaking. Staining her pale dress a royal blue.

By evening Frances is still asleep upstairs on her bed, her face crushing heavy scent from the lily of the valley. In the lower reaches, the decorations are down. They have eaten no supper. Mercedes consents to a cup of tea.

"The birth went smoothly." Mercedes lifts her cup but her hand shakes so badly that she sets it down again on the kitchen table. "Frances was very brave. The sisters said it was as though she felt no pain."

Lily and James wait for her to continue.

"It was a boy. He was, of course, quite dark. And very healthy."

"You saw him," says James.

Mercedes nods and the tears come. "He was beautiful. A beautiful baby with a lusty cry." She smiles a little at the recollection.

"Did you hold him?" Lily asks.

Mercedes nods yes.

"Did Frances?"

"He took to the breast right away, there was no problem."

Mercedes catches James's eye and he looks down, shaking his head.

"What happened to him?" Lily is confused. She seems to be the only one who doesn't understand. Mercedes turns to her and explains tenderly, "He just died, Lily. Sometimes it happens, a baby just dies in its sleep, they don't know why."

James nods, his mouth tightening. He says in a would-be matter-of-fact voice, "Crib death. That's what happened to the first Lily."

"Other Lily?"

"That's right," says James, rising to leave. "Was he baptized?"

Mercedes nods, starting to cry again. As James shuffles past he bonks each of them affectionately on the head with his bad hand and says without looking, "Night-night, girls."

"Good night, Daddy."

He shambles from the room. They hear him clear his throat once or twice when he reaches the hall.

Mercedes puts forth a hand and strokes Lily's hair, "Sometimes, if a child is very special, God might choose to spare it the pain and temptations of this world, and take it straight to Him."

"What was wrong with him?" Lily is suspicious.

"Why, nothing, Lily. He was perfect."

"You said he was 'special.' "

"Yes, specially beloved of God."

"That means there was something wrong with him, he was crippled."

"He wasn't crippled."

"I don't believe you."

"Lily. Look at me." Mercedes continues gently, "I have some nice news too."

Lily waits, not trusting. Mercedes takes Lily's hand and leans forward.

"While I was at Mabou I saw the bishop. He'd like to have a talk with you."

Lily looks up. "What for?"

"He wants to hear about your visions."

"You mean Ambrose?"

"Yes. And other things."

"What other things?"

Lily's hand cools and moistens in response to Mercedes' gathering warmth.

"Your special way with the sick and the lost."

"Who?"

"The veterans, for example. And Frances. And Daddy—" Mercedes' eyes have begun to shine, giving Lily the old creepy feeling of being a front for some figure situated immediately behind her, a figure she knows will disappear no matter how suddenly she turns—"And your special knowledge of God's plan."

The soft fur at the nape of Lily's neck stirs. She can no longer resist, she turns around in her chair but there is no one behind her—nothing to see but the oven, standing where it has always stood.

"What are you looking at, Lily?"

"Nothing. I thought I heard something."

Mercedes' gaze follows Lily's to the oven. And now the filaments at the back of Mercedes' neck likewise bristle to life.

"What does he want?" asks Lily, turning round again.

"Who?"

"The bishop."

"He wants to interview you. To find out if God has a special plan for you."

"How's he going to find that out?"

"By listening to you tell your story. And—Lily, this is the most wonderful part—you know how I've been saving so that we could go to Lourdes for your fourteenth birthday?"

Lily waits.

"Well, God has provided. There's more than enough money for us to go together and to stay as long as it takes to petition Our Lady for a cure."

"I'm not sick."

Mercedes flushes slightly and her eyes return to this world.

"Lily. Don't you want to have two good legs?"

"No."

Mercedes had not counted on this.

"But Lily. If you are blessed with a cure, it will be proof that God really does have a special plan for you."

"I don't need proof."

Mercedes is vexed, for Lily is, of course, right. She requires no proof because she has faith. But the bishop requires proof. Rome requires proof. And Mercedes requires that Lily's goodness—the essential goodness of this family—be revealed for all to see.

"Lily . . ." Mercedes lifts a lock of Lily's hair and slowly starts to wind and weave, "Do you know how pretty you are?"

Lily begins her habit of sucking in her lips one at a time, passing them back and forth over her teeth.

"I know you're afraid, Lily." Lily's hair is so smooth, her honey cheeks tinted rose, her lips flushed and full. "Change is frightening even when it's for the good. But Lily, I also know that you love your family and that, in the end, you'll do what's best for everyone." Mercedes strokes the long gleaming braid and lets it fall.

Lily remains still as Mercedes rises and takes her tea from the room. After a moment, Lily hears the piano and Mercedes' slender voice floating above it, " 'A-A-A-A-A-A-A-A-A-ve Mari-i-i-i-i-i-i-i-i-i-i-ia . . .' "

Like "Londonderry Air"—or, as Frances always called it, "London Derrière"—many people find it impossible to hear this hymn and not swell with sweet guilt at how they ought to have been nicer to their parents while they still had the chance. But for some reason it only makes Lily angry. Perhaps because she has always been so nice.

Lily rises and leaves the kitchen, past the front room—" 'gra-a-a-a-a-a-zi-ia-a ple-ena-a-a-a-a' "—where she can just see the top of Daddy's dry flaxen head above his parapet of books. She proceeds up the stairs, past the room where Frances has not stirred among moist sheets and up to the attic to do the one thing she can for Frances.

Lily is set to break the lock on the hope chest with her bare hands— she intends to remove the baptismal gown and dispose of it for good so that Frances need never come across it. But the hope chest isn't locked. The lid is down but not quite flush to the frame of the box itself. Lily lifts the lid. The cedar smell wafts up cloaking a second smell—in all likelihood another mouse entombed and decomposing. What light there is reflects feebly from the yellowed satin of the old baptismal gown. Lily remembers the garment spread lightly over Frances's beloved dolls, not wrapped about them, but she must be mistaken because, when she slips her hands beneath and lifts, the gown feels full and heavy. Too heavy for dolls. Cool fur. Trixie. Swaddled and entwined.

"Trixie." She must have leaped in for a nap and the lid shut. Oh Trixie. Oh no. She must have panicked and tangled herself up, winding and twisting until she finally came to rest. "Poor Trixie." Lily strokes the yellow eyes shut, but there is nothing to be done about the gaping jaw.

A truly terrible smell now, the body having been disturbed. Lily takes the shallowest of breaths to avoid her gag reflex as she carries Trixie down the attic steps. On her way past Frances's room, she sees Mercedes by the dancing light of a candle, seated on the edge of Frances's bed with an empty tray in her lap. Lily continues down the front hall stairs.

In Frances's room, Mercedes hears the kitchen door slam. She makes a move toward the window but stops when she sees Frances coming awake at the sound. "Frances?"

Frances looks up at Mercedes.

"Frances, it's time to make you fresh and dry, dear."

Frances blinks. Mercedes smiles.

"I've brought you your favorite dishes. Look."

Frances looks at the tray while Mercedes identifies its contents, "Blancmange, treacle, mead and mutton—"

"It's empty."

"Frances—" Mercedes' head starts to shake.

"Mercedes, what's wrong?"

Mercedes' fingers begin a blind search of her own face, probing her eye sockets—Frances reaches up and gently lowers her hands. Mercedes takes a breath and pulls herself taut. "I'm sorry, I didn't want him to—" but trembles and cracks all over like spring break-up—"die!—I—" Frances reaches up and draws Mercedes down into an embrace, soaking them both. Mercedes smells the new milk. "I'm sorry, Frances."

"He died. It's not your fault."

Mercedes grieves into Frances's neck. "Maybe if we had stayed here and let Mrs. Luvovitz—"

"Hush," patting her back. "Hush now, it's all right."

Mercedes mangles many words against Frances's neck, unintelligible to her sister but for "I love you, Frances."

"Shsh."

"Can I sleep here tonight?"

But Frances is looking past Mercedes' shoulder out the window. "What's Lily doing?"

Mercedes looks up.

They can see Lily on her hands and knees in the garden. Somehow she has rolled the big rock aside on her own. There is an object lying nearby—a brighter patch against the ground. Lily is scooping debris from a freshly excavated hole.

"She's digging," says Mercedes.

They watch Lily pause and rest for a moment against the garden stone.

"She's praying," says Frances.

They see Lily rise from her knees and pick up the dimly glittering bundle. She cradles it for a moment in her arms before lowering it into the hole. Mercedes rises and straightens her shoulders.

"I'm worried about Lily, Frances."

"Leave her be."

"You know, Frances, one thing looks very much like another."

"Mercedes—"

"What kind of a creature prefers to be crippled, Frances? Answer me that." Mercedes has entered a mad classroom, *i before e except after c, the time has come, the Walrus said, to give you forty whacks instead.*

"Mercedes, come back."

But Mercedes has left the room and now she is almost fainting at the evil smell enshrouding the hall. She follows the putrid cloud downstairs and into the darkened kitchen before Lily is halfway across the yard on her way back to the house. Mercedes waits with her hand on the electric light switch, trying not to breathe. One thing looks like another, but nose knows. There is the odor of sanctity. And there is the stench of hell.

The kitchen door opens and Lily steps into the sudden light.

"What have you done?" demands Mercedes.

Lily's hands are cupped together around a secret. She looks like a child with a robin's egg, *it fell out of the nest, I rescued it, really 'n' truly.*

"I've buried Trixie," Lily says.

Mercedes waits. Gives her one last chance. Lily walks to the kitchen table and deposits her treasure. Blackened with coal, nestled in a remnant of stained linen, a tiny human skull, fragile as a shell, with sutures still agape. Along with a few slender twig and pebble bones, the stuff of birds' nests.

"And I've found my brother."

She watches as Mercedes gets down on her knees, squeezes shut her eyes and, in a stage whisper, implores God to cast the Devil from Lily— " '*exorcizo te, immunde spiritus, maledicte diabole*' "—repeating the words until they are no longer words but sounds. She makes the sign of the cross over, and over, and over—Later she will contact the bishop so that Lily may be taken away to a place where a special priest will drive the unclean spirit from her by force of prayer and perhaps other means, cruel to the body but so kind to the soul. Later Mercedes will beg God's forgiveness for having flattered herself that she was the sister of a saint.

Lily walks past Mercedes, whose mouth is twitching and hissing like a puncture, and into the front room. She is ready to ask James a question. She has already forgiven him for what she does not yet know. The reading lamp is on. She steps through a breach in his wall of books to find him slumped as usual in the wingback chair with his mouth half open. Dante's *Paradiso* has fallen from his hands. Lily picks it up and places it carefully in his lap. She bends and kisses his forehead, but she doesn't ask him the question, because he is dead.

She returns to the hall, where Mercedes' whispers have risen to a buzz and whirr. Lily mounts the stairs and walks into Frances's bedroom, full of the scent, the innocent passion of wildflowers.

"Frances, I've buried Trixie and said a prayer for her. I've found Ambrose."

Frances says, "Lily, reach up and hand me *Wuthering Heights*."

Lily hands Frances the book.

"Remember when we buried the family tree?" asks Frances with a small grin.

"It decayed," answers Lily. "It was only made of paper."

"Did you find my nightgown?"

"A little piece of it."

Frances opens *Wuthering Heights*. The pages have been excavated in the center and replaced with a wad of cash. Frances hands Lily the money.

"Is this the Lourdes money?"

"No. I earned it honestly."

"Daddy is dead."

"I have a present for you, Lily. I was going to wait for your birthday but I want you to have it tonight."

"What is it?"

"It's in the hope chest."

"Frances—"

"What's that sound?" Frances tilts her head to listen. "Do you hear that? It sounds like a swarm of—"

"It's Mercedes. I'm afraid of her."

"She thinks you're a saint."

"Not anymore."

"I know."

"I don't believe in the Devil, Frances."

"Mercedes does."

"So?"

"I can't look after you anymore."

"It's okay, Frances, I can look after myself, I'm not scared of Mercedes."

"It's not just Mercedes. You have to go, Lily. Don't worry, I'll tell you where."

"No."

Frances cups Lily's face in her hands and looks her in the eyes. "Oh yes."

How can a person look into her own face and consent to be banished from it? For Lily, Frances is as first and familiar as the sky, as the palm of her own hand. The freckle on the nose, the green jewels in the eyes, the smart mouth, what does it mean to be banished from the face that first looked you into existence?

"I don't want to leave you."

Lily's forehead buckles but Frances insists, "You have to go, little gingerbread boy, 'run away and whatever you do, don't look back.' "

"This isn't a story, Frances." Anger ignites Lily's grief.

"Yes it is, Lily. *Hayola kellu bas Helm.*"

"It is not!"

"*Taa'i la hown, Habibti*—"

"No!"

"*Te'berini.*"

"Stop it!"

Frances reaches for Lily, but Lily flies into a rage, beating off the embrace until she forgets that Frances is not a book, or a porcelain figurine. Frances doesn't move except to protect her face and breasts while Lily exhausts herself.

When Lily crumples finally, the undertow gets ahold of her face and contorts it into a grieving clown. The same tide distends her voice, "I don't want to leave you, Fra-anc-ees." The corners of Lily's mouth run with clear saliva, she is incapable of closing her mouth or of taking the next breath. Frances touches Lily's fist, unlocking her throat. The air pours scraping in, and corrosive sobs begin.

"Come here, Lily."

Frances opens her nightgown and guides Lily's mouth to drink.

Shortly before dawn, Lily kneels before the open hope chest for the second time that night. She reaches deep down and withdraws a soft bundle wrapped in white tissue-paper. She lifts out a beautiful flowing dress of pale green silk. Then picks up the notebook that has fallen from its folds. Holy Angels Convent School.

Ten minutes later, the shed door opens and Lily walks in. It is not necessary to search, for there it is. Daddy's project. Finished. They are still mounted on the lasts. Two bright red boots. The small one, perched on its built-up sole, smiles out at her as does its big brother. Lily removes the new boots from their iron feet. She pulls them on, harnessing with care the left boot for its first taste of the bit. She wraps her ankles in the money Frances gave her, pulls tight the candy-cane laces and stands up. Calf leather. They enfold her feet like a second skin, no need to break them in. They go nicely with her beautiful new green silk dress—a little big for her, to be sure, and missing a sash as you can see from the empty belt loops, but lovely all the same. With her notebook under her arm, Lily leaves the shed.

The air is cool and moist with a hint of salt. The night is turning gray. It's the best time to see this town—the collieries, the tracks, the coal carts and company houses look best in the pewter dawn, likewise the ocean and the rocky shore. *Farewell*. Lily feels refreshed. As though she could walk for ever. *Farewell to Nova Scotia*. She closes the door behind her, and heads for the Shore Road. She looks back once. And keeps walking.

Book 8

HEJIRA

8 pm, February 29, 1918, New York City
Dear Diary,

No, I will not use that form of address. That is a relic of childhood. This book will serve as a record of my progress as a singer. I will record only relevant facts which will prove useful as my training progresses. No gush. Let other girls record their crushes and their dresses, their tresses and trousseaux. I am here to work. I will note scientifically everything I learn as in a lab book.

I will be objective and unflinchingly self-critical. I will not be distracted by the bustle of this city. And in this, my record book,

I will not allow emotion to color my perceptions.

1:12 am—I am burning. I have to live, I have to sing, I want to transform myself into a thousand different characters and carry their life with me onto the stage where it's so bright and so dark at the same time, just knowing there are three thousand people out there longing to be swept away by the passion that's about to flood out from scarlet curtains, to this I consecrate my body and my soul, I can give no more than all of myself, I feel my heart is a throbbing engine and my voice is the valve, like a wailing train, it has to sing or blow up, there's too much fuel, too much fire, and what am I to do with this voice if I can't let it out, it's not just singing. I am here as a speck, but I don't feel scared or about to be blown away, I feel like all New York is a warm embrace just waiting to enfold me. I am in love. But not with a person. I am passionately in love with my life.

Friday March 1, 1918—My voice teacher is someone I will simply call Herr Blutwurst. He is rude and, if my first lesson is any indication, utterly devoid of qualifications. I can only conclude he is a fraud. I will give him to week's end. He is a dry stick of a person. I feel dust in my throat just thinking about him. I was perfectly polite. He looked me over as though he were buying a horse. He has a horrible accent. He ordered me to "zing zomesink." I did, and he got an expression on his face as though he'd just et a bad oyster. Why did it ever even occur to this man to enter any field remotely connected to music since he obviously hates music? He said, after I had sung my *Quanto affetto,* "Vee haf a lot off verk to do." I should have said, *"Ich weiss das, Käsekopf, das ist warum Ich hier bin."* He wants me to cry but I won't, my daddy just finished killing a lot of his countrymen.

My first advantage: I have everything. My second advantage: this is just another island. My third advantage: I am bigger than it all.

March 2—I took a walk in Central Park. I didn't cry in front of Herr Kaiser. I didn't sing in front of Herr Kaiser because he hates singers who sing, he claims to be Hungarian but I know he's Fritzy, why hasn't he been arrested, there's supposed to be a war on.

Monday March 4—I ate the most delicious thing today. A pretzel. It's a baked thing tied in a knot. You eat it with mustard. Sounds unremarkable but is brilliant. Wrote pointless surprise theory exam for Kaiser.

Tuesday—Could someone please tell me what the point of "hissing" is? We have progressed, dear Diary! I am now forbidden, not only to sing, but to make any vocal sound whatsoever!

Wednesday—Museum of Natural History with Giles and fossilized lady friend Miss Morriss. Tea, then took me to see six girls doing modern dance in bedsheets swishing knives around. Maybe I should be a dancer. Take that back about Miss Morriss, they're both so nice and I'm so bored.

Thursday—Kaiser crept up behind me and put his skeleton hands around my lower back ribs and said, "For the purposes of these lessons I must ask you to loosen or discard your corset." Filthy *bodechean.*

Fri. March 8—Wearing my hair loose like Lady Godiva to feel less naked with no corset. Excellent feeling, though strange, like I'm always ready for bed or swimming. Came all the way to Island of Manhattan just to shed outmoded undergarment.

Sat.—Got perfect on stupid fake theory exam. Killed him to admit that. "You have virtually perfect pitch, Miss Piper." There's no "virtually" about it and he knows it. Asked him when I could sing again. He said, "As far as I can tell, Miss Piper, you have never sung in your life."

Sun.—Giles asked if I wanted to come sightseeing. No. Thank you.

Monday, March 11, Eighth Ave elevated train, squashed like sardine—"That which does not kill me, only makes me stronger."

tues.—My lower back is always aching. I have not cried, I'm past that, I'm numb, but I have almost fainted. *"Nein,"* he says. "Start again. Inhale, *ja, und . . .*" And then I "hiss."

Wed.—Oh joy! Today I got to make a sound! With my mouth closed. I have no idea what he's talking about most of the time and it isn't the language barrier: "Think that you must hold a boiled egg in the back of your throat." With or without the shell? Halfway through the lesson, as I was making a feeble little humming sound with my mouth closed, with my tongue in the "n" position, while I was trying "to put a smile into the sound," he said, "That's it." Apparently he has found the true placement of my voice. On the rear shelf of a disused library.

?—I wonder if anyone has ever committed suicide out of sheer boredom? Today I was permitted to open my mouth ever so slightly and release the faintest of "ee's." Then he told me to put an "ae" inside the "ee." "Ah" and "oo" come after but he wouldn't let me finish—he informed me that I had run out of air. I said I had plenty of air left and he told me that perhaps I had air enough to sustain life, but not the note. I have to learn to sing "on the breath," he said. Give me strength!

Giles just called me for supper. Everything she cooks is white or light brown. Except the boiled greens, which are gray. She said, in this voice that reminds me of dust on a doily, "Before you know it you'll have lots of friends and it will seem like a different city." I don't want friends, I didn't come here to make friends. She's nice, though. Why can't I just be grateful that there's at least someone who speaks kindly to me. Sometimes, though, she gives me a bit of the creeps. She'll look at me like she knows something and then she'll say something completely innocuous. This whole apartment reeks of lavender, there are lace curtains and praying hands everywhere. It's all like a fading photograph

except for me. I keep seeing myself whirling around, breaking everything without even touching it, it makes me want to talk louder,
breathe deeper, commit carnal acts!

I look at myself naked. Yes, this is my confession. In the full-length
mirror in the armoire in my room. I look at myself just to remind myself that I'm there. No, I look because I like to look and that's how I
know it's wrong. But how could it be? I feel an ache.

I want someone to see me and touch me before I'm old. Before it
wrinkles and fades and falls, I can't believe that will ever happen to me.

14th—Intervals of seconds. Up and down and up and down and up and
down and *lasciatemi morir*

15th—spent a month's carfare on a new dress—pale green silk chiffon,
très chic, très moderne, I look about twenty-five. I have no place to
wear it.

16th—Intervals of thirds

Sunday, March 17—No lesson today, no torture chamber. Also, I didn't
have to get up at the crack of dawn to WALK there on time owing to
the fact that I squandered a small fortune on that stupid dress I'll never
wear. But *oubliez* all that! I am happy as a clam because I'm in Central
Park all on my own, it's sunny, life is long,

I have all the time in the world and I will sing. He has put my
voice into a sad solitary cell but she will fly. I know because I can feel
her beating, getting stronger the longer she is silent. Could it be that the
Kaiser's training is working? Or is it possible my voice is thriving on ad-
versity? That is the perverse unbreakable Piper spirit. Thank you Daddy.

There is a couple "spooning" in broad daylight not three steps
away from me in full view of a nanny and a six-year-old girl with a face
full of freckles who keeps grinning at me—reminds me of Frances. Little imp just whipped her rubber ball at me, it bounced off the bench,
now it's landed in the pond

Fished the ball out, played like an idiot with her for the next hour
and a half much to Nanny's relief.

après diner:—Because this is my diary, I will ask this question:
Do you think Giles has ever been impure in thought and deed?
Why do I have to think that about a perfectly innocent old lady?! But

no one is perfectly innocent. A good singer knows that. I am terrible. I don't care. I want to make love with my voice to three thousand four hundred and sixty-five people at a time.

Tues. 19—I have been exiled to the *mezza di voce*. *Il passaggio*. He calls it "the no-man's-land of the voice." It is another of his sadistic techniques. I am being held prisoner an octave and a half above middle C between E and G.

Wed. 20—He wants to ruin my voice.

Fri.—*Il passaggio* is abandoned. *Il passaggio* is all but silent.
    Il passaggio is another word for limbo.

sat.—I was late this morning. Couldn't get to sleep last night and couldn't wake up this morning. Herr K worse than usual as a result.

Monday March 25—It seems *Il passaggio* is inhabited after all. Haunted is more like it. Full of ghostly sighs and groans.

2:00 am—I dreamt of Pete. He was wearing Mumma's apron and Daddy's pit boots and he was crying and wanting me to hug him. There is no such thing. The lights are on now. No such thing as Pete.
    I want to go home. I want to see my daddy.
    Kathleen, grow up.

3:30 am—don't write it down
    I can't stop crying.
    What if there's someone outside my door?
    Oh God. If I think about it, my door will open.
    "Let nothing disturb you; nothing frighten you. All things are passing." Saint Teresa, *ora pro nobis*.

thurs. 28—Giles made me drink a special tea so I could sleep last night. It worked. Has she been spying on me?

fri.—One heck of a middle C today. Felt like I was gorging on a chocolate éclair. Kaiser none too pleased—after all, I'm a soprano. Sopranos don't sing in chocolate.

sat.—Today I cried. he told me to sing the C-major scale, my first time allowed to put more than two notes together at a time. But still no consonants, just "ah." I felt like I was climbing stone steps in the dark and when I got a glimpse of light toward the top I started crying but I finished the ruddy scale.

APRIL FOOL'S DAY—Today Herr Knibs gives me that bloodless vulture eye and—no, he's more amphibian, he's probably covered in dry scales (scales, ha ha!) from collar to cuffs and dines furtively on furry creatures thrice daily. I can just see the squirming lump making its way down his narrow throat. Does he regurgitate bones every evening? Well today he says to me, "I vill accept you as a shtudent, Miss Pipah." Why didn't I say the perfect icy thing? I said—and I am being completely honest here, so I'll tell you—I said, "Thank you, sir." May I be struck dead.

Wed.—Daddy sent me a book today and Mercedes and Frances sent me saltwater taffy! I never thought I'd miss my little elves so much. I wish Daddy would put them in a special crate and mail them to me like kittens for a day or two.

Thurs.—*"La voix mixte":* In every head tone, the resonance of the chest. In every chest tone, the rarity of the head. Ascend directly to heaven.

Fri.—Giles asked me to sing something for her this afternoon and I had to say, "I'm sorry, I'm not allowed to sing anything but scales and arpeggios." The Kaiser says he can tell if I've been singing "ditties" on the sly. It's like I'm committing adultery with my voice or something, he's disgusting.

Mon.—He's making me wear my hair in a scalp-tight bun. What does he think I am, a ballerina?

Tues.—I have had an epiphany. I now know what people mean when they say you have to suffer for your art. I always thought they meant rehearsing till you drop, performing when you're not in the mood, starving until you get discovered and I always thought, "Great, I can't wait to suffer" but that's not it at all. The real suffering is this teacher trying to kill me with boredom by marching me up and down every scale known to man. Fine. I will beat him at his own game. I have begun repeating the entire morning's lesson three times every day.

Wed.—"Your vocal range is a freak of nature, Miss Piper, no more or less impressive than Mount Everest. It remains to be seen whether or not you have the stamina and skill to scale it." Scale!

Thurs.—I love the buildings. They're called skyscrapers. They're the closest thing to an ocean here. But it's an ocean that goes straight up, not flat out. They say that the body of water stretching away to the east of Manhattan is the ocean but it isn't. Not my ocean, anyway. It's weird because back home I just took it for granted, my gray-green sea. Now I have a granite ocean. It gives me the same happy-sad feeling I need sometimes. When I look straight up at the buildings I can feel alone in a good way. Not in that horrible way of no one knows me.

fri—This is not a city. This is a world with whole countries in it. You could go mad here if you were the type of person who thought you were sane in the first place. I have found something past the granite ocean. It's a whole amazing world. You can walk for an hour and never hear a word of English, you can eat in five different countries in five blocks, you can hear music everywhere. Why am I studying, why do I want to be caged on a stage when the real singers are out here, singing about fish, hollering out rhythm across wheelbarrows full of fruit to the timpani of Tin Pan Alley, a chorus of trams, horseshoes, knives and live animals, this is where the opera is. The Met is a mausoleum. The music room is a funeral parlor. God I don't want to wind up in a museum.

Mon.—There are places in Central Park that are better left unexplored and I won't scandalize you by telling you why.

Tues. April 16—Coney Island! Ate only pink things. Threw up. It was worth it.

Wednesday—Start at the South St. docks. Halifax times twenty. They better hope it never blows up. I see horses being winched up by their bellies in slings onto ships. They've been conscripted. That's what most of the ships are for. New York feeds the war. New York goes to the whole world and the whole world comes to New York. I love seeing huge crates with Chinese writing swing through the air and pile up on the dock alongside every other language known to man. I'd like to spend a whole day just watching the men and the cargo but I can't linger too long 'cause of all the tough customers wondering what a nice girl like me is doing . . . etc. What would they do if I said, "Hey pal, I think you're beautiful, you move like Nijinsky, you're my idea of a Greek god, in overalls." But I'm not allowed to say anything at all because they'd think I was asking for it. Men get to chat to strangers and learn all kinds of things. Women get to take a book out of the library. When I am a famous singer, I will talk to whomever I please.

On foot up through the Bowery, the Italian quarter—kids, carts, food, women in black, good-looking guys but don't let them see you looking, *opera verismo*—Greenwich Village, ladies and gentlemen, Tenderloin—get hungry here, buy a pretzel, have lunch in Hell's Kitchen—really! Why do they call it that? Seems perfectly nice, in fact you can have a *free lunch* at Devlin's Saloon Bar. It's true, a sign said "Ladies Entrance" so I entered and there were a whole bunch of women with red faces and gristly elbows and all you have to do is pay a nickel for a beer that comes with a hot heaping plate. Up Broadway a bit tipsy—not used to beer—the golden mile, Union Square, Madison Square, Herald Square, past the Met—genuflect—promenade through Times Square, Columbus Circle, buy popcorn for the pigeons to keep them in the statue business (where they perform a valuable civic service by keeping the glorious past in perspective), into the Park, zigzag through that immense chunk of countryside smack in the middle of the greatest show on earth, past the Pond, the Lake, the Castle, skip the Reservoir it's too big and too small, promise to go to the Metropolitan Museum next time, Haarlem Meer (sit down and decide I've walked far enough), out onto Central Park North, up Lenox thirty-seven blocks to the Haarlem River. It's night.

Take the Eighth Avenue elevated back, dead happy tired with the whole city around my head like a halo. There are no Dutch people in Haarlem. I have noticed on walks that colored people and foreigners in general are totally different here. In New York it's not like they're in someone else's city, at least not in their own neighborhoods. The neighborhoods are whole cities themselves. At home when I passed by the Pier or Fourteen Yard I always felt sorry and thought how lucky I was not to be born into that, but here when I went into Haarlem I felt weird for being white. It's full of churches, and families just out strolling in the evening. I felt conspicuous. But I never fit in down home either so what's the difference?

Everything in New York is a photograph. All the things that are supposed to be dirty or rough or unrefined are the most beautiful things. Garbage cans at the ends of alleyways look like they've been up all night talking with each other. Doorways with peeling paint look like the wise lines around an old feller's eyes. I stop and stare but can't stay because men always think I'm selling something. Or worse, giving something away. I wish I could be invisible. Or at least I wish I didn't look like someone they want to look at. They stop being part of the picture, they get up from their chess game and come out of the frame at me, blocking my view. What do they see when they look at me?

Fri April 19—Jesus, Mary and Joseph, last night I snuck out at midnight when Giles was asleep. Why didn't I do this weeks ago?

I thought there was music during the day, but the night consists of nothing but. The problem is I can't get into any of the interesting-looking places unescorted. But so far it's enough to drink up the night, the streetlights, the life on front stoops off Broadway, behind curtained windows, private clubs with shuttered doors, the faint sound of trumpets and drums, and the longest automobiles I have ever seen. I thought Haarlem would be asleep by the time I got up there, considering the number of churches, but maybe the churches turn into clubs at night like toys coming alive 'cause it was a different city—on the main streets anyhow. Daddy always says that in Ireland the number of churches is exceeded only by the number of pubs. Lenox Avenue was gorged with people dressed to the nines, lines of limousines, a fair number of white people, even mixed couples pouring in and out of places. It whitens somewhat at night. I'm on the verge of answering the next man who says, "Hey, sweetheart, where's your boyfriend?" just so's I can step inside somewhere, anywhere, so long as there's music, music, music. I did go to one place though. Jerry Chan's Chop Suey House at Canal and Bowery. Delicious. Here's my fortune: "You will meet a tall dark and handsome stranger." *Très romantique, n'est-ce pas?*

tues—Today the Kaiser made me stand barefoot in a basin of ice water while vocalizing.

Friday—This morning he brought out the *Vaccai Practical Method of Italian Singing!* I could have wept to see my childhood friend. I never thought I would be so happy to start at the beginning all over again. How the mighty have fallen. Kaiser opened to page one, "The Scale"—at least it's set to words—and said, "Vowels only, if you please." I told him I can read Italian, but he ignored me. So. It is still not yet given to me to chew solid food. NO CONSONANTS. I plot his death.

Have an accompanist now. She is a machine he imported to plod through the *Vaccai* while I gum the vowels. Why bother? And he has the nerve to tell me to pay attention to the "music" she is plunking out.

sat—I can tell when a piano is out of tune and, yes, it does matter.

mon—Why am I wasting my time and anyone else's? I can't sing, forget how, forget why I ever wanted to. Giles says I look pale—good. I'm staying in bed tomorrow.

wed, May 1—The Kaiser went nuts when I came in today, "Vere in Gott's name haff you been?!" "I was sick." "I don't care if you come here shpitting blood, you vill come! Next time you are indisposed I had better learn off it wia your obituary in ze papahs, do you understant me?" *"Ja, mein Kaiser."* He said he'd fling me out if I missed another class.

I didn't say, *"Ja, mein Kaiser,"* I said, "I'm sorry sir." Then I thought, what the heck, he's already wild at me, so I added, "Sir, I didn't think one day more or less of scales would be any grievous loss to the music world." And he slapped me. I looked over at the accompanist—that girl is made of stone. She didn't look at me. She just waited for him to give the command, "E minor, Miss Lacroix." And she started in like a player piano you couldn't give away. I sang but I don't know where it came from.

If I told my father, he would come and kill this man. Why didn't I hit him back? The strange thing is, today I felt like I was singing those ruddy scales for the first time. I can't explain it, it wasn't in words, it was this knowledge all of a sudden as though I knew it all along but didn't know I knew it, and it was: all the music is in this scale. The scale is just a safe place where all the music can fold itself down and get stored. Like seeds.

And the scale sounded so pure to me. Like in the end, if you had to be stranded on a desert island, you wouldn't take *Traviata* or *Bohème,* you'd take one scale. Because it has everything in it. I hope I don't have to be whacked every time just to learn one crummy, measly, huge lesson.

Thursday, May 2—Singing words!

Saturday—He asked me today if I knew the difference between sentiment and emotion.

Monday—Today he said, "Your voice is a beautiful face. Which you manipulate with the coarseness of a circus clown." My first compliment from the Kaiser.

Thursday, May 9—The Kaiser has set up an audition for me with Mr. Gatti-Casazza, *il numero uno* of the Metropolitan Opera! November 12. He is going to let me sing an aria! Aria? What's that? The Kaiser said if I'm lucky Mr. G-C will put me in the Met chorus next season. And I finally got up the guts to say I'd rather go back to New Waterford and have ten babies than tote notes in the Met chorus behind some Franklin stove of a superannuated diva. No, Diary—I must be honest. I said, "Sir, I am not chorus material." And he said, "That is the correct answer, Miss Piper."

Saturday—"Listen to the piano, you're not listening, Miss Pipah." I'm sick of the piano. It's time the piano started listening to the voice.

Monday—I asked the accompanist, perfectly politely, how long she had been playing piano and she raised one eyebrow and said, "I've always played." Oh, allow me to prostrate myself before thee, oh sphinx of the keyboard!

Tuesday—Miss Lacroix is in league with the Kaiser. She can do no wrong. She plays like an automaton and I'm supposed to follow her. I told the Kaiser I might as well go down to the Henry Ford plant and sing to the rhythm of the assembly line. I said exactly that and he just shrugged a bit. Maybe he's mellowing. Maybe I'm wearing him down a little, or maybe—oh horrors—he likes me. She still never looks at me much less says good morning, who does she think she is? Where did he dig her up? I thought colored people were supposed to have rhythm.

Friday—She has a first name: Rose. If you could meet her you'd know how unlikely that is. And what's more, she can actually play the piano.
    I came early today. I saw the Kaiser chatting with His Most Terrible Majesty Signor Gatti-Casazza out front and I slipped by and up the stairs. That's when I heard the most sublime, the most beautiful music. I thought it was Chopin at first, it was that romantic and thoughtful, but I knew it wasn't quite that, then I thought Debussy, it was dreamy enough but there was too much space in between some notes and not enough between others and time changes that slipped by before you

could pinpoint them and sudden catches of achingly sweet melody that would just end like a bridge in midair or turn into something else, and though there were many melodies, you could never hum the whole thing, nor could you figure out how they could all belong in the same piece and yet somehow they do, and you have no idea how or when it should end. In fact it doesn't end, it stops. Some modern composer I guess.

Anyway it was *her* playing! The sourpuss accompanist. She didn't see me. Someone should do something about her clothes. She dresses in pink, with puffed sleeves, pleated skirts and a hemline one inch above the ankle. Looks like she just came out of church around twenty years ago. Hand-me-downs maybe, from some rich battleaxe in the Temperance League. Anyhow, when she stopped playing I said, "That was nice, who wrote it?" And she just glared at me. If looks could kill. Just then the Kaiser came in, so our delightful conversation was cut short. He said his usual "Let's start with C Major, Miss Lacroix," and you'd never know she was a musician. But I know.

Wednesday—Miss Lacroix and I have a game we play. It's called Kathleen Arrives before the Kaiser and Listens to Miss Lacroix Play Piano Who Pretends Not to Know Miss Piper Is There. Why are the only people I've met in this city either senile, sadistic or eccentric?

Thurs.—After listening to Miss Lacroix play in the mornings before class I feel like a total impostor with no musicianship. (She'd love to know that.) I have figured out one of her secrets. She is the composer of the beautiful strange music she plays. If she even "composes" it—I think she just makes it up as she goes along because her pieces always come to an end the moment before I hear the street door open downstairs, which means she has seen the Kaiser through the window.

Saturday—This morning I got there even earlier and broke the Kaiser's rules. I sang whatever I darn well pleased. I sang Tosca! I felt like a criminal or a nymphomaniac. And when Miss Lacroix arrived I was dying to see the look on her face when she discovered she'd been beaten at her own game, but I didn't want to acknowledge her presence any more than she does mine. She left and I could have killed her except I suspect she just went out into the hall to listen, not wanting to give me the satisfaction of an audience.

Friday, May 31—Got her! This morning I came to the end of "Let the Bright Seraphim," then I got up silently and crept to the door and there was Rose, sitting on a chair tilted against the wall with her eyes closed. Her profile is imposing. I wish I could draw it. She is arrogant even with her eyes closed. Especially with her eyes closed. She has a tall round forehead and a high straight nose that flares out at the base of the nostrils, and her lips sit against each other like dark pillows. Almost purple. The only way my lips could remotely look like that would be if I puckered up for a kiss, but she doesn't look like she's expecting anyone to kiss her. Her eyes go up slightly at the outside corners almost as if she were Oriental. She has high cheekbones and a dimple in her chin which is entirely wasted on her, dimples being accessories to girlish charm. She reminds me of the pictures of African women on P. T. Barnum posters except she hasn't got the rings around her neck. And she's not wearing a colorful turban, she has her hair pasted to her head in two pigtails with little ribbons that look utterly perverse on her. Not to mention her Pollyanna dress with the ruffles. Doesn't she have a mother? Or a mirror? I noticed all this in the three seconds before she opened her eyes and looked at me. She didn't say a word, just got up and went into the studio and started playing. SCALES. Then she spoke, and I should have slugged her. She said without even looking at me, "You embellish too much. That's a thing of the past." Have I mentioned she's five foot ten?

2:30 am—The Harlem Rhythm Hounds!! But the sun is coming up, good night.

Sat.—Can you wail like that saxophone, can you walk like that bass guitar, can you talk like the trumpet and beat like the drum? Then what are you doing so far from home, little girl?

Mon, 3—David is too embarrassed to dance but there are lots of fellas willing to dance with me and I feel perfectly safe doing so because, after all, I have an escort! He was scandalized when I danced with a colored man named Nico but he got over it as well he should, I fail to see why color should cause such a commotion. I wonder if there's anything like this going on back in the Pier or Fourteen Yard? I was too much of a priss then to find out. Tomorrow night David's taking me to the Ziegfeld Follies. Maybe I'll introduce him to Giles.

tues—I want to be a show girl, I'm going to take tap-dancing lessons, forget the opera. I think this is an enchanted city where you hear with different ears and see with different eyes. I feel like I've been living in a graveyard till now. Reading dead books, listening to dead music, singing dead songs about dying. Beautiful, yes, but dead, like Snow White in her glass coffin—except the music I've been singing doesn't move when you kiss it. Or at least, if it could, I haven't found how to make it.

wed—I am so irresponsible, dear Diary, how could I not tell you who David is?

He's my soldier. He said, "Excuse me, miss, is this seat taken?" He's nineteen and he's on his way to the front. He is so debonair. At least his uniform is. To listen to he's very sweet. He's a farmer and his father is angry at him for enlisting but he's determined. He wants to live a little before getting hitched to a plow for life and who can blame him? I met him at Chan's, where I go to read and eat something that goes crunch. (D. is tall and quite nice-looking, but I don't think he could be the one from my fortune cookie because his hair is sandy and his eyes are blue.) Anyhow, we must have gone to fifteen clubs and we ended up at a place that was half theater, half bar, called Club Mecca. It's up in Harlem on Seventh Avenue and I had to drag my soldier in there. And that's where I heard JAZZ.

How can I describe it? I heard my mother play ragtime at home but jazz is something else.

fri. June 7—Sweet Jessie Hogan is a singer. I am not a singer.

Sun.—Had David over to meet Giles. He liked her. Ate everything on his plate. She showed him a decrepit photo album—a gallery of spinsters—and either he's a great actor or he was actually interested.

tues—Jazz.

wed—Razzmatazz.

thurs—I can truck. I can ball the jack, I May Be Crazy but I Ain't No Fool so Rock Me in the Cradle of Love.

fri–June 14—A riddle: how can I be singing scales for the Kaiser on the upper west side, while several blocks northeast of here, Sweet Jessie

Hogan, the Diva of Club Mecca, is sleeping off last night's jazz? Has Miss Hogan ever sung scales? Would she put up with this?

sat—She sings like twelve saxophones and a freight train, she wears about a pound of gold, the band just tries to keep up with her. She's no lady. Her songs are all unbelievably unhappy or lewd. It's called Blues. She sings about sore feet, sexual relations, baked goods, killing your lover, being broke, men called Daddy, women who dress like men, working, praying for rain. Jail and trains. Whiskey and morphine. She tells stories between verses and everyone in the place shouts out how true it all is. Imagine—the more interruptions, the higher the praise, like a *real* chorus. Picture Sweet Jessie Hogan at the Met. The best opera is just high-tone Blues.

Sun—David said what if he gets killed in the war, he doesn't want to die "never knowing what love is." Translation: he doesn't want to die a virgin. I don't believe he was a virgin, but I was, but that's all taken care of now. I don't want any fella thinking he's got anything special to "teach me" and besides, David is nice. We got a room for two hours. He said we were newlyweds but the man at the desk looked like he didn't care. Well, I liked the kissing part and the next part. And I didn't mind the rest too much but he seemed more—well, he went to the moon and I stayed here on earth. And he looked totally overcome like a sweet stupid puppy and said, "I love you." I felt like we'd just been to two different moving pictures and didn't know it.

Tues.—"Do not pretend to things that are outside of your experience, Miss Pipah. If you have never suffered, do not manufacture an imitation of suffering. If you have never been in love, do not insult your listeners with cloying counterfeit."

wed—I think I'm in love with David. Or at least, when we're alone to-gether I feel like I'm in love with him. But then I don't think about him again until I see him so can that be love? I realized something funny yesterday, I realized I haven't even told him I'm a singer. I wonder what he thinks I do all day?

sat—Sex is good for the voice. Why don't they teach you that in school?

Sunday—As for sin. I honestly can't believe God is so bored or so lech-erous as to care how close my body and its various parts get to someone else's various parts.

Mon—I can't stop thinking of David you-know-how.

Tues.—Today I got a letter from Daddy asking me if I'm okay because I haven't written in so long, I felt so badly, I wrote right away. Not about Mecca of course. Or David. About everything else. And I sent my two pets two matching sailor-boy dolls, one for Mercedes and one for Frances.

Fri–28—Today I started crying on the streetcar for no reason. It was crowded and I was looking at a little girl with dark blond braids like my own little Frances when a pair of woman's hands reached down to stroke the child's hair. They were Mumma's hands. With the soft wrinkled knuckles and the veins, and lines on the palms like blood dried in the sand. My throat got sore and I was crying before I knew it. And then I got a shock. The streetcar started to empty and I saw the woman's face. She was a colored woman. I am starting to not be able to picture Mumma's face anymore but I can picture her hands exactly. *"Salaam idEyyik,"* she used to say. Bless your hands.

sat—Today Rose Lacroix was there waiting for me when I arrived and she asked me why I hadn't been coming in early the past while. I said, "Did you miss me?" She blushed. You'd think it would be hard to tell because she's quite dark, but it wasn't hard at all. She wouldn't speak to me for the rest of the day and I regretted my flippancy, but at least I finally got some sort of human response out of her. David left for France. He cried but I didn't and that made me feel so mean so I told him I loved him. That's not really a lie, I loved him sometimes.

Mon–July 1—The Queen of Sheba still won't speak to me. Yesterday I asked if she'd like to come for a cup of coffee with me and she said, "No thank you," and I asked her again today and she said the same thing. I said, "Why not?" And she gave me one of her haughty looks like the cat just talked to the queen and answered, "I have responsibilities." As if I don't have *responsibilities.* As if conquering in the footsteps of Malibran and Patti were not a responsibility. As if animating the genius of composers from Monteverdi to Puccini were child's play. Lacroix will always have an excuse if she does not become the Paganini of the piano, but I have no such luxury.

tues—Got my period today, thank you, Jesus, Mary, Joseph and all the saints.

wed—The Kaiser says to me this morning, "Velcome back, Miss Pipah." I haven't been away and I said so, but he said, "Yes you have," and that if I couldn't be present in both body and mind from now on, he would cancel my audition. I will swear off all nocturnal ramblings until after November 12.

sat—Working.

mon—Working.

tues—Got a letter from David. He asked me to marry him!! I'm going to have to write him back as nicely as possible—but really. I'd as soon marry a coal miner. Can you picture me as a farm wife? In Montana? My God, that's under Winnipeg! But this is what gets me: for a while I thought more about playing with David in our pee-reeking hotel room than I did about my work. I cared more about a colored woman singing in a hundred-seat dive with a bunch of musicians who probably can't even read music, than my own career in the greatest opera houses of the world. My father did not send me here so I could get dragged down, I could have done that at home. From now on I'm only going out to hear real music at civilized hours. What really gets me is that I never even told David I was a singer, nor did he ever ask. He doesn't know anything about me but he's ready to marry me!

fri–12—She catches up with me on my way from the lesson and says, "You're working too hard." Who asked her? I pretended she hadn't said anything. She had her chance to be friends and she wrecked it.

sat—"Miss Piper, ze song is not your enemy."

tues—I have no pride. I asked Miss Music Authority what she meant by "You're working too hard" and she enjoyed it, I could tell. She paused, just to see me writhe a little on the pin, then she said, "I have to go straight home today, but tomorrow afternoon we could go somewhere and talk."

wed–July 17—She is the smartest person I have ever met! Except for Daddy. She's not like anyone else. She doesn't have a New York accent or a kind of Harlem southern accent. I wonder where she is from? Maybe she's rich.

sat—We go to Abernathy's Cozy Coffee every afternoon. She thinks music is already out there floating around and it's up to us to give it an opening into our world so we can hear it. As though the world were full of music we can't hear with "the naked ear." So today in class I thought, okay, the song as it should be sung is shimmering around me like air in the desert, and all I have to do is welcome it. So I closed my eyes and opened myself up and let the song pass through me and I thought, "Don't sing the song, just release it." When I finished, the Kaiser nodded. I looked at Rose and she gave just the most minute smile down at the keys.

mon.—She says I'm really a mezzo!!!! She must be out of her mind.

tues—I asked her if she likes chop suey. But she can't go anywhere or do anything except our half-hour coffee and she won't tell me why or where she lives or anything. She pretends it's boring and changes the subject but I am determined to find out what her secret is. Maybe she's so poor that she's ashamed to let me see where she lives. Maybe she's married. Maybe she has an illegitimate child.

wed—She said, "Malibran was basically a contralto with a very tough attitude." Malibran sang Desdemona *and* Otello. And Romeo *and* Giulietta. And everything in between. But that was almost a hundred years ago, no one's allowed to do that anymore. "They weren't allowed to do it then either," she said.

thurs 25—I invited Rose for supper. I thought, maybe she doesn't have money to spend on chop suey. She didn't even think about it, she just said no thank you.

fri–July 26—I followed her. She lives in apartment three at 85½ 135th St between Lenox and Seventh Avenue, over a second-floor church that's over a butcher shop that's tucked between a dentist and a haberdashery named "Dash Daniels Harlem Gentlemen's Emporium." Take the Eighth Ave. elevated.

sat—I followed her again today and she nearly caught me because she came running back out of her building five seconds after she went in. I ducked in a doorway and saw her make a phone call in the butcher shop. A little kid offered me a taste of his raspberry ice cream. I licked it and for some reason he thought I was hilarious.

The Lord's Day—Blessed Sunday. Church with Giles and Miss Morriss the only ordeal. I went up to 135th St to see if I could see Rose, and if she left the neighborhood I could follow her until she got far enough away for us to be able to meet "by accident."

I got there and there was music rollicking out the second-floor window—if church were like that where I come from, I'd be religious. It was fantastic. Someone was playing piano and there was, I presume, a minister leading the songs, and the congregation joined in, back and forth, back and forth, people taking solos, embellishments like you've never heard in a baroque opera, and I swear I saw the building rock. I guess that's rapture. The crowd in their Sunday best started pouring out onto the street and a big lady, in a hat with more flowers than grow in New Waterford in an entire summer, shooed me away saying, "This is a decent neighborhood."

But the church-sized lady served her purpose because she hid me from you-know-who, who also came out with the crowd, wearing an ice-cream-sundae version of her usual embarrassing clothes, and I wondered if that had been her whomping on the piano up there. Somehow I can't picture it—although I'd like to. Rose headed west and I followed her. She got on the Eighth Ave. I shadowed her all the way to West 14th, where she got off, walked down Greenwich, turned onto my street and went straight up to my building! I felt like I was in a play. The doorman was giving her a hard time so I went in and said in my snobbiest voice, "Thank you Ernie, that will do." And he said, "I'm sorry, miss, I thought the young lady was mistaken."

I was dying to tell her that I had just followed her all the way from her place, but something told me she wouldn't see the humor in it— I've seen her smile exactly one half a time. And never laugh. So I tried not to smile, and she was serious as usual when she reached into her leather schoolbag and brought out some sheet music. She handed it to me and said, "I think you ought to take a look at these." So I said thank you, and she said goodbye. She was going to go right home! But I said come for a walk, and she did.

I opened the sheet music when we got to Washington Square and it

was Carmen's "Oiseau Rebelle" and Rosina's "Una Voce Poco Fa."
She said they were a good contrast to Cherubino and "Let the Bright
Seraphim"—to say the least—and Mr. Gatti-Casazza will probably ask
me to sing something of my choice as well as what I've prepared and I
should just happen to have one of these. She gives a person a present
like she was giving them a black-edged telegram. I said, "Setting aside
for a moment the fact that I am a soprano, not a mezzo, why are you
helping me?"

   And she said, "You're going to be a star one way or another, it's
obvious." I said it's not obvious to me, at least not lately, and she said,
"Your teacher knows it, he's already told Gatti-Casazza what to expect.
There are a lot of singers but you don't get a voice like yours very of-
ten. As well as everything else." What everything else, I asked.
"Presence."

   She said all this as though she were a doctor diagnosing me with a
rare disease. I said, "You still haven't told me why you're helping me."
And she said, "People pay money to go and listen to stars. I think they
should at least hear the music the way it was meant to be heard." So
she's just doing a public service? She's awful sure of herself. I asked her
if she didn't agree with everyone else that the Kaiser is one of the best
teachers in the world. She said, "He's a brilliant technician. You can
learn a lot from him. And you can unlearn a lot from him, all that nonsense you were doing before. Now you're ready to stop singing the
words and music, and start hearing them." She could sell the Eiffel
Tower to a Frenchman. What she says is smoke, you can't get ahold of
it and it's basically meaningless. But it works. She couldn't stay for supper. She's nineteen; I asked.

Thurs.—I ran quickly after the lesson again, to catch her and get her
opinion on the day's work. She said to me, "You should be paying me
for this," so I offered to. I expected Rose to be insulted by the offer of
money but she actually looked as though she was considering it. She
said, "Do you really think I could teach for money?" So I said yes, but
that it would be an awful waste. "Why?" Because of your gifts as a
composer and musician, I said. Then she started walking again and said
to the sidewalk, "I'm not a composer. I just make it up." I told her
that's what is called composing, but she said she doesn't write it down.
That it's different every time.

"So write it down," I told her. And she said, "No." "Why not?" I asked. "Because then you kill the bird," she said.

She is so strange. But I know exactly what she means. I've never heard anyone talk like her or play like her but then, when I hear her play, I feel as though I'm hearing music for the first time. And the sound is so beautiful it hurts me. I asked her to come back to Giles's apartment and play. "Please," I said, "please, please, please." And she didn't say no right away, she said after a moment, "I'd like that. I'd like to take you up on your dinner invitation too. But I can't this evening." How about tomorrow? "I'll ask," she said. Ask who, I wondered, but did not inquire. I don't want the bird to fly.

evening—Frances sent me her own crayon drawing of me singing. It's adorable. And you know the strangest thing? Along with musical notes coming out of my mouth, there are little birds!

Friday August 2, 5:45 pm—She's coming for supper! She'll be here in fifteen minutes.

later:—At least Giles isn't prejudiced. She didn't act surprised when I introduced Rose as my friend, the accompanist. Rose—she finally told me to call her Rose, I told her to call me Kathleen weeks ago and she stopped calling me Miss Piper but now she doesn't call me anything at all—Rose was extremely polite, asking Giles all sorts of dull questions about her volunteer work at the convent. Giles has the most morbid job in the world. She looks after nuns who are on their way out. I'd be terrified if I were one of those old girls and saw her coming at me with a tray. Confession: I've had some wine. Giles actually poured us wine—apparently it doubles as a medicinal and a celebratory libation. So whether it's your birthday or you're having your leg amputated you can count on a swallow of Giles's chokecherry wine. I wonder if Rose was scandalized? We played the phonograph for a bit, then Giles took the needle off and asked Rose to play and me to sing. We were both embarrassed, but Rose asked Giles if she had a special request. "Yes, my dear," said Giles, " 'My Luve's Like a Red Red Rose.' "

I thought I would die! I couldn't look at Rose. But she didn't bat an eye, just turned to the song and started playing. And I sang. And after a while it didn't seem so silly at all, and I was glad Giles had requested it because it made me think of Daddy and of home.

Giles had her eyes closed at the end and she said, "Lovely, girls. Just lovely." I was going to ask Rose what she wanted to play next but she was already playing. Her pieces start like that—before you know they've started, they're just there and gathering. I can't talk about it. I don't know how long the piece went on because, remember when I said about how the time signature slipped and slid around imperceptibly? Well, all of time did that while she played. I lost time. I wanted to live in that music, no, to wear it loose around me instead of skin, and after a while I had this flooding thought that this was Rose just thinking. I'm sounding far too Irish for my own good. It couldn't be the Lebanese side could it? What's blarney in Arabic? *B'el Arnay?*

I thought it might be the wine. But it's the music. Giles was asleep when Rose stopped playing. I had tears all over my face, but it didn't feel like crying. Rose sat for a few bars of silence, then turned and said she had to go. I wanted her to stay and talk but I knew it would be wrong to ruin the music, so I walked her to the streetcar stop and we didn't say anything at all. At first it felt so right to be silent. Then it felt awkward, but I of all people couldn't think of anything to say. So I just said thank you. Finally the streetcar came and she slipped away.

Sat—You'd think we were total strangers. She called me "Miss Piper"! I wanted to catch her after the lesson but Kaiser kept me back to give me a present! It's a beautiful book, Emma Albani's memoirs, *Forty Years of Song*. He said it would inspire me, "she being your countrywoman," and at any other time it would have been the highlight of my whole life, but today it meant Rose had already caught the streetcar by the time I finished thanking the Kaiser.

He wrote in it, "For Miss Piper. One poised to clasp the torch. May you carry it another forty years." Wow.

Emma Lajeunesse changed her name to Emma Albani. Maybe I should change mine to something Italian-sounding too. Kathleen New Waterfordi. From Capo Bretoni.

mon—5—She barely looked at me the whole lesson. So afterward I wouldn't let her get on the streetcar, I grabbed her schoolbag with all her music in it and ran into Central Park. I was laughing my head off but she was furious. And she is very strong. Nearly took my arm off grabbing the thing back. Thought she was going to kill me but she stomped away with her silly hair ribbons bobbing so I made a scene. First I yelled at the top of my lungs, "I like you, I want to be your friend, why are you such a silly goose?" But she just kept walking. Then I caught up to her and started singing. I was laughing so hard by then I could hardly get the song out, "My Luve's Like a Red Red Rose." I don't know why I was laughing, I felt like a demon and I couldn't stop. She ignored me until we reached the park gate again, then she turned and clapped her hand hard over my mouth so water sprang to my eyes. It made me wild. I bit her hand, that got her moving, and I grabbed the schoolbag again and this time I didn't fool around, I ran all the way to the pond with her right on my heels, I knew she'd beat the can off me if I let her catch me. Thank God I got to the pond just barely ahead of her, I leapt on a rock and dangled the schoolbag over the water.

We were out of breath and I felt badly right away when she said, "Please." But I pressed on, "Please what?"

". . . Please, Miss Piper, don't drop it."

And I screamed back at her like a *banshee,* I don't know what got into me, "Please WHO?"

"Please . . ."

"What's my name?!"

"Kathleen."

I felt suddenly ashamed and she wasn't mad anymore, she was something else, I don't know what. But I didn't want to let her off that easy, I said, "Maybe I'll just have a wee look, find out what's your big mystery."

"No!"

She lunged and I dropped it. But just into my other hand, which made her yelp. I started to unbuckle it. And the strangest thing—she turned and started walking slowly away. I didn't have the heart to open it then. I followed her saying, "Here, you can have it back." But she wouldn't answer me. I caught up to her easily and that's when I saw she was crying. For the first time she actually suited the clothes she wears. I felt terrible. I wished she'd get mad again. I put the schoolbag back into her hand and I said, "I didn't open it." But she just wiped her free hand across her eyes and didn't look at me. I gave her my hanky and she blew her nose. I walked her all the way back to the streetcar stop and stood beside her, waiting, even though she never looked at me or said another word.

I tried not to watch her because she didn't stop crying. I couldn't stand the sounds she was trying not to make, or that she held her head up, why didn't she at least look down? I would. I felt so ashamed. I did it on purpose, I wanted her to cry. Why? There must be something wrong with me. She should never have to cry in front of anyone, beautiful Rose. I'm sorry. I love you.

Rose would hate me if she read this.

No wonder I don't have any friends.

tues—She didn't come today. Kaiser said she resigned. Said, "It's to be expected." I asked why, and he said, "She has a great deal of natural ability but she is essentially feckless." I said I didn't agree and she's the most feckful person I know. He said, "She's gone as far as she could go and it's best she redirect her gifts for her own sake." I said, "Music has no color." He smiled. I could have killed him.

But you know, he's right, music does have color but it shouldn't matter who plays it. Does Brahms turn black when Rose plays him? If he does, then it looks good on him and he should be so lucky. Why should she play that moldy old tripe anyhow, who cares? I care. I love Brahms. I love Verdi and Mozart, but I love the Rhythm Hounds and I love Sweet Jessie Hogan, she is the reigning diva of this city but the horse's arses who run this bloated burg would never know it and don't deserve to. This whole city stinks of music that the Kaiser has no idea about. I love it all. But I love Rose's music best.

She doesn't need any of them. I couldn't find my voice today and the Kaiser let me go, saying of course it put me off my stride to be so rudely dealt with by an accompanist who'd been lucky to have the job. I wanted to go see Rose but I know she hates me and it's my fault she quit. It's my fault the Kaiser thinks those awful things about her, so who do I think I am to say she doesn't need anything? She needed this job.

4 am—Just got home. Rode Giles's bicycle all the way uptown. Sat in a doorway across from Rose's building. What did I think she would do? Look out the window and invite me up for cinnamon toast?

There was phonograph music coming from the front room, scratchy ragtime, hot red and yellow lamps. The curtains were open. The windowpane was cloudy but I could see shadows of a man and woman dancing. They embraced. I heard laughter. Then they disappeared. Does Rose have a boyfriend? A husband?

wed—Aug 7—I told the Kaiser I was quitting today. I thought he'd get mad at me but he didn't. He was silent a moment, then asked me why. I told him I couldn't continue without Rose. He asked me to sit down, he's never done that before. I was beginning to think his furniture was all just stage props. I sat on a loveseat with pink and gray stripes and he told me quite calmly that I couldn't fixate on an accompanist, that I would have to learn that people come and go, it's part of the life I've chosen to lead. I have to realize that being a prima donna means being alone most of the time despite crowds of admirers. He makes it sound so horrible and romantic at the same time. Why should it mean being alone? He just said, "Do you want to sing?" I said it's the only thing I want to do. And he said, "Then don't ask any more of life, because you can either sing, or you can live."

He's trying to scare me but it won't work. I will sing. And I will live too. I've already had a whole life without a friend, with nothing but my music, it's not as though that's a big diva mystery waiting to unfold for me—the sacrament of loneliness. So I told him what I thought he needed to hear: "I'm prepared to make those sacrifices, sir. But I am also prepared to demand the best. That is why I am studying with you. And that is why I will not continue my studies without Miss Lacroix." I thought it all up at that moment and I said it just like that. He thought for a moment. And in that moment I wondered, just how far can I push him? I studied his black and navy cravat. He's really quite a natty individual, I don't know why I was so frightened of him. He said, "I'll see what I can do." And I wonder how much he can do, she's that stubborn.

Thursday—She's back. He must have bribed her good. But now I don't know why I bothered. She won't talk to me. Or look at me.

Sun.—I wrote Daddy and the girls a long letter. I told them all the good stuff. And there is mostly only good stuff. I don't care about that piano-plunking lump. I told Daddy how excited I am about my audition in November. It's coming up fast. It's my chance to show what I can do and when I think of that, it wipes away all thoughts of ingrate exfriends.

Monday—I've been working harder than ever and I've never been happier. I feel like a new sheet of steel fresh from the coke oven in the Pier. The sun goes blind when it looks at me.

Tues.—The revenge of *quanto affetto*. Welcome back, Gilda. Kaiser is pleased, I can tell. The corner of his mouth gets a small spasm like he's having a little seizure. And he adopts a manner that on most people would indicate anger, but with him it means he's happy. The more he barks, the more jerky his movements, the more he says, *"Nein, nein, nein, nein,"* as though I were sticking pins in him, the happier I know he is. He doesn't look like an albino lizard to me any more, he looks like an Afghan dog.

Thurs.—Kaiser asked me today what I would sing if Mr. G–C asks me for another piece. He said it could be a piece of my choosing and he would help me prepare it. So I said I would prepare Cherubino's love poem from *Le Nozze*. I looked at Rose but she pretended I hadn't said anything. Kaiser nodded and said I had made a good choice, "Entirely appropriate."

Today she was still at the streetcar stop when I passed by so I said, "Aren't you going to tell me I'm making a mistake?" She looked at me from a great height and said, "How should I know?" "Well you know so much about music, you're the authority on future stars or so I'm told." "Well that wouldn't apply to you, now would it?" That stung all right. But I couldn't care less what she thinks about me, and anyhow I know she's lying, it got to her that I didn't choose Carmen, that's all.

I knew I was digging my own grave, but I couldn't help it, I can't leave anything lie. "Why do you hate me?" I said. And she answered, cool as anything, "Girl, you ain't worth hatin'." "How come you have an accent all of a sudden, whatever happened to 'I'd be delighted to come foh dinnah, Miss Pipah'?" And she said this: "Fuck you."

I couldn't say anything back because no one's ever talked to me like that before, nor will they ever again, especially not some uppity dark brown girl in a borrowed dress.

Fri.—I could get her fired if I wanted to. I told her that today and she said, "I don't give a shit." And I said, "That's your problem, you don't give a shit about anything." "You don't know shit," she said. And I thought, here I am having a conversation in which every sentence contains the word "shit," if Holy Angels could hear me now! I can give as good as I get, she better look out, "I do so know shit," I said, which was a stupid thing to say and . . . she laughed.

Not snorted, laughed. Then caught herself. So I said, "And I want my fucking hanky back." At which she laughed some more. Fine, I'm hilarious, it's better than being utterly dismissed by the likes of her. I said, "Did you hear me? I want it back." And just as the streetcar pulled up she whispered to me, "I'll give it back to you. Just as soon as I've wiped my black ass with it." Then she was gone, puffed sleeves, ribbons, schoolbag and all. Maybe she's possessed by the Devil.

Saturday, August 17—This morning my hanky was neatly pressed and folded with the monogram facing up, all prim and proper on the piano when I arrived. Rose was warming up and the Kaiser was already there. I picked up the hanky and when I knew Rose was looking at me out the corner of her eye, I raised it to my nose and sniffed it. It was incredibly rude of me and so juvenile. Rose couldn't believe it. She forgot her policy of ignoring me, her chin dropped and she gawked straight at me and I grinned. She grinned back. And the Kaiser turned to us and said, "Miss Piper, shall we begin with a few deep breaths?" I got the giggles and Rose clapped her face into her hands. The Kaiser asked me what was wrong and that did it, I burst out laughing, which made Rose laugh which made me collapse onto his Persian rug. I could see the Kaiser's shiny black shoes a few inches away and that made it worse because who'd've thought my nose would ever be that close to his dainty feet? I sobbed into the carpet, Rose was howling, I thought we were going to die, I couldn't even remember what we were laughing at. The Kaiser gave up and I saw his fussy pant legs swish out the door and that made me scream.

Finally, when I could take a breath, I rolled over and looked up at the sober ceiling. And Rose dried her eyes and began to play—a piece that started slow, sad and foursquare like an Italian funeral, then became a big thumping tune like I'd heard coming out her church window, heavy on the left hand. She just went wild, bar after bar of variations, crazier and crazier till the only thing I could think of doing was dancing, because how could I possibly sing to that? Look out Isadora, we were groovin. I whirled like a dervish around the whole room, following the music, just doing what it made me do, I jerked like a catfish, my

shoulders had two different lives of their own, my feet went crazy, zig-
zaggy, I waggled my pointing fingers like I've seen the hep cats do, I
brought Mecca into the classroom! We went faster, faster, faster, till I
was just jumping, not even doing steps anymore—then the Kaiser came
back in.

He said in a quiet voice, "The temperature outside is ninety-seven
degrees. It is somewhat warmer indoors. Miss Piper, would you prefer
to adjourn for the day?" I apologized and agreed that the heat had indeed overcome me. Rose didn't give any excuse, just stared at the keys,
but I saw a drop of water splash onto F sharp.

I thanked him and agreed that it would be better to resume tomorrow. I was streaming sweat.

We went outside together and I started running ahead, not looking
back, just knowing she would follow me, willing her to. Into the park
all the way to the pond and I didn't hesitate, I ran straight in. My dress
puffed up like a big balloon with me floating in the center of it like a
ballerina in a music box. It was so refreshing. I looked back at the bank
and Rose was leaning forward with her hands on her knees, "You're
crazy!"

She stood there laughing at me, so I walked onto the bank streaming wet and I put my arms around her and soaked her. She tried to push
me away but I thought of a vise and didn't budge. She even walked a
few steps but she took me with her like a boa constrictor. She tried
tickling me but I know how to make myself dead. Finally she gave up
and just stood there while I hugged her. My face was against her neck.
She smells like a spice in Mumma's rack at home but I can't remember
which one because I never did any cooking. She smells like she looks. A
tall timber ship full of precious spices and silks from somewhere beautiful, bound for somewhere drab.

Finally she put her arms around me. I stopped squeezing the life
out of her and we hugged each other for a long time. She was so warm.
I said, "I love you." But not out loud. I felt her breath rise against my
chest, and feeling her heart beat made her so human that I didn't know
how I could ever have thought she couldn't be hurt by me or anyone
else. Dear heart. I felt her cheek against mine. I've never felt anything
so soft. I kissed her lips. In my mind. It felt so natural, but I knew it
couldn't be right. Even a kiss on the cheek—and anyone's allowed to
kiss someone on the cheek—but even that wouldn't be right because it

would be an impostor for the kind of kiss I want to give her. For that matter, it wasn't right to stand hugging each other for so long like that with other people around in broad daylight. She is so beautiful. My Rose. Finer than sculpture, softer than sand. Rose, I'm kissing you now. Oh God, I have to kiss her. I will die if I don't kiss her, I know that now. It is a fact. I will die. It will kill me.

When the hug ended I told her I was sorry about everything and she said she had been worse than I had and I said no she hadn't and let's not fight about that too. She smiled—her smile is . . . genius.

We walked back to the gate arm in arm just like any other girl-friends would, except I was drenched and she was damp. I was afraid of electrocuting myself because of the shocks that leapfrogged up and down me every time I glanced at her. Could she see my skin jumping? What would she think if she knew what I was thinking? I remember Sister Saint Monica warning us against "overly strong attachments." That doesn't apply to Rose. Not to adore her is the sin.

And, because this is my Diary and I tell you everything: I felt like I did sometimes when I was with David. Wet. Not just from the pond. That's how I know how bad I really am. Why can't I just love her with a pure love?! Not drag in things that don't belong?

I am going to be *normal* with her from now on.

Because if I can never kiss her, that would be bad enough. But if I lost my first friend because of that, it would be even worse. If I don't know how to have a friend, maybe I can find out how by pretending I do. And one other thing: no more mooning about her in this Diary.

12:17 am—I can't sleep. I'm going over there.

1:03 am—Giles's bike bloody flat. The cab driver didn't want to let me off here. He's Italian and kept rattling on about his horrible daughters back home in their beds and what kind of a girl was I anyway? Why, simply because I am awake while others are asleep, because I am white when the neighborhood is black, need it follow that I am either in trouble or looking for it? If I were a boy, he wouldn't look twice.

It's finally cool. I'm sitting on the steps in the doorway across from her building and there's no one here to shoo me away. Everything's very quiet. There are no clubs around here, "this is a decent neighbor-hood." The street has been washed today, it's glittering back at the moon like black diamonds, and windowboxes are giving off scent and scarlet. Harlem is cozy and dramatic at the same time. Rose's building is of burnt gray stone with an ornate entrance arch that bears a Latin inscription: *"Ora Pro Nobis."* Pray for whom? I wonder what the place was originally. Maybe a hospital of some kind. In the window of Dash Daniels Harlem Gentlemen's Emporium there's an empty suit and hat arranged like a jaunty scarecrow waving, a pipe stuck in his empty face. The butcher-shop window is full of upside-down carcasses, stripped of their skin and heads. In the dark it could be people hanging there. Pray for us. I just got a shiver. That's silly. This window would be a good place to hide a body in a penny thriller—right out in the open along with all the other meat. Ghoulish. Ha ha. But I'm not scared. The sky is almost purple. The moon is wearing a yellow veil. There is a cart full of watermelons parked nearby, cool green I can feel against my face. No one's afraid of it being stolen.

Someone just came out! I've tucked myself as far back into my doorway as possible. It was a man. I couldn't see his face under his hat. He walked away briskly. Bouncily, you could say. Her boyfriend? I can't imagine her with a boyfriend. I can't imagine her with anyone. But me. I'm going round the back of the building. That's where her bedroom must be.

4:53 am:—Giles is asleep, thank God. I'm not the slightest bit tired. I have a friend.

Glorious Sunday—I think the most beautiful sculpture in the world consists of fire escapes long-legging down buildings with their fancy fretwork, skinny black dancers creeping out their windows to the street below. By lamplight under a smoky moon. I'm on my favorite bench in Central Park. It's raining but there's a big chestnut tree over me, I have my umbrella perched on my shoulder and I've got my gumboots on. It's a perfect place to talk to dear old Diary. Utterly private and the world smells wonderful.

LAST NIGHT!

I walked down a pitch-black alley to a little courtyard behind her building with clotheslines crisscrossing overhead. The windows were all dark. I looked up to wonder which was her room and there was a man sitting on the fire escape outside the open window! He was wearing a fedora and nothing else but his long striped nightshirt. I froze because he looked right at me and said, "What the hell are you doing here?"

My eyes jolted in my head as Rose's face took the place of the strange man under the hat, and I answered I couldn't sleep and she said neither could she. And we just stood there for a moment looking at each other, not knowing if she would come down or I should go up or go home or what.

She stood up, walked down in her bare feet and swung the bottom steps to the ground for me so I climbed up. She was smiling. We didn't hug or anything. We sat outside the church window. I peeked in. It has Bible sayings painted on the walls but otherwise it's just chairs, a piano and, instead of an altar, a little stage with a pulpit in the center. It's her father's hat. She wears it when she needs to think. I asked, "Think about what?" And she said, "It's more like . . . It keeps the world out so I can be in my own thoughts." It's a charcoal-colored hat. Her father died before she was born. The hat suits her down to the ground. It brings out her cheekbones and her jawline. A hat can do that for you. She is not only beautiful, she's handsome too, but I'm not going to gush anymore, I have a friend and all wrong feelings are banished, they are not needed!

We talked for three hours, which sped by till I had to run halfway back downtown before I could find a cab. I don't care. The more I run the less tired I get, the less I sleep the more awake I feel. Rose was classically trained on the piano by tutors from the New York Conservatory. I was right. Child prodigy. She started playing when she was three years old. Her father was a musician. That's all she knows. And that he died of TB. Her mother has a friend who I guess is a quite prominent conductor who's been paying for Rose's lessons and connecting her to the right people since she was a kid. Rose is supposed to be the first colored woman to play with the New York Symphony at Carnegie Hall. She wouldn't tell me the man's name, though, and she wouldn't tell me why she wouldn't tell, either, she'd just say "a friend of my mother's." That girl keeps her secrets, but one by one they will be mine. I had such a great time.

If she were a boy we would be in love, but it's better this way. We can tell each other everything. She wanted to know all about home but I made her guess. She guessed that I came from parents I call "Mother and Dad," that I had "equestrian" lessons, that "Mumsy" is a "frosty blonde" with arch blue eyes and impeccable taste in porcelain and that "Fathah" is a judge from "old money." I played her own game right

back at her and didn't tell her if she was right or wrong. I'll let her think
she's smart for now. Then I'll show her my family photo. AND she
thinks *I* have an accent! She said, "Where you from, girl?" And I said,
"There you go again, sometimes you have an accent and sometimes you
don't, how come?" And she said, "I asked you first." I said, "Cape
Breton Island." And she said, " 'C'Bre'n Ireland'?" I said, "I don't talk
like that." She said, "That's exactly how you talk."

"Cape Breton is in Canada, not Ireland, what do they teach you in
school here?"

She said, "Useful stuff like how anyone can grow up to be president."

I said, "Don't you know anything about Canada?"

"Freeze your ass off, right?"

I never know when she's fooling but I do know now that she likes
to get me riled. What a pair! I told her I'd been to Club Mecca and she
was speechless. I love it when I can hit her with a zinger and she stops
looking like there's nothing new under the sun. I asked her to come
with me next time because I can't go alone. She said she couldn't do
that to her mother. I asked her how her mother was ever going to find
out if neither of us told her. She answered after a moment, "My mother
knows a lot of people."

So I told her about Sweet Jessie Hogan and her Harlem Rhythm
Hounds. Rose listened while I described the size of the Sweet's voice.
How can a voice that big be so agile, how can it groan gravel, then fly
up and outdance the band? Not to mention her costumes—look out,
Aïda. But best of all, the dancing. The cakewalk is tame compared to
what goes on there. It's not for the faint of foot. Rose looked at me as
though she were seeing me for the first time and said, "You're not
exactly a good girl, are you?"

I felt myself blush, I was actually a bit annoyed. "I haven't thought
about whether or not loving all kinds of music and loving to dance
means I'm bad."

She said, "I'm sorry. What I mean is . . . you've got moxie. You
know. Guts. You make me feel like a coward."

I was struck dumb because I can't imagine Rose being afraid of
anything.

"Then come with me," I said. But she just shrugged. "What can
your mother do to you?"

She wouldn't answer me, she just said, "You don't understand."

"Then tell me. Let me understand."

She clammed up and looked down. Her profile under the fedora. Three dark pyramids. "Tell me, Rose. Please."

She looked away and I thought, oh no, I've done it again. But the next instant she said in an icy voice, "The fact is, I'm not terribly interested in Darktown music." Then she turned to me with a polite smile, "But if you'd like to come to the symphony with me, I have tickets for Thursday evening."

I didn't want to upset the applecart again so I said, "Oh thenk you. I'd be uttehly delighted, rally I would." At which she grinned.

She doesn't have a boyfriend, I asked. I told her a bit about David. She asked me if I was in love with him and I said, "At times I thought I was. But now I know I wasn't."

"How do you know that?"

I couldn't look at her, but I did say the truth. "Because if he came back right now, I wouldn't leave this fire escape to go meet him." My face started to prickle because I didn't feel like that came out right, and I could feel Rose watching me, ready to hate me all over again, so I pressed on, "I'm a lot happier to have a friend." I finally looked at her but she turned her eyes forward and nodded. "Me too." I was so relieved. Thank God I didn't do anything really foolish the other day in the park. Thank God I only mortified myself in front of you, Diary.

Tues–20—Symphony divinely dull. Schumann. People stared at Rose. I'm beginning to understand why her normal expression is so forbidding. She has concert tickets but lives in a three-room apartment. Built like an Ethiopian queen with a dimple and a Roman nose. Draped in a flowered dress from 1905 fit for little girls and old ladies. La Mystère de la Rose.

Wed.—I'm not ashamed of my mother.

Thurs.—Stayed in bed today.

Fri.—I have no friends. I have only colleagues. The Kaiser is right. I suppose most people would run home about now but what is there to run to? It's the capital of nowhere. Only Daddy is there and when I'm rich and famous I'll sail him first class to all my performances. I feel so lethargic. I can't even muster any ambition. It all seems dead and flat. Yes,

I will work hard and get to all those places. I can see it stretching out, straight through to the triumphant end. I hate it when I can see through to the end of something. All that's left is the plodding to get there. Knowing too much is a kind of death. I pray that I don't know everything. That's my religious faith: to believe I really don't know. But it's so hard sometimes. And in my religion, the only mortal sin is boredom.

Sat.—My feelings about Rose that I wrote down seem like a dream. They happened to someone else in some other country.

Sun—Nothing ever happens.

mon—Ditto.

tues.—Ibid.

fri.—plus ça change

Saturday, August 31, 1918
Dear Diary,

I don't know where to begin. I have to get it all down now while it's fresh, I'm here under my tree in Central Park and we have all afternoon till supper-time. I'll have to go back a few days because despite all that whining about nothing happening, I realize now that tons was happening and it was all leading up to what I have to tell you which is EVERYTHING.

     But first things first: I'm working up Carmen. The Kaiser "objected strenuously" but gave in, for what choice does he have after all? He still snipes that I'm being "perverse" working against my "natural freshness and youth"—"My God, Miss Piper, you are an *ingénue,* Carmen is a whore." Thinks the idea that I'm a mezzo is professional suicide, "witches and bitches, dahling," he says, but I refuse to get stuck anywhere. I don't intend to be Gilda forever. Not when I'm a wizened thirty-two, and I certainly don't intend to take my final curtain a moment before I absolutely have to. Mezzos live longer. I'll sing Carmen and I'll sell Tosca. And there will not be a single pair of trousers left unsung. Kaiser doesn't know whether he is witnessing my first divinely inspired diva fit, or me falling on my face. Neither do I, but at least I'm no longer bored! He does see the wisdom in showing Gatti-Casazza the extreme outposts of my range, however, not just vertically but dramatically. Because that's where it really counts. It's not enough to have the most beautiful voice. If I have to sing ugly to put the feeling of a scene across, I'll do that. Opera isn't supposed to be "pretty." Women stabbing themselves and everyone else half the time isn't pretty, it's wild, it's passionate and gruesome and beautiful and you can't tell me that such women don't snarl as much as they sing. And that's not counting the comic roles, which are even more grotesque. But I digress. . . .

All right. Oh dear. Here goes. I have no shame in front of you, Diary, for you are me. You won't squirm, you can't be shocked, you know that nothing in love is nasty so I will try to be as free with you as I am in my own thoughts. Lest I forget, let me offer up a sincere orison of thanks for Giles. She is the least curious person on the face of the earth. Without her total lack of vigilance my life could never have got started. If Daddy knew what a lackadaisical gatekeeper she is he would be down here in a second to board me with the nuns. Which reminds me, I'd better write him. Oh but I'm teasing you, aren't I, Diary? You're in an agony of anticipation. Be still, open your heart, and I will begin at the beginning and unfold it for you as it unfolded for me. The joyful mystery of the Rose . . .

On the ferry in the middle of the Strait of Canso, Lily puts the diary down and looks behind her at Cape Breton because she will never see it again. She takes her last scent of salt island air, harsh, coniferous and cool, the indescribable gray that contains all things. Home. Farewell.

She wonders about the soles of her new red boots. Eleven days of gravel on Highway 4, a hundred miles to the Strait of Canso. Many people are kind so Lily is only a bit hungry. It is important not to spend any of the money in her boots. Not until she has arrived. She has sucked water from bright moss and slept beneath the low boughs of pine trees, their needles soft and young with May. The nights are cold but Lily is not. Every night as she falls asleep, she feels someone walk through the soft dew and cover her. And every morning she is warm and dry.

The ferry man took her coin and gave her a worried look. "What's your name dear? Who's your father?"

. . . My first class after our "tryst" on her fire escape, I was afraid Rose would treat me like a stranger again. But she didn't. She wasn't exactly warm, but she called me Kathleen and said, "Let's get to work," and that's what we did for days and days like riveters on a skyscraper.

I finally got her over for supper again—tore her away from her daughterly duties—and again Giles slept while Rose played and I sang the old-fashioned songs that Giles likes. Then I brought Rose to my room and tried to get her to take the ribbons out of her hair and do something less childish with it. But she wouldn't let me touch it. I decided I'd like to meet her mother and have a talk with her. Why should she have a grown daughter who's as tall as a man, and more beautiful than a woman, decked out like a Kewpie doll?

I waited for Rose to spot the framed photograph of Daddy and Mumma on my dresser. She said, "Who's that?" I said, "That's my father." She said, "Who's that with him?" And I said, "That's my mother." And she just stared at the picture, then looked back at me and said, "Not your natural mother."

"What do you mean?"

"Not your blood kin."

"Yes."

Then she looked back at the picture. "I can't see it."

"No one can."

"What is she?"

"Canadian."

Rose blushed. Hurray! But I put her out of her mystery;

"She's Lebanese."

"She's an Ayrab?"

"They don't like to be called Arabs. Especially not 'Ayrabs.' "

"What's wrong with that, that's how I've always said it."

"Well. Anyhow, a lot of Lebanese come from the coast and they're more Mediterranean, more European, you know. Not like Arabs."

"She musta come from inland." Then she looked at me and said, "Coulda fooled me."

I said, "I'm not trying to 'fool' anyone."

"You look pure white."

"I am pure white. My mother is white."

"Not quite."

"Well she's not colored."

She smiled—sneered is more like it—and said, "Don't worry, honey, you plenty white for the both of you."

"What's that supposed to mean?"

"Now you're mad 'cause I called you white." She was laughing at me.

"I like to be called by my name. Please."

She stopped laughing and looked at me for a moment and said, "Kathleen."

But I wanted her to get the point. "I'm not ashamed of my mother, but I take after my father. My mother is devoid of ambition and not terribly bright, although she is a devoted parent."

"Goody for you."

It was on the tip of my tongue to say "To hell with you" or worse when she got serious all of a sudden and said, "I'm sorry but you're not being honest with me. You are ashamed of your mother." I got a hot sick feeling in my stomach. "And I think that's a sorrowful thing," she added.

The feeling was coming up through my skin. I was sure Rose could smell it.

"Kathleen?" She looked so sorry for me, and that's what made me feel strange. In a sticky dream with my eyes on sideways and can't stand up.

"I'm sorry," she said.

I had to lean over.

"Are you okay?"

I thought, please, God, don't let me throw up.

"Want me to get Giles?"

I must have caught a bug. The floorboards were shifting. She put her hand on the back of my neck. "Breathe," she said. Her hand was cool.

"Good," she said. "But the idea is, once you've breathed out, it helps to breathe in again in the near future. . . . That's it."

I breathed and she kept her hand there until my head stopped spinning and my stomach cooled down.

"I'm okay now."

We lay on my bed and played Chinese checkers for an hour and Giles brought us cocoa and oatmeal cookies. I wanted Rose to stay overnight so we could tell ghost stories but she has to be home by nine or her mother worries.

The next day I told Rose she was in a state of social mortal sin because she had yet to invite me to her home. I have to come like a thief in the night and even then she doesn't ask me in. I asked her point-blank why not. She said, "My mother is an invalid."

She was lying, I could tell by the veil that came down over her eyes, but I went along with it.

"I wouldn't make any noise. You could just show me your room."

She said, "We'll see."

"Say yes."

". . . Okay."

"When?"

"I'll check."

Days went by and she still couldn't say when so I gave her the cold shoulder, but that didn't work—she's immune to her own methods. So last night I went over uninvited. At the decent hour of seven-thirty, when I knew supper would be through and it would be early enough to take the streetcar instead of a leering cab ride.

There were lots of kids playing in the street, and mothers everywhere, sitting on their porches in the cool of the evening.

Men too, in white shirtsleeves, some leaning against the buildings in twos and threes, others playing checkers, everyone chatting.

It reminded me of New Waterford, except Harlem is really prosperous. Not to mention that here I'm the odd one out. Everyone stared at me as I slunk by till I felt like something out of P. T. Barnum, "See the white slave princess, raised by wolves in darkest Canada!" A couple of young fellas sang a little song at me as I passed—softly, not nasty or anything, but it made me blush anyhow, calling me "sugar" and "baby," oh what I'd give to be invisible. Or to be taken for a man.

Before I got to her building I could hear Rose playing. It was coming from the church window, but church was not in session and this was definitely not church music, it was pure Rose. So this is where she practices. In exchange for playing on Sundays, I guess. I stayed under the window, sheltered by Rose's music, but I was soon disturbed by three women seated on kitchen chairs on the front stoop of her building. They didn't shoo me away, they gave me the low-down on Rose! They didn't know whether to feel sorry for her or to think she was nuts. I know the feeling. "Poor little girl," they were saying, "she bears her cross." "We all bear a cross." I wanted to say, "She's not a little girl," and I had to laugh because they went on, "And practicing twenty-four hour a day, but never can learn a piece of music top to bottom no matter how hard she try."

"That's right, just wandering on the keyboard, lost to the world."

" 'Cept Sunday, she plays like the angels come Sunday."

"That's the Lord's work."

"Thank you, Jesus."

Then one of them prayed that Rose would get some humility and they made jokes because they considered her too strange and—of all things—"homely" to get a husband, and what's the good of pride in a homely woman? I excused myself but the women didn't seem to notice, they just kept chatting as I picked my way past them up the steps and in through the front door for the first time.

The entrance has an echoey vaulted stone ceiling with turquoise and white tile mosaic. Maybe it was once a Turkish bath. I smelled a delicious stew. I followed a wide brass rail up marble steps worn to soft curves by a hundred years of footfalls, up to the second-floor landing, and was about to enter the church to surprise Rose when I had a flash. An evil one. I continued up to the third-floor landing and knocked at the door of what I knew must be her apartment. For a minute I thought there was no one home and I was halfway back down the stairs when a woman's voice stopped me.

"What can I do ya for, honey?"

I turned to the woman and said, "Sorry, wrong apartment."

"Who you lookin for?"

"Rose Lacroix."

"Rosie's downstairs practicing."

"Okay, I'll just pop down and say hello."

"She doesn't like to be disturbed."

"It's all right, she knows me."

The woman smiled in a sly kind of way and said, "You don't know her too well though, do you? Come on in and wait, she'll be up for dinner in a few minutes."

"Oh. Thank you." I was confused. "I don't want to intrude on your dinner."

"You won't if you join us."

I followed the woman into the parlor. It was fancy and shabby at the same time. Like a rich lady who's slept in her clothes. Velvet everything. A plushy plum sofa with shiny patches. Dusty curtains drawn—burgundy with gold tassels. And a huge gilt mirror over the mantelpiece. The stew smell mixed with her perfume and made me feel a bit queer.

I said, "I'm Rose's friend from singing class, Kathleen Piper."

"Oh yeah? I didn't know Rosie had a little friend."

I felt she was being ironic, not to mention rude, but I couldn't figure out why, no more could I figure out who she was. Although she clearly knew Rose.

"I'm sorry, honey, I'm Rosie's mother, Jeanne. Do sit down."

I guess my chin must've dropped a mile but I couldn't help it, I was speechless. She lit a cigarette and laughed at me in a lazy way. She was wearing a full-length evening dress—dull red satin, slim and loose with skinny little straps and a deep V-neck, black sequin flowers. And obviously no underthings. I think that shocked me more than the fact that she was white, with straight yellow hair falling anyhow onto her shoulders, and thin blue eyes. Tiny lines, she must be close to forty, but it was so dim in there I couldn't tell. You could see she used to be pretty. No face paint, oddly enough. She was enjoying my amazement. She offered me a cigarette.

"No thank you."

"Good. Keep your voice clean. Drink?"

"Yes please."

She smiled that rudely familiar smile again, as if my accepting a drink made us lowly conspirators, for there was something low about her and yet she acted like bored royalty. I don't go in for drinking but I didn't want this woman calling me "Rosie's little friend" again. She gave me a whiskey and leaned back in the sofa across from me. Her left strap slipped down but she didn't seem to notice.

I said, "Thank you."

"I know you're surprised, honey, everybody is at first, my God you're pretty."

I hate myself that I blush so easily. She was making me madder by the second, I thought, so this is what Rose lives with, I'd go around like a hornet too if she were my mother. But I said, "Thank you, ma'am."

And she laughed at me again. The word "languid" is always used in books, but I finally found a use for it in real life. Mrs. Lacroix was "languid."

"Call me Jeanne, baby."

I'm not your baby, I thought, but I said, "Jeanne."

And she chuckled again and looked me up and down and said, "Oh yes. Yes indeedy."

She made me most uncomfortable, the way she lounged there scrutinizing me like a bird of prey that's too full with its recent meal to be bothered to eat what's in front of it.

Rose came in. She paused when she saw me. I couldn't read her face, she just said, "Hi."

"Hi."

Jeanne grinned and said, "Rose, darling, your friend is simply charming. I insist you stay for dinner, Miss Piper."

"Please call me Kathleen, ma'am—Jeanne."

She winked at me. I blushed again. I looked at Rose, expecting her to be scowling at me, but she just said, "Want to see my room?"

I got up, relieved, although it crossed my mind that maybe Rose would murder me silently with a pillow once I got in there. Her mother stopped us on our way. "Did you get my prescription, Rose?" she asked without turning around.

"Yes, Mother, I got it."

"Good. We'll wait till after dinner, I'm actually feeling quite spry today."

"Good."

"You girls have a little gossip, I'll call you when dinner is laid."

"Thank you, Mother."

This was the strangest thing of all. To find out that Rose has not a "Mumma" but a "Mother."

***

It's raining on the Bay of Fundy. There's no particular ferry man this time, there's a crew. No one speaks to her as she boards, or asks her who her parents are, no one looks worried—although they do look a little askance. Twenty-eight days since New Waterford. What is Lily to do about the soles of her boots? She hugs the diary and looks over the rail. The Nova Scotia mainland is behind her, New Brunswick is in front.

★   ★   ★

Farewell to Nova Scotia, your sea bound coast,
let your mountains dark and dreary be.
For when I'm far away on the briney ocean toss'd,
will you ever heave a sigh and a wish for me?

Rose's room is as different from the rest of the apartment as can be.
She has a single bed with an absolutely plain white cotton spread and
no headboard. There's not even a rug on the floor. A wooden chair,
a small desk with a pen and a blank sheet of paper and, of all things,
the Holy Bible open at—but I didn't get a chance to see because she
flipped it shut the moment I glanced at it. You'd think I'd caught her
reading a racy novel. It looks like the nuns' rooms at Holy Angels. (I
know because I snuck into their wing on the last day of school,
hoping to find a long luscious wig in Sister Saint Monica's room but
no such luck.) The only difference is, instead of a crucifix on the
wall, there's a picture of Beethoven. And do you believe this? She
hasn't got a mirror!

Rose closed her door behind us and said, "So. Want to play
Chinese checkers?"

"Why didn't you tell me she's white?"

"Why should I?"

"I told you about my mother."

"What about her?"

"You said she's not white."

"She got a year-round tan, that don't count for colored."

"You said it did the other night."

"Yeah, well that's a moot point, isn't it, considering how you
come out."

"I can't win, can I?"

"Oh yes you can, there ain't nothin stoppin you, girl."

"You hate me 'cause I'm white."

"I hate you 'cause you're so fuckin ignorant."

"Then enlighten me."

"Why should I bother?"

"Because I'm your friend."

"Friends don't spy."

"I'm sorry. You give me no alternative."

"There's an alternative. Leave me alone."

"No."

"Why not?"

"I like you."

"Why?"

"You're the smartest person I know, except for my father."

"Is that supposed to be a compliment?"

"And you're beautiful."

That shut her up. She looked at me as though I'd told her she had a year to live. So I added, "But your mother dresses you funny."

"It doesn't matter what I wear."

"You're right, you're so gorgeous it doesn't matter."

"Shut up."

"Come to Mecca with me tonight."

"I told you I can't."

"Do you do everything your mother tells you?"

She sat down on the bed, folded her hands in her lap and quoted scripture, "She has my best interests in mind."

"Oh really? What are those?"

"Getting out of this dump."

I sat down next to her, I tried to be delicate. "What's wrong with her?"

"Nothing. She does her best."

"You're the one who's ashamed."

Rose got quiet and looked at me as though she were holding a puppy and begging me not to hurt it. "You think, because she lives here, she's not a fine person. Well it's only because of me that she has to live here. Do you know what that's like for her? They treat her like trash, they don't know anything about her. Ignorant niggers."

I couldn't speak. Rose went on, "She's given up everything for my sake."

"She seems pretty satisfied to me."

"She's too polite to seem otherwise."

"I didn't think she was the slightest bit polite."

Rose really looked bewildered. How can she know so much about so many things yet know so little about her own mother? But I just said, "Where's your hat?"

I followed her out across the parlor and past the kitchen, where
Jeanne was setting the table. That is, she was standing there with a fork
in her hand, staring into space. Rose took me into Jeanne's bedroom—I
should say boudoir. A mess of satin sheets in a huge mahogany bedstead
with claw feet. A big oil painting over the bed of a fat white woman
getting out of a tub. A vanity littered with silver brushes, pots of paint
and clumps of yellow hair—a crystal cocktail glass with lipstick smears,
an ashtray crammed with red-tipped butts, a jumble of jewelry, tweezers
and an eyelash curler. Clothes strewn everywhere, and too many smells
for one room. Rose opened a big wardrobe, rummaged through the top
shelf and pulled down the charcoal fedora.

"Rosie!"

It was Jeanne from the kitchen. She sounded like she'd just hurt
herself. Rose whipped the hat back onto the shelf and shot from the
room. I got it down again and put it on, and went back out to the parlor.
Rose's back was to me. But Jeanne was looking straight at me from the
sofa where she lay. She looked like she was in pain, but somehow still
slightly amused to see me in the hat. It gave me the creeps. Rose was
reaching into her schoolbag. I could see the sheet music inside. She
brought out a needle that she filled from a tiny bottle. Jeanne had her left
arm flung out and she was pumping her fist. The vigor of that action
didn't go with the swoon in her body. Her face was starting to tighten
and go even paler, she was looking at the ceiling now. Rose injected her
and Jeanne closed her eyes as though she were lost in prayer like the nuns.
Her fist relaxed, she gave a little moan, reached up and stroked Rose's
face. She murmured something then nodded off. Rose folded Jeanne's
arm across her stomach, stood up and saw me.

"She suffers a lot of pain."

I felt embarrassed for Rose having to lie again.

"Did she see you in the hat?" she asked me.

"I think so."

"Please don't do that again. It upsets her."

"I'm sorry." I handed her the hat. "Do you have a picture of
him?" I asked.

"No."

"Don't you have anything besides his hat?"

Rose looked at her mother on the sofa—out cold—and led me
back into the boudoir. And disappeared into the wardrobe. I had this

crazy idea that she might be gone forever into another time and place.
But she came out a moment later with a suit of men's clothes on a
hanger.

Black and tan pinstripe trousers. Black waistcoat and tails.

Tan cravat with black polka dots. Starched white shirt with
diamond studs.

"Goes with the hat," I said.

And she said, "Yeah."

And I said, "Try it on."

She didn't pretend to be shocked, which is how I know that in her
heart of hearts it had occurred to her before. It's also how I knew that
certain things between us were behind us now. Thank goodness. She
just said, "I couldn't do that."

"Why not?"

"It would be like—sacrilege."

"He wasn't God, he was just some fella."

"He was my father!"

"And all he left you were his clothes."

She hesitated. So I started to undress.

"What are you doing?"

I didn't answer because I didn't know, I just pulled my dress over
my head and got to work on my stockings and for some reason it
worked, and she said, "All right, all right." And I put my dress back on
as she undid the millions of buttons on hers and said, "Turn around."

I obliged. She took forever.

"Don't peek!"

"I'm not peeking."

Finally she said, "Okay. You can look now."

I turned around. Oh my.

She is a tall slim young man in a curious suit of black and tan.
There is nothing to beat her leaning against the bricks of any building
'twixt here and Battery Park.

She said, "How do I look?"

"You're coming out with me."

"I—"

"Look at yourself."

She hesitated so I closed the closet door to expose the full-length
mirror on the outside. I stood behind her as she looked at the beautiful

young man with the fine-cut face between hat and cravat. She looked at herself for a long time. And finally—"Do you think . . . ?"

"Oh yeah."

She nodded to herself and turned sideways.

I said, "Your own mother wouldn't recognize you. Much less your mother's friends."

"Do you have any money on you?"

"Two dollars."

"I've got carfare."

"Let's go."

"No."

I thought, "Oh brother, she's got cold feet," but she offered me her arm with a smile and said, "Let's dine first."

Jeanne had somehow managed to lay the table. It was just a kitchen table between the sink and the icebox but it was covered with a snowy lace cloth and set with silverware engraved with "J.B." Rose lit the candles. She filled our crystal goblets with bubbly root beer and heaped the bone china plates with what we call boiled dinner down home. Potatoes, carrots, pork hocks (she calls them "pig's feet"), doughboys, but instead of cabbage there were green leaves of some kind. Daddy was right. There has come a time when I think it's the most delicious dish in the world. We sat across from each other and clinked our glasses, "To Mecca."

"To Mecca."

And drank. There was a place set for Jeanne too.

"She doesn't eat much anyhow," said Rose.

"It's good luck to set an extra place at table."

"Why?"

"In case your guardian angel wants to join you."

"Don't spook me."

"They're not spooky, they look after you."

"You don't believe that."

"Oh yes I do."

"Why, what's your guardian angel ever done for you?"

"Sent me to New York. Made me meet you."

"Lucky you."

"We're going to know each other for the rest of our lives."

After a moment she said, "I don't think I have a guardian angel. I think I'm on my own."

"You have one as long as I'm around."

She listened and I could tell she wanted to believe me, and I didn't think about what I was saying, I just said it, "And if I die before you, I'll come back."

She got tears in her eyes and so did I, it always happens when you talk about ghosts. I had two helpings of stew. Would you believe Jeanne cooked it? "She does all the cooking." So I guess she's not a completely useless mother after all.

"What does J. B. stand for?"

Rose hesitated, then said, "Julia Burgess."

"Who's that?"

"My grandmother."

"She alive?"

"Yuh."

"Where's she at?"

"Long Island."

"Do you visit her often?"

"I've never met her."

"I've never met my grandparents either."

"To hell with them all."

"I'll drink to that."

We toasted again, then I raised my goblet for the third time. "Let's drink to the twentieth century," I said. "Because it's ours."

"To the twentieth century."

Do you think it's possible to get drunk on root beer?

Lily plucks big waxy leaves from a maple tree and replaces the lining of what's left of the soles of her boots. She walks across the United States border into Maine and the road turns from gravel to pavement. She kneels down by the side of the road and says a little prayer because, after all, she has entered a foreign country. This is at a spot near Calais, and if you go there now your watch will stop.

Lily knows where she is going, it is only necessary to keep to the coast. If she can see the ocean on her left she can't get lost.

We quickly washed the dishes, then Rose fixed a silver tray with two glasses, an ice bucket, a canister of soda and a bottle of whiskey, and put it on the coffee table next to the sofa where Jeanne lay. I was nervous that Jeanne would wake up and catch us but Rose said, "Don't worry. She won't wake up till her company comes." I didn't ask "What company?" because I didn't want to make Rose lie to me again. She led me to the door and opened it for me, *très galante,* saying, "Ladies first." As I stepped through the door, I turned my head to smile at Rose and caught sight of Jeanne in the mirror over the mantelpiece. She was lying perfectly still on the sofa, staring straight at me.

Do you think there's such a thing as a ghost who masquerades as a person? Do you believe that there are people whose bodies are still alive here on earth but whose souls are already in hell?

Lily loses sight of the water for days at a time, stopping to inquire, "Where's the water?" She is far from the only one walking the roads. She shares a meal of boiled potatoes with a slow thin man from Oklahoma, he's not going anywhere in particular. She asks him where the water is. He leads her to railway tracks that swing southeast until the ocean comes in view. That night, between the trees and the track, under a pure black sky, he talks about his home in the land of milk and honey and Lily asks why he left. "It blew away," he says. "What's that you're reading?"

"My mother's diary."

"Where's your ma?"

"She's dead."

"Well you hang on to that book, that's a precious re-membrance."

And he shows her a picture of his wife and baby.

"Are they dead?" Lily asks.

"Not so far as I know."

Lily is awakened by his bad chest. She watches him sleep and his wheezing stops, but when she nods off his torment resumes. So she stays awake. At dawn he sits up and forgets to cough. He scoops her up by the waist and pelts, years younger, toward the line of prehistoric boxcars lumbering by, all rust and thrust.

I didn't tell Rose that her mother had seen us.

What a feeling to walk arm in arm with Rose as a fella. People stared in a whole new way. I guess I've found the one thing that could make me look even more suspicious in this neighborhood. It was a breezy evening. Rose had polished her old black lace-ups to a high shine and I wished like crazy I had my new dress on. Oh well, next time.

I had to force her through the door of Mecca as though at gunpoint. The great thing about Mecca is that there's all kinds. I'd never soaked the place up like I did last night with Rose. I saw it all through her eyes and I was able to point out the regulars. It's mostly young colored men and not that many women. The fellas are all slick dressers except for the holes in their pockets where the money's burned through. They're earning more than miners, building tanks and artillery for "over there," I know because I've been told by the guy in the silk tie called Aldridge. I've never seen guys preen and present themselves the way they do. They lean against the bar like honey-drenched stamens, waiting for the women to buzz around, and you just know they're all breaking their mothers' hearts. They wear secret smiles and chuckle a lot when they chat with the white guys.

There are a couple of middle-aged men too, a famous jockey who eats five heads of lettuce a day, and a retired heavyweight champion with a bald head from Halifax. They're the only ones who bring their wives, two very serious looking women of a certain age who spend the whole time with their heads glued together, chatting. There's a group of West Indian fellas who stick together and wear pencil-thin mustaches. One of them's a lawyer and another is my acquaintance Nico, a little live wire who has made a fortune in real estate and can't stop smiling. He calls me *"chérie."* There's a studious young man who always sits alone and writes in a notebook and there are two tables pushed together of motley individuals who are delighted with each other and everything else and who turn out to be actors. There's a

Chinaman who holds court at the same table in the far corner every night.

Tonight I notice three or four other white girls sitting with their colored boyfriends and I say to Rose that at least we're not the only mixed couple in the joint and she says, "Yes we are." I say, "They don't look colored." And she says, "Say Negro."

As for the white denizens: a handful of tough-looking Irishmen in fifty-dollar suits with "dames" on their arms. A Jew who brings his barrel of hats into the club with him—he's a very formal older man who closes his eyes and nods slowly to the music no matter how wild the tune. Tonight there's also a high society table out for a low time— girls and boys who have no idea where they are and think themselves awfully clever for being there. They probably think the same thing of me.

There are also a few "working girls" of every shade who arrive alone and leave escorted several times throughout the evening under the watchful eye of the game-keeper, who lounges in the corner consulting his solid gold watch. I sometimes wonder, can it be any harder than washing floors? Or having seven babies?

Business must be booming because the management has installed a small stage, footlights and a sparkly purple curtain with "MECCA" written *à la* Araby in gold sequins against a silhouette of minarets. Ten minutes after we sit down, a man in a tuxedo comes out from behind the curtain and announces, "Ladies and gentlemen, Club Mecca proudly presents 'Ali Baba and his Forty Follies!' "

The curtain parts on a harem. Light-skinned girls and a very fat dark sultan lounge on striped pillows. The girls dance the seven veils while he sings a song of illicit lust for one of them—the lightest one— and the band plays snaky music. The tent flaps part and handsome Prince Ahmed pokes his turbaned head through and kisses the heroine. Then, bingo, you're in Gay Paree doing the cancan, and then the same young lovers flee the evil sultan all through the world's capitals while the chorus girls quick-change and outdance Ziegfeld's. We went to Hawaii, Japan, Holland and Canada, where they pretended to be Eskimos and Mounties! And although the girls changed costumes and countries every five seconds, they never wore more than half a dozen square inches, even when they were fur-clad in Canada's frozen wastes.

After the show the band played dance tunes but I couldn't for the life of me get Rose up on her feet. She did, however, graciously nod when other gentle and not so gentlemen requested her permission to dance with me. I danced with the busted-nose Irishman, built like a tree stump but light on his feet, boy. With the Jewish haberdasher, who made a waltz out of everything. With a lily-white boy from Long Island—I asked him if he was acquainted with the Burgesses and he answered importantly that they were his dear friends. I asked him if he knew Jeanne and he got a blank look—then said come to think of it there was a daughter years ago who "died tragically abroad." I laughed and he didn't ask for a second dance—just as well, he was like shifting sticks.

All the while, Rose slouched over her beer in that lovely suit. She didn't bat an eye until I danced with my pal Nico. It bothered her, I could tell, although why it should be any different than with the white fellas I don't know. Only difference I can see is, except for the stocky Irishman, the Negro men are the best on their feet. When I sat back down at the table while the band took a break, Rose said, "I'll dance with you if you teach me."

It was the first thing she'd said for an hour. I realized I had wanted to make her jealous. It bugged me that we had made it all the way to this club with her looking so gorgeous but all she wanted to do was sulk. I asked her how she liked the show.

"Irredeemably puerile."

"The dancing was great."

"The outfits are an outrage."

"Look who's talking."

"At least I'm fully clothed."

I made her take a sip of my whiskey, then I did something crazy— I kissed her on the lips. Just quickly, you know, but we both blushed. She didn't object, she simply raised her hand for the waiter and demanded two more drinks in a deep voice to make me laugh, then whispered desperately in my ear, "Do you have enough money?" I brushed my ear against her lips. She stayed perfectly still. I kissed her neck between the stiff white collar and her earlobe. I slipped my hand round the back of her head below her hat and stroked that gentle dip at the base of the skull. She turned slightly and kissed my mouth. So softly. I forgot where we were. That we were anywhere. We just looked at each other . . . so that's who you are.

The drinks came. And Rose looked away, shy again. What will happen to me if Rose ever ceases to be shy? I will have an attack of all the shyness I've been saving up.

Then something happened that I'd never seen before. The place flooded and turned overwhelmingly black, men and women both. I'll bet if I'd looked hard enough I'd've seen the ladies from Rose's front steps braving the Devil's music. The word must've spread since I'd been here. The house lights dimmed and the footlights shimmered on the minarets of Mecca. Silence fell over the whole joint and the impresario stepped up to invoke the Goddess of Blues, "Ladies and gentlemen, the star of our show: The Empress of the Blues. Cleopatra of Jazz. The Lowest, the Highest, the Holiest, the Sweetest, Miss! Jessie! Hogan!"

Applause and shouts to outdo the *bravissimas* of a grand finale though the curtain has yet to open. It parts purple and gold to reveal: pearls and peacock blue. Fourteen carats wink at every compass point. She starts off in a spotlight and emits a single moan. It goes on for minutes—growing, subsiding, exploding, until you're not sure if she's praying or cursing. She drags her voice over gravel, then soothes it with silk, she crucifies, dies, buries and rises, it will come again to save the living and the dead. People spontaneously applaud and shout, sometimes all together, sometimes singly. La Hogan is absolutely silent after the opening sacrament while God descends invisibly to investigate. Then, once He's split and the coast is clear, she spurts like a trumpet till the trumpet can't take it anymore and hits her back—they fight blow for blow till she raises her arms and calls a truce. She takes a step off the stage. The audience yelps, the trombone belts a shocked comment and she bursts into her song without words, quadruple time, strutting to the center of the hall, dancing, the band following her like obedient treasure bearers—except for piano—the drummer beats on every passing surface, people start clapping time as The Hogan somehow threads her stuff between the spindly tables and throngs of faithful. At the end of that first number she says, "Welcome and good evening," just as though she were an ordinary mortal. Sweat streams from her pearl headband and she flashes her ivory and gold smile. I guess she must weigh a good two hundred pounds.

I looked over at Rose. While everyone else in the place was swaying and rocking and beaming, she sat perfectly serious, listening and watching.

Afterward, you know what she said about the music?

"Crude but compelling."

High praise indeed.

Under a smoky streetlamp I stood face to face with my beloved and pricked my fingers against the diamond studs of her immaculate shirt front. Being tall, she slipped her hands naturally about my hips and pulled me close. And being bold, I put my mouth on hers and this time went inside and told her all the things I'd been longing to. Dark and sweet, the elixir of love is in her mouth. The more I drink, the more I remember all the things we've never done. I was a ghost until I touched you. Never swallowed mortal food until I tasted you, never understood the spoken word until I found your tongue. I've been a sleepwalker, sad somnambula, hands outstretched to strike the solid thing that could awaken me to life at last. I have only ever stood here under this lamp, against your body, I've missed you all my life.

She kissed my face like fire. And it happened, I grew shy and could only give her the top of my head, which she kissed anyway. She said in a voice I'd never heard before, "I didn't think you had a scent, but you do." Which made me laugh because what a thing to say! But she explained, "No. Everyone has a scent and you either like it or you don't or you're indifferent. And you had no scent. And I thought that was spooky."

"You're easily spooked."

I love talking with our arms around each other.

"It made you seem not quite human," she said.

"I'm not—"

"Don't—"

"Scaredy-cat."

She kissed me again and we didn't stop for a long time, except to lean out of the light when we heard horses coming. We slipped into an alley and I pulled her shirt out from her pants. I pressed my center into her and she sighed. It made me flood from inside, the sweetest music. We were finally dancing. I slid my hands under and up her smooth sides, I wanted to be slow to savor but we couldn't, she gripped me and moved under me. I felt her nipples under my palms and I think I died. Rose gasped as though I'd stabbed her and I felt like a savage robbing a sacred tree, her thigh between my legs. I found her hand and led it to a place I know, I kissed it with the mouth that I keep hidden, then took her inside and sucked her like the greedy tide that can't decide to swallow or disgorge. I lost track of everything. And even after I finally could stop, I knew that I would never be finished.

Oh Rose, it's not enough until I have all of you inside me, then give you back to the world fresh and new from my belly. She just said softly, "Oh," for the longest time.

Imagine, in an alley. It's not very romantic. But somehow it was. Terribly.

Crude but compelling.

The sign says "Lebanon." Could I really have slept so long? Lily wonders.

"I said out!"

Lily emerges from the gloom of the boxcar and the signal-man is remorseful.

"Need some help there?"

"Thank you, sir."

"Where you going, missy?"

"New York City."

"Well you're a bit off course in that case, ain't ya."

"I'm in Lebanon. Where's New York?"

"Eighty or so miles back the way you come, to Portland then turn right, heh heh—hey, where you going?"

"Back."

"You can't walk."

"Yes I can, don't worry."

Two hours later:

"Hello again, missy."

"Hello, sir. I forgot my mother's diary on the train."

He hand-pumps them over the rails twelve miles to the lumberyards. He climbs into twenty-nine boxcars.

"This it?"

"Yes. Thank you."

"You're welcome."

"Bye."

"Here."

"Thank you, sir."

"Don't wait too long to eat it, there's mayo in it."

"Don't worry."

September 6—Music class every morning. Mecca every night. It's clear which Rose is in disguise.

Sat.—7—Yesterday Jeanne leaned in close to me and said, "You remind me of someone, peaches."

I bit, I said, "Really, Jeanne? Who?"

And she said with her crooked smile that is, apparently, worth paying for, "Me."

I didn't say anything. She took a big drag off her fag, held it in, then exhaled. "I'll bet your Daddy's just crazy about you."

I've taken to saying a Hail Mary before I come into the apartment.

Mon—9—You have never seen two such professionals. The Kaiser is delighted with my progress. Sometimes he just says to me, "Sing," and to Rose, "Miss Lacroix, play if you please." And sits back. How the mighty have mellowed. We're just gently sculling till November.

I do sometimes get a jolting sensation—no sooner do I take leave of Rose in the afternoon in her ribbons and bows and dead composers, than I meet my lover in the snazzy suit for a night of jazz and jive. We tried it. It's made from a plant. Lovely aroma. Bought it from the Chinaman. Makes you lose time, makes you hear each note of music from every direction at once. Makes you make love slowly. But I haven't bought any more because I don't want my awake senses dulled. If all music is fascinating, then none is. And there's plenty of time to slow down, there's the whole rest of our lives.

For three nights we didn't go to Mecca. I went to Rose's place and waited while she doctored her mother and changed clothes. (I've given her the sash from my new green dress. I wound it around her charcoal hat to remind her. She said she doesn't require reminding. Then she kissed me in that way that makes me hate time.) We dined and went out. We can't stay at her place because of Jeanne's "company." We passed one of her gentlemen on the stairs the second night. An older light brown man with a paunch and a monocle. "He runs the credit union," Rose told me. I guess Jeanne does pretty well. Covers her doctor bills, anyhow. Enough men will pay for a blonde princess even if she's washed up and strung out.

It's not her job that bothers me, it's her. What I get from Jeanne is a big echo. Where is she really? She still hasn't said a word about having seen us. I'm used to being there now when Rose gives her her shot. That's all she cares about. She still cooks and sets the table for three every night, even though she is always horizontal by suppertime—come to think of it, I have never seen her eat. And I'm used to her sleazy stuck-up manner. The other evening she drawled at me, "I'm a Burgess, you know—I don't know if Rosie told you—one of the Long Island Burgesses. My father was George Morecombe Burgess."

And I drawled back, "Oh really. I'm a Piper, one of the Cape Breton Island Pipers. Perhaps you've heard of my father, James."

Her smile is now more sneer than leer, which is how I know she respects me somewhat. She plays cat and mouse: "Kathleen, dear, don't you have a young man waiting for you in torment somewhere?" And after a few more drinks, "Beware the dark fruit, darling. He'll leave you high, oh so high, but dry, baby, to the bone."

How am I different from Jeanne? She is addicted to morphine. I am addicted to Rose. A rose is not a poppy. That is how I am different from Jeanne.

Something happened after Boston. Lily kept to the highway with the water blinking on her left, and all was well until she noticed water on both sides. Then there was no more land. "Is this Manhattan?" It took a while before someone would answer her. A boy whipped a handful of sand and shells, "Fuckin moron." A clutch of ringleted predebs giggled behind their hands and ran away holding their noses. A long open automobile whizzed by.

The sea was very pretty here, so Lily sat down on a wharf to

read and wait until things became clear. A lobster fisherman told
her where she was and gave her a juicy claw out of his cauldron.

"The water's so blue," she said.

"Is this your first time seeing the ocean?"

"No. But my ocean is gray and green."

"Where you from?"

"Canada."

"Oh yeah? I have a cousin in Vancouver, maybe you know
her."

"Maybe I do."

Our first three nights after that first night: We stroll to Central Park. A
place near the Pond. Rose brings a blanket and I bring chokecherry
wine. There's a thicket that you enter like a rabbit. You crawl for ten
feet or so, then you can stand up and see the stars. And only the stars
can see you back. We spread the blanket, then we always share a glass of
wine before we touch. I thought I would get calmer, surer, but each
time we come close I feel almost sick at first. As though each time
vibrates with the times before. I feel a terrible sorrow coming up my
throat, I don't know why. And it can only be consoled against the
length of her body. Lying down with her for the first time—all the pain
I didn't know I had, till at her touch it disappeared like smoke. Is this
what purgatory feels like? To burn painlessly? If so, why isn't it called
heaven?

When my fingers slide against beautiful Rose, when they swell her
to a sweet unfolding and she puffs out like a sail at my every breath,
when they glisten into her and disappear, it's as though she were a
soldier fallen in the field getting healed by me, her head to one side. I
take off her uniform and she can finally come home. You don't know
how beautiful she is. Her hair finally released, black foam. Her skin,
nocturnal waters worshiped by the moon, her white lover. I fold her
clothes carefully and dress her with my tongue, my hands, my wet
center, the true balm of Gilead. Did you know it closes wounds and
opens hearts?

My pale green silk dress is what they'd call an undergarment at
home. I wear only it. It slips like skin and conforms to the slightest
caress like the shirt of a Mongol warrior meant to smooth the piercing

arrow's exit from the wound. It casts an arboreal shade when I kneel above Rose and invite her to refresh herself in this cool glade. "Look," I say. And I can feel the caress of her eyes. "Touch me." And it's the closest thing to having no skin. "Kiss me." She guides my hips, lowering me to her lips as though to sip from a legendary flask. The more you drink the fuller it gets.

Rose was a bit shocked at first. But I have discovered something about modest people. They're just waiting for the call. Then they are the first over the wall and into the temple. When she's inside me I sometimes think of her fingers on the piano. Wicked, I know, but I can't help it. She is endowed with a span of a tenth. I sometimes sing a line of *Traviata* between her thighs, which scandalizes her because she is as serious about sex as she is about music. Reverent.

When will she discover that I am from a lesser race of immortals? But the high deities have always needed pixies to persuade them down to earth. When she no longer needs an intermediary, will she still love me?

"I love you, Rose."

"I love you, I love you, love you."

"Who?"

"Kathleen."

Then we bathe in the Pond.

When I arrived home on the third night—morning actually—Giles was up already with the coffee perking. I thought, oh no, this is it. She was in her heavy brocade dressing-gown with the Louis IV sheep frolicking—somewhere there is a parlor with a naked armchair. But really, what am I to make of her? She put the marmalade on the table and said wispily, "Kathleen, dear, I'd really rather you brought your friend home nights."

I'm acting cocky here on paper but I nearly spewed. She said, "I know you two have formed an attachment and naturally friends lose track of time. There just seems to be so much to talk about."

My throat closed, I couldn't swallow the coffee. How much does she know? Does she imagine that we talk Verdi till dawn? That we plan to enter the convent together? But I said, "Thank you. It would be nice if Rose could spend some time here. Her home situation is not the most wholesome."

"Poor thing. She's welcome to stay and use the piano too, any time."

Jesus Murphy! "Gosh," I said, "that's awfully generous of you, Giles."

"No, Kathleen. It's selfish." She twinkled at me, sipped her coffee and crinkled the newspaper. I decided not to look a gift horse in the mouth.

"No wonder people in Cape Cod thought I was crazy," thought Lily. "No one would ever mistake the Island of Manhattan for any other place once they'd seen it."

The highway had become Broadway. She had crossed the Harlem River and asked, "Where's Central Park?" This time she was confident that it was a sensible question. But people still didn't want to answer for some reason, they looked quickly away. Finally, a big white lady with fruit on her hat said, "Come with me, child."

Lily wound up at a mission in the East Village where a volunteer lady tried to get her into a bath and a new dress. Lily bargained, "You may wash my dress, but I do not want a new dress, and you may wash me but I will not remove my boots, thank you."

"Your ankles are badly swollen."

"I've been walking a lot."

"You're actually quite pretty under all that grime, aren't you?"

"Thank you."

"Poor little thing."

"I'm not poor."

"God loves you."

"I know."

Lily's green silk dress began to disintegrate at the first hint of water. "This is fit for the trash," said the lady and the next instant shrieked in pain.

"What happened?" asked the matron, who came running, and the charity worker replied, "Little bitch bit me."

But by then Lily had her dress, her brace and her diary, and was out the door.

A pale man with long black hair, a top hat and curly sideburns pointed north.

She entered through the south gate of Central Park and found the pond as evening fell. She looked for the thicket but couldn't find it. She found an untenanted bench, curled up, hugged the diary and fell asleep. She moved several times, awakened by the crack of a billy stick on the soles of her feet, "Move along."

And more than once, as she rose and began to walk away, "I'm sorry, little girl, don't you have anywhere to go?"

"Yes, thank you, don't worry."

"Are you all alone?"

"No. My brother is with me."

Sept 23—She said, "There's a tree growing inside you."

In my little room with the Greenwich roofs beyond the window. Red geraniums, cool metropolitan night air, industrial blue. We lie next to each other a long time, looking. Lightly touching, as involuntary as breath. Black and white. Except she thinks I'm actually green.

"There . . . see?" She traces the green shoots of this alleged sapling, starting from behind my ear, down my neck, where it submerges then surfaces at the base of my breast, reaching up, cleaving in two twigs to encircle my nipple. She finds more evidence at my inner thigh.

"It's growing up to your belly button. I wonder where the roots are."

"It depends whether I'm a shade tree, or an aquatic plant."

"You're green."

"My eyes are green."

"You're so white, you're green."

"You say the sweetest things."

"You're beautiful."

"I'm green—"

"The Green Diva, la Diva Verde—"

"And I smell—"

"You have a scent."

"So do you," I said.

"What's mine?"

". . . Trade winds—"

"Ha—"

"—everything that's ever been worth stealing."

"Hm."

"What's mine?"

". . . Mineral."

"You know, it's because I know you that I'm able to translate. I know that what you're really saying is, 'Darling, you're ravishing, milk and honey are under your tongue—' "

" 'And the smell of thy garments is like the smell of Lebanon.' "

"Ha!"

She kissed me. And after a while she said, "Actually, you smell like the sea."

"What do you know from the sea, there's no sea in New York, there's a grubby harbor."

"I know you."

"Then what's it smell like?"

"Like rocks. Like an empty house with all the windows blowing open. Like thinking, like tears. Like November."

"What about the tree?"

"It's the part that goes on living."

". . . Are you cold?"

"No . . . Here."

"Thanks."

"I'm never going to leave you, Kathleen."

"Don't ever leave me."

"I never will."

November 1, 1918
Caro Diario,

This is my swan song. It's happened. I am too happy to write any more. There is one last event to record before I kiss and close you forever. Today the Kaiser took me to the Metropolitan Opera House.

Custodian let us in. All is calm, all is dark, awaiting the opening night of the season on November 11. The custodian raised the gold curtain and I stood center stage on the set of *Samson and Delilah* and looked into the house.

Beyond the pit, the dress circle and orchestra swept out before me, a varnished sea of gilded red rushing to the back and sides of the house to meet balcony upon balcony fanning up and around me like the decks of a grand seagoing vessel. Three thousand four hundred and sixty-five passengers, not counting the crew. This afternoon there was an audience of two. Rose and the Kaiser. Center orchestra. I sang *Quando m'envo* from *Bohème*. And received a standing ovation. I'll sing for Gatti-Casazza on the twelfth. I'll make my debut on this stage this time next year. But I had my maiden voyage today.

O Diary. My loyal friend. There is love, there is music, there is no limit, there is work, there is the precious sense that this is the hour of grace when all things gather and distill to create the rest of my life. I don't believe in God, I believe in everything. And I am amazed at how blessed I am. Thank you.

Love, Liebe, Amore,
Kathleen Cecilia Piper

Book 9

THE FAMILY TREE

"The sands of Mecca shape a rose"

THE THIEF OF BAGHDAD

THE INSCRIPTION IN THE stone archway says, "Ora Pro Nobis." So Lily does, folding her hands on the diary in her lap and bowing her head.

She has been sitting here for the past hour reading in the doorway opposite 85½ 135th Street. She is glad after all that the mission lady found her because, although her dress and boots are worse for wear, Lily's hair is clean and silky and her face is shining. Across the street, the church is still on the second floor, with four new stained-glass windows: the Holy Bible closed, the Holy Bible open, Jesus standing attended by sheep, Jesus sitting attended by sheep. The butcher shop is likewise there, renamed "Harlem's Own Community Green Grocer and Butcher Shop," but "Dash Daniels Harlem Gentlemen's Emporium" has been replaced by "Joyce and Cor-alee's Beauty School: Bonaparte System," the "A2Z Auto School," "Re-naissance Book Store," "Johnson's Photo Studio," "Johnson's Barber Shop" and "R.W. J. Johnson, Notary Public."

There are nests like this everywhere of buildings richly subdivided, bursting with business and smart signage yet flanked by those boarded-up and empty, "Danger Keep Out." The survivors seem to be clinging to each other for warmth, hoping to avoid the next sweep of the scythe through a neighborhood where at one time there seemed never to be enough space to house the dreams, the energy, the buzz of enterprise and thunderclaps of faith and music. More and more, Harlem depends on the tourist trade. The harder times get, the higher they get up here at a movable feast of dingy wangdangs and a string of glittering clubs where genius enters by the back door.

Lily watches three little boys in fedoras and long coats gathered round a wooden crate playing a mysterious game. A woman dressed like some type of nun passes by and scowls at her, then does a double-take and says, "God bless you." Little girls skip rope, there are children everywhere.

For a while now, the butcher has been leaning in his doorway across the street, considering Lily. He is a good-looking man of about thirty and he calls, "Are you waiting for someone?"

"No, sir."

He smiles. "Who's your momma, girl, where's she at?"

Lily smiles back—not since Cape Breton has she heard words to that effect.

"She's dead."

He nods. "You hungry? You look hungry."

"It's all right, thank you, I'm expected."

Lily rises, crosses the street and walks past him up the steps, through the stone archway and into the cool vaulted foyer. Up the stairs, her brace ringing out on the worn white marble. Second-floor church on the left. Lily pops her head in just to see what a Baptist church looks like. Three older ladies are cleaning and yakking, but stop dead when the oldest one looks up to see Lily's head inquiring around the door and screams the way anyone would if the Devil showed up in church. The other two women cry, "Sweet Jesus!" "Dear Redeemer on the Cross!"—they would bless themselves but they're not Catholic.

Lily withdraws, "Excuse me."

The bravest lady steals over to the door and watches Lily climb toward the third floor. Then she turns to her cronies and explains, "That red-haired devil who ruined our Miss Rose has come back to life as a shrunk-down raggedy cripple."

It's true.

Third floor. Open doors, a gauntlet of staring faces, mostly children, an old young woman on the verge of barking out the usual interrogation till she sees it's a lame girl. Hostility is replaced by curiosity. Lily makes her lopsided way in a wake of whispers and one giggle followed by the sound of a slap. Apartment Three. Lily knocks. And waits, turning to her audience, now silent. She smiles. The old young woman shoos the kids back into her apartment and slams the door. Lily knocks again. She knows there's someone home, she can hear a piano—soft, one-handed, as though that hand had fallen asleep and were now dreaming.

She knocks a third time. And finally gets a muffled reply: "Fuck off."

Lily puts her mouth to the crack of the door and formulates politely, "Miss Lacroix? It's Lily Piper. I've come to visit you, and I have something for you."

Silence.

Lily waits. It's a long silence but far from empty. Finally the scrape of a chair. Slow, firm footfalls. A voice just on the other side of the door says, "There's no Miss Lacroix here."

Lily waits.

The door opens. A man looks down at her. His face is all angles, handsome and severe, he's perhaps a bit too lean. Black hair shorn to the scalp, long neck, white shirt open at the throat. His baggy black trousers are worn to a shine, his impossibly articulated hands dangle, waiting to get back to their real life. But his eyes say he's forgotten music for the moment.

Lily waits while he looks and looks. One of his hands rises and a finger touches Lily's forehead—traces her eyelid, cheek, lips, chin. The man is crying. Lily asks, "May I come in?"

She enters when the man steps back. He closes the door behind her and she stands in the middle of the room looking round. There is a piano, a piano bench, one chair and a table. Lily turns back to the man and says, "Hello, Rose."

Rose takes a half-step toward her. Lily approaches. Rose puts forth her hands, slowly fingering the air as though searching for something in a dark wardrobe. Lily enters the embrace. When Rose shakes and shudders, Lily does not let her stumble. While Rose grieves, Lily takes more and more weight—she has held people up before when they were stricken and besides, she is in good shape from her walk.

Rose soaks Lily's neck and shoulder and groans into her ear as though something jagged and wrong were being drawn out of her body. She moans, "Oh no, no, no," because for Rose it has just happened.

It's important to attend funerals. It is important to view the body, they say, and to see it committed to earth or fire because unless you do that, the loved one dies for you again and again.

"No, no, no . . ."

Lily pats Rose gently on the back, the way you would a baby. Rose whimpers into her shoulder, "I'm sorry."

But what has she to be sorry for? A body doesn't need a reason to feel sorry. Sorry is a free-floating commodity.

"I love you," says Rose.

"I know."

"Never leave you."

"It's okay."

"Kathleen."

The word becomes a keening and Rose crumples in agony at the extraction of that last mortal shard. It's the one that hurts the worst, she tried to leave it where it was so it could kill her slow and numb, that last lethal fragment. Her name.

Lily guides Rose to the floor retching, past crying, until finally she begins to rock on her heels.

"It's okay. It's all right now, Rose."

And Rose takes her first unfettered breath.

Lily has made tea. She pours some hot into Rose's cup and asks, "Why didn't you save her?"

Rose could retreat to her usual safe cynical distance, but at this moment she can't remember what she ever had to lose or gain. She answers the question.

"I wrote and my letters came back unopened. I figured to hell with her. That's 'cause I wanted to think she was the one sending them back. I couldn't believe anyone could lock her up. Even though I'd seen her father."

Lily doesn't ask.

Rose stirs and stirs her tea, looking down until she picks up the thread again. "She always did what she wanted, you see. That was the great thing. It was better to think she was finished with me than to think anything could get the better of her. I thought, give her a couple months, she'll be back—her brilliant career, you know. She could quit me but not her music. . . ." Rose looks up. "But she didn't come back. By the time I got money for a train ticket to that what the hell island—"

"Cape Breton."

"Yeah," smiling, " 'C'Bre'n'—Giles found me and told me she was dead. Never said nothing 'bout babies. Said flu."

Rose looks out the window at a line of small clothes. Lily says, "You could've walked."

"Yeah. I could've walked."

They sit in silence for a bit. Then Lily asks, "What's the date today?"

"I don't know. June something—twenty-first. No, twentieth."

"It's my birthday."

Rose squeezes shut her eyes for a moment. Then opens them. Her voice is kind when she speaks. "Happy birthday, Lily."

"I'm supposed to be at Lourdes."

"You don't say."

There's a charcoal fedora with an emerald band hanging from a hook on the back of the door. Lily goes and gets it and hands it to Rose.

"Would you play me something?"

Rose sets the hat beside her on the bench, and plays.

When there is finally more silence than music, Lily looks up and says, "Thank you."

Rose returns to her cold tea and watches as Lily unbuckles her brace, pulls off her boots and turns them upside down on the table. A wadded heap: when the maple leaves wore out, Lily lined the sole of her left boot with newspaper photos of President Roosevelt because she trusted him, and reinforced her right sole with promises of "a new deal." The rest of the wrinkled papers on the table bear the likeness of King George V, which is why it takes Rose a moment to register the fact of three thousand dollars in hundreds.

"What do you figure it's worth in American money?" asks Lily.

"Where the hell'd you get this, child?"

Lily answers, "My sister Frances."

Rose nods and smiles and says, "Everybody should have a sister Frances."

St. Anthony, Patron Saint of Lost Objects

THE BEAUTIFUL COLOR PRINT of Bernadette and Our Lady of Lourdes has been nicely framed. It hangs over the blackboard in Mercedes' classroom at Mount Carmel High School. Mercedes never tires of telling the wonderful story of Bernadette, nor does she let many weeks go by without quizzing the class at random—"And how many times did Our Lady appear to Bernadette?" Bernadette is a saint now. She was canonized on the Feast of the Immaculate Conception, December 8, 1933—the year Lily went away. "And what did Our Lady answer when Bernadette asked, 'Who are you?' "

Mercedes stands ramrod-straight on her platform at the front of the class, anticipating the forties in her economy of line and preference for angles. April 1939.

"What's wrong with this sentence?"

She raps the blackboard with her pointer, taut hickory, parade-square quality. Chalked in her textbook longhand: *Do like your mother says.*

Her grade tens. Seventeen of them. God knows there'll be few enough by the time they hit grade twelve, and likely not a single boy among the graduating class. Only three left now. One of them, Bernie "Moose" Muise, shoots up his hand. Mercedes casts a withering eye and purses her lips, unaware that this has made her an easy schoolyard takeoff. *Who am I? Old leather-lips!*

"Well, Bernard?"

"See miss, it's like this: if every girl did like her mother said, the population of Cape Breton Island would be cut in half."

A burst of laughter bitten off and swallowed short by the class. Nervous titters as Mercedes strolls to the big boy's desk—he's grinning, actually kinda fond of old leather-lips. The blows rain down on him hard and fast, a hickory blur, before he can get his arms over his head he's bleeding from an eye, occasioning a new nickname.

"You need a bit of a rest, Mercedes."

"Yes, Sister Saint Eustace."

"Perhaps a brief change of scene."

"I have friends in Halifax."

Halifax County.

"Anthony, come here please."

The matron at the Nova Scotia Home for Coloured Children waits with her hands folded as the little boy throws a last clutch of grain to the hens. This is Mercedes' first trip to the mainland. She stands next to the matron. The little boy wears a red checkered shirt and brown corduroy pants with suspenders, sturdy boots. He looks healthy. The matron picks a little straw from his hair and says, "Anthony, this is Miss Piper."

The little boy looks down, on the bashful side, and says, ". . . Hello."

"Hello, Miss Piper," prompts the matron.

"Hello, Miss Piper."

Mercedes waits till he looks up. Then she begins: " 'Who made the world?' "

He hesitates, parts his lips, then, " 'God made the world.' "

" 'Who is God?' "

" 'God is the Creator of heaven and earth and of all things.' "

" 'What is man?' "

" 'Man is a creature composed of body and soul and made to the image and likeness of God.' "

" 'Why did God make you?' "

" 'God made me to know Him to love Him and serve—' "

" '—and to serve—' "

" '—and to serve Him in this world and to be happy with Him forever in heaven.' "

" 'What must we do to save our souls?' "

" 'To save our souls we must worship God by faith hope and charity that is we must believe in Him hope in Him and love Him with all our hearts.' "

" '—heart.' "

" '—heart.' "

Mercedes nods. "That is all. You may go, Anthony."

The little boy watches as Mercedes turns to walk away with the matron, then he stops her with a question. "Are you the nice lady?"

Mercedes turns back, at a loss. The matron helps. "The nice lady who sent you here and makes sure you have clothes and food? Yes."

Mercedes remains expressionless. Anthony says, "Thank you, Miss Piper."

And scoots, tickled and shy, back to the chickens.

"Lovely farm," says Mercedes to the matron.

"Come, I'll show you the school section."

Mercedes arranged for Anthony to be sent here before he was born. The first Nova Scotia Home for Coloured Children blew up along with half of Halifax in 1917, but they built another one out on the Preston Road. Mercedes did not expect Anthony to grow up as a charity child, even though this is a charity organization courtesy of the African United Baptist Association—some of the best women you'd ever want to meet on the Ladies' Auxiliary. There are even music classes. Anthony is learning violin. Mercedes pays for him out of the Lourdes money, asking only that he be raised a Catholic. The Baptist ladies have been as good as their word, as Mercedes ascertained just now.

He is six years old. Mercedes can see there is no devil in him. He has his mother's eyes.

Armistice Day

Of wicked and most cursèd things to speak I now commence.
Ye daughters and ye parents, all go, get you far from hence;
Or if ye minded be to hear my tale, believe me nought
In this behalf, nor think that such a thing was ever wrought.

OVID, METAMORPHOSES, BOOK X,

MYRRHA AND CINYRAS

JAMES GOT A LETTER from "An Anonymous Well-Wisher." He left that night. Three and a half days later, at 6:05 A.M. on November 11, 1918, he walked out of Grand Central Station. He walked all the way to where she was staying in Greenwich Village because he couldn't get a cab. There were crowds.

He knocks but no one answers. The apartment door is unlocked, in fact slightly ajar when he arrives. He pushes it open and calls, but no one answers. He enters the little vestibule and listens. "Hello? . . . Anybody home?" He looks into the old-lady parlor, "Giles? . . . Kathleen?" Quiet as the grave. He sets down his small black case. Cocks his head to a sound. Giggling. Removes his hat and hangs it on the hall tree. A shriek and muffled laughter from . . . across the parlor, down the hall—the smell of lavender—past the WC, treading softly. A closed door. He hovers. He places his ear to the panel of opaque glass.

It's Kathleen making those sounds. Impossible to see through the wavy glass. Shadows. He closes a hand over the china knob—pink rosebuds in milk. Turns silently. Opens the width of a human eye. Sees.

Spray of red-gold hair upon the pillow. His daughter's hands travel-ing over a black back, disappearing beneath the waistband of a pair of striped trousers moving between his daughter's bare thighs, his daughter's voice and not her voice, "Oh, oh-h, ohhh . . ."

A roar of blood behind his eyes and he's in the room, yanks the bastard off her with one arm to belt him across the face with the other and fling him into the wall, his daughter leaps naked at his back because he is going to kill her lover with the flat of his foot but no, James would never kill a woman. Arms up to cover herself, bleeding mouth, sliding down the wall, Jesus. James tears the spread from the bed, descends upon the dazed girl, enveloping her as though she were in flames, slings her from the room, down the hall, out into the corridor where he flings her, a mummy-sack of bones. Then he locks the door and slides the safety chain into place.

In the bedroom his daughter is crying, pawing the floor for her clothes.

"Why, Kathleen?" He is not feeling angry.

She looks up, a blind choking mess. He puts a hand down to her, she takes it, legs shaking badly, onto her feet, clutching the floor mat for cover.

"Why?"—the back of his hand—"Why?"—his speeding palm—"Why?"—closed fist.

Her head comes to rest facing forward, already puffing up. He looks at what he has done. He takes her in his arms. She is racked with shame, just wants some clothes, please—

"Shshsh," he says, kissing her hair, her injured face. It's his own fault—I should have never let her go far from home—an ecstasy beneath his hands, "It's all right, my darling—"

"Don't," she says.

He can't speak just now, he loves her too much—closer—oh so soft—

"Daddy—"

He will tell her after how much he loves her

—her palms against his shoulders, fighting to stay on her feet—

Ohh my darling

—falling, fists against his back, enmeshed between his weight, the mushy bed, struggling only shakes the web, the sheet and all its threads conspire, she can no longer find her feet—

The iron taste of her mouth where he's made it bleed, dreadful sorry, I'll take you home again—"Be still," he pleads.

"Stop it."

I'll never let anyone hurt you again

"No!"

never let anyone *touch* you

"NO!"

No one *No* one *No. One.* Will *ever ever*

She has stopped screaming.

Hurt you *Ever*

she is lying perfectly still now

Again!

He shudders. "Shshshsh. It's all right now. Hush, my darling. It's all right."

James unhooks the safety chain and lets Giles in. "Hello, Giles."

"Who . . . ? Excuse me—"

"I'm sorry, it's James."

"James!"

He takes her net bag of groceries and helps her off with her coat.

"James, why I haven't seen you since—" A little flustered. "Was I—? Am I forgetting?"

"No, no, I'm here unannounced—thought I'd look in, see how the world-famous singer's making out." He smiles and blinks twice in quick succession.

"Does Kathleen know you're here?" Suddenly alarmed lest—

"Yes, oh yes, we've already had a visit," says James.

Giles starts down the hall, "Kathleen, dear—"

James stops her. "She's having a bit of a nap—not feeling too spry."

"Oh." Giles hesitates. "Oh dear. Was—did you meet Rose?"

"Yes, oh yes."

Giles strip-searches his face. Then says, "I'll just look in on the girl."

"She's sleeping, really, look, I've made myself useful." There's a pot of tea and two cups set out in the tiny dining room.

"Oh. Well. That's lovely, James, thank you . . ."

On their way to the table, Giles chats politely, "You know I just popped out to the corner to get some—where did I put my—?"

James holds up the net bag, "Right here."

"Oh good, thank you, James, yes I just popped out for a jiffy but I was delayed, you know, caught up in the celebration, swept quite out of my way."

"Oh?"

"Oh yes. Haven't you heard?"

James gives her a sociably blank look, pours tea, his hand shaking only slightly. Giles breaks into a big papery smile. "Oh James, the war is over. This morning at eleven o'clock. Oh wait till I tell Kathleen it's over. It's all over."

Rose fought her way through the victory crowds and holed up in Central Park till dark, ticker tape in her hair, confetti drying on her bloody face.

Around nine, she walks into the apartment on 135th, past Jeanne, who's reading on the couch, something in French. Jeanne actually sits up.

"What happened to you?"

"I got beat up."

Rising, "Who did this thing?" Summoning her upper-crust command, "Answer me, Rose."

Rose splashes water on her face at the kitchen sink. "Kathleen's father."

Jeanne swallows the smallest of canaries. Then slides back into her sweet drawl, "Don't worry, honey. Momma will make it all better."

Rose watches as Jeanne heats water on the stove. She sits still while Jeanne dabs at her fat crusty lip. "Poor baby."

"Don't you want to know why, Mother?"

"Oh honey, you don't have to talk right now."

Jeanne doesn't comment on the bloodstained bedspread or the trousers peeking out below its fringe. She picks up the phone and cancels tonight's visitor. She lights candles and lays the table for "a prodigal feast." She postpones her injection—"The pain is a little better tonight."

Jeanne sits across from Rose. And eats. She talks with well-bred animation of Rose's brilliant future. It is as though she had never left Long Island—she can almost feel the phantom servant at her right elbow poised with his crystal decanter.

"You'll be more celebrated than Portia Washington Pittman, darling."

Rose does not reply but Jeanne seems not to notice as she enumerates the triumphs that lie ahead: Rose will perform for royalty as did Elizabeth

Taylor Greenfield, the Black Swan. She will perform for the president as did Sissieretta Jones, the Black Patti who came so close to singing at the Met. She will play with the greatest orchestras of Europe, and Carnegie Hall will be on its knees, begging. "After all, Rosie, someone's got to be first and it may as well be you." Jeanne gives two pats to her lips with her linen serviette. "And Mother will be so proud of you." She reaches out to squeeze her daughter's hand. "Not that I'm not proud already, I am, Rosie, you're my life, you're all I have left and I love you." Jeanne gives Rose her most wistful look across the candles. "Really I do, dear."

"What's the occasion, Mother?"

Jeanne looks politely baffled. But she's in too good a mood to dissemble. She is feeling girlish tonight. Positively flirtatious. She shoots Rose a cupid's-bow smile and leans forward in the candlelight.

"Listen to me, my love. You have more talent in your little finger than twenty Kathleen Pipers, and one day you'll thank your *pauvre petite maman.*"

"For what?"

Jeanne winks and lights a cigarette, inhaling with a sly eye on Rose, shaking the match well after the flame has gone out. An Anonymous Well-Wisher.

Rose begins a mental list of things to do and starts with item one, "Who was my father?"

A pained smile from Jeanne—an unfortunate remark from her dinner guest. "Rose, dear heart, you always did love to hear the story—"

"I know the story, I want the truth."

Jeanne taps her cigarette, arches her brows slightly and sighs, really this is a little tiresome.

"Who was he?"

"He was Alfred Lacroix, darling, as you perfectly well know."

"And what did he do?"

"He was a preacher, a man of the cloth and a credit to his race."

"And where is he now?"

"He's in heaven, my treasure."

The catechism finished, Rose leaves the table. It's a long list. There is no time to lose.

"Kathleen has gone home, Rose."

"When's she coming back?"

"Her father didn't say."

"What did she say?"

Giles looks tired. "She didn't say anything."

Rose gets up. "I think I left some clothes here."

"By all means dear, have a look."

"Did he hurt her?"

Giles looks away. "I don't know what he did. She wouldn't speak."

Rose pauses, momentarily forgetting her errand.

"Rose. Do you need a place to stay?"

"Thank you, Giles. I'll be okay."

Rose stands in front of the bathroom mirror at home and cuts her hair to the scalp. She changes out of a dress for the last time, wakes up her mother and says, "I'm going now."

Jeanne takes a while to come out of a bad dream that starts when she opens her eyes. Rose doesn't wait, just conveys information, "I'll let you know wherever I'm playing. I'll send you money every week whether I have it or not. When you die, I'll come back and live here."

The road starts at Club Mecca. Sweet Jessie Hogan loves spaghetti and meatballs and beer and sweet young things who tear up the keyboard and don't know when to stop. A hot blues streak, the twenties.

Until boom goes bust and Rose starts playing her own stuff. Doc Rose. And his trio.

"a garden inclosed is my sister . . . a spring shut up, a fountain sealed"

THE SONG OF SONGS

WHEN FRANCES DIES IT'S safe for Mercedes to put Anthony's picture on the piano. Framed in filigreed silver, he stands proudly at attention in the uniform and broad trooper's hat of the Boy Scouts of the Zion African Methodist Episcopal Church. He is still a Catholic.

Mercedes contemplates the cover of the record album in her lap. Frances amassed quite a collection. Ralph Luvovitz sent her one every Christmas and whenever he visited his mother, always the same request. Frances died early this morning. The kitchen counters are still heaped with her baking.

Mercedes never was a big eater and Frances less so. Through the thirties, people came to the kitchen door and carted it away—big stews, pork and beans by the bucket, molasses cookies, oatmeal cookies, date squares, Nellie's Muffins, johnnycake, rhubarb upside-down cake, jelly-rolls, pies, blueberry grunt, yards of shortbread, hundreds of tea biscuits. Nowadays there aren't as many people going hungry but Frances still cooks for an army—Mercedes has had to organize pickups by the hospital, the rectory, the convent. Young single miners have been taking care of the rest, wolfing down huge meals, hardly noticing the old girl at the oven with her three cigarettes on the go and her glass of Irish. Frances looked very old at the last, though she took care to henna her hair from time to time.

For twenty years Frances listened to her records. Cooked. Smoked. Drank. Watched the street. Slept on the attic floor. Walked the shore. She no longer walked the Shore Road because it fell into the sea—they've replaced it with a paved one that runs a sensible distance from the water, but it's just not the same. She read newspapers and saved them all. Scared children without knowing. Led home cats. Tried never to change her clothes. Spoke little. And then yesterday she up and said, "Don't you ever wonder where Lily is?"

And when Mercedes didn't reply, Frances got up from the sofa in the front room—"Frances, what do you need, dear, I'll get it." But Frances made her way to the piano bench and bent down, which made her cough—"Frances, dear, use your hanky"—opened it and took out her newest long-playing record album. She handed it to Mercedes and lay back down on the sofa, exhausted.

Mercedes pushed a blotched tabby off Frances's chest and looked daggers at a cross-eyed Siamese who never shut up—"Shut up," said Mercedes. And glanced down at the album cover: *Doc Rose Trio, Live in Paris: Wise Child.* A handsome black man, the angles of his face reprised by a fedora wound round with a gleaming emerald band.

"You might want to look her up someday, Mercedes, you never know."

"Why would I want to do that?"

"So you can die in peace."

Mercedes hates it when Frances says things like that. She's usually so good except when she's drunk and then Mercedes just lets her alone, shutting the door on whatever room it is so she doesn't have to hear what Frances is saying to herself.

"My conscience is quite clear, Frances."

"Daddy died in peace."

Mercedes gets up to leave and close the door—

"I'm not drunk, Mercedes. I quit drinking."

"Since when?"

"This morning."

"Oh Frances, here, have one, I'll join you, perk up the appetite."

"I've quit. I want to die sober."

Mercedes turns stony. "You're not going to die."

In the schoolyard Mercedes is no longer "old leather-lips"—there is not enough affection to inspire a nickname anymore. Just fear. Everyone fears Mercedes, except Frances. If Mercedes could have terrified Frances into going to a sanatorium, Frances would be well now. Frances could have gone to the best sanatorium money could buy, in the States, in Switzerland, but Frances refused. And Mercedes has had to watch. And now it is too late—*damn you, Frances, how is that any different than suicide?*

"Don't be ridiculous, Frances, you're not going to die."

"Daddy died in peace because he made his confession." Frances reaches a hand to the floor for a white blue-eyed kitten. "He confessed to me. And I forgave him."

"You are not invested with the power to dispense the Sacrament of Penance—"

"Yes I am."

"Frances, I don't know about you but I'm just going to have a wee dram—"

"I want to make sure you know who Lily's parents were."

Mercedes covers her ears. Frances uses her last sprint of energy to pry the hands away, and to speak the words.

A hacking agony of basins and blood and mucus—little songs, the two bright spots on Frances's cheeks, a trip upstairs to get the dolls. A story about two tiny girls with tartan housecoats and cinnamon toast, "I love you Frances." A flagon of port or would you prefer blancmange?—a kiss on the cheek, ring around the rosy, "Forgive me."

"Don't cry, Mercedes."

"Don't be afraid."

"Will you sleep with me tonight?"

"Frances, remember the time you dressed Trixie up in the baptismal gown?"

"Don't make me laugh!"

A cool cloth, Frances your eyes are so pretty—always so pretty—feel better in the morning, *Habibti . . . "Te'berini."*

"Mercedes, remember that song?"

Forgive me, Frances.

"Sing it, Mercedes?"

" 'Oh playmate, come out and play with me, And bring your dollies three, climb up my apple tree. Shout down my rain barrel, Slide down my cellar door, And we'll be jolly friends, for ever more. . . .' "

In and out of sleep—that's right, you rest now.

"It's all right, Mercedes."

Forgive me, Frances.

Frances is so thin it's no problem for Mercedes to stretch out next to her on the couch, so light in her arms like a child, so hot like coals. The terrible wheezing starts and goes on for a long time, how can such a small body make such sounds—don't be afraid. All things are passing, love never changes. *Angel of God, my guardian dear, to whom God's love commits me here, ever this day be at my side. . . .* The last of Frances leaks out her mouth warm and thick. Mercedes has never been sick a day in her life, is unafraid of disease as her father was of bullets, holds Frances all through the dawn though her chest has stopped heaving. Stroking her damp forehead, cool now like the grass; kissing her temple no longer throbbing. A child asleep, my sister.

Mercedes puts the picture of Anthony on the piano, closes the piano bench over the record album, kneels down and folds her hands upon the lid. She asks the Blessed Virgin Mary what she must do.

MAY JESUS HAVE MERCY ON THE SOUL OF

Frances Euphrasia Piper
Died April 25, 1953
Age 40

"We have loved her in life. Let us not abandon her, until we have conducted her by our prayers into the house of the Lord." ST. AMBROSE

Solace Art. Co.—202 E. 44th St. N.Y.

Sister Saint Eustace attends. Mr. MacIsaac attends. Mrs. Luvovitz attends, she is a widow now. Ralph and an altar boy carry the coffin. Teresa meant to keep a low profile but it's difficult amid so few people. Mercedes pointedly ignores her—don't come to me asking for forgiveness. Among Frances's absent former cohorts there is surprise—not that she up and died, but that "I thought she died years ago."

At the cemetery, Mrs. Luvovitz bends and places fresh flowers on

Materia's grave, as is her habit. Benny is buried at the far end in a little patch blessed by a rabbi from away. Mrs. Luvovitz comes and chats to Benny every day when she's not in Montreal.

Ralph helps his mother back to her feet. Mercedes finds the sight of him indescribably sad. He is almost bald. He has a paunch and a foolish smile. Ralph is happy. He is an obstetrician. He loves his family and he survived the war. The second one. When it broke out, he joined up as a medical officer. He promised his mother he would not fight and he didn't—although by 1936 it was clear to Mrs. Luvovitz that, although she had always considered herself a German, Germany no longer considered her so. Nonetheless, she armed Ralph with a slew of addresses of relatives in Germany and Poland. Ralph spent the aftermath of the war treating people in DP camps and it was there that he came to realize that the addresses his mother had given him were of no use.

Now Mrs. Luvovitz squeezes her son's arm and remembers birthing the woman who is being buried today. Born with the caul. Mrs. Luvovitz looks at the sea and thinks, when did this become my home? When I buried Benny here? When the second war came? She cannot discern the moment. She just knows that every time she returns to Cape Breton, she feels in her bones, this is my home. That is why she has declined to move permanently to Montreal. She spends half the year there. She loves her daughter-in-law, would you believe? And her five grandchildren who are only each perfect. They speak French at home, English at school and Yiddish with every second shopkeeper. Real Canadians.

Mrs. Luvovitz watches the casket being lowered into the ground and says a prayer for the wild girl. She was smart. Maybe the smartest. What happened? I should have done something. Gone over there. He didn't deserve to have daughters, there was something wrong there. . . . Mrs. Luvovitz looks east at the horizon and reminds herself of what she has learned: that nothing in life is not mixed. That it is something to know where your dead are buried. That they are buried. Little Frances. *Aleiha Ha' Shalom.*

Dirt hits the casket. Mercedes listens. She watches the ocean. She will go on teaching, of course. Pray for the souls of her loved ones, for their speedy release from purgatory into heaven. But who will be left to pray for her? To speed her reunion with her sister? No one, thinks Mercedes. Hopeless.

Hope is a gift. You can't choose to have it. To believe and yet to have no hope is to thirst beside a fountain. Mercedes watches the ocean. Chill green today, and rough. Purple farther out. She wonders when it was that she began to despair. All these years she mistook it for pious resignation. Now she sees the difference. Such a fine line between a state of grace and a state of mortal sin. What is the good of believing fervently in God if you wind up hating Him? How long have I hated God, Mercedes wonders. When did I first believe it was all up to me?

Which are the sins against hope?

The sins against hope are presumption and despair.

What is despair?

Despair is the loss of hope in God's mercy.

Mercedes says to herself, "I am damned."

Her face has eroded to shale, her brown eyes are dry with sorrow. The ocean sorely tempts her like a lover—she longs to shave her body and walk stinging into salt, naked and anonymous, battered and embraced by rage, nothing personal. Drown. The word is melodious. Beckoning.

Standing back from the gravesite, Teresa looks at Mercedes looking at the ocean and starts to pray for her. For the sake of the girl in the ground. Teresa stays and prays until everyone but she and Mercedes have left the grave and night has begun to fall. Finally Mercedes hesitates . . . then turns away, and walks home instead of into the ocean.

That night, the Virgin Mary tells her what to do.

Sudden Light

I have been here before,
But when or how I cannot tell:
I know the grass beyond the door,
The sweet keen smell,
The sighing sound, the lights around the shore.

''SUDDEN LIGHT''
BY DANTE GABRIEL ROSSETTI

ROSE IS SIXTY-FIVE. ANCIENT for a jazzman. Rock 'n' roll reigns and there are fewer gigs now. She has attained that thankless high status, to wit: Doc Rose is the jazz pianist most often cited by famous jazz pianists as their favorite jazz pianist. Knowledge of Doc Rose is a litmus test of connoisseurship. The records are hard to come by now and cherished by those in the know. The rarefied fan club knows everything about Doc Rose except that he and his manager live hand to mouth on 135th Street.

Lily cleans churches, including the one on the second floor. Rose plays chess and checkers on the corner with the other old men. Lily has never cut her hair. It hangs down to her knees, streaked with gray. There are lightweight aluminum braces available nowadays, but she never thought to buy one when they had the money. Her face is fallen but still sweet, her eyes the same. She is forty-five.

It's just after eight on Sunday night. They're watching "The Ed Sullivan Show" on television when the knock comes at the door. Lily opens it and Anthony smiles, embarrassed.

"Hello. Miss Piper?"

"Yes."

"You don't know me, although we actually have the same name, I knew your sister, Miss Mercedes Piper. My name is Anthony Piper."

Lily looks at the young man. Rose doesn't take her eyes off Topo Gigio while growling out the side of her mouth, "Someone cack and leave us money?"

"I, no, I don't think so, heh."

"Then go away."

Eddie, kees me goodnight.

Lily says to him, "Aloysius."

Anthony says, "I beg your pardon?" convinced now of his mistake, wrong apartment, a senile old couple, ancient smell of cabbage . . .

Lily says, "Come in."

He says, "You are Lily Piper?"

"That's right."

"In or out, make a decision," Rose is beginning to enjoy herself.

He steps in. What a day. His first time in New York City. Subway to the black metropolis so strange and familiar, he belongs everywhere and nowhere. Anthony has experienced the feeling before—no matter where he is, there is something about people's struggles to keep their memories that bruises his heart, because it's too soft to break. The world is his orphanage. Why he should feel so sorry for the other people on the planet is a mystery to him. He's actually a very happy person. It's just that he doesn't know there's a difference between love and empathy, nor does he question why he should be overcome so frequently with nostalgia for times and places not his own. He can't see differences. Only variety. He travels well.

The soft heart feeds a wire frame that is never still. He plays spoons, fiddle, mouth harp, and is learning the bones from a man called Wild Archie—odd, Archie came out of an orphanage too—whom he met at the Cape Breton Club in Halifax. Anthony is wearing desert boots, white jeans, a black turtleneck and an Afro. Slim and eager, a bright penny. Green lights in his hazel eyes.

"You grew up to be happy," says Lily.

He looks at her more closely, not trusting his sense that he's met her before, which happens to him so often. As does the reverse. So familiar.

"I guess you must know," he says carefully, "Miss Piper passed away. Quite recently."

"No, I didn't know that."

Lily mourned Frances long ago, on the night she left, but she never imagined Mercedes dying, although she has prayed for her soul every night.

"I'm sorry," he hands Lily his handkerchief.

"That's all right . . . she was my sister. . . ."

"I don't know what you're blubbering for," snarks Rose, "she tried to have you extradited."

"Exorcized."

Where am I, thinks Anthony, and who are these people?

Lily blows her nose, "Aloysius, did you know Frances? Did Frances ever get to see you?"

"Actually, my name is Anthony. Um—Frances who?"

"What do you do for a living, Tony?" Rose probing for a percentage.

"I'm a musician—"

"Shit," shifting back to the TV.

"—and I teach ethnomusicology."

Rose turns up the volume. Another damn rock 'n' roll band from England.

Anthony is not giving up. "I should explain that Miss Piper more or less adopted me from afar, if you know what I mean, and when she died she left me her house, and she asked me to—"

"Any money?" Rose's last attempt.

"No. I think she spent all her money on me. I don't know why. She was a nice lady."

"Our Lady of Lourdes," says Lily.

Our Lady of Loonies, thinks Anthony, instantly contrite, can't help the things that pop into his head, his love of humanity notwithstanding.

"The cocoa tin," says Lily.

Cuckoo, thinks Anthony. Then he remembers his errand. He opens his knapsack and takes out a sealed cardboard tube. "When Miss Piper died, she left me a note with your name and address, and instructions for me to give you this personally."

He hands the tube to Lily. She breaks the seal at one end and withdraws a paper scroll. She spreads it out on the table.

Anthony asks, "What is it?"

"It's the family tree," Lily says. "Look. We're all in it."

Rose flicks off the TV, scuffs over on her dilapidated slippers, fishes for her glasses.

"See?" Lily tells Anthony. "You have quite a few brothers and sisters. Your father's still alive, although, oh that's too bad, your stepmother Adelaide is gone."

" 'Leo (Ginger) Taylor,' " he reads aloud.

"That's your father, dear. And your Aunt Teresa too, she's still living according to this—and look, you have a cousin too. 'Adele Claire.' "

"I don't understand."

"There you are, there."

Lily points to the issue of Frances Euphrasia and Leo (Ginger). Sprouting from the union of their branches is his name in green ink, "Anthony (Aloysius)."

Ambrose is there too, twinned with Lily, and under his name the words "died at birth." Brother and sister hang by a twig from a branch that joins James to Kathleen. Rose looks at Lily. But Lily just folds her hands.

Next to Kathleen, an "equals" sign joins her name to Rose's. Rose takes off her glasses.

It could be the stale air, the reeling sense of the familiar awash with the foreign, the ocean finally giving up her dead—Anthony is suddenly seasick.

"Sit down," says Lily.

He drops to his haunches and puts his head between his knees. Lily gets a cool wet cloth from the kitchen and places it on the back of his neck.

"Breathe," she says.

He does.

That's better.

"What the hell is ethnomusicology?" Rose wanders off to the piano.

Anthony stands up carefully. "Sorry—"

"Here, dear," says Lily, "sit down and have a cuppa tea till I tell you about your mother."

THE END

Permissions

Every effort has been made to contact copyright holders; in the event of an inadvertent omission or error, please notify the publisher.

Ambrose, Sister Mary, O.P., "For a Happy Death," from *My Gift to Jesus,* copyright © 1929 by Adrian Dominican Sisters. All rights reserved. Reprinted by permission.

Baum, Bernie, and Stephan Weiss, "Music! Music! Music!" copyright © 1949 (renewed), 1950 (renewed) by Cromwell Music, Inc., New York and Warner/Chappell Music, Inc., Los Angeles, California. All rights reserved. Reprinted by permission of the Richmond Org. (TRO).

Florence, Nellie, "Jacksonville Blues," copyright © by Enterprise Music Corp. All rights reserved. Reprinted by permission.

Grainger, P., and E. Robbins, " 'T Ain't Nobody's Business (If I Do)," copyright © 1922, 1949, 1960 by MCA Music Publishing, a division of MCA, Inc. All rights reserved. Used by permission. Copyright renewed. International copyright secured.

Lashley, Clarence, "Sly Mongoose," from *Cape Breton's Magazine,* no. 18, copyright © 1977 by Ronald Caplan. All rights reserved. Reprinted by permission of the publisher.

Ledbetter, Huddie, and John A. Lomax, "Goodnight, Irene," copyright © 1936 (renewed), 1950 (renewed) by Ludlow Music, Inc., New York, N.Y. All rights reserved. Reprinted by permission of the Richmond Organization (TRO).

Mercer, Johnny, and Harry Warren, "Jeepers Creepers," copyright © 1938 (renewed) by Warner Bros., Inc. All rights reserved. Reprinted with permission of Warner Bros. Publications U.S., Inc.

Montrose, Percy, "Oh, My Darling Clementine," copyright © 1884.

Paton, John Glenn, *Vaccai: Practical Method of Italian Singing (for Mezzo-Soprano [Alto] or Baritone) vol. 1910,* copyright © 1975 by G. Schirmer, Inc. (ASCAP) International copyright secured. All rights reserved. Reprinted by permission of Music Sales Corp.

Rexford, Eben, and Hart P. Danks, "Silver Threads Among the Gold," copyright © 1873.

Verdi, Giuseppe, "Rigoletto," copyright © 1955, 1986 by EMI Records Ltd. Translated by Dale McAdoo, copyright © 1956 by EMI (U.S.) Ltd. All rights reserved. Reprinted by permission.

Westendorf, Thomas P., "I'll Take You Home Again, Kathleen," copyright © 1876.

Whitson, Beth Slater, and Leo Friedman, "Let Me Call You Sweetheart," copyright © 1910 (renewed) by Shawnee Press, Inc. (ASCAP) and Shapiro Bernstein & Co., Inc. New York. International copyright secured. All rights reserved. Reprinted by permission of Music Sales Corp. and Hal Leonard Corp.

Yellen, Jack, and Milton Ager, "Ain't She Sweet?" copyright © 1927 (renewed) by Warner Bros., Inc. All rights reserved. Reprinted by permission of Warner Bros. Publications U.S., Inc.